Peeking through the crack from behind the bedroom door, Kate was surprised when the man stepped into view. He was a tall, slender but muscular man with shoulder length, light brown hair and a scruffy beard and mustache. He was dressed all in black, from his shirt to his shoes and was pacing the floor. He seemed worried and angry as he moved around the room.

Her fear rose when Mike responded "What's wrong with you man?"

The man's voice only became angrier as he shoved Mike into a chair and started ransacking the small apartment.

Kate watched as the man threw things out of the cabinets in the small kitchen. Dishes were breaking as they crashed to the floor. He then turned over everything in the living room, cursing and threatening Mike the entire time.

Her whole body froze and she held her breath as the man headed toward the bedroom where she was hiding. Fear took over, paralyzing her as she tried to think of what to do; but didn't have a clue. *Lord, help us!* She mentally screamed.

It took all of Kate's willpower to keep from screaming out loud, as Mike looked toward the bedroom then jumped up and bolted for the door. The man quickly pulled his gun and shot Mike. Kate watched as Mike first hit the entry door then stumbled back in a daze. He looked questioningly at the man, while blood was quickly staining his shirt. Kate was afraid to move. She was terrified as the man walked over and grabbed Mike.

"Where is it?" he screamed. "The next one won't be so healthy for you."

Acknowledgements:

In memory of my husband, Herman, for encouraging me to write and my son, Ryan, for encouraging me to publish my stories. I also want to thank my cousin, Jeanne Hawkins, for taking the time to read and edit my books.

ISBN: 9798398512168

DUDE RANCH PROTECTORS

Colorado Dude Ranch Series

By: Barbara Clay

Chapter 1

Before heading to the Las Vegas airport, Kate was looking forward to spending a few more minutes with her half-brother, Mike. She hadn't seen him in a couple of years and he seemed to be doing much better than when she had last seen him.

He had been working hard on getting off drugs; which had made a huge difference. He was hoping to move back home to Indiana once he was sure he had kicked the habit for good and Kate was hoping that would happen.

Kate and her friend Jessica had flown to Las Vegas on Friday, for a weekend vacation to celebrate Kate's graduation from Purdue University. She had taken her certification tests for her veterinary license and was waiting on the results.

They had stayed very busy and had a great time checking out the different casinos on the strip as they all had different themes. They also enjoyed seeing the Las Vegas parks over the weekend and Mike had been a great tour guide.

Kate was glad she had stayed an extra day to spend more time with Mike. It had been great reminiscing about growing up on their family's farm in Indiana and catching Mike up on what the family was up to, and how things had changed over the years, since he had been gone.

Kate and Mike had just returned from dinner and Kate had walked into the bedroom to get her backpack, when the door to the apartment crashed open. With her heart pounding she quickly looked around for a place to hide. She didn't understand what was going on as she stepped back against the wall, afraid to move. She was afraid of what might happen if the person who had crashed in the door saw her.

The closet was across the room and the bed was directly in front of the open bedroom door, so she couldn't hide there. She tried to control her fear and force her legs to move, but the moments seemed to take forever. She finally managed to slip behind the bedroom door, praying the person hadn't seen or heard her.

Kate's heart was beating hard and fast and every nerve in her body seemed to be on edge as she listened to the low angry voice. "Where's the money? Dylan knows you've been holding out on him and he wants his money now."

Peeking through the crack from behind the bedroom door, Kate was surprised when the man stepped into view. He was a tall, slender but muscular man with shoulder length, light brown hair and a scruffy beard and mustache. He was dressed all in black, from his shirt to his shoes and was pacing the floor. He seemed worried and angry as he moved around the room.

Her fear rose when Mike responded "What's wrong with you man?"

The man's voice only became angrier as he shoved Mike into a chair and started ransacking the small apartment. "Where is it?"

Kate watched as the man threw things out of the cabinets in the small kitchen. Dishes were breaking as they crashed to the floor. He then turned over everything in the living room, cursing and threatening Mike the entire time.

Her whole body froze and she held her breath as the man headed toward the bedroom where she was hiding. Fear took over, paralyzing her as she tried to think of what to do, but didn't have a clue. *Lord, help us!* She mentally screamed.

It took all of Kate's willpower to keep from screaming out loud, as Mike looked toward the bedroom then jumped up and bolted for the door. The man quickly pulled out his gun and shot Mike.

Kate watched as Mike first hit the entry door then stumbled back in a daze. He looked questioningly at the man, while blood was quickly staining his shirt. Kate was afraid to move. She was terrified as the man walked over and grabbed Mike.

"Where is it?" he screamed. "The next one won't be so healthy for you."

The man's phone began to ring and he shoved Mike to the floor. The man started pacing again as he answered the phone. He stated he would be back, as he walked out, slamming the door behind him, but without a latch, the door flew back open.

Kate didn't understand what had just happened, but was relieved the man was gone. It only took a few moments before she pulled her thoughts together and moved from behind the bedroom door. She then ran to check on Mike and slowly closed the door. The door wouldn't latch but it did stay closed.

Blood was still oozing from the bullet wound onto Mike's shirt and Kate knew she had to get it stopped. She checked the site and fortunately it appeared the bullet had gone through and not lodged below his shoulder. It was awfully close to his heart though, which worried her.

She jumped up and ran to the bathroom and found a small towel and some tape. Her whole body was shaking as she knelt beside her brother and placed the towel to the gunshot wound with pressure. "Who was he? Why did he have a gun? Why did he shoot you?"

Kate could hardly hear Mike. His words were broken and almost in a whisper. She could tell he was in a lot of pain as he spoke. "His name is Ryan... He's a DEA agent. I've been working with him to get to the drug-lord, supplying this area. I don't understand what was wrong with him. Something must have happened. Unless..." He didn't finish the sentence, but it didn't really matter at the moment.

"Come on Mike, you have to stay with me. We have to get out of here before he returns." Kate replied.

"You go." Mike responded; his voice barely more than a whisper and his words broken. "You'll be safer without me; I have somewhere I can go. Take my guitar home. I'll join you there as soon as I can. Don't let it out of your sight. I found it at a pawn shop a couple months ago. I'd hate to lose it again."

Kate didn't want to go, she knew Mike was right, but she couldn't just leave him. They had to act fast in case the guy returned. "Come on, I'll drop you at the hospital on my way to the airport. You can't stay here." She said as she quickly taped the towel on the wound, and then grabbed her backpack and his guitar case. She couldn't believe he was so worried about losing his guitar again, but she didn't want to disappoint him.

Tears came to Kate's eyes, but she was afraid to stay there with Mike and take the time to call the police. Since the man who had shot Mike was DEA, he might be monitoring the police radio and hear the call to the police. Ryan might come back, if he was even gone; or just finishing his call outside.

Kate knew their lives were in danger if Ryan returned and found them. He had no logical reason for shooting Mike, unless he had sold out and was no longer acting as a DEA agent.

If he was supposed to be collecting money for the druglord, he also could be in trouble with him for not getting it. The only thing Kate could think to do was run. She needed to find someplace safe for them to hide, but she had no idea where that would be.

Kate helped Mike as he struggled to his feet. She quickly grabbed his coat and baseball cap that were beside the door, in case he would need them later when the temperature dropped. She had heard the door leading out of the building close shortly after the man left, but knew he could return at any time.

As they hurried out of the apartment, she heard the window shatter in the kitchen and wondered why, but she didn't have time to think about it now. They almost knocked over the neighbor Kate had met earlier when she arrived, and stopped for just a minute.

"A man just shot my brother. We're afraid to stay here because he said he would be back and I need to get Mike to the hospital."

4

"I already called the police when I heard what sounded like a gunshot. They should be on their way." The little gray-haired lady stated worriedly.

Kate could tell Mike was struggling to keep his voice calm as he spoke to her. "It's okay Mrs. Miller. You should go back into your apartment, lock the door, and wait for the police. I'll be okay." He then wrapped his arm tighter across Kate's shoulder and they headed down the stairs as quickly as they could manage. She could tell Mike was really struggling, but they couldn't stop now.

Just as Kate started to open the door, they heard a car door slam and then a siren and flashing lights shining through the window at the top of the door. She knew the police had arrived, and her thoughts were racing as she looked around, terrified since all the doors were closed.

She then felt a tug on her arm, and realized Mike was trying to quietly get her attention. She quickly followed as he pointed to an opening under the stairway. She pulled him into the small area just before the entrance door opened.

Kate's heart was still pounding and her hands shaking as they stood in the small space with all the odds and ends and bicycles that had been stored there. She listened intently as two men entered the building and the man, she assumed was a police officer, asked questioningly. "Hey Ryan, what are you doing around here?"

Kate then heard the voice of the man she had seen and heard earlier in the apartment. "I was just in the neighborhood and heard the call so I thought I'd see if you needed any help. With all the drug problems we've had lately, it could be another drug deal gone wrong."

"It does seem as if drug problems have gotten worse lately." The officer replied.

As they continued up the stairs, she heard Ryan say, "Although, the neighbor probably just heard a car backfire?" then he laughed.

Right, Kate thought. They listened as Ryan told the officer, "I can check the apartment and speak to the neighbor who called in the gunshot if you need to get back to work on something else."

"Thanks Ryan, but I'm already here so I might as well check it out, although I'm not looking forward to the paperwork." He said jokingly, then his voice became serious. "Hey, Ryan, that door looks splintered at the frame and it looks like a possible bullet hole in the doorjamb. Maybe the lady did hear a gunshot."

Kate heard what sounded like someone pulling his weapon and shuffling, then a knock and the squeak of the door opening. Footsteps followed as the officer and Ryan walked into the apartment. "That looks like blood and this place has been ransacked. I'd better call this in." The officer stated.

Kate could still hear them shuffling around and was a little surprised when the neighbor stepped out of her apartment. "Mike and his sister left for the hospital. His sister was afraid, since she saw the man who shot her brother."

Ryan hesitated for a moment before he told the neighbor to go back into her apartment and lock the door. The police officer then came out and told him no one was in the apartment.

Kate could imagine Ryan's shock at finding out she had been in the apartment when he had shot Mike. She wondered what he would do although she didn't have to wait long.

As Ryan quickly responded. "The neighbor just said a woman, who claimed to be the sister of the guy who lived here, ran out shortly after she heard the gunshot. She was half dragging the man as he slumped against her and told the neighbor someone shot her brother and she was taking him to a hospital."

Kate couldn't believe it when Ryan then told the officer, "She probably shot him herself and took him to get rid of the body." As she continued to listen, Ryan asked the officer to wait there and call in a possible homicide, even though they didn't have a body yet.

He might also want to have all the hospitals in the area checked, just in case a gunshot victim showed up. Ryan then said he would check the roof.

The officer replied that he thought Ryan might be right and would get a description from the neighbor so he could get a warrant out for the supposed sister. They listened as the officer went into Mrs. Miller's apartment, shortly after.

As soon as Kate heard footsteps above them on the stairs, she didn't waste any more time. She helped Mike up, knowing they had very little time before Ryan would reach the roof. It only made sense that he thought they had gone up the steps, since he hadn't seen them leave the building.

She prayed they could get away before he was able to reach the roof and look over the side. Kate had no doubt he would be looking for them both now and they both needed to disappear.

Kate motioned to Mike to be quiet as they exited the building. Fortunately, she had found a close parking spot earlier, just outside the building entrance, so they didn't have to go far.

She then helped Mike as he stumbled into her rental car, praying no one saw them. She threw Mike's guitar, jacket and baseball cap, along with her backpack into the back seat, then quickly jumped in and started the car.

It was dark and very few people were on the street, which Kate hoped was to their advantage. As she pulled out of the parking place, she noticed a couple of men running toward them in the alley next to Mike's apartment building. She didn't think it had anything to do with them, but she didn't want to take any chances. She quickly hit the accelerator and sped down the street.

Mike told her he didn't feel safe going to a hospital and gave her directions where to go instead. It turned out to be a mission with a clinic, only a few blocks away. The people there were great and told her not to worry; they would take care of him and keep him safe.

Mike then told her they were the people who had helped him get off the drugs and he trusted them. He encouraged her to leave and to be careful, and then collapsed and passed out. The people at the clinic went to work fast, placing him on a gurney and wheeling him to a room in the back. They immediately started an IV and plasma and were checking the wound.

Kate didn't want to leave Mike, he looked terrible and he was so weak. He had lost a lot of blood, and the color in his face was pale. She hoped leaving him there was for the best, and although she didn't want to leave him, she now needed to disappear.

The people at the clinic were encouraging and gave her a card with information and a password, so she could contact them later and they would know it was her. She was hesitant, but finally told them her parents would possibly call and she would give them the password; she then left.

Kate made a quick call to her parents to let them know what had happened as she drove toward the airport. She asked them to contact the police with the information about the DEA agent, Ryan, being at the scene and shooting Mike, and told them she and Mike were safe; for now, she thought.

Her parents said they were catching the first flight out to Las Vegas to bring Mike home. Kate didn't think it was a good idea, especially with the shape he was in and the fact Ryan was looking for him.

She knew they wouldn't listen though, so she told them where to find him. She also gave them the number at the mission from the card and the password they had given her. She then told them not to tell anyone where he was; not even the police, as she didn't know who they could trust.

Kate turned off her phone and drove to the rental agency at the airport and dropped off the car. She was glad she was able to leave the car in a check-in line rather than having to speak with a representative. She was sure they were going to see the blood on the seat when they checked it in.

As she grabbed her backpack out of the backseat, she noticed Mike's coat and hat. Thinking she might need them if the temperatures dropped and possibly to make a good

8

disguise; she grabbed them too. Her thoughts were still scrambled making it difficult to think of what to do next. One step at a time, she thought, as she stepped up into a shuttle heading to the airport.

Money; she had to have money so she wouldn't have to use her charge card again before she got home, just in case they were able to track her transactions. She quickly found an ATM and withdrew enough money to hopefully get her home; as it was all she had.

Kate knew she couldn't follow her plans to fly home; her flight wasn't scheduled to leave until midnight and it was only nine. The police were going to be looking for her or possibly already were, since the police officer was putting a warrant out, that she was wanted for questioning as a suspect for a possible murder she didn't commit. She only hoped they would lose her trail and spend time at the airport or at the car rental where they were sure to find blood on the seat.

It suddenly dawned on Kate she had given a copy of her graduation photo to Mike and it was sitting on the dresser in his bedroom. The photo was signed. "I made it! Love, Kate."

If the officer had found it, it wouldn't take long for them to put out a description of her and a photo for the warrant. The neighbor could identify her as the woman with Mike, from her photo, which was definitely a disadvantage to escaping notice.

Mike had also put her phone number in his phone and she hoped they wouldn't find her number to track her phone's location. She wasn't sure though, if Mike had his phone when they left his apartment. If the police found his phone and he had a password on it, maybe that would at least slow them down.

Kate hadn't noticed any police looking for anyone yet at the airport, but she had noticed several men in dark suits, who appeared to be looking for someone; and hoped they weren't looking for her.

9

She quickly ducked into a restroom, and changed into jeans and put on a clean sweatshirt; then threw her blood-stained clothes into the trash. She didn't think carrying them around was a good idea and hopefully it would slow down the police if they found them; and they would possibly waste time looking for her on flights.

Since she had taken Mike's jacket and baseball cap out of the car, she put on the jacket, then pulled her long hair up and placed the cap on her head. She quickly looked in the mirror to be sure no hair was hanging down around the cap and was surprised when she noticed her appearance was totally different. She hoped the disguise would help.

Looking around before exiting the bathroom, Kate headed towards the departure area. Fortunately, it had cooled off a little, but she was still rather warm. She changed her mind about catching a shuttle downtown to the bus station, and thought a taxi would be quicker, and maybe cooler. She was thankful there were no police cars in sight as she climbed into the taxi.

She did however notice a man dressed in a dark suit looking around, and wondered if he was looking for her. Hopefully he hadn't seen her or was looking for someone else, but he looked a lot like one of the men she had seen running down the alley when they had left Mike's apartment.

She asked the taxi driver to drop her off at the Freemont Casino downtown, because she had remembered from their earlier tour that the bus terminal was downtown. She hoped it would be easy to find.

Fortunately, the taxi driver was a foreigner and wasn't talkative, giving Kate a chance to try to figure out what to do once she got to the bus terminal. Her thoughts were jumbled. Everything had happened so fast; she couldn't focus. She had never been in a situation like this before, and had never been on the run from the police or anyone else.

She needed time to figure out what to do, but right now, it would have to wait until she was out of Las Vegas.

10

Perhaps she would have time to come up with an idea on the bus, if she was able to get on one.

Kate thought maybe she should go to the police, but couldn't imagine the police would believe her word against that of a DEA agent. If Ryan was the one to find her, she was pretty sure he couldn't afford to let her or her brother live. They both knew he had shot Mike and that he was working for the drug-lord, and working both sides wasn't good for his career.

Kate didn't trust Ryan, even though he was a DEA agent. Her brother had said Ryan had changed recently, and unfortunately, she felt it wasn't for the good; perhaps he had been bought out by the drug-lord. Whatever it was, it was making it very bad for her brother, and now her.

When the taxi dropped Kate off at the casino, she walked inside until he drove away. She then got directions to the bus terminal from a person standing near the door. She walked to the bus terminal and was thankful she didn't see any police cars around. She was surprised at how busy it was, even though it was late, but hoped it would work out in her favor.

Kate knew getting her own ticket wasn't a good idea, even with her disguise, as they would ask for ID. She walked around for a few minutes, and noticed a young man sitting in the corner. He looked very sad. His hair was long and unkept and his beard was long and scraggly. His clothes looked dirty and wrinkled as if he had been wearing and sleeping in them for a while.

She had little doubt he was homeless as she knew there were a lot of homeless people in Las Vegas. It was sad, so many people had lost so much from gambling and drugs. He looked so much like Mike had the last time she had seen him; when he was strung out on drugs.

Kate wasn't sure she could trust the homeless man, but she approached him hoping he could help her. He was soft spoken and polite when she offered to pay him to buy her a bus ticket for the next bus getting ready to pull out.

She asked if he had identification and he showed her his driver's license. The license showed his name was Paul Hayworth and he was from Shreveport, Louisiana. He said he would be happy to help.

Kate prayed the bus was heading east toward her family's home in Indiana, but it didn't matter where it was headed, she had to be on it. Kate was thankful and maybe even a little surprised when Paul came back with a ticket and a receipt. He said the next bus getting ready to leave was headed to Denver, which was good for Kate since it would give her several hours to decide what to do next.

Kate's thoughts were racing as she thanked Paul and gave him enough money for a bus ticket, hoping he wouldn't use it for drugs. She then suggested he use the money for something to eat and to go home. She told him she felt his family was probably ready to help if he would let them.

She also suggested he check in at the mission that had helped her brother, which was close by and she told him how to get there. He looked tired and sad as he told her he would try the mission to see if they would help him, like they had her brother.

He hadn't been home in a couple of years and didn't want his family to see him the way he was now. He said things just hadn't gone as he had planned trying to break into the entertainment business, but he hoped he would still be able to be an entertainer someday.

Kate understood how his dreams had been crushed; so much like her brother's. He looked so lost and alone. She didn't know how he had gone from trying to get a job in entertainment, to getting into drugs, like Mike had, but drugs had been their downfall.

She hoped he would follow through and go to the mission and they would be able to help him; however, she knew that was unlikely before he hit rock bottom, if he wasn't already there; and then only if he survived it. She could only pray.

She talked with him for a few more minutes, trying to give him encouragement, then headed outside toward the bus. She stopped when she noticed a police car pulling into the terminal. When the two officers got out, she hid in the shadows, wondering if she should say something to them, but was hesitant. Although it hadn't been long, she worried they were looking for her.

Kate was shocked when she heard the description they were giving as they walked toward the terminal. It matched her description except for her six-foot height. Her thoughts went wild; she wasn't ready to go to jail. If Ryan found out she was anywhere he could reach her, she doubted she would make it through the night, even in jail.

Kate wondered if Mike was alright or if Ryan had found him yet, but there was no time for worrying about it now, since the bus would be leaving shortly and she had to be on it. She wasn't sure what she would do when she got to Denver, but at least she would be out of Las Vegas.

She pulled out her cell phone and stepped back into the shadows of the building, but within sight of the bus. She needed to be proactive, so she dialed the police station and asked to speak with a homicide detective.

A gruff voice answered the phone, "Homicide, Detective Dodd speaking."

Hoping Detective Dodd would believe her, she quickly explained what had happened, but when he asked where she was, she quickly hung up. She was beginning to feel she would be safer on her own since she didn't know who she could trust.

Kate called her parents and told them who to contact at the police station, and that her phone would be off for a while as her battery was almost dead. She said she would call them later and wished them luck on getting to Mike and told them she loved them, before hanging up.

She then turned off her phone before placing it into her backpack. Kate slung her backpack over her shoulder, picked up Mike's guitar and stayed in the shadows as she watched the officers search the terminal and then head toward the buses.

Her bus was about to leave, but she couldn't take a chance on boarding with the officers checking it out. Even with her disguise, she didn't want to take the chance. She had to be patient, but it was hard knowing her best chance of getting out of town was about to pull away without her.

Kate watched worriedly as the officers exited the bus she needed to board. She ducked back quickly as they looked around the bus and checked the luggage compartment. As soon as the officers boarded the next bus, she walked quickly, staying close to the bus to avoid being seen, then stepped in. Trying to act shy and keeping her head lowered, she smiled at the bus driver as she handed him her ticket.

She was thankful to see the bus was only half full when she walked down the aisle. She found a seat near the back of the bus with no one sitting close to bother her. Fortunately, the bus driver closed the doors and started off shortly after she was seated.

Kate found herself thanking God for helping her get this far. It had been a long time since she had thought about praying and relying on God, perhaps too long, but she had to try something. She felt that praying for guidance from God was her only hope.

Kate thought she could get a flight or another bus from Denver to Indiana, but then realized Indiana would be the first place Ryan would look for her. She wasn't sure what she was going to do, but at least she was on her way out of Las Vegas.

Fortunately, it was dark and most of the people on the bus were sleeping. She had to concentrate and figure out where to go. Staying with anyone in Indiana, where most of her family and friends lived, would be too obvious and possibly put them in danger; and her friends at school had already gone home.

Kate finally had time to think, but still didn't understand why the DEA agent had suggested a warrant be put out for her for murder. Was he hoping to have help with finding her and hoping someone would shoot first and ask questions later? That was a scary thought.

Did it mean he was planning to find her brother and kill him first, then come after her? With all his connections, it probably wouldn't be hard for him to track her down. Ryan probably knew about the mission and where Mike would go, which is what worried her the most. There had to be somewhere else for her to go, but where?

Being on a bus to Colorado reminded Kate she and her friend Jessica had plans to be near Colorado Springs for a two-week vacation at a dude ranch, in a little over a week. Perhaps she could find a place to hide out near there while she waited for Jessica to arrive. It was a long shot, but hopefully better than going home.

Maybe she could try to find a bed and breakfast or a small motel near the ranch, where she could pay cash and might not be seen. She wondered if staying in a larger city like Denver or Colorado Springs would be better and harder for Ryan to find her.

She didn't know how long her money would last if she had to pay much for a room and food. Her problems kept mounting and she wished she had some answers and wondered if things could get any worse.

It would help if her hiding out was only for a short time, but that would only happen if the police believed her, which was doubtful. It was only wishful thinking, but she hoped someone would believe her and Ryan would be arrested, instead of her.

Kate kept running different scenarios through her mind, but nothing seemed feasible. She tried to close her eyes and rest, but thoughts of Mike and the blood on his shirt, kept appearing when she closed her eyes.

The sound of the gunshot woke her several times when she had dozed off, so she found it hard to get any sleep, even though she was extremely exhausted. It had been several days since she had gotten much sleep with exams, vacation, and then what had happened last night.

Kate must have dozed off for a short time though, as she was startled awake when the bus came to a stop. It was still dark when the driver announced they were near Salt Lake City, Utah, and were stopping at a small café. They would be there for a half hour to gas up and if anyone wanted to, they could enjoy an early breakfast.

Kate went to the bathroom on the bus as the others got up and left. She grabbed her backpack and the guitar; afraid someone might take it if she left it. She remembered Mike had made her promise not to let the guitar out of her sight and she planned to keep her promise.

As she stepped off the bus, the wind was so strong it almost blew Mike's baseball cap off her head, and she had to quickly grab hold of it. She could tell a storm was brewing as the temperature had dropped considerably and she could smell the moisture in the air.

She was glad she had thought to grab Mike's jacket, although not in the best of shape, it had worked well as a pillow, even if it was lumpy. It worked somewhat better now against the weather and in hiding her figure. Although she was tall and thin, she wasn't shaped like a boy under the jacket.

Kate fought the wind, hanging on tightly to Mike's cap as she walked to the side of the building to try and block the wind. She pulled out her phone and turned it on. Thankfully, there was a signal, and she made a call to Jessica.

She was glad when Jessica answered quickly. "Jess, I only have a little battery life left on my phone, so just listen. Mike was shot by a DEA agent, but he's okay for now. At least I hope he still is.

I saw the agent shoot him, but he didn't see me and I know the agent is trying to blame the shooting on me and saying that I killed Mike. He had the police put out a warrant with my description and possibly my photo, as I gave Mike my graduation photo.

I caught a bus heading east. I'll make it to Colorado and hide out, then hopefully meet you at the dude ranch as planned. Please call and tell mom and dad I'm alright. They may already be on a flight to Las Vegas or will be soon, but maybe at least you can leave them a message.

I haven't spoken with them since I left Las Vegas last night. They were hoping to convince Mike to talk with the police, then to come home with them, but I'm not sure he will be in any condition to travel. He lost a lot of blood.

I just hope the agent doesn't find out and try to use them to get to me or Mike. At least Mike has a different last name, so that might slow him down in finding mom and dad and the agent may not expect mom and dad to fly out to Las Vegas.

Please pick up some clothes for me since I only have my backpack with a few things. Tell them not to let anyone know where I might be and to call and leave a message when they get there and find Mike."

Kate could tell Jessica was shocked by the sound of her voice. "Are you sure you're, okay? Do you want me to meet you somewhere and pick you up? I can leave right now."

Kate's phone was beeping letting her know her battery was almost dead. "My battery is gone. As soon as I can recharge, I'll give you a call. Otherwise, just plan to meet me as scheduled at the dude ranch. Bye."

The phone went dead and Kate hoped Jessica heard the end of the message. She quickly turned off the phone and stuffed it back into her backpack, then fought the wind again as she headed to the door and entered the small café.

Kate felt every eye on her, as she worked her way to an empty booth near the back, next to a window facing the parking lot. As soon as she sat down, she felt around the edge of the cap, hoping, the strong wind hadn't blown any stray hair loose. She really needed her disguise to work.

The waitress startled her as she walked up to the booth with a coffee pot in her hand and asked if she could take her order. It took Kate a moment to get her nerves under control. She wasn't hungry and doubted she could eat, even if she was, but felt she should order something.

Trying to talk in a lower voice, she ordered toast and coffee. The waitress turned over a cup on the table and filled it, then left to get the toast, which didn't take long.

As Kate drank the coffee and nibbled a little on the piece of toast, she listened to the wind now howling outside. She noticed two cowboys at the booth in front of hers, laughing and talking about cattle and horses. The cowboy facing her was really cute with sandy blond hair and gorgeous blue eyes. The other cowboy had dark brown hair, but his back was to her so she couldn't see his eyes.

She glanced up a few times thinking the one facing her might be interesting to get to know. Now wasn't the time to be thinking about that, though, especially since she was in so much trouble and would never see him again.

The next time she glanced up, she caught the cute cowboy looking at her. Their eyes held for just a moment before she quickly looked down. She couldn't take a chance on anyone being able to recognize her.

Kate had barely touched her toast when she noticed a sheriff's car pull up in front of the café. Her heart began to pound as she watched the sheriff get out and walk into the cafe. She froze as panic swept through her. The panic increased as the sheriff first looked around the café then began showing a photo around.

When he walked up to her and showed her the photo, her breath caught and she was terrified; it was a copy of her graduation photo, she had given her brother. It was hard to believe they had gotten her photo out so quickly, although with all the new technology, she knew it probably wasn't too hard.

She kept her head lowered and it took a moment before she could find her voice to speak. Using a low voice that wasn't much more than a whisper with a knot caught in her throat, Kate told the sheriff she hadn't seen her; then holding her breath she prayed he had believed her. He hesitated for just a moment and she thought she was going to pass out, but fortunately the sheriff moved on and she finally let out her breath.

Kate was thankful she had thought to grab Mike's jacket and cap when they had left his apartment, and her disguise as a boy had worked, at least this time. Fortunately, her thin build and six-foot height wasn't apparent in the picture, and she was sure it helped with her disguise.

She had tried to keep her head lowered, but looked up as the sheriff walked toward the table where the cowboys were eating. She was surprised to see the cowboy facing her, staring at her. The sheriff then handed her photo to the cute cowboy. She was caught off guard by his comment after looking at it. "Haven't seen her, but wouldn't mind meeting her."

The sheriff replied. "Not sure you'd want to get mixed up with this one; she could be armed and dangerous. She's wanted for a possible homicide in Nevada for killing her brother. This photo was faxed a few minutes ago and I knew there was a bus from Las Vegas scheduled to be here, so I thought I'd check it out. It doesn't look like she was on it, though."

"Guess that goes to show, you never can tell anything about a woman by the way she looks. Looks can be deceiving." The cowboy commented. He looked at the other cowboy and then back at her once the sheriff walked away. He must have noticed her fear because he looked at her strangely before resuming his conversation with the dark-haired cowboy.

Kate's thoughts went wild with worry that the cowboy may have recognized her, but then thought he would have mentioned it to the sheriff if he had. She was also worried about not being able to contact anyone who might know about Mike, now that her phone was dead.

Homicide? was her brother dead? Did Ryan find him already and kill him? Armed and dangerous, was Ryan hoping someone would shoot first and ask questions later? Was he already after her?

Kate was worried and couldn't slow down the questions. Too many questions and no way of finding out the answers was really frightening. Her attention was drawn back to the sheriff as he stopped at the counter after talking with the other people in the diner and asked the bus driver if anyone else was on the bus.

The bus driver said he thought everyone had come in, but they were getting ready to load up so the sheriff was welcome to check it out. He then announced they would be leaving in ten minutes, then headed out with the sheriff to check the bus and the passengers as they boarded.

Kate knew she couldn't get back on the bus with the sheriff checking everyone as they boarded. He hadn't spent much time looking at her in the café, but that didn't mean he wouldn't if she boarded the bus.

Kate wasn't sure what to do. She couldn't stay at the café with the sheriff already looking for her. She didn't really want to battle the storm, but it looked as if she had no other choice. Her thoughts were running wild trying to figure out what to do now. Perhaps she could stay at the café until the storm passed over or another bus arrived, but she didn't know how long that would be.

Fortunately, Kate had brought her backpack and Mike's guitar in with her when she left the bus. She worriedly looked out the window where the wind was whipping around the flags in the parking lot and huge drops of rain were starting to slam against the window.

Kate had to do something, so she quickly got up. She hesitated for a moment as she looked first at the women's restroom, then went into the men's restroom, hoping it was empty. She hid in a stall and stayed there until she heard the bus drive off a few minutes later.

Kate couldn't just stay in the restroom forever; she had to move, go somewhere, even if she had no idea where or how, especially in this weather. She grabbed her things and slowly opened the door, checking for the sheriff. She didn't see him in the café, so she looked out the window catching a glimpse of his car as it pulled away.

She was surprised to see the two cowboys were still sitting in the booth drinking coffee when she walked out and picked up the check from the table. She was dreading the thought of walking out into the storm, but she didn't know what else to do.

The cute cowboy was looking at her questioningly, but she was afraid to speak or acknowledge him. She couldn't take the chance. Kate wished her circumstances were different. His comment had surprised her and he was so handsome, and something about him intrigued her, but she didn't have time to think about it or anything but getting away right now.

***

Sam had watched the kid from the time he had walked into the café and sat in the booth facing him. He seemed to be alone, tired, and frightened, and Sam wondered why. He had only ordered toast and coffee, so he probably didn't have much money and he had hardly touched the toast or the coffee.

Sam had noticed the panic on the kid's face when the local sheriff had walked in and wondered why, although it seemed the officer hadn't been looking for him. The kid had been especially nervous after the sheriff had stopped at his table and shown him the photo of the woman.

No matter what, he thought the kid needed help and hoped he wasn't running from the law. Perhaps the kid was just running away from home with his guitar to start a new life, but whatever it was, Sam could tell the kid was really scared. He wasn't totally surprised when the kid ran into the restroom after the sheriff walked out with the bus driver or that he missed the bus.

Sam was worried about the kid, so he mentioned it to, Nick, as he started to get up. "Why don't we wait a minute; I'm kind of worried about the kid, he looks like he might need help. If he doesn't come out of the restroom soon, I'll go check on him. Maybe we can help him out and give him a lift since he missed his bus."

"You know it's against the law to transport a minor across the state line; or a convict." Nick replied.

"I don't think he's a minor and he doesn't look much like a convict, just a scared kid. The sheriff didn't appear to be interested in him, so there's a chance he's not wanted by the law. I do think he's afraid of something though and we should help him if we can, especially since that storm outside is probably going to last a while. I'd hate to see him caught out in it."

"Whatever you think; if there's anything we can do, I'll go along with it." Nick responded hesitantly as he sat back down and picked up his coffee cup.

The bus had just pulled away and Sam was getting ready to get up, when he noticed the restroom door open slowly, so he picked up his cup and took a drink. He watched as the kid walked out of the restroom, looked out the window, then picked up the check from the table where he had sat, and started toward the cashier.

"You just missed the bus kid and the weather's pretty nasty out there. If you need a ride, we can get you as far as Colorado Springs, if you don't mind the smell of cattle."

Kate was startled and frightened at first, but his voice was soft and he really seemed concerned. What made him think she would consider accepting a ride with two strangers? She thought, but the café was almost empty, the storm was raging and she didn't know when another bus would stop. What other choice did she have, especially with the sheriff here already looking for her?

The two cowboys had been polite and respectful to the waitress, and the cashier, who was the owner; and had stopped to talk with the cowboys earlier. All she could do was pray God would watch over her and hope He listened. She felt safer being disguised as a boy, at least she hoped she was safer.

Kate took another look out the window at the pouring rain and then tried to keep her voice low as she replied. "Thanks mister, I'd appreciate a ride. I really hadn't meant to miss my bus. It's just, I um… got sick and didn't realize I took so long in the bathroom." Kate didn't want to lie to him, but was unsure of what else to say, so she had said the first thing that came to mind.

Kate was surprised when the cowboy stood as he was a few inches taller than her. He introduced himself as Sam and the other cowboy as Nick then grabbed the check from her hand. She tried to protest and hand him some money, but he refused, so for a couple of dollars, she didn't argue. She watched as he paid her bill along with theirs before he motioned toward the door.

Kate had noticed when Nick had stood, he was closer to her six-foot height. She also noticed he was nice looking and very polite. As Sam paid the bill, Nick took off running toward the truck to unlock it. They were not far behind and Kate was happy when they reached the truck that Nick had already started it.

The rain pelted them as they ran. It was pouring and the wind was whipping it around. Kate really felt they were fortunate the truck hadn't been far. Mike's jacket wasn't much help against the cold rain and she had to hang on to his cap, to keep it from flying off. Fortunately, even with the wind it had stayed on her head.

Sam opened the front passenger door and motioned for Kate to get in. He quickly threw her backpack and guitar in the back seat, before he jumped in the front beside her. She would have preferred sitting in the back, but there was lots of stuff already back there, so she didn't mention it.

They were soaked, but the truck was dry and it didn't take long for the heater to warm the cab and to start drying them off. Kate felt strange sandwiched between the two cowboys, but she hadn't been given a choice. She tried to hold her arms in and not touch them, especially since Sam seemed to have had a strange effect on her when her arm had accidentally touched his.

Kate really didn't feel like talking, so she pretended to be tired, but unfortunately Sam was inquisitive. "What's your name kid?"

23

She simply stated "Kit" which wasn't really a lie since that had been her dad's nickname for her since she was young; it was short for his kitten.

"Where are you from?" Sam asked.

"I grew up in Indiana." Kate replied.

"Is that where you're headed?" Sam asked as he was really curious about the boy and what had frightened him.

Kate tried to maintain a low voice as she responded. "I'm on my way to a place near Colorado Springs, before heading home." It actually was the truth, although not her original destination. She also omitted being in Las Vegas and fortunately, he hadn't questioned where she was coming from. Although, the Las Vegas hat, she had on probably gave it away.

"Do you have a job lined up in Colorado to play your guitar?" Sam asked.

Kate didn't want to lie to him, so she told him the truth. "No, it belongs to my brother and I'm taking it home for him. I'm just making a short stop in Colorado first."

Sam wondered why he was taking his brothers guitar home, but he didn't ask. "You seemed pretty worried back there at the café when the sheriff walked in; you aren't wanted by the law are you?"

How did she answer that without lying to him? She couldn't tell him the truth. They would probably throw her out and leave her or worse, turn her in to the police, which might truly seal her fate. "I haven't done anything to cause the law to be after me. I'm just heading back home after a vacation with a friend to visit my brother. I hadn't planned to miss the bus. I really appreciate you guys giving me a ride."

"Not a problem Kit. Glad we could help, but if you've got a problem, you need help with, all you need do is ask. Did you have a good vacation?" Sam asked.

"Yes, it was nice visiting with my brother." Kate replied.

She could tell Sam didn't completely believe her story, but at least he didn't question it, and just offered to help,

24

which was really thoughtful. He seemed like a nice guy and she wished there was time to get to know him better. Too bad the timing was so totally off.

Kate needed to find a way to change the subject and get him to stop questioning her. "Thank you, but I'm fine, just really tired. What do you guys do?"

She sat quietly trying hard not to fall asleep and have the nightmare of what had happen return. Her short, restless naps on the bus hadn't helped. Memories of Mike covered in blood and thoughts of how he was, had kept her awake most of the time.

She listened as best she could, as they told her stories about a ranch in Colorado where they were taking the cattle. They did most of the talking then and she enjoyed their stories about the ranch; and was surprised they lived and worked on a dude ranch.

They had a lot of funny stories, but her mind kept wandering to what had happened last night and what she was going to do next. She was thankful Sam and Nick seemed to be very nice and thoughtful and wondered if somehow, God had placed them at just the right place and time to help her. Maybe He hadn't given up on her after all.

Chapter 2

Kate thought it would be impossible for her to fall asleep, but she must have, because when she opened her eyes, the sun was up and shining beautifully. She noticed the phenomenal majestic mountains surrounding them. "WOW!" was all she could think to say.

"Amazing, isn't it?" Sam laughed and responded. "We are near Vail, Colorado."

"I've never seen anything like this before. It's breathtaking." Kate replied.

"It's one of my favorite places, especially in the winter as skiing is terrific here. If you ever have a chance, you should check it out." Sam said.

"Believe me, I think this will be my next vacation." Kate responded in awe, while trying to keep her voice low.

Wanting to keep Sam from asking too many questions again, Kate then asked if the mountains, near where they were from, were anything like these. She was glad Sam was willing to carry the conversation by talking about the hills and mountains around where they lived, rather than asking her questions.

Sam then went on to tell Kate more about the dude ranch where he was foreman. She especially loved the funny stories about people who had stayed there, which lifted her spirits, at least a little. It made her wonder if the ranch Sam talked about could possibly be the same dude ranch, she and her friend Jessica had scheduled their vacation at almost a year ago.

Their vacation was supposed to start in a little over a week, and she really hoped it was the same ranch since Sam and Nick seemed so nice. She wondered if she and Jessica would have funny stories to share after their stay; if she was even able to go. She knew Jessica would be able to go, but what about her. Would this nightmare be over by then, she wondered sadly.

Kate hoped that if the ranch she had made reservations at, wasn't the same dude ranch where Sam and Nick worked, it would at least be a lot like their dude ranch. It sounded like so much fun.

She wondered if there would be any great cowboys like them, especially Sam, but she doubted she would find another Sam. She wished things were different and she had time to get to know him, but it wasn't possible now.

Unfortunately, Kate wasn't even sure she would be able to go on her vacation to the dude ranch: due to still being on the run or worse. A lot could happen between now and then.

She wondered what would happen if Ryan found her and what she needed to do next. Once Sam and Nick dropped her off, she would be on her own again. She knew she had to find a safe place to hide, but she didn't have a clue where that would be.

***

It was nearing noon when they pulled into a truck stop to grab a bite to eat and get some gas. Sam turned to Kate and asked. "Hey Kit, you getting hungry?"

At first, Kate said she wasn't, but then her stomach began to growl, which totally embarrassed her.

Sam laughed. "I guess that answered my question."

Kate knew she hadn't eaten since dinner the night before, so she was hungry, but she was worried about going in and possibly someone recognizing her. She looked around and didn't see any police cars, but that didn't mean they wouldn't stop by or hadn't been there already with her photo. She just couldn't take the chance.

"Yes, I guess it does." Kate finally answered quietly. "Would you mind bringing me back a hamburger and a coke? I can give you some money. I'm really tired and would rather just wait for you here and rest; if you don't mind?" As she replied, she put her hand in her pocket to get some money.

Sam hesitated for a moment, then placed his hand on Kit's arm to stop him from dragging out any money. "My treat Kit."

27

Sam had watched Kit as he looked around the parking lot with a worried expression. He also thought back and remembered how Kit had awakened several times from his short naps, during the trip, confused and frightened. His dreams must have been terrifying and Sam wondered why. He wished the kid would confide in him, although he understood why he possibly was afraid to confide in a stranger. It didn't mean he liked it though. He was worried about the boy and just wanted to help.

Sam also remembered how frightened Kit had been earlier at the café, especially after the sheriff had arrived, and how tired he looked now. "If that's what you want. I'll bring a burger and coke back for you and don't worry about the money, I've got it. What would you like on your burger?"

Kate could see the concern in Sam's eyes and was thankful he was turning out to be a really nice guy, but she was going to have to find a way to repay him. She wished things could be different, but they weren't, so she simply responded. "Lettuce, tomato and mayonnaise, please, and thank you."

"It's raining pretty hard here, so you might want to stay in the truck and stay dry. Don't feel you have to leave now Kit. We'll get you to Colorado Springs, you don't have to worry." Sam responded, hoping Kit wouldn't take off while they were eating and planned to watch the truck while they were inside.

He wanted to trust the kid, but couldn't be sure he wouldn't take anything. He worried about the truck and the load of cattle they had in the trailer, although it wouldn't be very easy to steal without the keys, unless the kid knew how to hotwire a vehicle.

Kate had thought about getting out and taking off, but she didn't know where she would go. She hadn't figured that out yet. As soon as Sam and Nick left, Kate slid down in the seat, so hopefully she wouldn't be seen, but could watch for any police cars that might arrive. She had to stay awake and figure out what she would do once they got to Colorado Springs where they were planning to drop her off.

Everything was such a mess and she didn't have any way to find out about Mike. She prayed he was still okay and then continued praying for help, guidance, and faith to trust God. Even though she doubted He would listen to her after her lack of faith the last few years; she knew God was her only hope of surviving this horrible ordeal.

Kate was startled as she heard the truck locks click, and then soon after the doors were opened. She was frightened at first as she hadn't seen Sam and Nick walking up, and then relaxed a little when she realized it was them.

In a way, she was relieved they were back and they could get back on the road, but in other ways she was worried. She still wasn't sure what she would do once they dropped her off.

Kate was surprised as Sam handed her a large bag and looked at him quizzically as he said. "Thought you might like some fries to go with your burger." He then placed a drink in the cup holder in front of her. "And Kit, this is for you too."

Kate had to smile, but couldn't take the chance of looking at Sam as she replied. "Thank you. It all smells great; and I love fries."

As the truck started off, Kate opened the bag and was surprised at how many fries there were and how large the hamburger was. She knew there was no way she was going to eat it all, but she was going to try to at least eat some. She offered fries to Sam and Nick, but they refused stating they were full already from their burgers and fries, which there were a lot more of than they had expected.

After eating a few fries, Kate unwrapped the sandwich and took a big juicy bite, savoring the flavor, but after just a couple more bites, she had to give up. It was great, but it was all she could handle so she wrapped it up and placed it back in the bag. She had been hungry, and it was good, but she really didn't feel much like eating. She ate a few more fries and drank part of the coke, and then gave up. She had more important things she needed to be thinking about.

Sam was surprised Kit had eaten so little, as the food had really been good. He was hoping to get him talking again and maybe drop his guard and tell him what was wrong. He didn't know why, but he really wanted to know what was causing Kit to be so frightened and hoped he could help. "Done already?" he asked.

"Yes, thank you. It was very good, but way too much for me to handle. I figure I can save the rest for later." Kate replied.

Sam worried Kit was afraid he wouldn't be able to afford to eat later, once they dropped him off in Colorado Springs. That was sad. He really wished there was something he could do to alleviate Kit's problem, whatever it was. "I'm glad you liked it."

Sam hesitated for just a few moments before he stated. "You know Kit, it often helps to talk about things when we have a problem. We're really open to hearing about what is bothering you and hopefully we can help. You can trust us, Kit."

Kate thought for a minute. It was uncanny, but for some reason, she felt she could trust them, and wished she could tell them, but there wasn't anything they could do. She wasn't even sure they would believe her story. And with a man hunting her down to kill her by now, it would only put their lives in danger too.

"Thanks Sam, but I'm okay and there's nothing you could do to help. I just need to get some rest before you drop me off in Colorado Springs." Kate replied quietly. She then laid back in the seat, pulled the cap down a little and closed her eyes. She wasn't really expecting to sleep, but hoping it would help keep Sam from questioning her any further.

Sam didn't really like the idea Kit felt there was nothing he could do to help him without even trying. It only made him wonder more what was terrifying him. He just wished there was something he could do, so he prayed.

When they reached Colorado Springs, Kit was sleeping and Sam really felt he needed it; and he wasn't ready to give up on him yet. He knew it was probably a long shot, but he wanted to help, so Sam whispered to Nick that he didn't think Kit really had any place to go and to drive on to the ranch. If needed, he could bring Kit back later. The ranch wasn't far, so Nick agreed and continued on.

***

Kate was startled awake when the truck came to a stop. Her head was lying against Sam's shoulder. She hadn't thought it possible, but she had fallen into a dreamless sleep. Not thinking clearly, she quickly jerked back, knocking the baseball cap off her head. Panic ran through her as she felt her long hair hit her shoulders then quickly cascade down her back.

Sam looked at Kate and immediately recognized her from the photo the sheriff had shown them at the diner. He then realized why she had seemed so frightened. "Do you think there's something you might want to tell us before we call the sheriff?"

Kate wanted to jump out of the truck and run, but she was sandwiched between them and couldn't move. Nick looked at her strangely before he commented. "You're the woman in the photo, the police were looking for this morning. The one who killed her brother."

"But I didn't kill him. I saw the guy who shot my brother and my brother said the guy was a DEA agent. I tried to stop the bleeding then got my brother out of the apartment and to a mission clinic where he thought he would be safe." She said worriedly as she looked at each of them, but with little hope of them believing her.

"Mike, my brother, told me it wasn't safe to stay with him and to get out of town and find someplace to hide, so I am. I know you don't believe me, but it's true. I wouldn't shoot my own brother." She could feel the tears welling up in her eyes, but she fought to keep them from falling.

"Why didn't you go to the police?" Sam asked.

31

"Would you if you'd just seen a DEA agent shoot your brother? He also appeared to be good friends with the police in Las Vegas and with a drug-lord."

"I guess not." Sam slowly replied.

Kate then continued, speaking quickly trying to explain, yet knowing there was no way they would believe her. She told them the neighbor had heard the shot and had called the police, so she and her brother had hidden under a stairway when they heard a car door slam as they had started to leave the building. We heard the siren and saw the lights of a police car outside. "The agent was still there when the police officer arrived." She emphasized.

Then she told them the officer who responded seemed to know the DEA agent and she had heard them joking around with each other. She told them the agent had taken a call right after he shot her brother, and then left the apartment to talk with the person and must have been sitting in his car.

She had heard the neighbor tell the officer and the agent she and her brother had left for the hospital. The agent told the officer the women must have pretended to be his sister and had shot the guy and took the body; and was trying to blame it on someone else. "I didn't shoot my brother!"

Kate was trying hard to hold back the tears as she remembered all that had happened, she continued, with little hope it would help. "We didn't know what to do other than run. My brother was afraid for us to stay together. I dropped him off at a mission with a clinic. He thought they would be able to help him since he had lost so much blood.

I then went to the airport and dropped off my rental car, took a shuttle to the airport, changed clothes, then caught a taxi to a casino downtown near the bus terminal and got on a bus. I did contact a Detective Dodd while I was at the bus terminal and told him what had happened, but I don't know if he believed me."

"Weren't you afraid to show your ID to get a bus ticket? That would make it easy for the police to trace where you were going." Sam asked.

Kate hesitated for only a moment before telling them about the homeless guy who had helped her by purchasing the ticket. She then went on to tell them about the graduation photo she had given Mike that he had placed on his dresser. It was the same photo the sheriff had shown them at the café. She explained that the neighbor must have confirmed it was her.

"I hadn't thought about them finding the photo and getting it out so quickly. Mike also had my phone number in his phone. I don't know if Mike had his phone on him, but I'm hoping Ryan didn't find it. Just in case, I've tried to keep my phone turned off, it doesn't have any battery life left anyway."

Kate was frantic as she continued. She didn't think Sam and Nick were believing her bizarre story, but she had to try. "If you'll let me, I'll leave. You've been nice to me and I don't want to put you in danger.

I know the agent will be looking for me so I can't identify or testify against him. If I can leave now, maybe I can find some place to hide out. I can't go home because I know that's the first place he'll look and I'd be putting my family in danger."

Sam could see her worried expression and the tears in her eyes, and although her story sounded crazy, he wanted to believe her. "Maybe we can help."

"But what could you do? Nobody can help." She said as the tears began to run down her cheeks.

Sam hoped he wasn't making a big mistake, as he looked over at Nick who gave him a nod, so he finally responded. "The sheriff here is a friend of ours and I know he will help if he thinks you're telling us the truth.

Under the circumstances, it might be risky having you in a jail cell if a DEA agent is really looking for you. If the sheriff agrees, I'll tell him I'll be responsible for you so no one can find you, if you promise to work with the sheriff and don't try to run off or shoot us."

"I can't stay here. I would only be putting you guys in danger; and I can't do that." Kate responded.

"If the DEA agent can't find you, then none of us would be in danger." Sam replied.

Kate was surprised, but wasn't sure what else to do or where to go and for some unknown reason, she wanted to trust Sam and Nick. They had only been nice and helped her so far.

"I'm not armed and I'm not dangerous, I promise, and I would never shoot anyone. I would be happy to talk with the sheriff and hopefully get this straightened out. Maybe he can contact Detective Dodd in Las Vegas after we talk to confirm what I've told you and hopefully check out the DEA agent."

"What made you decide to hide out in Colorado?" Sam asked.

"I'm supposed to meet a friend a week from Sunday. We have plans to meet at a dude ranch we made reservations at several months ago, and if we're near Colorado Springs, it shouldn't be far."

"Do you know the name of the ranch?"

Kate hesitated for a few moments, not really sure if she should let them know where she would hopefully be going, but she had already told them everything else, so it wouldn't make much difference. "Yes, it's Jake's Dude Ranch near the Black Hills northwest of Colorado Springs."

She noticed the strange look on Sam's face as he looked over at Nick. "Well Kit, you don't have far to go."

"What do you mean?" Kate asked.

"Welcome to Jake's Dude Ranch. Can you give me the name the reservations were made under so we can check it out?" Nick responded.

Kate was so surprised; she looked at him in shock, before she finally found her voice, "Kate, Kate Davis."

"So. are you, Kate Davis?" Nick asked.

"Yes, my dad nicknamed me Kit when I was a kid; short for his kitten. So, I didn't lie to you about my name and I'm not lying to you about what happened either."

Kate could hear the concern in Nick's voice as he spoke. "We'll set you up in one of the cabins. You should be safe here, as it would be hard for anyone to find out where you are. We'll let the rest of the guys know though, so they can keep an eye out for anything unusual or anyone they don't know, just in case."

"I couldn't ask you to do that." She responded. She definitely didn't want everyone at the ranch thinking she had shot her brother, but she understood why Nick didn't want to take a chance in case there was a DEA agent looking for her. At least maybe he did believe some of her bizarre story.

"You didn't ask, I offered, but you have to promise not to leave or shoot us, and to talk with the sheriff today. Sam can give him a call." Nick responded.

Kate was amazed they were willing to help her; they didn't even know her. "Thank you. I really appreciate your help. I had no idea where I would go and I feel safer here than on my own. You guys are truly an answer to a prayer.

I promise not to leave or shoot anyone, and I'll be happy to speak to the sheriff as soon as possible. I just hope he doesn't put me in jail and let the agent know where I am."

Sam couldn't believe how attracted he was to this woman. She was even more beautiful than her photo. How could he be so attracted to a person who had possibly shot or killed her own brother?

At least her brother was still alive, if she was telling the truth. "Come on Kit, I'll show you to a cabin and watch out for you until the sheriff arrives and he can decide where would be best for you to stay."

"My name is Kate, not Kit."

Sam just grinned as he replied. "I think I like your nickname. It seems to fit you."

Kate smiled, but couldn't blame Sam for not trusting her, although he was trying to make it sound as if he was worried about something happening to her rather than her disappearing. He seemed so caring, and she wondered if she really could trust him with her life or if she would be putting him in danger by allowing him to help her.

As they got out of the truck, Nick turned to a ranch-hand who was walking toward them and asked him to get help and unload the cattle into a nearby corral. He then turned and Kate noticed an older man walking toward them. He walked up to Kate with a wonderful smile as he held out his hand. "Well, what do we have here boys, are you going to introduce me?"

Sam began the introduction. "Jake, this is Kit... I mean Kate Davis. She's a guest that was planning to arrive a week from Sunday, but she ran into some trouble and we picked her up on our way home."

"Well Kate, it's very nice to meet you. I'm glad the boys were able to help you out. I'm Jake and welcome to my ranch."

Jake was very handsome for an older man and his smile was genuine. Kate really liked him, but she knew once he found out the rest of her story, his impression of her would probably change. "It's nice to meet you too and I'm really thankful for their help. I just hope it won't be a problem, but please let me know if it is."

Nick then spoke up. "It won't be a problem, Kate; I'll let him know what happened. We'll see you later."

Nick then turned to Sam. "Why don't you take her to the cabin closest to the barn, it will probably be the safest and easiest for us to keep an eye on."

Kate watched as Nick and Jake walked up the hill toward the huge house near the top then turned to Sam and spoke softly. "Thank you."

"You're welcome." He replied as he grabbed her backpack and guitar from the backseat and another duffle bag before directing her toward the nearest cabin.

It was turning dark, so Kate couldn't see much, but she could hear water running nearby and noticed a small stream as she started up the steps to the cabin. Sam was so near; she could smell the scent of his musk aftershave. It bothered her that she was so attracted to him, which was something she couldn't deal with right now.

Kate was amazed as they walked into the small cabin. It was very nicely decorated with a rustic flare. There was a large living room with a fireplace and above it was a beautiful painting of a deer, feeding near a stream. There were two bedrooms with a bathroom in between.

Beside the second bedroom was a closet and some louver doors, she hoped were hiding a washer and dryer, as mentioned on the website she had checked out. She needed to do her laundry since everything she had with her, which wasn't much, had been worn and the only jeans and sweatshirt she had with her, she was wearing.

Sam noticed the amazed, but worried expression on Kate's face as they walked into the cabin. "Don't worry; you don't have to be afraid of me. Actually, if anyone should be afraid, I think it should be me."

Kate looked at him and tried to smile. "I've never had any desire to use a gun, and hopefully will never have the need to do so. You will be safe, and if you'd like to check my backpack for a gun, you're welcome to."

Sam returned her smile. He had planned to do just that, but wasn't exactly sure how to approach her, so he was thankful she had suggested it. "That does make me feel a lot better."

He then showed her around the small cabin before he placed her backpack and guitar case on the bed in the bedroom furthest from the door. "I hate to ask you this, but if you don't mind, I would like to take a look in your guitar case too. And would you please empty your jacket pockets onto the bed?"

As he unzipped the side pocket of the backpack, Kate asked if he would hand her the phone and charging cord, which he did. He then pointed to an outlet where she plugged it in as he unzipped the main compartment, first pulling out her computer before reaching back in.

As Kate watched Sam, she turned on her cell phone and wasn't surprised when it showed she had three messages.

She expected the first two as they were from her friend, Jessica, and her parents, and she planned to call them as soon as Sam left the room.

The last message was from an unknown number, so she checked the voicemail to see who it was from. "You can run Kate, but you can't hide, not you or your brother. The boss has too many connections, so it won't take us long. You'll both pay for what he did."

Kate dropped the phone like a hot potato as fear raced through her at the sound of the voice of the agent who had shot her brother. She knew it was a threat and had no doubt now he was looking for her and hoped he hadn't found Mike yet.

Sam was surprised when he heard the phone hit the floor and then noticed the terrified expression on Kate's face. "What is it? What's wrong?"

Kate picked up the phone, put it on speaker and replayed the voicemail. She could see Sam's expression change from surprise to concern as he listened to the short message. It surprised her, but perhaps Sam now believed at least part of what she had tried to tell him.

Sam tried to mask his concern as he looked at Kate and could tell she was worried. He wanted to take her in his arms and comfort her, but he knew that would be a mistake; it would probably only frighten her more. It surprised and worried him just thinking about wanting to take her into his arms. He wasn't sure what had come over him, but it was definitely unexpected.

"It's okay Kate. You're safe here and we'll get the sheriff working on the case as soon as he gets here. Don't erase the message. We need the sheriff to hear it and it may be evidence later on. Try to get some rest; you look like you need it. Your short naps in the truck were restless, so I'm sure you didn't sleep well."

Kate's thoughts were racing. She had to get out of here. She couldn't put them in danger too, but where could she go? She then looked up and was embarrassed as Sam returned to her backpack, and started throwing out her

38

clothes. The few clothes in her bag were shorts, t-shirts, and underwear, that had been worn, so they were all wrinkled from being tossed in her backpack.

Sam didn't seem to notice though or make an issue of it, just briefly felt around in the pack. Once finished, he turned to her and told her there was a washer and dryer behind the louver doors next to her room. He told her there was also laundry soap and dryer sheets, if she wanted to use them, which she was glad to hear.

Kate emptied the pockets and pulled out the pocket lining of Mike's jacket, which only contained a few dollars. Afterwards, she took off the jacket and turned around so Sam could see she wasn't concealing a weapon. Considering how snug her jeans were, it would have been impossible anyway.

Sam's breath caught as she turned around, but he tried to hide it. She was drop-dead gorgeous and her tight-fitting jeans made it difficult to look away. What was he thinking? This woman could possibly be a killer and here he was gawking at her, with an attraction he had never thought possible.

He tried with difficulty to shift his attention as she opened the guitar case, which he only glanced in before he closed it again. He tried to avoid her eyes, hoping she hadn't noticed the way he had been looking at her and was thankful she hadn't seemed to notice.

Kate had noticed briefly the admiring look he had given her as she turned around and tried to hide the way it made her feel. If only they had met under different circumstances, she thought sadly. She understood the meaning of his actions in checking her backpack and the guitar case, even though she didn't like it.

"Is there anything else you need to check out?" She asked pointedly, although trying not to show her irritation. She knew if the circumstances had been reversed, she would have done the same, but it didn't make her feel any better.

Sam quickly looked over at her, if she had noticed him gawking at her, she wasn't letting on. "No ma'am. I'm sorry I had to check, but I hope you understand. I'll leave you now to get comfortable and get some rest. I'll be in the other room if you need me and I'll call the sheriff now. He really needs to hear that message."

Kate didn't like the idea Sam was planning to stay in the cabin with her, but it was definitely better than a jail cell. "I understand, thank you." She said as she sat down on the bed and watched Sam turn to walk out the door.

She did feel safer here, and thought it would be more difficult for Agent Ryan to find her. She had little doubt he would eventually find her, but at least he didn't appear to know where she was now.

Kate planned to keep her door locked, although Sam probably had access to a key if he needed it. She wanted to trust him, which was odd since she didn't even know him or anything about him. He was at least willing to help her, even though he didn't know her either, and that meant a lot.

***

Sam doubted Kate would sleep, but at least maybe she could rest until the sheriff arrived. He didn't know why he felt so infatuated with her. It was the same way he had felt when he had first seen her photo. He was almost thirty, but had never had a long-lasting relationship, well maybe one that hadn't worked out, and he had no intention of going through that again.

His girlfriend, who he had met in high school, had been living with him for over a year, before she left. He had asked her to marry him, but she had kept putting off the wedding, which should have given him a clue.

He had thought she liked living on the ranch and their relationship was strong, but he had been wrong. She started having an affair with a guest at the ranch and had run off with him. Before she left, she told him she didn't like ranch life any more than his mother, who had left when he was young.

Sam thought about his friend, Nick and what he had gone through with his wife who had been running around on him, and then died suddenly in a crash that was still under investigation. Nick's last girlfriend had also been a disaster, that would make anyone leery of a relationship.

Kate, however, was giving him second thoughts. Just what he needed, feelings for a woman who had possibly killed her own brother, boy was he losing it. At least the phone message had given more credence to her story, unless it was just someone working with her.

***

Kate's thoughts began to wander to Mike and the last few hours she had spent with him. She had never been close to her half-brother, as he was four years older and had left home when she was young to pursue a music career in Las Vegas, which apparently hadn't worked out. It didn't make his being shot any easier though, and she wondered if he had run to the door to save her life.

At least Mike had been trying to turn his life around. It had been easy to tell the difference from when she had seen him a couple of years ago. He had told her about waking up one day in a small mission clinic where the people had saved his life and had helped him get off the drugs and find his way back to God.

They had convinced him to undergo treatments and meetings to come off the drugs and were helping him through it; but had he only gone from using to dealing? Is that why the agent had been looking for money? Why would he do that? Her thoughts kept wandering. There were too many questions and no way to get answers.

In a way Kate was glad, she had a chance to see and talk with Mike before this mess had all happened, but her emotions were mixed on whether it had been a good idea. She had enjoyed their visit and getting to know him better, but had her being there caused him to get shot? Would he have given the agent the money and still be okay if she hadn't been there?

41

There were too many unanswered questions she might never have answers to now. Her visit had almost cost Mike his life and maybe had or still would. She could never forgive herself for that; or forget about him. She felt the tears welling up in her eyes, but she didn't have time to cry, she had to think, she had to figure out what to do now.

Kate checked her other messages, then laid back, but when she closed her eyes, all that had happened came rushing back. She remembered how scared she had been, hiding behind the door in the bedroom after the door of the apartment was kicked in. The fear as the agent ransacked the living room and kitchen, before heading toward the bedroom. The gunshot as Mike ran to the door; and the blood.

Had the phone call the agent received right after shooting Mike, saved their lives? She would probably never know the answer to that, but wondered who had called and why he had left so quickly; and why had the kitchen window shattered as they were leaving the apartment.

Had Ryan been trying to finish the job and kill Mike and possibly her? Unanswered questions kept spinning in her thoughts. The worst of them being whether Mike was still alive or if Ryan had already found and killed him.

Kate was worried about her parents and brother and prayed they were all safe and Ryan hadn't found them. Her parents were supposed to let her know when they found Mike. Had something gone wrong? Should she try to call them? Their brief message had only said they had just landed in Las Vegas, so she hoped they would send another message soon and let her know if they had found Mike and how he was.

The message from Jessica had also been brief, and she had just wanted her to call. Kate was afraid to turn her phone back on again as she had turned it off as soon as she had listened to the messages. She was sure everyone at home was worried about her, but she had found a safe place to stay, at least for now and would let them know soon;

after she met with the sheriff. She had to be patient, which for her was really hard.

Kate couldn't sleep, or even rest. She couldn't close her eyes without seeing her brother lying on the floor with blood oozing from his chest and covering his shirt, and the threat of another bullet. What had caused the window to shatter as they left the apartment? Her mind wouldn't stop and kept replaying the phone call from Ryan, over and over.

She wondered how soon he would find her and what would happen then. She tried praying, but it didn't help. She wanted to believe God would help her; for her faith to be strong, but she worried she had drifted away for too long. Sam had mentioned she would be in his prayers. Perhaps his faith was stronger and God would listen to him.

Kate was also worried about meeting with the sheriff and if she would be sleeping in a jail cell tonight. Sam had said he would offer to be responsible for her, but it didn't mean the sheriff would let him. It would also make it very easy for Ryan to find her if she was locked up in jail or the sheriff sent her back to Las Vegas.

There was no doubt in her mind she wouldn't live to see Nevada again; not that she would ever want to. Kate reached for her phone, unable to wait any longer to check with her parents, but as she picked it up, there was a knock on the door.

"Kate, the sheriff's here." Sam said.

Kate hesitated for a moment and looked around the room. There was no place for her to go. She was so afraid her next hours would be in jail, but there was nothing she could do about it now. "Thank you, I'll be right there."

As Kate walked out of the bedroom, she noticed Nick and Jake were also there. She couldn't blame them. She would be putting all the people on the ranch in danger too, if she stayed.

After Sam introduced her to Sheriff Dave, Kate told him about the shooting and their narrow escape, then realizing she was still fumbling with her phone, she mentioned the voice mail message. She turned on her phone and put it on speaker so they could all hear the message Ryan had left.

She could tell the sheriff was skeptical about her story, but was sure the message had helped in his decision. He agreed to check out her story and asked if she could look at photos of DEA agents, if he could get them, especially if this agent was undercover. She agreed and told him the agent's name was Ryan, according to her brother; but she didn't know his last name.

Kate could tell the sheriff really didn't want to leave her there and she also felt it was a bad idea with so many people being put in danger, but Sam, Jake and Nick said they would be responsible for her. She couldn't believe people who didn't even know her, were willing to help her.

The sheriff then asked, "Do you know what he was looking for?"

"The agent said someone wanted his money. I think the name was Dylan, but I'm not sure. I never saw any money other than a few dollars Mike had in his coat pocket. I know Mike was a heavy drug user when I saw him a couple years ago, but he said he was getting himself straightened out and off the drugs and he did seem better.

Here are a few photos I took while we were sight-seeing in Las Vegas and Monday night when we were at dinner." She said as she pulled up the photos on her phone and showed them to everyone, along with the last photo taken after Mike had been shot, she had forgotten about.

"Mike was alive when I left him with his friends at a mission. They said they would take care of him and keep him safe. I just hate to think he went from using to dealing, but I guess it's a possibility. Mike said he was working with Ryan, the DEA agent, to help him get to the head of the organization, but he said something must have gone wrong."

"In theory, that's definitely a possibility, but it's hard to say. I'm sorry you had to go through this Kate, but it sounds like you may be right about your brother dealing. At least it looks like you may have had a good visit with him prior to him being shot. Why did you take the last photo, after he was shot?" The sheriff responded.

"Thank you; we did have a good visit and I'm glad we had that chance. I took the last photo as it showed a footprint in the blood. I thought it might help show that someone else had been there." Kate replied sadly as her thoughts of Mike returned to haunt her.

"I'll be sure to pass on this information, the message, and the photos, to the detective in Las Vegas, if you don't mind forwarding them to me. You said the detective's name was Dodd, correct?" The sheriff commented.

"Yes, I don't think I got his first name. I just called the main number for the police in Las Vegas and asked for a homicide detective, since the warrant for me was for supposedly killing my brother. I have the number here if you want it." Kate said as she showed him the recent call history.

"I promise not to leave here, although I hate possibly putting other people's lives in danger, if you have a better idea, I'm willing to work with you."

"Don't you worry about that Kate." Jake responded. "God sent you to us for protection and that's exactly what we plan to do. There's always safety in numbers and there are a lot of people working here and we don't have to worry about any guests for over a week."

Kate could feel the tears welling up in her eyes as she tried to control her voice. "Thanks Jake, that means a lot. I'm so sorry to put you through this."

The sheriff then asked. "And you're sure your brother didn't mention anything about any money or where it might be, even after he was shot?"

Kate wasn't surprised he asked, so she responded. "No. He never said anything about any money or where it was. If I knew anything about it, I wouldn't hesitate to tell you and give it to you. I definitely wouldn't want anything to do with any dirty drug money."

Kate was happy when the sheriff, Nick and Jake finally stood to leave and told her to get some rest. The sheriff also said he would be back the next day to check on her, which she had expected, as she knew he hadn't really been comfortable leaving her there, but Jake had convinced him, she would be safer staying with them.

Kate was tired, so when everyone left except Sam, she turned to him. "I think I could use some sleep. I don't want you to feel you have to babysit me. I won't run away, I promise. I don't have anywhere to go and you've made me feel safe here; thank you."

Sam still had reservations, as her story was definitely strange, but he wanted to try to ease her worry. "It's been my pleasure, Kate. I believe you, but until your friend arrives, I feel better being with you. I kind of like the idea of being your bodyguard. I hope you don't mind."

"I don't mind, I kind of like having you as my bodyguard; it makes me feel a lot safer having you here. I'll see you in the morning." Kate responded as she turned to go to her room. She knew Sam didn't totally believe her any more than the others, but at least he was trying to ease her mind and she appreciated it.

"How about something to eat first?" Sam asked. "I don't think you've had anything since we stopped for lunch earlier and if I remember correctly, you didn't eat much then."

Kate thought back about lunch and how little she had been able to eat and how she doubted she would be able to eat anything now either. "No thank you, I'm fine. I just need some rest and need to make some calls." She wasn't sure she could eat or sleep, but at least the rest might help, especially since she was at least out of jail for another night.

"I hope you get a good night's sleep. You look like you need it; goodnight." Sam said worriedly, hoping she would get some sleep, but wished she would eat something.

"Goodnight." Kate responded as she walked into the bedroom and shut the door, then looked over at the clock. She realized she needed to call her parents and Jessica before they went to bed, but first she checked another

46

message from her mom and was happy they had made it to the mission and found Mike. She also said she wanted Kate to call as soon as she had a chance.

Kate quickly dialed her mother's phone, but it went straight to voicemail, then she tried her dad's, with the same result, causing her to panic. Suddenly her phone began to ring. She didn't recognize the number and was skeptical, but she answered it anyway. When she heard her mother's voice, the tears began to flow although she tried to hold them back, as her mother filled her in on what had happened.

Thankfully, they had found Mike, who had been patched up by the mission workers at the clinic, but was weak from losing so much blood and was still on IVs and receiving plasma. Her mother also told her how the mission workers had hidden Mike, before Ryan had stopped by. He had searched the house with his buddy, and threatened them all; thankfully, not knowing who her parents were.

Kate's parents had called the police station and had spoken with Detective Dodd. Although he was reluctant to let Mike leave Nevada, he had approved it. He had agreed with them that flying home might not be to their advantage, if Ryan was looking for Mike, and flying also might be a problem, especially in Mike's condition.

Detective Dodd had said he would rent a car so it wouldn't be in their name and would bring it to them. They were planning to leave in a day or two, depending on Mike's condition and planned to use cash instead of credit cards.

They had turned off their phones and removed the batteries, so they couldn't be tracked, just in case, but had been checking them occasionally waiting for her call. They had bought the burner phone they were calling from, which had also been suggested by Detective Dodd, so she could reach them at any time. They suggested she get one too, so she planned to, as soon as possible.

Kate then updated them letting them know she had found a safe place to stay, with wonderful people who were willing to help and protect her. She also told them, the sheriff where she was staying would be contacting Detective Dodd too. She didn't tell them about the voice mail message, as she didn't want to worry them anymore than they already were.

Her mother mentioned that a young man named Paul had come to the mission shortly before they arrived. He had said a guy at the bus station, had told him the mission had helped his brother and he was hoping they would help him. "I know he said a guy at the bus station had suggested he come here, but were you dressed like a boy and suggested he come here?'

Kate was so happy to hear Paul had taken her advice, as she confirmed to her mother that he was the young man who had helped her get a ticket at the bus station. Before she had a chance to hang up, she heard her dad's voice. "We have you in our prayers Kitten."

"I've been praying too." Kate replied.

"You have to turn your problems over to God and let Him handle them. Until you can turn loose of them, you won't get much rest." He responded.

"I'm trying dad, but it's really hard with all that's happened."

"Hold on to your faith Kitten, and trust God. We're all praying for you and we know God will take care of you, Mike, and us." He replied.

Kate was trying to hold back the tears. She wished she had her dad's faith and could just turn over her problems, but that was so hard to do. "Thanks dad, I'll try. You all are in my prayers too. I'll pick up a burner phone so you can call me every day, and so I'll know you are all safe. Love you."

The tears began to flow freely as Kate hung up the phone trying hard to get her emotions under control. At least they were safe for now and hopefully all the way home, but what if Ryan found out and was at their house when they got there. Her mother had said arrangements had been made for the kids at home to go stay with family and friends until they got there, but Kate also hoped they wouldn't go straight home either.

Finally, emotions under control, or at least somewhat, Kate dialed Jessica's number and wasn't surprised she seemed in a panic, which was totally out of character for her. The multitude of questions came off so fast Kate couldn't get a word in.

She finally had to laugh, which eventually caught Jessica's attention and she stopped. "I'm sorry; I'm just so worried about you. Are you alright? I can come pick you up?"

Kate told her what all had been happening and she was fine and safe with people who really seemed to be going out of their way to help her. She also let her know she was hoping this ordeal would be over by the time they were supposed to start their vacation. She promised to keep in touch before she hung up. She was glad she had called Jessica as she had put her in a better frame of mind or at least stopped the tears.

***

Sam hadn't meant to eavesdrop when Kate had talked with her parents and Jess, whoever he was, that had made her laugh. Could he be her husband or boyfriend? It shouldn't matter, but for some reason it bugged him. He was glad he had overheard her though as he felt better after hearing she felt safe here.

He waited until Kate was finished with her calls then tapped on her door. "I thought you might be hungry, so I had one of the guys bring over some food. Would you like to join me?"

Kate really hadn't even thought about food, but now with the aroma coming from the living room, she realized, she actually was hungry, so she decided to join him.

The conversation was great. Sam had so many more great stories of ranch life, and the food was terrific. She didn't know if it was the food or the fact, she was so hungry, but it really didn't matter, because she ate it all.

Sam seemed really concerned about her family and hoped they were well, so she told him what she had found out about them finding Mike. Sam then asked if she had been able to reach her friend and if he was who had made her laugh, as he had heard her laughing.

She was surprised at first but then told him about all the questions and being so out of character for 'her,' which seemed to catch Sam off-guard. He seemed a little embarrassed, so she had to smile. She really was tired though, so she thanked him and headed to her room in hopes of getting at least a little sleep.

Sam had loaned her a shirt to sleep in, so she threw her clothes in the washer, before heading to bed. She had just sat down on the side of the bed when her phone rang. Afraid something had happened to her parents or Mike; she quickly reached for the phone. The caller ID was 'unknown' and since she had spoken with her parents a short time ago and put their burner phone number under their name, she let it go to voicemail. She thought she had turned her phone off, but evidently hadn't.

Once the person hung up, she checked her voicemail. The sound of Ryan's voice caught her off-guard. She hadn't expected another call from him today.

"Thought you'd know better than to leave your phone on Kate. I would think you would have bought a burner phone by now and taken the battery out of yours. Slip-ups like that really make it easier for us to find you. We'll be on our way soon, so don't get too comfortable, we need that money."

"I don't have your money." Kate shouted, although knowing quite well he couldn't hear her. She just wished he could.

The words were tumbling over and over in her mind as she quickly turned off her phone and removed the battery as her parents, and now Ryan had inadvertently suggested. She was startled as she then heard a tap on her door.

Sam's voice sounded concerned as he asked if she was okay. She wasn't okay, but she couldn't tell him that, could she? She hesitated trying to find the right words, but then told him to come in. She put the battery back in the phone and turned it on, then replayed the voicemail message.

"How could he know where I am?" Kate asked.

Sam hesitated for just a minute before saying, "I don't think he does, since he said they would be on their way soon. He's just trying to scare you."

"Well, he's doing a good job of it." Kate replied.

"I'll call the sheriff and let him know. Why don't you try to get some sleep, it's been a long day?" Sam then walked out and closed the door, trying to make sense of the call and what he should do next.

Sam quickly made a call to Dave and told him about the message Kate had received. Sam still wasn't sure about her story, but now was leaning more toward believing Kate and wanted to keep her safe, but wasn't sure how he could do that if the agent did show up.

He told Dave what the agent had said about being on the way soon, which hopefully meant he didn't know where she was yet, which was good to know. He had also mentioned she could be tracked by her phone. She was planning to turn her phone off and take out the battery, but was worried about her parents not being able to reach her.

Ryan had said, 'we' would be on the way soon, which could mean he wouldn't be alone. Sam wasn't surprised when Dave agreed and told Sam to be sure Kate didn't erase any of the messages, as they could really help in her defense.

Sam's thoughts were troubled, but he knew Kate's were even worse. There was no doubt in his mind of why she couldn't sleep; and now, he wasn't sure he would either.

Kate checked to be sure her phone was off and the battery was beside it on the nightstand, then curled up under the covers. She couldn't charge it that way or receive any messages from her parents, but she felt better knowing Ryan was unable to trace it that way either.

How could she have been so stupid. She had left her phone on and he could have easily traced it already and

51

now know where she was. She wasn't sure what she could do now, but she knew she had to do something. She couldn't put Sam or anyone else's life in danger.

She tried to go to sleep, but every time she closed her eyes, she would see Mike lying on the floor and the blood covering his shirt. Her mind wouldn't turn off, and she kept replaying all that had happened and what Agent Ryan had said.

Kate wondered how soon Ryan would find her and come after her. At least hopefully, he hadn't found out where she was yet, since he said they would be on their way soon. Did that mean there would be more than just him coming after her; and if so, how many others?

She also wondered if Ryan would be flying or driving as it would make a difference in how long it would take for him or them to get there. Once he found out where she was; if he did.

If Ryan didn't want the DEA office to know where he was and that he was coming after her, she guessed he would probably drive, which would take him longer, she hoped. Too many ifs and unanswered questions were driving her crazy.

She was also worried about Mike. He had lost so much blood. The clinic had given him two pints of blood, that she knew of, but was that enough? Would he be able to make the trip home with her parents, and would they all be safe? And what about the other kids at home, were they safe, or would Ryan be after them to get to Mike?

At least Mike's last name was different, but did Ryan know that and be able to find out their mother's last name now? Where could she go so no one else would get hurt if Ryan did find out where she was. It was all such a mess, so finally Kate broke down and prayed, hoping God would protect them all.

Chapter 3

Kate awoke and looked around, unsure of where she was. Flashbacks of what had happened at Mike's apartment had terrified her and even more so when she heard someone moving around in another room. She froze, unsure of what to do, but then memories of the ranch and Sam came back to her.

She was safe, or at least she hoped she was. She hadn't slept well with thoughts of what had happened and what she needed to do next. She was worried about her family and if they were safe and if she and the people she was staying with were safe. She really didn't like the idea of putting their lives in danger too.

Kate slowly got up as she heard a door close and hoped whoever had been there had left. The bed looked as if she had battled the pillows and covers all night, but she needed to get up and figure out what she was going to do. She hoped the person she had heard earlier, was Sam, and wondered where he might have gone.

Kate opened the door slowly and peaked out. She didn't see Sam or anyone else, so she stepped out to check on her clothes she had thrown in the washer before going to bed. She was surprised as her clothes were dry and folded on top of the dryer.

Sam must have stayed up and finished it for her. It was embarrassing that he had folded her underwear, but she was grateful it was something she no longer had to worry about. Thank God for Sam, Kate thought.

Unfortunately, she only had a couple of t-shirts and shorts, as well as, the one sweatshirt and pair of jeans she had on yesterday. She and Jess had only gone to Las Vegas for the weekend, where the weather was warm, and she hadn't expected a detour, especially one almost two weeks early to the exact dude ranch where they had made their reservations.

The few things Kate had needed for her trip, had been further depleted when she threw away the clothes that were covered in Mike's blood. Fortunately, they had been shorts and not her only pair of jeans.

She could only hope there would be somewhere she could get some clothes to last her until Jessica arrived and brought her more warmer clothes. She quickly grabbed the clothes and put them in her room, then picked up the jeans and a t-shirt and headed for the bathroom to shower and change to start the day.

When Kate came out of the bathroom, she was surprised to see Sam sitting on the couch. She had forgotten how handsome he was. She stopped her thoughts as the timing was bad for considering a relationship; especially with someone so far from home; as well as all the problems she was dealing with.

She didn't need a distraction like him while trying to figure out what to do. She needed to get her head on straight, which was difficult when Sam stood and smiled. "Are you hungry? I thought we could get some breakfast then get out of here for a bit. We have some really nice horses."

Kate thought for a minute, unsure of what else she could do, before replying. "I'm starving and definitely ready to get out and check out the ranch, if that's okay?"

"Great! We'll eat and then go for a ride. Do you know how to ride a horse?" Sam said, surprised she was wearing a t-shirt rather than something warmer.

"I've been riding horses since I could walk, and maybe even before that. I love horses and love to ride. I grew up on a farm, so I've had a horse of my own most of my life and have ridden almost every day, except when I was at college. I'm really looking forward to getting back in the saddle." Kate responded, and was glad to see her response seemed to please Sam.

"By the way, thank you for taking care of my laundry. It was thoughtful of you and I really appreciate it." Kate said.

"No problem. Just didn't want you to have to worry about it when you got up." Sam replied.

"It was nice of you, especially since I wouldn't have had anything to wear today until my clothes were dry. You're a life saver."

"Any time Kate. We aim to please around here. How about we go to breakfast, but first, you should put on your sweatshirt or a jacket. It's a little cool here in the mornings. But usually warms up later." Sam responded.

"Thanks, I definitely will do that." Kate said as she walked back into her room and put her sweatshirt on. Sam is so thoughtful Kate thought and she was grateful he was there and willing to help her out.

Kate looked around as they walked onto the porch. She hadn't had a chance to see much of the ranch last night, but now, with the sun shining beautifully in the clear blue sky, she could see more of it. There were several barns to one side and what appeared to be a bunkhouse and a few cabins.

Several horses were in the corrals, possibly being worked and ready for the guests, and cattle and horses were in the fields surrounding the barns. Kate could hardly wait to be on the back of one of the horses.

To the other side, were two rows of cabins like the one she was staying in. Sam pointed out a large building about halfway down the row of cabins; and told her it was the gathering hall, where meals were served, and where there was entertainment on Friday and Saturday nights.

Further down, at the end of the row of cabins, Kate saw a large building she thought must be the lodge she had read about on the website. It was all very rustic, but fantastic, just like she had imagined.

Kate had seen the photos on the website, but it was so much better seeing it all in person. The babbling brook she had heard and seen last night was wonderful and she watched the water flowing over the rocks for a few moments.

Up on the hill was the large beautiful house she had seen when they had arrived, but in the daylight, it looked magnificent. She was surprised to see a small church, a short distance from the house, she hadn't noticed before.

She was glad it was there as it gave her some peace to know they worshiped God on the ranch.

Kate finally turned to Sam. "This is amazing; so much better than what I expected from the photos on the website. I can't wait to go for a ride and see more of the ranch."

Sam smiled, understanding what she meant, he had always loved it here. "So, are you ready to eat so we can pick out a horse for you and go for a ride?"

"Yes, I'm starving." Kate said quickly as she walked down the steps.

Sam led the way and headed toward the gathering hall where they would have breakfast. Kate had mentioned seeing the website where there were lots of photos, but he wasn't surprised to see the expression on her face when she saw the layout of food.

It wasn't as big a spread as it would be once the guests arrived, but still it was quite a bit of food, since most of the ranch-hands also ate there. After they filled their plates, they sat at a table full of cowboys and Sam introduced Kate to everyone at the table, except Nick and Jake, whom she had met the night before.

Kate was happy everyone seemed really nice, but guessed they probably hadn't heard why she was there. She had been amazed at the variety of food and everything tasted wonderful. She also enjoyed the comradery and banter between them all.

There were fascinating and funny stories, which made her smile, something she hadn't expected under the circumstances. The gathering hall was all she had expected and more, with tables circling halfway around the small stage, where Sam had said they have entertainment on Friday and Saturday night and every night once the guests arrived. She could hardly wait for it all to begin; and hoped the nightmare she was now caught in would be over, she thought sadly.

Sam noticed Kate still looked very tired and it bothered him, although he wasn't surprised. He doubted she had slept much, if any, after the call from the DEA agent who had upset her last night, and all she had gone through the last couple of days. He doubted anyone would have been able to sleep.

At least, she seemed to be enjoying the stories everyone was sharing. He knew he wouldn't have slept much facing her circumstances, although he actually hadn't gotten much sleep either; he hadn't been able to turn off his thoughts of the call from the agent, Ryan. He also caught himself thinking an awful lot about Kate, which was something he definitely needed to stop doing.

The fear that had been so apparent last night was gone, or at least well-hidden for now. Kate had easily carried on a casual conversation with an occasional smile that really set off her beauty. She was tall and thin with gorgeous hazel eyes that sparkled when she smiled and her long dark brown hair shown beautifully, even pulled back in a ponytail.

Sam was surprised at how attracted he was to her, but he couldn't remember ever meeting anyone like her before. She could easily have been a model on the cover of a magazine, yet when she talked, she seemed sincere and down-to-earth instead of snobbish and stuck on herself like Nick's last girlfriend had been.

Sam had to stop staring and get his mind off her. She probably wasn't the type to be satisfied living on a ranch, in a small cabin with a cowboy; what was he thinking? She was a college graduate and way out of his league. He had no intention of getting tied down anyway, so he wasn't sure why he was even thinking about her that way.

Sam needed to get away from Kate for at least a few minutes and readjust his thoughts, so after he finished eating, he excused himself to call the sheriff. He asked Dave what time he would be stopping by. He wanted to be sure before they left for their ride that they had enough time to enjoy it.

He didn't want to worry Dave by letting him know they were going for a ride, since he didn't want him rushing out and arresting her, before he had all the facts. Sam wasn't positive he had all the facts himself, but he wanted to believe her story. He did plan to tell Jake and Nick where he planned to ride to, before they left; just in case.

As soon as Sam hung up the phone, he walked back to the table and sat down across from Kate. "The sheriff said he won't be able to make it until later this afternoon, so are you ready to go for that ride and check out some of the scenery?"

"I'd love to, but aren't you afraid of being alone with me?" Kate said teasingly.

Catching the gist Sam said. "You don't have a gun stashed anywhere on you; do you, Kate?"

"Haven't packed in the past and don't plan to start now. I don't have any boots with me though. I guess I can ride in my sandals."

"That's not very safe. What size shoe do you wear? I'll check around and see what I can find. We have lots of things guests have left behind over the years." He knew there was a large stash of items that were kept in a room in the back of the gathering hall, although a lot had already been donated to charity. He hoped checking it out and going through that mess would be a distraction. Something he really needed to get his mind off Kate.

For the first time in a long time, Kate was actually embarrassed about her shoe size. Of course, when you are six feet tall, shoe size does tend to be a little larger. She figured Sam probably wore an even larger size considering he was a few inches taller than her. She looked up at him and said sheepishly, "I wear a size ten."

His voice was teasing as he responded. "Well, I could probably just loan you a pair of mine then."

Kate couldn't help but laugh. "Right, I didn't say I wore boats."

Sam was surprised, but loved her smile and her laugh went straight to his heart, which surprised him since no one had ever affected him that way. "Are you insinuating I have big feet?"

"No more than you are insinuating the same about my feet." Kate responded.

"Sorry about that; I'll check and see what I can find. My younger brother, Joey, will stay with you in case you need anything. He can show you around and help you pick out a horse. I'll meet you at the barn in about a half hour. I need to freshen up, but shouldn't take too long."

"Yes; that might be a good idea." Kate said kiddingly. "We'll see you at the barn."

"Are you insinuating something?" Sam responded as if shocked, trying to keep the conversation light, as everyone at the table started laughing.

"Wouldn't think of it." Kate replied innocently.

Sam had to smile as he walked away. She had a good sense of humor and he liked that; actually, there wasn't much about her he didn't like; other than being a murder suspect.

***

Kate was glad to have someone to show her around. Joey was young, maybe sixteen or seventeen, but tall and thin like Sam; and he was very nice and polite. He pointed out the main house where Jake lived, the small chapel on the hill near the house where services were held on Sundays, and then they went to the lodge. It was beautiful and very rustic.

He pointed out the meeting rooms where a lot of the introductory gatherings were held and the indoor and outdoor pools, which she was anxious to try out, once they opened. There was also a small café, that was available for guests if they missed a meal or wanted something to eat between meals.

As they headed back toward the barn, Joey showed her the small store attached to the end of the gathering hall where they had been eating, which gave Kate an idea. "Do they sell boots here?"

"Sure, they don't have a big selection of anything, but they do have a little of just about everything. They aren't

59

normally open before the season starts, but it looks like someone is in there and I'm sure they would be happy to help you out. Would you like to go in?" Joey asked.

"Yes, please. Maybe I can find some boots so Sam won't have to worry about finding some for me. I'd really prefer not to wear someone else's boots anyway. I could also use some more clothes to get me through my stay here. I don't have much of a selection with me and what I have is definitely more for warm, summer weather, than for cooler weather and for riding." Kate replied.

The jeans she had on were actually the only pair she had with her and she was rather chilly, even though she had put her sweatshirt on over her t-shirt, which she was glad Sam had suggested. She was hoping the temperatures would get warmer during the day, but for now, even a light jacket would help.

Kate found a pair of boots she liked in her size and sat down to try them on. She was surprised they fit perfectly and were so soft and comfortable. They were made of very soft leather, possibly deer skin, and nothing fancy, but were comfortable even though they were new. It was so unusual, as it had always taken a while to break in new boots in the past.

The price was a little more than she was used to paying and she didn't have that much money with her, but she felt they were worth it and decided to splurge. She figured she could use her charge card, if they would accept it. Hopefully she would get her license and be working soon, and could pay the charge card balance off quickly.

Kate also purchased a hat, a couple pairs of jeans and a couple t-shirts, sweatshirts and a hooded, zip up sweatshirt she thought might come in handy and hopefully it would be enough to get her through until Jess arrived with her clothes.

Everything she purchased had horses on them. She also found some undies with horses on the back and socks with horses, and she couldn't pass them up.

Since she had seen the swimming pools at the lodge, Kate decided to look at swimsuits too, and found one she loved. It had horses running around it, which surprised her. She loved the selection of clothing in the store. She had been lucky since the store hadn't officially opened yet, but it did mean they had a full supply of all the new merchandise.

They accepted credit cards so Kate paid for her purchases and left the store. While walking back to her cabin, it dawned on her, it had probably been a mistake to use her charge card. She wondered if Ryan would be able to find out where she had used it and then know where she was. It was too late now; there was nothing she could do about it. She could only pray Ryan wouldn't find out.

Kate dropped her new clothes off at the cabin, except for the boots, the hooded sweatshirt, and the western hat she had already put on. She and Joey then headed to the main barn where there were several horses. There was every color of horse imaginable in the corral just outside the barn, and especially a lot of paints and appaloosas.

Kate told Joey her favorite color horse was a palomino. She was surprised by the look on Joey's face. "What's wrong?"

"I don't think you want a palomino; you should try something else. The paints we have are really nice and so are the appaloosas and there's a nice variety to choose from."

"Why would I not want a palomino?" Kate replied curiously.

"I probably shouldn't say anything, but Nick had a girlfriend here last year who rode a palomino. Everyone was really glad to see her go, and I'd hate for anyone to compare you to her. You seem like a nice person; and believe me, she wasn't."

Kate smiled, figuring he hadn't heard yet why she was there, or his opinion of her would more than likely, be different. "Thank you. I appreciate the advice and I think a paint horse would be wonderful; how about that beautiful dark brown and white one over there?"

"Oh, you'll love him. His name is Choco and he is really gentle and nice to ride." Joey responded.

"That's great! I haven't had a lot of time to ride for the last few years, while I was away at college, so it will be nice being able to relax and enjoy the scenery." Kate said as she smiled at Joey.

Joey then ran out into the corral and placed a rope around Chocó's neck and led him into the barn. Kate was really impressed with how easy to handle and calm Choco seemed to be and how good Joey seemed with all the horses in the corral. It was easy to tell Joey had been raised around horses and his love of them was apparent as he petted and talked to Choco.

"Where did you go to college?" Joey asked as he handed Kate the rope so he could brush Choco.

"Indiana; near where I grew up. I attended a really great veterinary program and just graduated and took my licensing exams last week."

Kate was surprised when Joey answered "Really? I want to be a veterinarian too. I decided to go to Purdue in Indiana and I've been accepted there. I heard they have a great program."

"They do; that's where I graduated from. My friend Jess, who will hopefully be joining me here in a couple of weeks, went to school there too. She's a computer consultant or you might say, an IT guru. Computers and I don't always get along well, but Jess is phenomenal with them.

Veterinary school is a lot of hard work Joey, but I think it was definitely worth it since I love working with animals so much. Will you be graduating from high school this year?" Kate asked.

"Yes, at the end of the month. I've been taking some entry college courses at the community college here, so hopefully it won't take as long to get my degree. We're on spring break this week, but we start back on Monday."

"I did the same thing and it really helped in shortening my time in college. Since I'm still waiting on the results of my license exam, I'm not sure where I will be working yet.

All of my family is in Indiana, not too far from Purdue, so you would always be welcome to visit our farm if you get homesick for horses. I even have a sister around your age who will be graduating from high school this year and starting classes at Purdue this fall to be a veterinarian. Most likely you will probably run into her."

"Thank you, Kate. I'll look forward to meeting your family and if your sister looks anything like you, I'll definitely look forward to meeting her." Joey responded.

Kate laughed. "Just remember, school must come first if you plan to be a veterinarian. There's a lot of studying and you have to keep your grades up."

"I will, I have always kept my grades up. That's how I got my scholarship and I plan to come back here to work. Doc Porter, the county veterinarian here, said I could help him in the summers when I'm not in school. He's always needing help." Joey replied.

Kate was surprised at how easy it was to talk with Joey. He seemed like such a good kid. "That's great, it would give you some good experience, although I'm sure you've had a lot of experience working with horses and cattle, here already. I wish you luck, and I'll only be a phone call away if you need help." At least she hoped she would.

"Thanks, I really appreciate that." Joey replied enthusiastically.

"I worked with a local veterinarian back home during the summers and the experience really did help. He offered me a partnership once I get my license, but I'm just not sure yet if I want to stay in Indiana or try somewhere totally new. Guess I'll find out soon." That is if I survive this nightmare. Kate thought sadly.

Sam had walked into the barn and was glad to see Kate was getting along so well with his kid brother. He had found a pair of boots he hoped would work, but was surprised to see she already had on a pair, as well as a hat.

He walked over to them and questioningly asked, "I thought you said you didn't have boots with you?"

Kate was startled and quickly turned around, as she hadn't heard Sam come up behind her. It didn't take long to recover, although her heart was still pounding and it took a moment to calm down and speak. "I did, but Joey was nice enough to show me the little store at the end of the gathering hall and they had a pair just my size, as well as a couple pairs of jeans, a jacket, shirts and a hat, as you can see."

"Sorry, I didn't think about that. It usually isn't open before the guests arrive. I'm glad you were able to find something that fit, did you also find a horse you'd like to ride?"

"Yes, I think this horse is beautiful and Joey said he's really nice." She replied as she smiled at Joey and rubbed Chocó's face.

"You have a good eye for horses, I think you'll really enjoy riding Choco. It looks like you're ready to go so I'll saddle my horse while Joey saddles Choco for you."

"That won't be necessary; I can saddle my own horse. I rode a lot when I was younger and have still ridden every summer and break since I started college." Kate replied.

Sam wasn't surprised, especially after she had mentioned she had grown up on a farm. "You're a guest and Joey needs the practice to get ready for when the season starts and he'll have a lot of horses to saddle for guests who don't know how to at first."

"But I'm not a guest yet." Kate responded.

"Sure, you are; you're my guest. Just give us a minute and I'll take you out to see some beautiful country."

Kate was so glad Sam was considering her a guest rather than someone he was having to watch for the sheriff, to keep her out of jail or at least he was putting on a good act. "Thank you, that sounds wonderful."

They mounted their horses and rode along for a while with Sam simply pointing out the abundant wildlife and areas, he found interesting. The variety of colors of the wildflowers starting to bloom in the valley and the horses and cattle calmly grazing was wonderful to see.

The landscape was so beautiful, especially the hills surrounding the valley that were also in bloom. The snow-covered mountains in the distance made a phenomenal contrast, and she loved the way Sam admired the beauty of it.

Kate wasn't surprised when Sam finally started questioning her, but for some reason, she didn't feel threatened by it. He had been so nice. "I heard you talking to Joey about school; how much longer do you have?"

"I just graduated." Kate responded.

"Where did you go to school?"

"In Indiana, like I mentioned last night." Kate replied.

"Sorry, I forgot. What was your major?" Sam asked.

"Veterinary medicine, I took my licensing exams last week, then Jess and I decided to fly to Las Vegas for the weekend, since my mom wanted us to try to talk my brother, Mike into coming home with us." Kate hesitated for just a moment before continuing.

"We flew into Las Vegas Friday, then hit almost every casino on the strip to check them out on Friday night and Saturday. Neither of us gamble or drink, but it was really fun seeing the different themes of each casino.

I think my favorite casino was probably the Bellagio. Out front, they have a water fountain show put to music. I think they called it Waltzing Waters. They also have a beautiful garden inside the casino, that they change to a different theme each month.

The Venetian had a gondola ride in the shopping area and the ceiling was painted blue with white clouds to look like the sky. We also went downtown and watched the light shows at night. It was like walking through a tunnel of lights that changed colors and music every half hour. They even had a zipline, which we did, that was really fun.

We met up with my brother Mike on Saturday and Sunday and he showed us all kinds of neat places he had visited when he first got to Las Vegas. He would have

65

made a great tour guide. We went to the Valley of Fire Park, where the red rocks actually looked like they were on fire when the sun hit them right. They also had some really amazing rock formations. I think my favorite was the elephant rock.

When we left there, we took a road going to Lake Mead. We stopped at a few places that used to be boat docks, but they were all dried up. You could tell they had tried to move them a few times, but had finally given up. It was so sad. When we got to the beach area, there was what used to be a boat dock, really high in the air. It was hard to believe the water had once been that deep.

From there, we went to the Hoover Dam, which was interesting to go through and we finished on a dinner cruise on Lake Mead that went up near the dam. The food and service were great. Afterward, we took Jess to the airport as she had to be back at work on Monday. I stayed an extra day to try to convince Mike to come home with me, but he said he wasn't quite ready, although maybe soon.

On Monday, Mike and I went to Red Rock Canyon and I was surprised to see wild burros, then up to Mt. Charleston where the view from the restaurant near the top was phenomenal. We later had dinner at a restaurant at one of the casinos downtown near where Mike lived, then I took him home.

It really was a great weekend and we had a lot of fun getting to know each other again. Until…" Kate's voice broke and she couldn't hold back the tears any longer, as it finally sunk in that she might never see Mike again.

Sam pulled on the reins of both horses to stop them. He jumped off then pulled Kate down and into his arms. "It's okay Kate; I know it has to be hard dealing with what you've been going through, but you're safe here. I'll take care of you. I promise." And he meant it. He believed her; at least, he wanted to believe her, and she felt so right in his arms, but that was crazy and scary.

Kate tried hard to regain her composure, but it took a while as she hadn't taken time for it to all sink in until now.

She was thankful Sam didn't try to rush her, just held her close.

She was surprised at the way it felt being close to him. It was calming, yet stimulating once she was able to stop crying. She had never realized a person's touch could have such an effect on her, but then she realized she was out in the middle of nowhere, with someone she really didn't know and she didn't want him to let her go. How crazy was that?

"Thank you. I'm sorry, I didn't mean to break down. Everything is just such a mess and I'm worried about my family and whether Ryan has found them yet. And if he's coming after me, I don't know what I'll do." Kate said as she tried to control her emotions.

"I understand Kate. I'm here for you any time you need a shoulder." Sam replied teasingly, trying to lighten her mood, as he handed her his handkerchief.

"Thank you for being here, and for everything. The ranch is really beautiful and you've been so nice to me. I'm just sorry I had to get you involved in this nightmare."

Sam wasn't sure why, but he didn't want to let her go, although he knew he had to. He wasn't sure when the sheriff would arrive and he wanted to be sure she was at the ranch when he did, so he slowly stepped back.

"We'd better get back. It won't be long before it's lunchtime; and Kate, don't worry about me. I'm just glad we've been able to help you out and you're at this ranch now where we can all protect you, if that rogue agent does show up."

"Thank you; I'm so glad you and Nick were willing to rescue me from the diner and bring me to this ranch. However, I hope Ryan doesn't find me here and put you all at risk."

Kate slowly stepped back, while wiping the tears from her eyes. She felt strange when Sam released her, as if she wanted to be back in the comfort and safety of his arms. That didn't make any sense, she didn't even know him that well. How could she feel safe in his arms? Perhaps it was because she was still so tired. She hadn't slept much last night or her night on the run.

During the crazy weekend in Las Vegas, she had also been busy and gotten very little sleep. Due to everything that had been going on recently, it was no wonder she was exhausted. Normally, she would have crashed and slept for a couple of days following her exams and her trip, but unfortunately that hadn't happened.

"I'm not really hungry, but I think I'd like to rest for a while. I haven't had much sleep for over a week with cramming for my license exams and then a weekend in Vegas and…, everything else." Kate finally said.

"Not a problem." Sam replied as he reluctantly stepped away to get the reins of her horse and hand them to her before she mounted.

They rode quietly for a short time then Sam finally broke the silence. "It sounds like you had a great time in Vegas. I've only been there once, to get Nick, but definitely didn't see all the things you did. Actually, I only saw the airport and one, small and not so interesting casino, that Nick was at. Sounds like there's really a lot to do there."

"There is, but I never want to go back." Kate replied.

To change the subject, she asked. "What do you do here, Sam?"

"I'm the foreman."

"What about Nick?" Kate asked.

Sam knew Nick didn't like guests to know his father owned the ranch, so he replied. "We share the responsibility since there is so much to do here, especially once the guests start arriving. He handles the guests and I handle the livestock."

"It's a beautiful ranch. I'm sure Jess is going to love it too."

"Is Jess your boyfriend?"

Kate looked at Sam and smiled. "Are you asking if I have a boyfriend?"

"Well, let's just say I'm hoping he's not, as I enjoy your company and think I'd like to get to know you better.

Although you're probably way out of my league since you're a college graduate and soon to be a licensed veterinarian."

"College doesn't teach you half of what real life does, so if anything, I don't fit into your league." Kate responded.

"That's debatable, but you still didn't answer my question."

Kate smiled and replied. "Jess is short for Jessica. We have been friends for quite a while and we both love to ride. With school, it has been difficult to occasionally date, much less have time for a relationship, so no boyfriend."

Sam smiled as he remembered Kate had said Jess was a 'her,' last night. "That's really good to know."

Kate laughed. "Does that mean you might consider me worth spending a little time with, even if I'm not in your league and you think I might be a possible murderer?"

Sam's voice was serious as he responded. "I don't think you are a murderer and I'd never consider you out of my league. I hope we have a chance to spend a lot of time together and get to know each other better."

"I'd like that, but I don't want to take a chance on getting anyone hurt. I'm afraid the agent who shot my brother is planning to come after me so I can't testify against him. I don't want you or anyone else to get hurt.

It would probably be better if I left so I wouldn't be putting anyone else in danger. I made the mistake of using my charge card today and I'm afraid he might be able to figure out where I am now."

Sam understood how she felt, but there was no way he was going to let her fight this alone. "Using your charge card was definitely a mistake, but using your phone probably gave him a way to track you anyway, so I doubt it really made that much of a difference.

You don't need to worry Kate, I can take care of myself and I have a lot of friends to help me take care of you, so just don't get scared off. There's always safety in numbers and there are a lot of men and women working here. If you have any problem, just come to me and we'll take care of it together. I also think you'll find it more comfortable here in a cabin than in a jail cell."

Sam was right, Kate knew that, but it didn't keep her from worrying about everyone at the ranch. "You're right, I definitely do prefer the cabin to a jail cell. Thank you, Sam. I don't know how I can ever thank you enough for what you've already done."

"I'm sure when the time is right, I'll think of something." He said teasingly with a smile as he winked at her, trying to ease her worry.

Kate was surprised. She knew she was attracted to him, but couldn't believe he actually seemed to be flirting with her. She sure didn't have time for that since her life was such a mess. Even if it wasn't a mess, she didn't have a clue as to where she would set up her practice and settle down. If she survived this ordeal, it could change everything, which was a scary thought.

Kate had thought she would set up her practice somewhere around home in Indiana and had already been offered a job with a veterinarian. It was also near her family, which was a plus; however, she had been playing with the idea of trying someplace new, but hadn't decided where that might be, yet.

Indiana was pretty far from here, which might be a problem, but she guessed it didn't have to be, if the right offer came along. It was really beautiful here and she loved the hills and mountains, especially now when everything was starting to bloom.

It was so different from the flat land in Indiana, where she lived. Even if she did consider moving to Colorado, she had to avoid leading Sam on. It wasn't good for either of them to get involved, especially not until this nightmare was over.

They stopped on a small hill overlooking the ranch as they were riding back and Kate looked around, amazed at how fantastic the layout was. Someone had really put some thought into it and she could see why it was busy during the open season.

70

The hills that surrounded the area were covered with trees starting to bud and the snow-covered mountains towering behind them were majestic. The fields that were full of wild flowers, horses and cattle were amazing, as were the people scattered around working. It was all so fascinating to watch.

"This is really a beautiful place Sam. I see why you love it here so much."

"I was raised here and wouldn't have it any other way. My dad was the foreman before he retired and my kid brother, Joey was raised here too."

"I forgot the Joey I met this morning is your brother."

Sam was proud of his brother and glad Kate liked him. "If you need anything and I'm not around, feel free to go to Jake, Nick or Joey."

"Did your dad move away when he retired?" Kate asked.

"No; he's still here. You met him at the table this morning, but he was rather quiet. Dad was sitting on the other side of Joey." Sam said, although trying not to mention why he had been so quiet. His dad definitely didn't like the idea of him watching out for someone he thought should be in jail. He just didn't understand.

"You mean John? He seemed nice, but he was awfully quiet." Kate was almost afraid to ask, but she had to know. "What did Jake say about my being here after Nick told him about me?"

"He said our first priority is keeping you safe." Sam replied.

Surprised, Kate responded. "He doesn't hate me and want me to leave?"

"I've never known Jake to hate anyone, and he believes God sent you here for protection. His faith is very strong and he believes people come into our lives for a reason." Sam responded.

Kate knew she had been lucky to end up at this ranch. "I agree and I'm thankful God put you all in my life. I just pray He keeps you all safe in the process."

Kate was relieved, and was glad Jake felt that way, she had always believed it too, especially after she had lost her husband. She believed God has a purpose for everyone, whether to bring them into our lives or to take them home.

Sam looked up at the sky. The clouds had grown dark and he felt a few drops of rain on his arm and turned to Kate. "It wasn't supposed to rain until later today, but I think it has arrived sooner than expected. We'd better make a run for it."

Kate quickly agreed and they took off at a run. The wind was getting stronger and the rain was coming down hard. She could hear thunder in the distance and flashes of lightning, lit up the sky. Suddenly, a loud clap of thunder filled the air and a lightning bolt hit a tree nearby, splitting it as it burst into flames rising high above it.

Choco suddenly stopped and reared, throwing Kate out of the saddle, then ran off. She hadn't expected it and hadn't been prepared. It had been a long time since she had been thrown from a horse, so it was a shock. She didn't feel as if she was hurt, but it had taken her breath away.

Sam stopped and quickly ran over to her. She could tell he was worried as panic was apparent on his face. "Are you okay? Do you feel like anything is broken? Can you get up?" He asked frantically.

After a minute, Kate was finally able to catch her breath and told him she was fine and not to worry. She watched as he pulled out a phone and told whomever he had called, about the tree and for them to send someone out to be sure the fire didn't spread, because Choco had been spooked and thrown Kate and he was taking care of her.

He also said to have someone watch out for Choco and take care of him. He knew Choco was probably now back at the ranch, or soon would be and in the barn where it was dry, where he wished he and Kate were.

With the torrential rain, Sam didn't think the fire in the tree would be a problem, but wanted to be sure it was taken care of. His priority was to get Kate back to the ranch and out of the rain, where he could get her checked out. He knew she had to be cold, since he was, so he helped her onto his horse, then got on behind her. "Let's go; we need to get out of this rain."

It wasn't long before they rode into the barn. They were both soaked and Sam was worried about Kate. He quickly jumped off his horse, helped Kate down, grabbed a saddle blanket and wrapped it around her.

She was shivering and he wasn't sure what else to do, but knew he had to get her to the cabin and warm her up before anything else. They took off running to the cabin, which thankfully, wasn't far. After reaching it, Sam coaxed Kate into taking a long hot shower to warm her up, then started a fire in the fireplace.

Kate stood under the hot shower for several minutes before the shivering finally stopped. It had been a long time since she had been in a storm like that, and she couldn't remember ever being that cold. Although the rain had washed some of the mud out of her hair, there was still mud that needed to be washed out. Once finished, she wrapped a towel around her then stepped out of the bathroom.

Kate noticed Sam standing in front of the fireplace rubbing his hands together. She was sure he was cold too, so she quickly said. "You're turn. I think you probably need to warm up too. Thanks for letting me go first. I feel much better."

Sam replied. "Thanks; I think you're right."

Kate wasn't surprised when he quickly walked into the bathroom and it wasn't long before she heard the shower start. She only hoped there was still some hot water left for him.

She threw her wet clothes in the washer, along with her new clothes, but left the lid up so Sam could add his wet clothes too; if he wanted to. She then decided to lie down while waiting for Sam.

She knew she really needed some rest, as she had been exhausted last night but hadn't slept much. Each time she had closed her eyes, her brother's body was all she saw, and the sound of the gun going off, kept resounding in her head.

She also knew she hadn't gotten much sleep in the cab of the truck yesterday. They had stopped for lunch before she had fallen asleep, although she had possibly dozed a little before that. She had only meant to close her eyes so Sam would stop questioning her, but she had dozed a little, as exhaustion had taken over.

Kate knew she really needed sleep in order to think straight, especially about the way Sam was making her feel. She couldn't let herself get involved with him. Not with all that was happening in her life right now. If circumstances were different, she might think differently. No; she couldn't think about that right now. She had no idea where her job and future would lead her. She just prayed she still had a future.

***

Kate bolted up, startled by the knock on the door, waking her from a sound sleep. Disoriented and confused, she looked around the room; then she heard Sam's voice telling her it was time for dinner.

Her nerves began to calm and her mind focused as she realized where she was. She then looked at the clock next to her bed and couldn't believe she had slept all afternoon. Her stomach was telling her she was hungry as she responded. "Give me just a minute and I'll be ready."

Kate was thankful when she noticed her clothes were dry and folded on the dryer as she walked out of her room. She quickly dressed, then ran to the bathroom, and threw cold water on her face to help get fully awake. Once ready, she walked into the living room to meet up with Sam. His smile touched her heart, which surprised her, but she tried not to let it show. "I'm starving, are you ready?"

"Just waiting on you, sleepy head." Sam responded. He was happy to see she looked a little more rested.

"It was truly needed as I don't remember anything after hitting the pillow. What's for dinner?" Kate asked.

"We have some really great cooks around here, so I'm sure you'll find something you will like." Sam replied.

"Sounds good to me. Let's go. I know anything will be better than the Raman noodles, TV dinners and pot pies I've been living on the last few years at school." Kate responded teasingly.

Sam then asked. "How are you feeling? I'm so sorry Choco threw you."

"I'm fine; just had the wind knocked out of me for a couple of minutes, but the ground was soft from the rain, so nothing is broken." Kate said. She was a little sore from being thrown, but she wasn't about to let Sam know, and worry him. "And I'm starving and ready to eat, so please lead the way."

Sam was glad Kate was feeling good or at least she had said she was, but he was hoping the doctor would come out tomorrow to check her out. He didn't want to take any chances. He laughed as it appeared she was always starving, so he was happy to show her the way.

Fortunately, the rain had stopped, at least for a short time allowing them to get to the gathering hall without getting soaked again. He was glad Kate had seemed happy to have her clothes and jacket, as he had added his wet clothes with hers and had finished the laundry before waking her.

Kate was really surprised when she saw all the food that had been prepared. There was a large roast beef being sliced, barbequed ribs, shredded barbequed pork, and grilled chicken as well as fried chicken and ham.

There were all kinds of side dishes and a large salad bar. The dessert bar also looked very tempting with several cakes, pies and even cobbler, and of course ice cream to top them off. She couldn't imagine anyone not gaining weight at this ranch.

Kate tried getting small amounts of each item as she wanted to try everything, and then wondered how in the world she was ever going to eat it all. She could hear Sam laughing at her, but his plate looked pretty much the same.

75

They finally sat down to eat with Nick, Jake, John, Joey, and Sheriff Dave. Kate really enjoyed their stories about things that had happened over the years at the ranch.

The food was terrific and she managed to actually get most of it down. She was looking forward to Jessica arriving and having a chance to really enjoy the food and horseback riding at the ranch. Hopefully the nightmare she was living in now would be over by then.

As Kate was finishing up, her phone rang and she answered it. Not thinking ahead, she had put the battery back in the phone to charge it and then turned it on hoping her parents would call since she hadn't been able to pick up a burner phone yet. Panic hit her as she put the phone on speaker and listened, along with the others at the table.

"Using your charge card wasn't too bright Kate. Unfortunate for you, the boss seems to know someone who was able to get the information for him. Hope you're having a good time in Colorado. Better make the best of it. We'll see you soon and I'll need the money."

It was like a lightning bolt struck her sending a shock wave of tension through her body as she listened to his low voice, before screaming, "I don't have any money." then quickly hung up. She looked over at the sheriff, unsure of what to say as he stared at her with a questioning expression. "Was that him?"

"Yes." Kate replied

"If he's in Las Vegas, it will take him a couple of days to get here?" Sam stated.

Kate hadn't thought of the consequences this morning when she used her charge card. It hadn't even dawned on her not to use it. How dumb could I have been? She thought.

"He doesn't know where you are Kate. You could have just done some shopping here and moved on for all he knows." Sam replied.

Dave then responded. "You're wrong Sam, they can pinpoint exactly where the card was used. We need to investigate moving her, but I'm not sure where that would be. I just wish I knew how soon he will get here."

"I think she is still safer here at the ranch. With all the ranch-hands, armed and on the lookout, it would be hard for him to get to her." Sam said, not willing to let her leave.

Kate cut in, "But it may not be hard for the agent to get to one or more of you. No, I don't want to put you all in danger. Sheriff, what do you think? Can you take me somewhere today?"

Dave looked at her thoughtfully as he spoke. "I actually think Sam may be right. The jail would probably be way too easy for him to get to you and I'm starting to question if you belong there anymore. I'd have to make some arrangements to put you somewhere else, but it sounds like we may have a couple of days before he gets here, so it should give us time.

I can have my deputies circle the perimeter starting tonight and with the ranch-hands watching from inside, I think you will be a lot safer here. I'm sorry I questioned your story last night and I really do want to help you." Dave said apologetically.

"But he knows where I am and he may not worry about who gets in the way. I think you need to move me." Kate responded.

"He may come anyway, since this is where you were today when you used the charge card and when you answered your phone just now."

"Maybe I could leave my phone on and just leave, so he could follow me away from here."

"I'm afraid his being able to track you may have gotten a lot harder. He hasn't checked in for a few days, and his department is looking into his activities based on your statement. Coming here may be our best way to catch him before he hurts anyone else."

"It sounds as if he isn't using his own connections to find me. He said his boss had connections and had gotten the information for him, so it looks like there must be a leak in the Las Vegas police department or somewhere." Kate responded.

"You're right, but finding a mole is often very hard. I'll contact the DEA when I get back to the office and see what they can find out." Dave said.

Jake finally spoke up. "The sheriff is right, Kate. You are safer here with our help and I'll make sure all of our men are ready for him. He won't have the slightest idea what he's walking into. Don't you worry Kate, we have you covered and Sam will stay with you at your cabin to keep you safe there."

Kate didn't like the idea of staying. The thought of getting anyone else shot or killed didn't sit well with her, but what was she supposed to do? At least they would be more prepared to capture him, knowing he was coming there.

It also meant he wasn't going after her family and for now they would be safe. She sat quietly listening to the plans being made, hoping they would work, but it didn't make it any easier, especially being the bait for a trap.

After the sheriff left, Kate finally accepted Sam's suggestion to return to the cabin and try to get some rest. She doubted she would be able to get any sleep again tonight even though she was still totally exhausted.

They had just walked into the cabin when her phone rang again. Kate was hesitant not recognizing the number, but answered. She was happy to hear her mother's voice telling her Mike was doing better and they were safe. He was regaining his strength little by little each day.

They were planning to leave in the morning if all went well, and were expecting to be back in Indiana within the next few days. They wanted to take it slow. They had also made plans to stay with friends until Agent Ryan could be caught.

They had sent the kids that were still at home to stay with family and friends nearby, so they would all be safe too. It was good news, something Kate really needed and if the sheriff and Jake's ranch-hands could capture the agent, perhaps life could get back to normal, whatever that was going to be now.

Kate didn't tell her mother what was going on or where she was, just that she felt safe and had made some really good friends. She promised to call her from a burner phone in a few days, but for her mother to call her if anything came up or happened. She didn't see any reason to worry them, just to let them know she loved them and was praying for them.

Kate then joined Sam in front of the fireplace where he had started a fire earlier that was now burning bright. She loved watching the flames flicker and the soft crackle of the embers. Her conversation with Sam was casual and light hearted and she loved hearing about his life, growing up on the ranch.

She was having difficulty staying awake, so she finally excused herself and went to her room to try to sleep. She just hoped she would be able to rest as well as she had during her afternoon nap.

Chapter 4

Kate awoke with rays of sunshine streaming through the window. She felt more refreshed and alert today, which was a nice change. She remembered waking up a couple of times during the night, but had fallen right back to sleep. Exhaustion had finally been the ticket for a good night's sleep.

Kate heard someone, she hoped was Sam, moving around in the living room. She jumped out of bed, grabbed some clothes, and ran to the bathroom to get ready. It seemed the cabin was always cold in the mornings, so once out from under the covers, getting dressed quickly was a necessity.

Kate wasn't disappointed to see Sam as she walked into the living room. His smile was so nice, but she couldn't let him know how much she looked forward to seeing it; or seeing him. She was still unsure of her future, but she had to pretend, everything was alright, so she pasted on a smile. She hoped she and Sam would be going for a ride again today.

"Good morning sleepy head. Ready for breakfast and a ride?" Sam asked.

"Yes, definitely yes, and good morning to you too."

"You look a little more refreshed today. Did you sleep well?"

"Yes, mostly. I think the exhaustion helped. I do feel much better today and I'm really looking forward to another ride. I will be better prepared today, in case we run into any surprises again." Kate replied.

"I'm really sorry about yesterday. Do you still want to ride Choco? Or would you like to ride a different horse today?" Sam asked apologetically.

"Choco, of course. He's wonderful to ride and it wasn't his fault for being frightened yesterday. It scared me too when the lightning hit that tree, so I don't blame him." Kate replied.

"Then Choco it is. I'm ready for breakfast, how about you?" Sam asked.

80

"Definitely!" Kate replied as she headed for the door and then walked on out.

The breakfast was amazing and Kate felt she had never seen so much food prepared at one time before, as she had the last few days, and it was all delicious. She couldn't imagine what it was going to be like after the guests arrived, if this was what they fixed for the ranch-hands.

After breakfast, Kate and Sam headed toward the barn. Sam had told her they were going to check for strays today. A couple of small foals had been brought in and Kate couldn't help stopping to take a look. They were so cute. She stepped into the first stall and checked out the mare and colt. She was glad to see they were both doing well, but when she went into the next stall, she became worried. The mare seemed to be fine, but the colt was weak. She tried holding the colt up to eat, but it was having trouble nursing.

Kate looked up at Sam. "This colt isn't doing very well. Do you have a bottle and a pump so we can pull some milk from the mother and bottle feed it until he can drink on his own? It will keep the mare from drying up, in case the colt pulls through."

Sam quickly called for one of the guys to get the needed supplies, which thankfully didn't take long. Every minute counted if they were going to save the colt. Kate quickly attached the pump to the mare, which the mare didn't like at all, but as Sam held her, Kate was able to fill the bottle most of the way.

It took a little coaxing, but Kate was finally able to get the colt to drink. It wasn't much, but at least she hoped it would work for now. "I think I need to stay with him, Sam."

"That won't be necessary. We have plenty of people to help, and Joey is the best. He loves these young foals as if they were his own and he has bottle fed many over the years, whether they needed it short term or long."

Kate was hesitant at first, but with a ranch this size, she was sure they had run across this problem before. She was surprised when she saw Joey walk up and stand in the doorway to the stall. "I hear you're the bottle-feeding expert around here." She said to Joey jokingly.

"Yes ma'am. I love taking care of the foals. You don't have to worry." Joey replied.

"That's wonderful to hear, but I'll check back in with you when we return from checking for strays today."

"I'll be here; or one of the other guys who helps out with the foals, in case you're gone a while." Joey said as he picked up the bottle and tried to get the colt to drink a little more.

Kate was so proud of Joey. His love of horses was evident. He was going to make a great veterinarian some day and the experience he was getting now, was going to be a big help. She knew her experiences working with the veterinarian back home had really come in handy around the farm.

Sam had the horses saddled and ready when Kate walked out of the stall, so it didn't take long to be on their way. He told Kate they were going a little way out, into the hills, to a place he thought she would really love.

Since it was going to take a while and since Sam had told her so much about his life, Kate decided to tell him more about hers. "You told me a lot about growing up here last night, so I thought I would tell you a little about my life."

"I'd like that." Sam replied.

"I was married to my childhood sweetheart, right out of high school."

Sam was shocked finding out Kate was married. He thought she was single. She didn't have a wedding band on her hand, so he was really confused. "You're married?"

Kate smiled. "No, not any more. My husband joined the military shortly after I started college. He served for a couple of years, then on his last mission, he didn't make it back."

"Kate, I'm so sorry. It takes someone very brave and special to serve in the military." Sam replied.

"He was a special man. Just like the other men and women who serve are."

"You seem alright with it now though; are you?" Sam asked.

"Yes. It was rough at first and I threw myself into my studies, but my faith got me through. I believe God has a purpose for each of us and brings people in and out of our lives for a reason.

The ones who go home to Him are truly the lucky ones. I feel I'm still here because he still has a purpose for me. I'm just hoping Ryan doesn't get the chance to send me home, before I can fulfill whatever God has set as my purpose, but it's up to Him."

"Wow, Kate. That's a wonderful way to look at life and death and it's kind of the way I think too. I really believe God brought you into our lives for the purpose of helping you through this challenge in your life."

"I want to believe you're right, but I hate putting you all in danger along with me." Kate replied.

"He's watched over me this far, so I don't expect him to stop now."

"It doesn't keep me from worrying though, although I know it should. So don't you want me to tell you more about me?" Kate asked.

"Definitely." Sam replied.

"Well, for my family, I'm the oldest of five. Mike is actually older and would make six, but he is a half-brother. Our mom had him when she was very young and before she met my dad. I have three younger brothers and one younger sister. My sister is graduating from high school this year, like Joey, and is planning to go to Purdue in the fall to be close to home.

I think Joey is looking forward to meeting her and maybe they can help each other out studying for classes. I'm sure Joey will like knowing at least one person when he gets there, and I think Emma will like him, especially since he likes to ride."

"Kate, I think it's great Joey might know someone there. I hope you have a chance to introduce them when he gets to Indiana." Sam said.

"Me too." Kate replied as she tried not to let Sam know how much she still worried about her future and if she still had one, but it was hard.

Kate continued to tell Sam about her family and how she considered Jess a sister, since her parents had taken her in when Jess's parents were killed in a car accident. "She was only sixteen and she had been taking riding lessons from me for a couple of years. We became good friends and my parents felt she needed us, especially since her brother was stationed overseas in England at the time.

Her brother had come home for the funeral and was going to get out of the service to take care of her, but Jess took the loss pretty hard and they didn't get along. I think he was glad when my parents offered to let her stay with us.

It worked out well, especially when I went away to college and only went home on weekends and summers to ride. Jess is a couple of years younger than me, but finished college in four years, since she didn't go on to graduate school. She has been taking care of my horses, while I've been in graduate school and has picked up a couple of her own.

We took a lot of camping trips and Jess started going to church with us and I think her faith finally got her through the trauma of losing her parents. She's really great and I think you will like her."

"I'm sure I will, especially if she's anything like you." Sam replied.

"Oh, you mean a murder suspect?" Kate asked kiddingly.

"I don't think you shot or killed your brother anymore." Sam said seriously. "It's all your other attributes, I like."

Kate then went on to tell Sam about the horses she'd had over the years and the ones she now had and how much she had always loved riding and camping. She had also helped her dad with the cattle, especially when they needed to round them up to change pastures, since they didn't have a lot of land or when they somehow managed to get out and were blocking the road.

Sam laughed. "We've had that happen a few times too. It's hard to believe the cows think the grass is always greener on the other side of the fence, even with all the land here."

Kate was surprised when Sam stopped. She looked at the beautiful lake in the middle of a small valley and when she caught sight of the snow-covered mountains reflecting in the lake, she was amazed. "Oh Sam, it's fantastic here."

"I thought you would like it. Would you like to have lunch here?" Sam asked.

The view was phenomenal, so Kate didn't hesitate to respond. "Sounds wonderful!"

"I brought plenty to eat, if you don't mind sandwiches. We'll have a real meal tonight at the gathering hall." Sam said as he dismounted.

Sam retrieved a tablecloth from his saddle bag and then handed Kate a couple of sandwiches and bottles of water, along with a small bag of chocolate chip cookies, which she had already figured out were his favorite. He spread out the tablecloth and they sat down. They had just finished eating when Kate noticed some movement by the lake. She watched for just a few moments, before mentioning it to Sam.

Sam was surprised to see horses there, but then noticed there were three riders circling them and leading them toward the fire tower. Sam quickly called the sheriff and let him know about the riders he thought might be rustlers, since he didn't recognize any of them.

Dave told Sam to stay put, until the rustlers were out of sight, and not try to go after them as he and some deputies were on the way and could hopefully catch them red-handed. He asked Sam to go down and if he could find out where they had parked their rig to get a plate number, just in case.

He said for Sam to call Nick and have him meet them at the base of the fire tower road with his truck so he could hook up to the trailer to take the horses to the ranch. Dave then emphasized that Sam should not try to apprehend the rustlers.

Sam understood and anyway, he didn't want to take a chance on getting Kate hurt. As soon as the riders disappeared into the trees, Sam told Kate to stay put and he would be back shortly, but Kate refused. She wasn't about to stay there alone with bears, mountain lions and hard telling what else around.

She also didn't trust Sam to not try and apprehend the horse thieves if she wasn't there. If something happened to him, she didn't have a clue of how to get back to the ranch, although Choco probably did.

Sam finally agreed and told her to stay behind him as they slowly descended the ridge and headed toward the lake. The horses and riders were gone, so they quietly rode into the woods toward the fire tower where they had seen the riders disappear.

Sam suddenly stopped and whispered to Kate to dismount and hold the reins of both the horses and she didn't hesitate. She could hear voices nearby, although they were not close enough to make out what they were saying.

It wasn't long before they heard an engine start and knew the men were pulling out. Sam quickly called Dave to make sure he was in place, then they mounted up. They rode through the trees staying near the road leading away from the fire tower, but out of sight.

They were nearing the exit from the fire tower road when they noticed the truck pulling the horse trailer stop. There was little doubt why, as Dave had said they were in place to catch them.

Sam pulled his rifle from the sleeve and got down, then handed Kate his reins, "Stay here. I just want to make sure nothing goes wrong when they meet up with Dave."

Kate was now worried as she watched Sam slowly walk to a large tree near the back of the trailer. She heard and saw the men exit the truck with rifles aimed toward the road where she knew Dave and his deputies were waiting. She froze and held her breath as the men started shooting toward Dave. She then heard Dave shout for them to put down their rifles as they were surrounded.

Suddenly, Kate watched as Sam took a shot, hitting the side-view mirror next to one of the men. The man quickly dropped his rifle and held up his hands. She then heard another shot, that seemed to come from the other side of the truck and watched as the three men walked toward Dave with their hands in the air. All she could think of was, Thank God it's over.

Once the men were in handcuffs, Kate rode to where Sam was standing next to Dave and was happy to hear no one had been hurt, especially Sam. They talked for a few minutes before hearing a truck headed their way, and were glad to see Nick driving up to get the horses.

Sam walked over and helped Nick hook up to the rustler's trailer. One of the deputies was taking pictures of the truck, the horse trailer, and the horses with Jake's brand on them. The deputy then climbed into the horse rustler's truck to pull it out of the way, then proceeded down the road toward town. It was amazing how quickly they were able to get it all done. Nick then told Dave he would drop off the trailer in town after he unloaded the horses.

Kate and Sam said goodbye to everyone and watched as they all pulled away. Nick said he would see them later at the ranch and thanked them for all their help.

Sam turned to Kate and asked. "So, are you ready to continue our ride back to the ranch with the rest of the horses left by the lake?"

"Yes, and I think we've had enough adventure for one day. Just think, we even managed to get some horses back to the ranch before us."

Sam laughed. "You're right; and I'm also hoping we don't have to face any more trauma today. I'm ready for a nice quiet ride back to the ranch now."

They mounted up and rode back to the fence where it had been cut. Sam quickly repaired it as Kate watched and looked around at the beautiful surroundings. It was truly amazing up here. They rounded up the horses which were still by the lake and headed them through the pass.

Kate was worried and watched the rocks diligently as they rode through, since Sam had told her they sometimes spotted mountain lions in the area. She was thankful she hadn't seen anything moving, except a few birds and rabbits that had possibly been startled by them.

As they rode on, they found another small herd of horses and headed them all toward the ranch. It had been so easy, Kate was surprised. Suddenly a shot rang out and then another, not far from where they were and the horses stampeded.

Sam and Kate rode hard trying to keep the herd together and finally was able to slow them. Sam quickly rode over to Kate and she could tell he was worried. "Are you alright?"

"I'm fine, but it's been a long time since I've ridden that hard and never with a herd of horses. It was definitely exciting." Kate hesitated for a moment. "Did you hear a couple of gunshots? Do you think it could have been Ryan?"

"I did, but I'm not sure where they came from. I don't think Ryan has had a chance to make it this far yet. I'm going to send some men to check out the area and have some of the others help us bring this herd in, so we don't take any chances at losing any." Sam replied before making a call to the ranch.

Kate was hoping Sam was right, but she had doubts. She kept looking around for any movement in the trees around where they were, hoping not to see anyone or anything that could stampede the horses again. It wasn't long before she noticed riders heading toward them and was happy to have the riders join them for the rest of the ride.

Sam spoke with a couple of the men, telling them approximately where they were when they had heard the shots. They hadn't been too far from the road at the time, so it could have been anyone. He doubted they would find anyone, but he would rather be safe than sorry.

Sam told Kate he doubted it was Ryan as he didn't think he had time to make it to the area yet, but now, he wondered if maybe it had been him. He was going to have to keep a closer eye on Kate and make sure the guys were armed and ready in case Ryan had made it this far and found her.

Kate was happy when the ranch came into view and nothing else had happened along the way. Thankfully there adventure today had taken her mind off Ryan and her dilemma, at least for a while.

She was looking forward to dinner tonight at the gathering hall and spending more time with Sam. She knew she shouldn't feel that way and definitely didn't want Sam to know. A relationship with him now would be a mistake, especially since her future was up in the air. She had to keep her guard up.

As soon as they entered the barn, Kate immediately went to the stall to check on the young colt that had been so weak, that morning. She wanted to see if it was any better, and if the bottle feeding was working. She was surprised to see Joey was in the stall and bottle feeding the colt. It was a good sign that the colt was eating again.

Joey looked up and smiled as she entered the stall. "He's doing a lot better."

"I'm so glad. Do you need me to take over so you can go get something to eat?" Kate asked.

"No. Not necessary. I just got back from dinner and relieved my friend. There are four of us taking turns, so he will be well taken care of. How was your day?" Joey asked.

"A little more eventful than I was expecting, but we had a nice ride."

"I heard about the rustlers; and then the gunshots. It's definitely not a typical day around here. I'm glad you weren't hurt."

"Me too, but I am starving, so please call me if you need me for this little guy." Kate replied as she patted the colt on the side of the neck.

"I will. You'd better get going if you don't want to miss dinner." Joey said.

"On my way." Kate replied as she walked out of the stall. She was surprised to see Sam waiting for her. They ran to the cabin to wash up, before heading to the gathering hall.

The food line was just getting ready to close when they got there, but there was still a great variety, so they quickly filled their plates. The food was terrific and Kate couldn't believe she ate so much, but it had been quite a while since they had stopped for lunch. Sam and Kate kidded around as they ate since Jake, Nick, Joey, and the other ranch-hands had eaten earlier.

Before heading back to the cabin, they took another walk to the barn to check on Joey and the colt. Kate had to smile as she looked in the stall and saw Joey and the colt curled up together, asleep. They decided not to bother them.

Once they returned to the cabin, Kate decided to check her voice mail to see if her parents had called, while they were gone. There were two messages. The first message was from her mother, who said they were doing fine and were hoping to be near home some time tomorrow. Kate was glad to hear Mike was also doing better.

Kate hesitated when she noticed the next message showed as an unknown number.

"What is it?" Sam asked.

"I think the next message might be from Ryan."

"I'm here for you Kate. You can put it on speaker, if you'd like."

Kate brought up the message and put her phone on speaker. She hadn't been wrong. It was Ryan.

"I need the money, Kate, so you'd better start looking harder. We'll see you soon; real soon."

Kate had hoped Ryan would say whether or not they were there yet, but he hadn't. It was still a guessing game and how could she look harder for something she didn't have. Why wouldn't he believe her?

Sam then said. "Well, it doesn't sound like he has made it here yet, so maybe he won't show up for a few more days. We checked everything out when you got here, so I don't know where else you could look for money. Have you tried asking your brother about it?"

"No; not yet. He hasn't been in any condition to talk much according to mom and dad. Maybe in a couple of days, he'll feel more like talking and I can ask him. I'm not sure it would stop Ryan though. I'm still a witness to him shooting Mike."

"You're probably right." Sam responded, but still wondered who had shot at them or near them, earlier today, if it wasn't Ryan.

Kate finally told Sam she was tired and thought she would turn in. She thanked him for the beautiful ride today. Even though it had been a little more exciting than she had expected, she had still enjoyed it.

Sam told Kate he had really enjoyed the ride too; and especially learning more about her. He then told her rain was in the forecast for tomorrow, so it would be a good day to go into town. They planned to head to town after breakfast to meet up with the sheriff and see if he had heard anything new about Ryan. He then told her goodnight and watched as she headed to her room.

Sam couldn't believe their ride had turned into such a mess. They had run into problems with horse rustlers before, but it had been quite a while ago. Why did it have to be when he was trying to protect Kate. He was also concerned about who had shot at them. Could Ryan be here already? There were mountain lions, bears, wolves, and cougars in the mountains, maybe someone was shooting at one. At this point he doubted he would ever know.

Sam decided he was going to have to be more cautious and aware of their surroundings, because he didn't want anything bad happening to Kate. He hadn't planned to fall for her, but he had, and hard. He knew she was right for him, but was he right for her.

Is it possible she could feel the same way about him; he doubted it. He had never met anyone like her before, and after getting to know her better, he didn't believe she could have shot anyone, especially her own brother. The messages from Ryan had helped him believe her story, so now his only problem was figuring out the best way to protect her.

Chapter 5

Kate hadn't slept much and what little sleep she did get was interrupted by terrifying nightmares. She had awakened several times during the night in a sweat. The last nightmare was so vivid she was still shaking and gun shots were still ringing in her head.

As she opened her eyes and looked around the room, she was unable to place where she was at first. She began to panic, but then remembered she was in a cabin at the dude ranch and her body began to relax. She had to pull herself together. There was no reason to let Sam see how stressed out she was. It would only worry him and she was sure she had worried him enough already.

Kate needed to think positive. Just knowing Sam was watching over her, lifted her spirits a little. She really liked him, but she couldn't let him know how much. She would have to keep her feelings from getting any stronger; it wouldn't be fair to Sam with being so unsure about her future.

She was thankful things had worked out so well and she had ended up in this wonderful place where she felt safe with supportive people all around her, especially Sam. She knew the danger wasn't over yet and she was still putting everyone on the ranch in danger, even more so now since Ryan knew where she was.

It was raining outside, which put a damper on Kate's hopes of riding today, but she was sure Sam would have something for them to do. He hadn't failed yet in keeping her busy. She then remembered them planning to go in to town today to talk with the sheriff. She was hoping he had an update on Ryan.

Sam was nowhere in sight when Kate came out of her room, so she quickly got ready for the day. By the time she had showered and dressed, Sam was back wearing a rain slicker and carrying another slicker over his arm. She couldn't help but smile as she looked at him; he was so tall and handsome, even in the huge rain slicker. He had such a wonderful smile; it melted her heart. "Good morning."

"Good morning to you too. Did you sleep well?" Sam replied.

"Yes, thank you. Hopefully I'm all caught up on my sleep now." Kate responded, not wanting to let him know about the nightmares and how worried she was.

Sam could tell Kate hadn't slept well. The bags under her eyes were back and her pretense of a smile was noticeable, but he felt it better not to make an issue of it. Perhaps she would have a chance to rest later. "So, are you ready for breakfast?"

"Definitely; is that slicker for me?" Kate asked.

"Yes; I thought you might need it. It's pretty soggy out there and chilly, so you should put your coat on under it." Sam stated.

"Thanks, I'll get a jacket." Kate said before she walked back into the bedroom and retrieved her brother's jacket. She already had on her hooded sweatshirt so she felt he didn't think it would be enough.

When Kate returned, she noticed a strange look on Sam's face. "I only have my brother's jacket with me. I know it's a little worn out, but hopefully Jess will bring mine when she comes. It was warm in Las Vegas, so I didn't need a coat."

"Not a problem." Sam told her remembering she had worn the jacket the night he and Nick had thought she was a scared boy and had given her a ride. They had really been surprised when it had turned out to be Kate.

"Let's go and after breakfast we'll go into town to see Dave and see if he has any news." Sam responded.

"Thank you. Sounds like a good plan for this rainy day. At least with this rain slicker on, no one should be able to recognize me."

"You might consider wearing your brother's baseball cap as well and putting your hair underneath while we're there, just in case. I don't think Ryan is around, but just in case he does show up, he might ask questions around town." Sam hated having her put on the baseball cap, he loved her long hair; it was beautiful, even in a ponytail, and he had to fight his desire to pull her into his arms again and run his fingers through it.

"Not a problem," Kate replied as she quickly retrieved the cap and stuffed it in her pocket. She then walked to the door where Sam was standing, and for a moment, their eyes met. She wondered why it was so hard for her to turn away.

Finally, she forced herself to stop looking into his eyes. She had to keep reminding herself, this was no time for her to get involved with anyone; even if he did have a wonderful effect on her and his sky-blue eyes were entrancing. She couldn't let him get to her; not now, so she quickly turned her back to him.

Sam helped Kate on with the rain slicker, then they ran to the gathering hall where breakfast had been prepared. The slicker covered her from her head to almost her feet and she felt like she was covered in a huge, heavy plastic bag, but it did keep her dry.

Kate hadn't noticed before, but pegs had been placed along the wall, just inside the door, which was really handy for everyone to hang their slickers or coats while enjoying breakfast. The food, as usual, was great, especially the coffee that she so desperately needed.

After breakfast, Sam told Kate to wait by the door while he went to get his truck. She thought it was unnecessary, but she didn't argue as the rain was really coming down hard.

She didn't have to wait long before Sam drove up in a very nice gray crew-cab pickup. She almost hated getting in, because she was drenched by the time she got to the truck. Sam insisted she didn't need to worry. He said it had been through a lot worse than a little water. Kate wondered what, but she didn't ask.

Sam told her the drive into town wouldn't take long, but it gave Kate time to check out the scenery, which was beautiful even though she couldn't see very far with the rain, but she still loved it. The light conversation with Sam was wonderful and he didn't bring up the problems she was having, but instead shared more about his life growing up on the ranch. She also shared a little more of her life growing up on the farm.

As they rounded a curve, suddenly a stalled pickup truck appeared in the middle of the road in front of them. Sam hit the brakes and his truck began to slide and spin. It finally came to a stop facing the opposite direction. Fortunately, it hadn't hit anything, but by the time Sam's truck had come to a complete stop, the pickup in the road, had vanished.

Kate was still shaking as Sam turned to her. "Are you alright?"

"Yes, I think so." She replied, although her heart was still pounding.

She looked around and asked. "What happened to the other pickup? Where did it go?"

Sam looked around and was surprised the pickup was nowhere in sight. "I don't know. It must have taken off. Did you get the color of it or anything?"

"No, it all happened so fast, but I think it had a camper on it. You don't think it could have been Ryan, do you?" Kate asked.

"Hopefully not, but I don't think he would have known it was you in my truck. I do however think he has had time to get here. We'll let Dave know about the pickup with the camper when we get to his office, just in case." Sam replied.

95

Sam wished he had been able to get a description of the pickup, but getting his truck under control had been more important at the time. He was relieved he hadn't hit anything or gone down into the ravine. It had scared him and he knew Kate had been frightened, but thankfully they were both okay. He couldn't understand why anyone would stop a vehicle in the middle of the road, but after Kate's remark about Ryan, it made him wonder.

If Ryan somehow had known she was in his truck or that they would be going to the sheriff's office today, it might make sense, but how could he have known? Was he tracking her phone and able to know she had left the ranch? Had Kate even brought her phone with her? Why would Ryan try to wreck them, unless he was just trying to get to Kate? Sam didn't like having so many unanswered questions.

***

Fortunately, the rain finally slowed to a drizzle as they drove into town. The town was small and quaint, but larger than Kate had expected. It didn't take long to get to the sheriff's office, and Kate wasn't really looking forward to going in. She was afraid she may have to stay if the sheriff had changed his mind. She put her fears aside, walked in, and then entered the door to Dave's office.

Dave seemed nice and cordial as they entered, but seemed very concerned as Sam told him about the pickup that had been stopped in the middle of the road on their way into town. Sam also mentioned, that Kate was afraid it might have been the DEA agent, Ryan, and then about someone shooting at or near them the previous day when they were near the road leading to the ranch.

Dave quickly told one of his deputies to put out an alert to watch for an out-of-state pickup with a camper on the back. He also told him to let everyone know, to be cautious and not stop the truck but to get a better description instead, and if possible, the license plate number.

Kate understood why Dave was being so cautious, and she was sure he was now worried that it had been Ryan. Dave knew Ryan was armed and dangerous and he didn't want any of his men getting hurt or killed. She hated it was her fault Ryan was possibly there and someone might get hurt, but she didn't know what she could do. She could maybe identify Ryan, if Dave had been able to get his photo and hoped it would help.

Dave sat down at his desk, then turned the computer screen around for Kate to look at the photos he had received. Kate looked through them and immediately recognized Ryan out of the bunch. Although the person in the photo was more clean-cut with the long hair, scruffy beard and mustache gone, it was Ryan. She let Dave know, but also told him how he had looked when she had seen him.

Dave picked up the phone and began to make a call. He said he was calling the DEA office to speak with the agent he had spoken with the previous night.

Kate listened intently as Dave relayed the information that she had identified Agent Ryan Scott as the person she had witnessed shoot her brother. He also told the agent what Sam had said about the incident that had happened on their way in to town. After listening for a few minutes, Dave handed the phone to Kate. "This is Agent Matt. He wants to know everything that has happened, in detail."

Kate couldn't believe, Agent Matt had so many questions, but she tried to answer them all. It worried her because he sounded as if he didn't believe her. He did, however, say he would try to see if he could find out if Ryan was on his way or was there already. He said he would be coming to town later today to help find Ryan, then asked to speak to the sheriff again.

After hanging up, the sheriff turned to Kate. "Kate, Agent Matt is not totally buying your story, but it seems the agent you identified is under investigation, as he has been out of contact for over a week now." Dave's voice then became serious. "He thinks you should be behind bars,

97

but he's leaving it to my discretion whether to lock you up or let you stay at the ranch.

He definitely doesn't want you leaving town. He realizes it could be risky having you in jail, if what you said is true, since it would be easier for Agent Ryan to find you. I'm leaning toward believing your story Kate after hearing the messages Ryan has left."

The sheriff hesitated for only a moment and turned to Sam before continuing. "But Sam, it's your call if you want to be responsible for her, I'll turn her over to you and continue with our plan, otherwise, I'll have to lock her up."

"Sheriff, he left another message last night." Kate said as she pulled out her phone and found the message, then played it for him.

"It does sound like he is definitely coming, if he's not already here. Have you thought more about the money he's asking about?" Dave asked.

"No. I don't know where it could be and my brother is not up to talking yet. The trip back to Indiana has been hard on him. I do plan to ask him as soon as I can though." Kate replied.

Sam looked at Kate and then back at the sheriff. "I don't think she shot her brother. According to her parents, Mike has been able to handle the trip, but it hasn't been easy on him. I looked through Kate's things when she arrived and didn't see any money, other than a few dollars, she pulled out of his jacket, she was wearing."

"I haven't found any money and I don't know where to look. I would guess it was somewhere in Mike's apartment, if anywhere." Kate stated.

Sam hesitated for only a moment before turning back to the sheriff. "I believe her and I'll take full responsibility. I think she will be safer at the ranch anyway, since Agent Ryan may already be here."

"You're probably right, but if she disappears, you will be considered an accomplice and I'd have to lock you up." Dave said.

"Thanks Dave, I'll take my chances." Sam replied.

"Okay then, just try to keep her out of sight, or where there are a lot of people around so he won't be tempted to try to get to her." Dave said apprehensively.

"Will do." Sam said before turning to Kate. "Put on your cap, we need some lunch and serving time for lunch at the ranch will be over by the time we get back. I know a great place to eat."

Kate had put her hair in a pony tail earlier, so it was easy to pull it up and put on the cap before she turned to the sheriff. "Will that be, okay?"

"Well, with that disguise, I can see why the officer, who showed you your photo in Utah, didn't recognize you. I think if you keep on the cap, you should be fine." Dave said.

"Thank you. I promise I won't leave the ranch once we get back. I feel safe with Sam." Kate replied.

"I think the question is; does he feel safe with you." Dave responded.

"I hope so; I've never had a use for guns and hope I never have to." Kate said.

Kate could tell Dave was still worried as he responded. "I'll let you know if I get an update. I want to believe you Kate, but you must admit it is a pretty bizarre story, even with the photos and messages. And remember, Sam is putting his reputation at stake by being responsible for you. If you run, he goes to jail."

"I know and I promise I won't run. I'd never do anything to hurt Sam or the others at the ranch. I wish this had never happened. I feel like I'm living in a nightmare, especially seeing my brother…" Her voice caught and she had to turn away to hide the tears surfacing in her eyes, but Sam quickly pulled her into his arms.

"I'm not worried Dave, and I'll take care of her. We'll see you later." Sam responded, as he and Kate walked toward the door. He had noticed the worried look Dave had given him, which had grown more intense when he had taken Kate into his arms, but he wasn't going to let Kate down. She needed someone she could count on.

It was only a couple of blocks to the café, so they decided to walk, giving Kate a chance to regain her composure. "Thank you for believing in me Sam, you don't know how much that means to me."

"Things will look better soon, just hang in there. I'll be here for you, for as long as you need me. Come on, let's eat, they have some really great breaded tenderloins and pecan pie here, I know you'll love. The owner is originally from Tennessee, so her menu is a little different, but I love the southern cooking." Sam responded.

Kate wanted to believe him and have this nightmare behind her, but she was afraid it wouldn't be over for a while; not until her brother's shooter was behind bars for good. She tried to hide her fears as she responded. "Breaded tenderloin sounds great. I haven't had one in a long time, but one of the small cafés back home serves really good ones. Do they also have fried okra?"

"I don't know, but we can sure check. It's something I've never had, so if they have it, we'll definitely get an order so I can see what it's like." Sam replied.

When the waitress came over, Sam ordered for them both and was surprised they did have fried okra. The waitress looked at Kate and asked. "Got you a new ranch hand Sam?"

"Yep, a little young, but we think he might work out. Sadie, meet Kit, he started this week."

"Nice to meet you Kit, anytime you get tired of eating at the ranch, feel free to come in for some good old-fashioned country cooking, and our desserts are something to die for."

Kate kept her head lowered and her voice low as she responded, hoping the waitress would just think she was shy. "Thank you, I'll keep that in mind, but the foods pretty good at the ranch too."

The waitress laughed, then turned and left, which relieved Kate. They didn't talk much, especially with other customers around, but the food was great and she definitely enjoyed the tenderloin. She had forgotten how much she loved breaded tenderloins and even though it was huge, she ate the whole thing.

Sam really liked the fried okra and was going to check with the cooks at the ranch to see if they could get some and fix it up. Kate told him it was best fried up in cornmeal, like they did here, and very easy to make. The waitress had also been right, as the pecan pie was to die for.

As they left the cafe, Sam asked if there was anything she needed while they were in town, but she said she just wanted to get back to the ranch where she felt safe and no one else would see her. She then remembered she hadn't gotten a burner phone yet.

"Wait! Is there any place I can pick up a burner phone? I'd like to have a way to keep in touch with my parents and the rest of the family without having my phone tracked."

Kate and Sam stopped in the general store where fortunately they carried prepaid phones. She purchased one with cash, and also got a few cards with extra minutes, so she wouldn't have to worry about how long she talked.

As they were walking out of the store, Kate noticed a clearance rack of coats, so she asked Sam if he would mind if she looked at them. She was surprised to find one with horses that she really liked, and it was just the right size.

She was sure it wouldn't only look better than Mike's jacket, but would probably be warmer too. She purchased it as well, again using cash. She didn't want Ryan trying to track her in town and possibly put anyone else in danger. They then headed toward the truck.

Kate noticed Sam looking around. She was sure he was just being cautious, but she also thought the pickup from this morning could be in town. It worried her that they might encounter it on the road back. When she noticed the sheriff's car pull in behind them as they started out, it put her mind more at ease.

***

The drive back to the ranch went without incident and Kate was glad when they arrived safely. Sam asked if she would like to check on the colt, since it had finally stopped raining, and she told him that would be great.

"Since we've already had lunch, we could help with some of the work around here rounding up horses again, though hopefully without incident; if you'd like. I need to update Jake and Nick first." Sam stated.

Kate laughed. "Yes; that would be nice."

Once they found Jake and Nick, Sam filled them in about the incident on the road. They also thought it might have been Ryan, but weren't sure.

He let them know what Dave had said about putting everyone on alert, and how the deputies were keeping a lookout for a pickup with a camper and out-of-state plates. Dave had also said he and Agent Matt would be out some time today or tomorrow, depending on how soon Agent Matt arrived.

Sam finally turned to Kate after answering all their questions. "Are you ready to check on the little colt now?"

"Yes, I'd love to see how it's doing. I might as well earn my keep." Kate replied, hoping it would help keep her mind off of her situation for a little while.

They first stopped by the cabin to change and drop off her purchases, then Kate made a quick call to her parents and Jess to give them the number of her burner phone, before they headed toward the barn.

Just before they got there, Sam was surprised to see Nick with a worried expression. "What's wrong?"

"We have one of our mares down, and she's having difficulty birthing. I'm afraid we're going to lose her if doc can't get here soon."

"I can help." Kate quickly responded.

"What can you do? The foal is probably going to have to be turned."

Sam then spoke up. "She just finished school to be a veterinarian."

Nick looked surprised. "But have you worked with large animals?"

102

"Yes, it was my major and what I plan to practice. I grew up on a farm with horses and cattle, and I've been working with the vet at home in my spare time, so I've had some experience."

Nick was a little hesitant, but then took her to the stall. The mare was in distress and going down as they walked in. Kate quickly checked her then asked where she could wash up and if they had some long gloves. Nick went to the horse's head as Sam quickly took Kate to wash up while he got the gloves.

Kate was able to turn the foal and was pulling it out when she noticed an older man standing back watching. The foal was a beautiful dark brown and white filly with a light mane and tail.

It hadn't taken long for Nick to get the mare to stand, so Kate felt the mare would be okay, although she would still need to check her. It took only a short time for the filly to stand on its wobbly legs after Kate finished rubbing her down. Kate then checked the mare, before she told Nick they seemed to be fine.

Nick was smiling as he replied. "Thank you, Kate, you've got a job here any time you want one. I think I'll call this little gal, Katie, since you probably saved both their lives."

"Thank you, Nick, I'm glad I could help." Kate replied.

The older gentleman who had been watching then walked over to Kate and said, "You did a right nice job their girl, looks like you might have had a little practice delivering foals before."

"I just finished veterinary school and I grew up on a farm in Indiana where my parents raise cattle and have a few horses. I worked for a vet near home on breaks and summers, while I was in school, so I've had a little practice. I don't think we've met, I'm Kate."

The older gentleman extended his hand and took hers. "I'm Doctor Hank Porter, the local veterinarian. Thank you for taking care of my patient. I was tied up at a ranch on the other side of the county when Nick called."

"I'm glad I could help." Kate replied.

"You're new around here, aren't you? I don't think I've seen you before." Doc asked.

"No, actually, I'm just visiting. I'm taking a vacation while waiting on the results of my license exams and tying up some loose ends." Although she felt her situation was far more than loose end, she didn't see a need to share the issue with him.

"Once you have your Indiana license to practice why don't you give me a call. If you think you might be interested in working in Colorado, we can get you licensed here as well. I could sure use some help and we could have a chat." Doc Porter said as he handed her his card. "At least that way I might not lose one of my best customers." He smiled as he then looked over at Nick.

"Thank you, I'll keep it in mind. It was nice meeting you, but I think I'd better get cleaned up." Kate said.

Kate then turned and headed for the cabin with a smile on her face. She was excited thinking of the offer from Doctor Porter. She wondered if Colorado might be a good place to work. Her thoughts then turned sad as the thought of Ryan being after her surfaced. She had no chance of getting a job if the chance of her being killed for money, she didn't even have, was hanging over her head.

After reaching the cabin Kate quickly showered and changed. She joined the guys back at the barn and was surprised to see Doc Porter still there. He shared several stories about his practice and things that had happened, and she thoroughly enjoyed listening and talking with him.

Once Doc left, Sam asked. "Are you ready to go for a ride now? It would be awfully hard for Ryan to get to you without a horse as there are no roads around here other than the main road, and we can avoid that area."

Kate quickly replied, "I'm always ready for a ride."

They saddled their horses and left for the ride they had planned earlier. They rode for a little while talking about the ranch before running across a small herd of horses.

104

They decided to round the herd up and take it back to the ranch.

There was a beautiful black gelding in the herd and Kate thought of Jess and how much she would love it. "Jess loves black horses and that one is magnificent. Do you think it will be ready to ride by the time she gets here?"

"I don't know. I'm not sure if it's ever had any time under the saddle, but we can have the guys work with it and see if it's possible. Is she an experienced rider, who could handle a green broke horse?"

"Jess has been riding for a while now and is truly a natural when it comes to riding, with or without a saddle. I haven't ridden as much since I went to college, but Jess has been home and exercising my horses for a few years now and has been training a couple of colts she picked up a couple of years ago, so I'm pretty sure she could handle any horse."

"We'll let him rest tonight, then I'll get the guys to try him out tomorrow. I'll ask them to wait until we get there so we can see how he does."

"That would be great." Kate replied. "I can't wait."

As they were riding toward the back side of the herd, Kate noticed a movement a short distance away in the trees and alerted Sam. He took out his rifle, looking through the scope and then fired, catching Kate off guard.

Panic shot through her as she looked over at Sam while trying to calm Choco. She was surprised the gunshot had affected Choco, but at least he calmed quickly. She was sure the horses on the ranch were trained to the sound of a gun, but perhaps only when someone on their back fired the shot, or maybe her fear at the unexpected sound had affected him.

As Sam lowered his rifle he looked over at Kate. He hadn't thought to warn her first and panic was written all over her face. "Kate, I'm sorry. It was a pack of wolves. I had to scare them off. Wolves can do a lot of damage to a small herd. I'm so sorry."

It took Kate a few moments to calm her fear so she could speak. "It's okay Sam; I just wasn't expecting it. Did you frighten them away?"

"Yes. They hightailed it up the hill, but we need to check and see what they were after. Are you up to it?" Sam asked.

"I'm fine. Let's go. There may be an animal in trouble." Kate replied.

They nudged their horses into a canter as they headed toward the trees, but quickly pulled up and jumped off when they reached the area. A mare was down and struggling and appeared to be pregnant, so they had to act fast. Sam ran to the head of the mare to try to calm her thrashing, while Kate tried to get into position to check her and help without getting kicked.

As soon as Sam was able to calm the mare a little, Kate went to work checking her and wasn't surprised, she had numerous bite marks and was in labor. The wolves had probably spotted the mare away from the herd, making her vulnerable. Battling the wolves had no doubt thrown the mare into labor and she was struggling.

Kate was finally able to get into a position to help the foal out as she prayed it would live. It was hard to believe this was happening twice in one day, but this was a large ranch with lots of horses, and this was the birthing season. Something she was going to have to remember if she took the job with Doc Porter and worked in Colorado.

It took a few minutes, but Kate thanked God as she pulled out a very small, but beautiful white colt. The colt was a preemie, but it appeared to be breathing on its own and doing ok for now.

Sam threw her his handkerchief and she used it to wipe the foal's face, then checked it before setting it aside. She then started checking the mare and was worried because she hadn't gotten up yet.

The mare could have twisted her intestines while thrashing and fighting off the wolves, but hopefully was just tired from struggling. Kate and Sam needed to get the mare up so Kate could check her and find out how much damage the wolves had caused.

Sam struggled a few more minutes to get the mare on her feet then, thankfully, she stood. The mare had several noticeable bite marks, but nothing that looked life threatening, if they could avoid an infection.

Kate could check her out further once they were back at the ranch. The mare looked as if she could walk okay, so Sam threw a rope around her neck to lead her to the ranch, He then told Kate to mount up and handed her the small colt.

They had to take it slow with the mare so weak, but fortunately they weren't far from the ranch. Sam had called ahead and ranch-hands came out to help bring the small herd in. Once they got to the barn, Joey came out immediately and helped them get the mare and colt to a stall.

Kate worked with the small colt for a while and was happy when he finally stood on his own, but just barely and for only a very short time. She then checked the mare, who was now eating, which was a good sign, but there were numerous bite marks that needed attention and she definitely would need antibiotics and perhaps a rabies vaccine; just in case.

Kate held the colt up for a few minutes, but then let it lay down. She knew the colt wouldn't be able to nurse yet, as it was too small, and the mare hadn't dropped yet either.

She asked Joey to see if he could get some milk so she could try to feed it, while Sam called Doc Porter. Doc said he would be out soon, so Kate stayed with the mare and colt.

Sam had excused himself for a few minutes to send some men out to look for the wolves, but as soon as he returned, she told him about the problem. "This one will have to be bottle fed for at least a few days. It's not able to nurse yet and can barely stand."

"Not a problem Kate, we can take care of that. Why don't you go get cleaned up for dinner, I think you've done

107

an amazing job in keeping him alive and getting him to stand. As you know, Joey is really good at bottle feeding and is looking forward to the challenge. He loves working with the young foals and so does his friends."

Kate looked up and saw Joey standing behind Sam, with a bottle in his hand, which he handed to her. He then started applying salve to the mare's wounds. She could tell Joey was really worried about the small colt; and she was too.

"That's great, but I want to wait and talk with Doc Porter and see if the colt will drink some milk. You can go on if you'd like Sam. I'm sure Joey can help if needed.

"I'll watch for Doc and bring him here as soon as he arrives." Sam replied as he walked out of the stall.

It wasn't long before Doc appeared with Sam. Kate had gotten the colt to drink a little, but was still very worried about it. Doc agreed that the next 48 hours were crucial and suggested prayer. He then checked the mare and gave her antibiotic and rabies shots, then said he would leave the antibiotic there to be administered for the next few days.

Joey quickly took it to the refrigerator in the tack room, then returned as Doc left. "I can take it now Kate, if you'd like to go to dinner before they shut down the serving line."

Kate was hesitant as the colt was still in bad shape. Joey had done great with the other colt, so she finally handed him the bottle. "If you have any problem Joey, don't hesitate to send for me. I'll come back later and check on him too."

"I'll take good care of them and I promise I'll come get you if there's a problem." Joey responded.

"Okay, I guess I'll catch you guys later." Kate said as she smiled at Sam and whispered. "He's a good kid."

"I know. I think he'll make a great vet someday, just like you." Sam said.

"Thank you. I just hope I get the chance to be one." Kate responded sadly.

"You will. God will take care of you and we'll all be there to help out too." Sam said with concern.

Kate wanted so much to believe him and trust God. She knew she should. He had been with them today to save the life of the two mares and the foals. It gave Kate hope, but it was so hard to let go and turn her problems over to Him.

***

After dinner, Kate was surprised as a group of guys got up, went on stage, and started playing country music. "Do we get entertainment tonight?"

"Sure; the band has been practicing all week to get ready for the guests arriving next Sunday, but this is a typical Friday night here. We all enjoy Friday and Saturday nights together with our families. Would you like to dance?"

Kate smiled as she replied, "I'd love to." She loved to dance, so even though she was tired from the long day working, she took his hand when he offered and they walked out to the dance floor.

She had a great time dancing mostly with Sam, but occasionally with Nick and Jake. Although Jake spent most of his time dancing with an attractive lady, with shoulder length light brown hair and appeared to be around Jake's age. She had arrived shortly after the music started and they had danced most of the evening.

Kate was surprised when they went back to the table for a few minutes to take a break and Jake introduced the woman he had been dancing with. "Kate, I'd like you to meet Doctor Lorrie Houston. She's a doctor at the hospital in town, but usually comes out on weekends to enjoy horseback riding, the music and dancing."

"It's nice to meet you, Doctor Lorrie. I'm going to be here, hopefully for another three weeks, so I hope we get a chance to know each other better." Kate responded.

"I'd like that. You can drop the doctor, just Lorrie is fine. I hear you are a veterinarian and have been helping out a lot around here." Lorrie replied.

"Well, almost. I took my license exams a little over a week ago, and I'm praying I passed. I've really enjoyed the experience I've been getting here though."

Lorrie laughed. "I'm sure you passed, although I don't doubt, they were probably as bad as the license exams I took, but I love what I do. Coming out here on weekends though really helps me relax."

"I think that's great and it's wonderful meeting you." Kate said, as a slow song started and Sam pulled her up and into his arms. It felt so right, she didn't want the music to ever stop, but as soon as the song was over, she stepped back out of his arms. She couldn't let down her guard, not now.

Unable to look into his eyes, afraid she would lose the control she was fighting to hold, she softly said, "I think we should go check on the mares and foals then I'd like to turn in. I'm pretty worn out from the workout today."

Sam didn't want to let Kate go. He wanted to keep her in his arms and never let go, but he didn't want to push her. "I'm pretty tired too, it's been a long day, and I guess you did get quite a workout."

"Great practice and I loved it." Kate responded.

They returned to the table where Jake, Lorrie, and Nick were sitting, watching the dancers. Kate was surprised they weren't on the dancefloor, but expected they needed a break too. Jake and Nick, both thanked Kate again for saving the horses today and said goodnight.

Kate and Sam said goodnight, then walked to the barn, where they found Joey asleep in the stall with the small white colt curled up in his arms. She hated to bother him, but wanted to check the colt before she left, although she decided to let them sleep a little longer and went to check on the other mare and Katie, the filly she had delivered earlier before their ride.

The filly and mare were both doing fine, so she checked on the small colt from yesterday and was surprised to see a young boy bottle feeding him. She checked out the colt and was happy to see he appeared to be standing better. She was starting to get a collection of patients and she loved it.

Kate then headed back to the stall where Joey was sleeping. She tried to be quiet as she checked the mare, but

110

when she turned to check the colt, she noticed Joey staring at her.

"You're a great vet, Kate. I hope I'll be as good as you some day." Joey said.

"I'm sure you will. I can tell you love animals and that's what it takes to be a great vet."

"I do, and I got the colt to drink a little from the bottle, so I think he'll be okay. I have the alarm on my phone set so I can try to feed him every two hours."

"That's good, but don't you think you should get some sleep?" Kate asked.

"I'll be fine. I'm catching a few naps between feedings and I have a guy relieving me in the morning so I'll get some sleep then. This little guy's worth missing a little sleep." Joey replied.

"He is adorable. I'm glad we were able to save him. I'll check on them in the morning and see you tomorrow after you get some sleep. By the way, have you named him yet?" Kate asked.

"Yes. I'm calling him Snowball, because he's solid white. I haven't been able to find one bit of color on him."

"Then I think it's a very suitable name. See you in the morning." Kate responded.

***

Kate had just gotten to her room and closed the door, when her phone rang catching her off guard. She had been thinking about the way she had felt in Sam's arms, so the ringing phone was a shock.

She had left her phone on in case Ryan called so she would know if he was there and if it had been him that morning who had almost caused them to wreck. She quickly pulled out her phone and wasn't surprised the caller ID was 'unknown'.

Kate had already given her family and Jess the number for her burner phone, so she wasn't expecting anyone else to call. She knew it was probably Ryan, so she let it go to

111

voicemail. She could share the message with the sheriff later rather than trying to relay the message. She waited for the notification that she had a message, then went to her voicemail. She was still shocked at the low voice she recognized immediately. "Don't get too comfortable with ranch life, Kate. Nice little town though. By the way, I hope you had a nice ride yesterday. You handled those horses pretty good when they took off. You were awfully close to the road though. Anything could have happened. You didn't by any chance, go in to town today, without any serious incident, did you. I hope you weren't hurt. As you can see, it is possible to get to you, just remember, I have patience, but my boss's patience is running out and you definitely do not want to deal with him." The message ended with, "And don't forget, I need the money and soon."

Unfortunately, Ryan's calls were never long enough to trace, but the sheriff had put a tracer on her phone, just in case. At least now she knew it was him yesterday, who fired the shots; and this morning he had caused them to almost wreck. She wished there was some way to find him so he and whomever might be with him could be thrown in jail.

Kate could see the concern on Sam's face as he quickly walked into the room and asked. "It was him again; wasn't it? What did he say?"

Kate hesitated for a few moments trying to gain composure and then replayed the message from Ryan. "I can't believe he is here already and he knows I'm on this ranch."

"At least we now know he's the one who shot at us yesterday. He said we were too close to the road, so we need to avoid that area. It was also him this morning, so we need to keep you near the ranch where there are always lots of people. If we go riding, we need to go up into the hills, where he would need a horse to get near you." Sam replied.

Sam was worried, but he tried not to let it show. "He's not going to get close to you Kate, I promise. I'm going to leave for just a few minutes to tell Jake and Nick about the call then I'll contact Dave and update him. Can I borrow your phone for a little bit? I'll bring it right back."

"Sure. I don't think he'll call anymore tonight anyway and my family and Jess have my burner phone number to reach me."

Sam then pulled Kate into his arms and held her close for just a moment. He was really worried now, but couldn't let Kate know and worry her more. "At least we know Ryan is here and can be prepared. Try to get some sleep, we're all here to help you through this, so don't be afraid. God will take care of all of us and the people here will help Him take care of you."

"Thanks Sam. I appreciate all your help." Kate replied. She wanted to believe him, but it was too hard to believe this nightmare was going to end without anyone getting hurt. She had too many doubts and wished she could think of another way to handle all of this.

"We'll all be keeping our eyes open, so get some sleep Kitten; I'll be back shortly." Sam then reluctantly released her and walked out the door. He was surprised she didn't balk when he called her Kitten. He liked the nickname her dad had for her, but maybe it was because she was so upset. The lousy agent sure had bad timing.

Sam first contacted the sheriff regarding the phone call and played the message for him. Dave had seemed surprised, but he also had received an update. The agent Kate had identified as Ryan, had been on an undercover assignment for several months, but hadn't checked back in for several days, which was unusual for him.

The DEA was doing some investigation from their end and found evidence from the ballistics report on the bullet found in the door at Mike's apartment was linked to Ryan's weapon. The best news was they had cancelled the warrant for Kate's arrest.

Sam was so relieved and knew Kate would be too. He updated Jake and Nick when he got off the phone with Dave. He played Ryan's last message and they were both happy to hear the news that Kate was no longer a suspect, but worried about the agent showing up at the ranch. At least the ranch wasn't open for business yet, so there weren't guests to worry about.

Jake said they would put out the word for the ranch-hands to watch out for anything unusual or any strangers. Sam then told them Dave said he would be out in the morning to check on Kate and introduce them all to Agent Matt who was the DEA agent now working with him to find Agent Ryan.

Dave had also suggested they all be armed in case they ran across Ryan. Everyone on the ranch was usually armed anyway, for chance encounters with wild animals stalking the herds, like the wolf pack Sam had run off earlier, as it had been much too close to the ranch.

Sam was getting ready to head back to the cabin when he remembered Dave's last comment and knew it was important to share with Jake and Nick. "Dave also said to remind everyone, the agent is armed and dangerous, so rather than try to take him on, they should call him, unless there was no other alternative."

Jake and Nick both agreed. As Nick headed to the bunk house to talk with the ranch-hands, Sam ran back to the cabin to tell Kate the good news. He was sure she would appreciate hearing everything the sheriff had said.

Kate's door was shut and the light was off, but he knew she wouldn't be asleep yet. He knocked lightly then opened the door and walked over and sat on the side of the bed. "Kate, I have some good news."

Kate opened her eyes but avoided looking at him, hoping he wouldn't notice her tears in the dark. "Have they arrested Ryan?"

"No, but they have cancelled the warrant on you since the ballistic report on the bullet turned out to be from Ryan's gun." Sam responded.

Kate threw her arms around Sam's neck and hugged him. "That's wonderful. You don't know how relieved I am, to know I'm no longer a suspect. I just hope they catch Ryan soon."

"They will, don't worry. The other DEA agent has arrived and everything's going to be all right." Sam replied as he continued to hold Kate close for a few more moments, not really wanting to ever let her go. As he finally pulled back and looked at her tear-stained face, he couldn't hold back his feelings any longer.

Kate was surprised as Sam's lips met hers, at first very soft and gentle, then deeper with a desire that matched her own. He finally ended the kiss, but continued to hold her close in his arms where she felt safe. She wanted to stay wrapped in his arms, but she had to pull away.

She knew getting involved with him would only make it harder on both of them when she left or if something should happen to her. She couldn't take the chance of him getting hurt because of her. She already cared too much.

"Thanks Sam. I appreciate all you've done for me, but I really need some sleep. Please close the door on your way out. I'll see you in the morning." Kate knew it sounded cold and it wasn't the way she felt about him, but it was the only way she could think of to keep a distance between them. She couldn't let down her guard.

Sam reluctantly got up. He didn't know what had come over him. He hadn't meant to kiss her, but the tears in her eyes had caught him off-guard. He had been surprised when she had responded to his kiss rather than backing off and he thought he had felt the desire in her, he felt in himself, which had given him hope, even though she had pulled away.

As Sam walked out of the room, he wondered if Kate had backed off because of her predicament or had realized she wasn't interested in getting involved with a dumb cowboy. He had finished high school and taken a few college classes during the winters when they were not busy, but it was nothing compared to Kate's education.

He really couldn't blame her for not wanting to get involved with him. He had nothing to offer her. He lived in the small foreman's cabin with his dad and brother, which was definitely not suitable for a wife, even though his brother would be leaving for college in the fall.

Wife! What in the world was he thinking? He was a confirmed bachelor. He had seen enough marriage problems at the ranch; his mother, his ex-girlfriend, and especially Nick's unfaithful and unhappy wife. Heck, half of the guests seemed to have problems. He didn't need any of that in his life.

He enjoyed being with Kate and she made him feel…that was the problem, she made him feel something no one else ever had, but he wasn't ready for marriage and doubted he ever would be. It didn't mean he couldn't enjoy the time they had to spend together though, and he was looking forward to a lot more time with her. He also still wanted to protect her and that required being with her.

Chapter 6

Kate awoke feeling better. The memory of Sam's kiss still lingered. That kiss had helped her sleep and she had dreams of Sam instead of nightmares of Ryan. She now knew for sure Ryan was here, and that worried her. She had to be careful and hoped Sam would keep safety in mind if they rode today. She jumped out of bed and quickly dressed for a ride. Sam had promised her they would take a ride today to get her away from the ranch and she was looking forward to it.

After breakfast, Sam turned to Kate and spoke. "Sun's coming up; we're burning daylight, are you ready to ride?"

"Sure am. Let's saddle up." Kate replied.

They walked to the barn, checked on the mares and foals, and then saddled their horses. They headed away from the ranch and up into the hills that surrounded the valley where the ranch was located.

It took a while, but the scenery was beautiful and the wildlife abundant, which Kate loved. It was hard for her to focus since she kept thinking Ryan could be watching them right now. She was thankful Sam didn't push her for conversation.

Kate was surprised at how dense the area was as they rode, but as they climbed higher, the trees thinned out and the majestic snow-covered mountains beyond them, were breath-taking. Although the scenery as they came out of the dense trees was all fantastic, Sam had mentioned he was taking her to an especially beautiful area and she wondered how soon they would get there.

"Just a few more minutes, when we get to the top of that crest, you'll see why I brought you here." Sam said.

Kate wasn't disappointed. It was the place they had stopped for lunch two days before; they had just taken a different route to get there, away from the road to the ranch.

She really loved it here. It was so beautiful with the mountains, reflecting in the lake. There were a few horses grazing near the lake they must have missed the other day.

She was sure they would probably get them today. "I thought we got the rest of the horses yesterday."

"We must have missed a few, but we'll get them when we head back, but how about lunch first?" Sam asked.

"Sounds wonderful. I love the view from up here, and I don't have to worry about any unwanted calls from Ryan while we're here either."

Sam laughed. "That's right; we can just enjoy our time. Let's eat some lunch and then get those horses moving toward the ranch."

"Sounds great to me; I'm starving." Kate responded.

Sam then laughed and replied. "We aim to please at this ranch, especially when we know you're 'starving'."

"Well, you definitely know how to please me." Kate said briefly thinking about the kiss from the night before. "It does seem I've been starving before every meal since I arrived here.

It must be from all the exercise and fresh air I've been getting or maybe it's the smell of the great food. I must say though, I've eaten a whole lot more these last few days because of all the great food. Maybe I should start cutting back before my clothes stop fitting."

Sam looked over at her. "I don't think you have anything to worry about. I'm sure you've been getting plenty of exercise to work the food off and you will be having a lot more fun and exercise over the next few weeks. I'm sure you will remain as beautiful as you are."

"Thanks Sam. I'm really looking forward to being here the next few weeks. I just hope nothing happens to prevent it, now that Ryan's here and the sheriff hasn't caught him."

"Don't worry Kate; nothing's going to happen and I'm here to make sure of it. Just trust me and the rest of the folks at the ranch; and Dave's a great guy and he won't stop until he catches Ryan, and neither will I. I plan to protect you until all of this is behind you."

Kate was glad Sam had so much confidence in Dave, and in his ability to protect her, but she still worried about something happening to him or someone else at the ranch.

118

She knew, as a DEA agent, Ryan was probably trained in many things including self-defense and probably how to stay out of sight, and that could make a big difference.

Sam wanted to change the subject, so he started unpacking his saddlebags. He took several packages out, along with a tablecloth and two large bottles of water. Kate was surprised when she opened one of the packages to find fried chicken, potato salad, slaw and of course Sam's favorite, chocolate chip cookies. She had expected sandwiches like they had yesterday, so this was a pleasant surprise. They talked for a while about the activities that were planned once the guests arrived.

Sam decided he wanted to know more about her. "You mentioned, you were one of five kids, plus Mike, and later, Jess. You must have lived in a very large house."

"Not really. It's an old four-bedroom country farmhouse. Mom and dad had one room, the boys shared one and the girls, another. The fourth was the quiet room where we did our homework or played games, although we weren't always quiet.

My parents felt by sharing a room, we would learn better, how to get along and about team work. We each had our chores, including doing our own laundry, once we were old enough. My sister and I got wise and continued doing ours together, even after she was old enough to do her own, that way we could take turns. Jess liked the idea too, once she joined the family, and joined in on our arrangement.

In the morning mom and dad would get up first, then the boys, so they could help dad in the barn. Then us girls would get up and ready for school and helped mom with breakfast. The worst part was only having one full bathroom upstairs and a half-bath downstairs.

We had to take turns. The boys would clean up after they finished their chores in the morning. Luckily it was a fairly large bathroom and mostly us girls showered at night. It worked and we all survived it."

"Wow, and I thought I had it bad just sharing my room with my kid brother and only having one bathroom. It seems like your parents were well organized."

"Yes; I think they had to be, especially with keeping the farm running with two to three dozen head of black angus cattle. There also were usually eight or so horses or ponies, as we each had at least one. It's a pretty good-sized farm but not nearly as big as this ranch.

They only have a couple hundred acres, but it's made a good living for them. Two of my three younger brothers are still home to help with the farm. The oldest of my younger brothers, Donnie got married a couple of years ago."

"He still helps out at the farm though?" Sam asked.

"Yes, he and his wife, Amy, have a home down the road and help out, but he's also taking classes to become an electrician. He really loves it."

"It's good to have a career you enjoy." Sam responded.

"I agree. I'm hoping Mike will stick around and help when he's better, since his music career never took off. My sister, Emma is also there, until she leaves for college in the fall.

Jess stayed at my parents' home for a little while after college, but then found an apartment near where she works. It's still close to my parents' home, so she's kept our horses exercised, with the help of my sister, while I've been away at school."

"You weren't able to live at home while going to school?" Sam asked.

"I lived on campus, since my workload was so demanding, but spent the summers at home and worked with the veterinarian, whose office was nearby. I had worked there part-time when I was in high school and my sister is working there now. I've been offered a partnership there, if I want it, but I'm not sure yet.

It would be nice to stay near my family, but after my time here, it opened my eyes to other possibilities. Jake and Doc Porter have both offered me jobs, but I'm not sure where I want to set up practice yet. I was also thinking maybe Texas or Wyoming." Kate said.

"Well, if it were me, I'd consider Texas to be too hot and Wyoming to be too cold. I saw Indiana, when I took Joey to check out Purdue, and it seemed awfully flat.

Colorado however, has decent weather most of the year, although four definite seasons. The scenery is really beautiful with the hills and mountains, so it would be my first choice if I were you." Sam responded. "And you've already made a lot of friends here, especially one in particular who would love to have you move here."

Kate laughed. "I think you may be biased. I am leaning that way too, but there are too many factors to consider right now. If Ryan finds me, I may not have a future."

Sam stood and pulled Kate up and into his arms. "We're going to protect you, Kate. Trust us and have faith that God put you here to protect you. Don't give up on us."

Kate wanted to believe God still cared about her, but it was so hard. She wanted her faith to be strong, like it used to be. She didn't know why she had stopped going to church and stopped relying on God while away at college.

She hadn't meant to pull away from her faith. It was just easier to find excuses with so many other things going on in her life. But she still believed in Him and prayed He would forgive her and keep them all safe.

Kate and Sam cleaned up and mounted for the ride into the valley to gather the small herd of horses they had seen by the lake. Kate nudged Choco toward the lake, following Sam. When they were just about in position to start the herd, a shot rang out. The shot was so close it not only frightened them, but also spooked the horses. Fortunately, the horses headed toward the pass so Kate and Sam rode hard trying to get out of range of the shooter.

As soon as the horses started slowing, Sam quickly called Nick and told him to call the sheriff and park ranger as the shots appeared to be coming from the area near the fire tower. He hadn't thought about anyone else finding the access road so soon.

He hadn't expected anything to happen today, since the horse thieves had been captured the other day. It should have been safe. His only thought, was that it was possibly Ryan, but he couldn't believe Ryan had already found the access road to the fire tower.

As he hung up the phone, he prayed Kate was alright as he looked around for her. He finally saw her and was heading toward her when he heard another shot and saw Choco suddenly rear, then take off at a run; and it worried him. He nudged his horse into a run and took off after Kate and Choco.

***

Kate had pulled Choco to the side, below a large rock that jutted out narrowing the pass, where she could hopefully avoid bullets. She hadn't been there long when she heard a loud scream, like that of a terrified baby. When she looked up, she found herself looking into the narrowing eyes of a large mountain lion crouched above her, ready to pounce.

Suddenly, the lion leaped into the air above her. At the same instant she heard a gunshot and watched as the lion came closer and then fell landing beside her. Kate was surprised and terrified, and unfortunately, so was Choco. He reared almost throwing her out of the saddle and then bolted into the herd of horses that were now running again from the sound of another gunshot.

Kate used her legs to hold tight as her feet had slid out of the stirrups. It took a few minutes to work Choco to the edge of the herd again and then calm and slow him as she looked around at the rocks for any sign of another mountain lion before stopping. Her heart was beating fast and her whole body was shaking.

Sam was beside her shortly after she stopped. "What happened? Are you okay?"

Kate was still having trouble catching her breath from being so terrified, as she replied. "Gunfire; mountain lion; I'm okay. Wasn't it you who shot the mountain lion?"

122

"What do you mean did I shoot a mountain lion? What mountain lion?" Sam asked worriedly. "I didn't shoot it. Maybe it was whoever was shooting earlier, but if it was Ryan shooting earlier, why would he save your life?

I don't know how Ryan could have found the access road to the fire tower, if it was him. That road is closed off to the public and seldom ever used except in the summer when the weather is dry and the rangers go up to watch for fires."

"When I pulled over to wait for you beside a large rock, I heard a loud scream and looked up to see a mountain lion above me. As it jumped out, I heard a shot and it fell right beside me. Choco reared, then bolted and I just hung on. You didn't shoot it?" Kate asked.

"No, but I'd sure like to know who did. Thank God, whoever it was, shot the lion before it got you. He had to be a good shot if he got it mid-air; and probably saved your life. At least we should be out of range now of the shooter. Do you want to get off and rest a few minutes?" Sam asked.

It didn't take Kate long to reply as she was ready to get out of the narrow pass as soon as possible. "No, I'll be fine. I think we should get the herd out of this passage and headed back to the ranch, before anything else happens."

"Sounds like a plan. Let's head them out." Sam responded.

It wasn't long before some of the ranch hands met up with them and took over taking the horses to the ranch. Kate and Sam were able to relax and enjoy the ride once they no longer had to herd the horses.

After a few minutes of riding, Sam noticed motion in some brush not far from where they were. He wondered if it was the same wolves, he had run off the previous day. It wasn't far from where they had seen them, so he was worried. Sam told Kate about the movement and they quickly headed in that direction.

Sam's guess had been right, so he quickly pulled his rifle from the sleeve and fired at the wolves. He was relieved to see that this time, Kate hadn't been frighted, so warning her had made a difference. They watched the wolves scatter and then noticed a young calf was down and its mother wasn't around.

They quickly jumped off their horses and ran over to the calf. It didn't look good. Bite marks were all over it and it was bleeding. Sam doubted it could be saved, but wasn't surprised when Kate went down on her knees beside it and asked for water and a rag.

Kate knew Sam always carried a handkerchief and bandana with him and knew she had to act fast. She was glad he had understood, and had quickly handed his handkerchief to her. She then started checking the calf as Sam went to get the canteen from his saddle.

She first checked the calf to see if it was still breathing and was relieved to see it was. She checked for possible broken bones and thankfully didn't find any, then started on the bite marks. She hoped none of the calf's injuries were life threatening, but at this point, it didn't look good.

She was horrified to find so many puncture wounds. Thankfully the calf was unconscious; it must have been terrified and in severe pain. Some of the bite wounds were deep and bleeding, but she hoped she could save the calf's life.

After her inspection of the calf, she stood up and asked Sam to hand the calf to her once she had mounted Choco. She could tell Sam was skeptical, but he didn't hesitate to place the calf on Kate's lap. Fortunately, the ranch wasn't far and she prayed the little calf would make it until she could better administer aid.

As soon as they rode into the barn, Sam jumped off his horse and then removed the calf and placed it in a stall. Kate quickly followed behind him. He then told some of the men to get mounted up, find the wolves, and take care of them. He knew having wolves that close to the ranch wasn't good for the ranch-hands any more than it was good for the horses and cattle.

While Kate was looking after the calf, Sam went to look for Joey. When he found him, he asked him to get some salve and to help Kate. Sam checked with Kate to see if she thought the calf had any chance of making it, before calling Doc Porter. He could tell she wasn't sure of the calf's chances, but said she was going to try her hardest to save its life.

The calf had regained consciousness and was starting to move and bawl in pain. Sam knew she was worried, and if it did survive it would need tranquilizers to rest and meds to ease the pain, as well as antibiotics and probably a rabies vaccine. He didn't know if any of the wolves were rabid, but he knew Doc Porter wouldn't take a chance and would do the safest thing, just in case.

Kate was still working with the calf when Doc Porter arrived. Sam could tell she was worried as she stood to talk with Doc Porter regarding the calf's condition. Doc then checked it out and said it didn't look good.

He gave the calf a shot of an antibiotic and a rabies shot. He also gave it a tranquilizer and something to ease the pain and help it sleep. He then asked Kate if she would be willing to keep an eye on the calf. Once she agreed, he handed her a bag of syringes and a vial of the antibiotic and a couple of other vials for her to administer as needed.

Kate was glad Doc trusted her. She hoped she could save the calf, but had doubts. She was relieved when the calf calmed down and hoped it could now get some rest. Joey offered to stay with it while she and Doc went to check on the foals Kate had delivered the previous day, and she accepted Joey's offer.

She remembered how helpful Joey had been with the small white colt she had delivered, and she trusted him. She quickly went to the basin close by and washed off. She knew it wouldn't help with the blood on her new clothes, but that wasn't important now.

Sam joined Kate and Doc as they walked to the horse barn to check on the foals and mares. Doc asked Sam if he had found the calf's mother, but Sam told him he hadn't, but was planning to have a couple of guys go out and see if they could find her. He asked Doc if he thought the calf

125

was going to live and wasn't surprised when he said he wasn't sure.

Sam knew he could get milk from one of the other cows in the barn or field and bottle feed the calf, if necessary. He also knew the calf would need to be bottle fed initially, considering its condition, but felt its mother would be best if the calf was able to stand and nurse any time soon.

Kate and Doc checked on Katie, the breach filly Kate had delivered and were happy to see her and her mother were doing fine. They next went to check on the little white colt, Snowball, and his mother and found one of the boys from the ranch bottle feeding Snowball.

They were surprised to see salve had already been placed on the wounds of the mother and she was peacefully eating. It seemed she was doing good and not in pain from her ordeal with the wolves.

Kate then took Snowball from the boy and stood him next to the mare to see if it would nurse, but it still couldn't seem to figure it out, so she gave Snowball back to the boy so he could finish feeding him.

Kate and Doc took a few more minutes to check out a few other foals and horses in the barn. Doc excused himself and started to leave, but before he left, he told Kate he was impressed with the job she was doing and hoped she was considering his offer to join him in his practice.

Doc respecting her work and trusting her so much really made her day. She hoped it would still be a possibility since she truly loved the ranch and all the beautiful surroundings, but only time would tell what she would be able to do.

Sam stopped Doc to tell him it was dinnertime and he should join them. Doc said teasingly, that he was sure there would be something he would like and didn't hesitate to accept the offer. Kate was unsure of leaving the calf, but Sam convinced her that Joey would watch over it and would find her if anything came up.

Kate finally agreed and they headed toward the gathering hall for dinner. Kate laughed to herself as she realized she was starving, which seemed to be usual since she had arrived at the ranch. They made a quick stop at the cabin so Kate could get cleaned up and change then headed to the hall.

The food was fabulous as usual and Kate thoroughly enjoyed talking with Doc about his practice. She was amazed at how he was able to handle so many ranches on his own, and felt he really did need help and hoped she would be able to join him in the future. She had fallen in love with Colorado and the ranch, and although she was trying hard to fight it, she knew she was falling in love with Sam too.

She couldn't tell him or even show him how she felt as she didn't want to hurt him. With her life in such a mess, there was no way she could let down her guard. She had to stop her feelings from growing stronger, but if Sam should start having feelings for her too, it would make it harder.

Unfortunately, she felt Sam caring about her, might already be happening. She had to be strong and fight her desire to build a relationship with him, but it was getting harder every day she was with him.

Kate also enjoyed getting to know Lorrie better and really liked her, but after eating, Kate finally excused herself to go check on the calf and Snowball; and Sam joined her. They both were praying it was still alive, so they were quiet as they walked to the cattle barn.

Joey had the head of the calf lying in his lap and it seemed to be resting quietly. Kate hated to disturb them, but she sat down next to Joey and asked him to get a bottle of milk from one of the cows and then to go get something to eat for himself while dinner was still being served.

Joey hesitated for a moment as he told Kate that one of the other boys could bring him something to eat. When she gave him a stern look and didn't appear to be backing down, he finally got up to leave. He pointed to the bottle that had been lying beside him and spoke. "He hasn't been awake yet, but I thought he might need it when he woke up."

Kate smiled at him. "And you thought right. I'll stay with him until you get back, but take your time. I'll be fine. I'm glad you found help feeding Snowball."

"Several of the guys were willing to help. They all think he's really cute; and I think they will help me with this calf too, so you don't need to worry. We'll take good care of them."

Kate wasn't surprised. "I know you will, but you need to take care of yourself too, so skat. Go get something to eat."

Sam watched and enjoyed the comradery between Joey and Kate, then excused himself to check on the horses that had been brought in earlier. He also wanted to see if the guys who had gone after the pack of wolves had returned, as well as, the ones who had gone to check on the mother of the calf.

He told Kate he wouldn't be gone long. Sam didn't especially like her having to take care of the calf even though he knew she didn't mind. She had already done so much and he hated that a guest would think she had to work around the ranch. Even if she wasn't an actual guest yet, he didn't think it was right.

The guys were back from going after the wolf pack and said they had taken care of them. They had been able to tranquilize all of them and load them up to be taken to the reserve, which was an area in the mountains, where they could be turned loose away from the cattle and horse ranches around. A couple of the guys had already left to take them to the ranger station to have them tagged and taken to the reserve.

Sam also found the ranch-hands who had gone after the mother of the calf and was happy to hear they thought they had found her and had placed her in the stall next to the young calf. He then decided to check on the horses they had found by the lake and was happy to see they appeared to be fine.

The big job would start on Monday when they would be checking all the horses that were being brought in, worming and branding, gelding the ones old enough, and inoculating any that hadn't been branded yet. It was a big job and he was not looking forward to it. He was sure Kate would love the experience, so he was going to surprise her.

Sheriff Dave called and told Sam they hadn't found anyone near the fire tower, although they had found some tire tracks and were going to keep an eye on that road. Problems on two days in one week was more than the sheriff's department had dealt with in the last year.

Sam still didn't know who shot the mountain lion? Could it have been Ryan? Had he been up near the fire tower and Dave not seen him? He figured he would probably never know, but was glad whoever had shot the mountain lion had been a good shot and Kate was still alive.

Sam finally headed back to the stall where he had left Kate and sat down next to her to wait for Joey to return. He was surprised the calf was nursing from the bottle, which was definitely a good sign. They talked for a short time, as Sam filled her in on finding the wolves, that were now on their way to the reserve or would be soon.

She had already seen the cow that was brought in and placed in the stall next to where she had the calf. Someone had told her they thought the cow was possibly the mother of the calf. They had found it near where Sam had said they had found the calf. The cow was a nursing cow but there was no calf nearby.

When Joey returned from dinner, Sam got up to leave, but Kate asked Joey to get the antibiotic and other vials so she could administer them before leaving. She was hoping it would help the calf to rest.

It didn't take Joey long to bring her the medicine and syringes, then after Kate injected them, he disappeared to put them back where they were kept. Kate was relieved when Joey returned with another young man who had offered to help.

Kate wanted to check on the white colt, Snowball, before they went back to the cabin and was happy to see the colt standing beside a young boy who was petting and talking to him. It was someone different than the boy they had seen earlier, and Kate was happy to know Joey had been fortunate enough to find some others to help. She thought it probably wasn't unusual to have so many boys on a ranch this size.

It was getting late, so Kate and Sam decided to head to the cabin and get some rest. Kate heard music coming from the gathering hall and Sam asked if she wanted to go to listen for a few minutes, since the band would be playing for a little while longer. Kate said she was too tired, but even if she hadn't been, she didn't want to take the chance of being in Sam's arms again.

She had loved being wrapped in his arms, but it was something she knew she had to avoid until her nightmare was over. It had been a very busy day, and thankfully everything all turned out well. She was content knowing she would soon be curled up in bed and could hopefully get some sleep.

They had just entered the cabin, when Kate's phone rang. She let it go to voicemail and when it pinged to let her know she had a message she had little doubt who it was. She checked the message, while Sam listened in. Kate recognized Ryan's low voice right away.

"Hope you enjoyed your ride today, Kate. Beautiful up by that lake, isn't it? You do realize it would have been just as easy to shoot you as that mountain lion, don't you? I just thought you could help us find the money better, if you were still alive, at least for now. See you soon Kate and don't forget I need the money, before anything else happens."

Sam hesitated for just a moment, then pulled Kate into his arms. "At least we know who shot the mountain lion. I can't say that I like the fact Ryan's here, but I'm thankful for him saving your life today. It appears he's a skilled marksman, so I hope we don't run into him again. We're just going to have to avoid being anywhere he can get near us."

130

"I'm happy he saved my life, but I'm not too happy that he's here and has found me. He's after me Sam, not you, and I want to keep it that way. Maybe you shouldn't be with me all the time since I no longer have a warrant out for my arrest and you no longer have to make sure I don't run away."

Sam thought for a moment before he responded. "God put you in our care to watch over and protect you, and that's just what I plan to do. Don't give up on me Kate. I want to help you get over this horrible ordeal, just trust me."

Kate stepped back, out of Sam's arms, trying to put at least a little distance between them. "Thank you, Sam. I truly appreciate you wanting to protect me. I do trust you, even with my life, but I don't trust Ryan.

You've been wonderful, but I don't want anything happening to you because of me. I'd never forgive myself." Kate hesitated for just a moment then said. "I'm really tired and hopefully I can get some sleep tonight. Goodnight, Sam." She then turned and headed toward her room.

"Wait Kate. I'm sorry, but I forgot to tell you Dave called earlier when we were at the barn. He said they didn't find anyone near the fire tower, so Ryan must have left the area, right after shooting the mountain lion. I'll give Dave a call and let him know we now know for sure it was Ryan."

"Thank you for letting me know." Kate replied, before going to her room. She hadn't heard Sam move to his room as she closed her bedroom door, but hoped he would go to bed soon and get some sleep. It had been a rough day for him too and she knew he had to be as exhausted as she was.

131

Chapter 7

Kate awoke from a deep sleep. She didn't remember anything after her head had hit the pillow last night. She hadn't really expected to sleep after all that had happened, but she had been exhausted and was grateful to have finally gotten a good night's sleep.

She was looking forward to checking on the calf they had brought in last night and the little white colt, Snowball. She hadn't expected either of them to live, but at least she had more hope after they had both started nursing from the bottle. It was fun having actual patients; she loved it.

She was also grateful that Ryan had saved her life by shooting the mountain lion, but it was a catch-22 situation, as his next bullet might be to kill her rather than to save her. She didn't know how long she had before he would shoot to kill.

She wished she knew where the money was so she could give it to him. It didn't mean he would let her live, even if he got the money. She couldn't dwell on it; worrying about it, wouldn't make it go away or even prolong the inevitable. She got up and dressed to go to the barn.

Sam met her in the living room as she headed to the door and asked where she was going. She told him she was going to the barn to check on the calf and Snowball, then hopefully to get breakfast.

Sam laughed. "I know. You're starving!" He then joined her for the walk to the barn.

Kate smiled. Her own words were coming back to haunt her. She was definitely going to have to stop saying that she was starving.

She was happy to see the calf standing and had hopes that her prayers had been answered and it now had a chance to live. She gave the calf a shot of antibiotic, tranquilizer, and pain med, with the help of the young boy who was with the calf. She felt it still needed rest to fully recuperate and was sure the meds would help.

She then checked on Snowball, who was curled up next to Joey; and both were sleeping. She didn't want to wake them, so she asked Sam if he was ready to head to the gathering hall for breakfast.

While they were eating, Sam asked Kate if she would like to ride after church. He had taken it for granted she would want to attend the church service, so he was surprised when she hesitated.

Kate hadn't even realized it was Sunday, the days had all run together. She hadn't been in a church since Christmas Eve when she was home last. It was part of her family's tradition to attend the Christmas Eve service, and Christmas morning, unless it was a Sunday, they would have a big breakfast before opening packages.

It wasn't that she felt the roof was going to fall in or anything, but she wasn't sure God would forgive her for being away so long. She used the only excuses that came to mind. "I don't have anything to wear to church and somebody might see me."

"You don't have to worry about what to wear. Everyone is always dressed to ride; and until the guests arrive, only ranch-hands and their families will be there.

Pastor Thomas will be preaching today and he's really good. You'll like him." Sam wondered why Kate seemed hesitant. He knew from comments she had made that she believed in God, and her personality and actions also made it apparent she was a Christian, at least the ones he'd seen.

It was comforting to Kate to know Sam was a Christian. She wondered why her faith had faltered since she had been away at school, especially this past year, with the heavy workload. She felt God had been with her this last week. Perhaps now was a good time to renew her faith and get back to church, so she replied. "That's good. I haven't had a chance to go to church since Christmas with my family. Thank you for inviting me."

"They don't have churches near the university?" Sam asked.

"Yes, but my life was very busy while I was in school, especially this past year, so I just didn't make time for going like I should have. Hopefully now I can make it part of my routine again. I know God has been with me this past week and I'm thankful He brought you and everyone else at the ranch into my life."

"I'm glad He brought you into my life too." Sam replied. "We'd better go if we want to find a seat with Jake and Nick."

As they approached the church Kate was surprised to see Sheriff Dave and a stranger, that she thought could possibly be the DEA agent who had arrived to help capture Ryan. Dave quickly introduced Agent Matt and then added. "I figured most everyone would be here, so I thought it might be a good place to catch Matt up on everything that has been going on and discuss what our plans will be."

"It's not fair to put all these people in danger by me staying here Dave. I think you should take me somewhere, where no one else can get hurt while you hunt Ryan down." Kate stated frankly.

Kate hadn't noticed Jake had walk up behind them. "God put you in our care Kate. Everyone here feels the same way and would be very upset if you left. With God's help, we'll all get through this without a hitch. Just trust Him; and trust us. We want to do this for you. There's always safety in numbers, that's probably why God sent you to us."

"I just don't want to get anyone hurt Jake." Kate responded.

"God will protect us and you too. Just have faith Kate, we do." Jake replied.

Kate finally agreed to stay at the ranch, although she was still worried as they entered the church. Before the service started Sheriff Dave went to the front and apologized. He then explained what had happened to Kate's brother and showed the photo of the agent, Ryan, but told them Ryan's hair could be long now and he may have a beard and mustache. He also explained they were making plans after church and he would keep them updated.

134

Even though Jake had already explained to everyone about Ryan, Sheriff Dave wanted to make it clear for them not to confront Ryan, because he was most likely a rogue DEA agent, armed and dangerous. Instead, they should contact Dave as soon as possible, if they saw him. He then introduced Agent Matt who explained that he was there to help find Ryan and take him in.

Kate was amazed at the comments from the guys and even some of the women. She thought their faith must be very strong.

"She's safe here. We'll protect her."

"He'd better not try coming around here. We'll take care of him."

"God sent her to us to protect her and that's just what we'll do."

These were a few of the comments but there were also others, which brought tears to Kate's eyes. People she hardly knew and ones she didn't know at all, cared enough to want to protect her. God had brought her to the right place; she knew that now.

Kate was happy when the sheriff responded. "Just remember, the agent is armed and dangerous. He has already shot one person, we know of, so be very careful. Don't try to apprehend him. Don't even let him know you know who he is. Just call me as soon as you can. Let me, Agent Matt or my deputies take care of him. The state police are also working with us so hopefully we can apprehend him before he even finds out Kate is here."

Sam then stood up. "Actually, Ryan does know where she is. He killed a mountain lion yesterday, that almost got Kate. We're not sure exactly why he saved her life, but we're thankful he did." Then he sat back down.

Sam knew Ryan had saved Kate's life in hopes of getting the money first, but didn't think it a good idea for anyone else to know there possibly was money involved. They hadn't found it when she arrived, so he doubted she had it with her, or if she even knew about it before Ryan had told her.

Pastor Thomas then took over. "I think we all need to keep Kate in our prayers; and all her family who are trying to protect their loved ones that are being threatened, especially her brother, who was shot. Let us bow our heads in prayer."

Kate really enjoyed the service as Pastor Thomas was an excellent preacher and even with all that was going on in her life, he held her attention. She felt as if he was talking directly to her as he spoke about God's love.

How God is always there for us, even when we least expect it or feel we don't deserve it. Believing in Christ and trusting Him to be there for us was all that was necessary, but letting go and allowing Him to take over was the hardest thing to do for everyone.

God had truly proved it to her over the past week and she felt as if He had inspired the pastor's sermon today, especially for her. She just wished she knew what to do now to keep her new friends from harm.

It was something she was going to have to pray about. She knew they would be safer if she left, but she didn't know where else she could go without putting someone in danger. Everyone here seemed to want to help and protect her, and she was thankful.

After the service, Sam introduced Kate to Pastor Thomas. Kate thanked him for his inspiring message that truly had meaning for her.

"I only preach what God tells me to and I'm glad it was inspiring to you. It's nice to meet you Kate, please call me Tucker, most people do."

"Tucker's an odd name; I don't think I've heard it before."

"It's Scottish for Thomas."

"You mean your name is actually Thomas, Thomas?"

"Well, yeah, you might say that or Tucker, Tucker."

They all got a laugh out of that and Kate could see why Sam really liked him. He wasn't only a good preacher, but also had a great personality. They talked for several minutes then Jake invited the pastor to stick around for some entertainment and lunch, which he gratefully accepted. The sheriff and Agent Matt also decided to stick around.

Dave then pulled Kate and Sam aside. "Why didn't you call and tell me about the mountain lion, and that Ryan had shot it? How do you know it was him?"

Sam then responded. "I'm sorry, I just forgot with all that has been going on. We were trying to get some stray horses from up near the fire tower. Kate was almost killed by a mountain lion, which fortunately, Ryan killed.

Afterwards, we found a wolf pack, which have now been tagged and sent to the reserve. The calf they were attacking when we got there, was in bad shape. We had to get it back to the ranch quickly so Kate could take care of it. It was really crazy around here for a while."

"It sounds like you two really had an eventful day; and here I thought my day had been bad. How do you know Ryan killed the mountain lion though?" Dave asked.

"Because Ryan told us." Sam said, then turned to Kate and asked her to play the message Ryan had left last night.

Kate could tell Agent Matt was upset by the message, but hoped he now better understood what she had been trying to tell everyone. He said he still didn't understand why Ryan would save her life, if he was only there to kill her anyway.

Agent Matt then asked Kate point blank. "If you have the money, why haven't you given it to him?"

It made Kate angry, and she didn't hesitate to respond. "Because I don't have any dirty drug money or have any idea where it is, or if it even exists. If I did, I would have given it to him.

I doubt it would have changed his mind about killing me, since I can identify him as the person who shot my brother." She then turned and headed back toward the cabin. She couldn't believe the agent had confronted her like that. He had no right. She was the one Ryan was stalking and planned to kill; not the other way around.

137

Sam quickly caught up with her. "Kate, I'm sure he didn't mean to offend you."

"Yes, he did." Kate replied angrily.

"He had no right to ask you that, but you have to understand. Ryan's his friend and co-worker and he's having a hard time understanding why he would have changed, even for money."

Kate understood what Sam meant, Mike had wondered about Ryan's change too. But none of that was her fault, especially the money Ryan was after. She didn't have it, although it seemed Agent Matt didn't believe her either. She could tell. She hoped Agent Matt would stay out of her way the rest of the day. She didn't have to tolerate his rude behavior; and she didn't plan to.

Kate then turned to Sam. "I need a few minutes to freshen up, then I'll meet up with you for lunch. Just keep that man away from me, okay?"

Sam wasn't surprised at how upset Kate was. Agent Matt's remark had upset him too, although he tried to understand. He knew it would be hard to accept that a friend had changed so drastically. He just wished there was something he could do to calm Kate down and ease her mind about Ryan. "Okay, I'll wait for you here. You don't have to hurry, but I have a full day planned and I don't want you to miss it."

Sam then made a quick call to Dave asking him to keep Agent Matt away from Kate since she was so upset. Dave understood and had already spoken with Matt, who wanted to apologize. Dave said Matt was just upset about Ryan and couldn't understand why he would be after her or any money. The whole situation just didn't make sense to him.

Sam went and stood outside Kate's closed door and relayed the message from Dave to her. In some ways, she understood how Matt felt, but she still wanted nothing to do with him. She did hate that Sam was going to miss out on whatever was going on today.

Kate had heard something earlier that week about a rodeo, but she had thought it was still a couple of weeks away. She knew Sam didn't want her to miss out on whatever he had planned for them today though.

Maybe it was just a ride he was planning, but it didn't matter what it was, it wasn't fair for her to keep Sam from enjoying the day. She waited a few more minutes before walking out to join him. She didn't say much to him, but felt he understood, as they walked out of the cabin and closed the door.

Kate was surprised as they walked toward the lodge. There were games like croquet, volleyball, horseshoes, cornhole, and others, that had been set up in the large area beside the lodge and everyone seemed to be having fun.

It didn't take long for Nick to call out to them from the area where the volleyball net was set up, and they quickly got a team together to play a game. Kate hadn't played volleyball in a long time, which showed with all her fumbles, but it was fun and had taken her mind off Agent Matt and Ryan, at least for a while.

Around noon the dinner bell rang and everyone raced to the gathering hall for lunch. Kate was out of breath but laughing as they walked into the hall. "That was fun, but I sure can tell I'm out of practice."

"I'm glad you enjoyed it." Sam replied, "How about some riding after lunch?"

"I'd like that; it's such a beautiful day for a ride."

Kate noticed the smirk on Sam's face, but didn't have a chance to ask what was going on since they had reached the food and were filling their plates. She was glad when she noticed Dave and Agent Matt were sitting at a different table and hoped then didn't try to join them.

They approached their usual table where Pastor Thomas was also seated, with Jake, Lorrie, Nick, John, and the other regulars. The pastor carried most of the conversation and Kate found him quite entertaining. When they finished eating, they headed to the barn, but Kate was surprised as almost everyone was taking their horses to the arena or gathering in the stands. She turned to Sam. "I thought we were going for a ride?"

"No, I didn't say we were going for a ride, I asked if you'd like to do some riding. The rodeo is only a couple weeks away, so we're taking some practice time, since Sunday is not totally a working day. I thought maybe you'd like to try some barrel and pole racing for fun. Something I figured you may have done in 4H when you were younger."

"Yes, but I haven't competed since high school. I'd love to try though. Is it okay to use Choco for it?" Kate asked.

"Sure; and if you want to use him during the rodeo, that's fine too since you and Jess will be here for a couple of weeks." Sam responed.

Kate hesitated for a few moments before she replied. "That would be great; thanks." But her thoughts were different. She should leave until Ryan was found, but that might take a while. She felt she was only putting everyone's life in danger staying at the ranch though. She felt uneasy with so many people around; as if someone was watching her, but she didn't want to let on and ruin the time for the others.

Sam noticed her hesitation, just as he had noticed her looking around all day and the uneasy tension in her face and body. He felt she was worried about Ryan showing up, but he knew everyone here and with so many people around he doubted Ryan would make a move even though he had made it to Colorado. He was hoping the mini-rodeo today would help eliminate her fears for at least a little while, so he pulled her aside.

"Relax and enjoy yourself Kate. I know everyone here, and there are no strangers, other than the agent with Dave. I doubt Ryan would come close to the ranch, especially with all the people here. Trust me and trust God to watch over us; this is His day."

Kate hadn't realized her feelings were so transparent and she knew Sam was right; she should have more faith and trust, but it was hard. At least knowing Sam knew everyone here, did help. She was determined to try to put her fears aside, at least for a while, even though she still had an uneasy feeling that someone was watching her.

"Thanks, Sam. It really does help to know you know everyone here. I'm sorry if I'm putting a damper on your day. I don't mean to. If you'd rather, I can go back to the cabin."

"I'd rather you stay right here with me, but under the circumstances, I think we should go out and show the others how to ride and have a good time, okay?" Sam asked.

"Okay, let's saddle up and head out. I'm ready to do some riding." Kate responded, trying to ease Sam's worry.

Kate did find running the poles and barrels exhilarating and it did take her mind off her problems for a while. It also helped watching Sam as he raced with Nick to rope and tie a calf and then later as he rode a bronc. Her mind was really taken off her problems as she watched Sam ride out on a really wild bull and she caught herself holding her breath until he was finally off, but the seconds had seemed like hours.

The events took most of the afternoon and had really been fun. Kate had been surprised to see the pastor and the sheriff compete with all the other cowboys and they had done great.

When the events were over, she couldn't believe the fear she had felt when Sam had flown off the bull and landed on the ground. The other riders hadn't affected her that way, which made her realize her feelings were becoming much too strong for Sam. She couldn't let that happen; not now. She needed to back away; she didn't want to hurt him the way she was going to be hurt, from missing him when she left the ranch.

At the end of the competition ribbons were handed out for each event. Kate was surprised she had won third place in the barrels and fourth place in the poles, which was much better than she had expected. Sam or Nick had taken first or second in most of the male events they competed in which didn't really surprise her.

After most of the people had left the arena, Sam asked one of the ranch-hands to bring out the black gelding he and Kate had brought in a couple days ago. The horse had seemed very calm in the corral, but Sam wanted to see how he responded to being ridden.

The horse seemed docile when he was led out into the arena, although he held his head high. The ranch-hand then saddled him and climbed into the saddle without a problem. It wasn't until the rider lightly touched him with his spurs that the horse went crazy. Kate had never seen a horse twist and fly into the air so high and she wasn't surprised when the rider was quickly thrown to the ground.

A few others also tried, but with the same results. Sam finally told them to put the gelding back in the corral. It was hard to believe it was the same horse since he was so calm without a rider, but so crazy once someone was on his back.

Sam wasn't about to put Kate's friend on that wild horse's back. They definitely didn't need a guest getting hurt. "I'm sorry Kate, but I think we'd better look for another horse for Jess. I don't think he is going to be ready to ride in a week, if he ever is."

"I understand. It's so sad though. He's such a magnificent horse." Kate responded

As Sam headed to the barn to check on the black gelding, Kate walked toward the gathering hall and saw Sam's father, John heading in the same direction. She had never really talked with him, even though they usually ate at the same table, so she thought it might be a good time. She hastened her pace and quickly caught up with him.

"Hi Mr. Nelson! Did you enjoy the rodeo?" Kate asked.

"It was okay." He said gruffly, before continuing toward the gathering hall.

Kate could tell Sam's father was upset about something and she thought it might be because of her. He had always seemed to enjoy talking with the other ranch hands at the table, but had never spoken a single word to her.

"Mr. Nelson, have I done something to offend you?"

"You mean like, putting my son in danger?" John responded angrily.

"I'm sorry. I didn't mean to do that and I definitely don't want him to get hurt." Kate said apologetically.

"Well, you have. Every minute he's with you, his life is in danger and I'll never forgive you if anything happens to him." He shouted before he stomped off.

Neither would I, Kate thought, as she watched him walk away. She knew now that her plan to leave was definitely the right one.

It had really been a wonderful day and Kate was so happy she had a chance to enjoy it with them. She wished she could be here for more great days like today, but that couldn't happen. She had to leave, no matter what everyone else thought and Sam wouldn't be put in jail as an accomplice now that charges against her had been dropped.

When Kate got to the gathering hall where she was to meet Sam, she looked around for his father and finally saw him sitting at a different table. He still didn't look happy, but she couldn't blame him. She was putting his son in danger, but that was going to change.

It didn't take Sam long to join her and they got in line to fill their plates. She didn't tell him about her encounter with his father since she knew it would only upset him and wouldn't change anything.

The food was great, as usual, and Kate could tell everyone had worked up an appetite. She was amazed afterwards, when the band started playing, that most of the people still had enough energy to get on the dance floor.

She was exhausted, but when Sam asked her to dance, she didn't hesitate. She wanted to dance with him, one last time, so she danced with him until the music stopped for the night. She loved being in his arms where she felt safe, and she was going to miss him terribly.

Sam could tell something was bothering Kate, but she hadn't said anything and he didn't want to push her. He

143

wished he could keep her in his arms forever, but felt it didn't make any sense.

He wasn't right for her, just wished he was. Kate was everything he had always dreamed of and more. He hadn't wanted to fall in love with her, but after holding her close most of the night while they were dancing, he felt he had failed and had fallen head over heels in love with her.

When the music finally stopped, they headed to the barn to check on the foals and calf, before going to the cabin. Sam knew Joey would have let them know if there had been a problem, but he was sure it wouldn't have stopped Kate from checking anyway.

Once they reached the cabin, Kate tried to force herself to stop Sam from kissing her goodnight, but she just couldn't. She needed to be alone, so she could sneak out later. It was time for her to go so no one at the ranch would be hurt by Ryan coming after her.

Shortly after she entered her room and shut the door, she heard her phone beeping, letting he know she had another message. She wasn't surprised the caller ID was 'unknown.' Ryan's low voice didn't shock her this time. She now knew he had arrived and found her at the ranch.

"You seemed to enjoy yourself at the little rodeo today, but remember, there won't always be a large group of people around you. Hope you've found the money. We'll be meeting soon."

Kate's feelings of being watched hadn't been wrong; someone had been watching her today. Although everyone had been busy having fun, she wondered why no one had seen him. Perhaps, he had hidden in the trees near the road and had left the area before anyone else. Although, there weren't many who had actually left the ranch, since most of the people at the mini-rodeo, worked and lived there.

She wished her life could be different now instead of this horrible nightmare. She loved it here and had enjoyed her time with Sam, but unfortunately, it was time for her to leave. She hadn't expected to meet the man of her dreams, and then have to let him go, and it was going to be hard to never see him again, but there was no other way.

***

It was late and the ranch was quiet when Kate got up and packed her backpack. She could hear Sam softly snoring in the other room and hoped she could sneak out without waking him. She had seen a path leading beside the creek that appeared to go toward a lake in the valley below or toward the road in the opposite direction, so she started up the path toward the road, running most of the way. She didn't know where she was going to end up, but at the present time, anywhere was better than here.

Her fear escalated as she quickly ran up the path. Strange sounds were all around her and she struggled to keep control of her fear as she kept glancing around. She heard gravel crunching and the sound of a vehicle close by, but then it stopped.

She wasn't sure what to do so she hid behind a tree for a few moments. She didn't see anyone on the path ahead, so she worked her way slowly toward the road and then spotted a pickup truck parked on the shoulder.

The truck didn't have a camper like the one the sheriff had been looking for, but it didn't mean it wasn't Ryan. He could have changed vehicles. Her mind was racing trying to figure out what to do. She really didn't want to face Ryan; not now, not ever.

She was afraid to move, then was terrified when someone came up behind her and put their hand over her mouth, smothering her scream, which was silent anyway as her voice was gone from her fear. She was momentarily paralyzed but then started to fight as she bit his hand.

"Ah! Stop Kate, I won't hurt you. You've got to play along. I'm not after you. I just need the money so the boss doesn't come out here. Dylan's man, Kevin, is in the truck, and he's not a nice guy, so please work with me. If you know anything about me, please don't say anything. I'm trying to protect you." Ryan said.

"I recognize your voice, Ryan. You shot my brother, yet you say you're trying to protect me. That's rich." Kate responded.

"I can't explain right now, but Kate, you have to believe me." Ryan replied as he heard footsteps coming toward them from the road and had no doubt it was Kevin.

"What's taking so long. Hurry up and get her up to the truck, before someone sees us and tie her hands so she can't put up a fight." Kevin said.

"That's what I'm doing, you idiot. Why aren't you watching the road. It's not going to do us any good if we lose the truck. Come on, let's get out of here." Ryan responded angrily.

As Kevin got in the driver's side, Ryan helped Kate into the truck and threw her backpack in the back. She wasn't sure what to do or if she believed what Ryan had said about helping her, but she decided to stay quiet and not mention that Ryan was supposedly an undercover DEA agent. She was sure it wouldn't help her situation anyway.

They didn't go very far, before they turned up a drive. Kate noticed a 'Do Not Enter' sign, but didn't know where they were. It didn't take long before Ryan started questioning her.

"Where's the money, Kate? We really need it before things really get bad."

"I don't know anything about any money. Mike didn't say anything about any money, before you shot him." Kate responded angrily, not wanting to let him know Mike was still alive.

"Did you check his guitar case? We know you took it with you." Ryan responded.

Then Kevin piped in. "You're lying. Why would you take the guitar case of a dead guy if you didn't know it had money in it?"

Kate was furious. "I don't know anything about any money and if it's drug money, I wouldn't want anything to do with it anyway. The guitar was a gift from his mother that he had taken to Vegas with him a few years ago.

He had pawned it and had lost track of it, while he was strung out on drugs, but had found it recently. He wanted me to take it home with me and I thought his mom would appreciate it, after losing him." She didn't want them to know they had the same mother and tried to make it sound like his mother was someone else.

"And you expect us to believe that?" Kevin remarked.

"Shut up Kevin." Ryan finally said, then turned to Kate. "Have you checked out the case and the guitar?"

Kate had opened the case when she first arrived at the ranch so Sam could check it for a gun, but all they saw was the guitar and closed it back up. She hadn't opened it since, but she thought she might consider it now, if she got the chance. "I just glanced in it and saw the guitar, when I first got to the ranch. I haven't paid any attention to it since. It's just been under the bed and out of sight."

It was quiet in the truck for a few moments, before Ryan finally spoke up. "If we take you back…."

Kevin didn't let him finish before he interrupted. "We can't take her back. She'll have the cops all over us. She's seen my face now too, so I'm not about to let her go."

Kate could tell Ryan was trying to hold back his anger while he thought of a way to convince Kevin to go back; although she wasn't sure why. She remained quiet, hoping Ryan would win out and she could get away.

"How do you expect to get the money, if it is in the guitar case and we don't take her back to get it?" Ryan asked.

"Didn't she just say it was under her bed, so we know where it is. We just need to sneak in and get it." Kevin responded.

Ryan was losing patience with Kevin, but tried to keep his voice calm. "And how do you plan to sneak in with a ranch full of armed men hanging around? You've seen them; and we don't even know what cabin she has been staying in. The telephone trace doesn't show that."

"We can't trust her. She can tell us what cabin she's been staying in and we can take the path she did just now.

147

That way we can go ahead and get rid of her." Kevin shouted.

"Sure, we can, but I think we can trust her if she knows that the ranch will become a firing range when the boss gets here and we don't have the money. If she tells anyone, we can be sure to kill them too. Isn't that right Kate. I'm sure you don't want all your new friends at the ranch to pay for you not keeping this to yourself." Ryan said as he turned toward Kate.

Kate was afraid he was right. She didn't want anyone at the ranch getting hurt. She had to do what he said and hope it worked. "Okay, I promise. If you let me go, I won't tell anyone and I'll check the guitar case and see if I can find the money. If you call tomorrow, I will let you know if I found it."

She could tell Kevin wasn't convinced, but he finally gave in and started the truck. She had hoped Sam wouldn't wake up and notice her being gone, but knew he had when they heard on the police scanner in the truck that the sheriff and his men were starting a search for her.

Kate was terrified when Kevin pressed the accelerator to the floor and sped off; however, he only went a short distance down the road and stopped. Ryan let her out of the truck and handed her the backpack.

"You'd better get that money and keep your mouth shut." Kevin shouted angrily at Kate as she got out of the truck.

Ryan spoke to Kate softly as he quickly untied her hands. "Please don't tell anyone. Tell them you got lost. Try to find the money. I don't want anyone getting hurt." He then told her the trail was only a couple of miles down the road, but they needed to disappear before the sheriff found them.

***

Sam was frantic. It had taken a few minutes for him to put on his clothes and boots after hearing the door shut and he had looked out the window and saw Kate heading up the

148

trail behind the cabin. It led to the road and anything could happen to her, especially if Ryan found her.

He had run part of the way and then walked fast hoping to catch up with her. He couldn't imagine what she was thinking. She had to know she was safer at the ranch. He had finally made it to the road, but there was no sign of her. She had just vanished.

There were no vehicles in sight and he couldn't imagine her walking so fast that he hadn't caught up with her. He called for her, but there was no answer. He didn't know what else to do, so he back-tracked to the cabin, hoping to find her along the trail or at the cabin, but unfortunately, she wasn't there.

Sam wasn't sure what to do, but he couldn't just wait around. He made a call to Nick and told him what had happened. Nick told him to meet him at the bunk house so they could get a search party out and told him to contact the sheriff.

Everyone at the bunk house was ready to help and they all headed to the barn to saddle up. Sam and Nick decided to head back up the trail Kate had taken. Once they reached the road, they split up and headed in opposite directions.

Sam hadn't been riding long when he saw something ahead on the side of the road. He wasn't sure at first what it was, but as he drew closer, he realized it was Kate, sitting on the side of the road. He jumped off his horse and ran to her. "Kate, what are you doing here?"

He then heard a vehicle on the road heading toward them and pulled her up and told her to hide behind the large tree a short distance from the road and for her to be quiet. He prayed she didn't disappear again.

Kate watched as the SUV stopped and Sam walked over to it. She tried to listen as they talked, but couldn't hear what they were saying as they were speaking softly and were too far away.

The man in the SUV was one of the deputies and Sam told him they could call off the search, as he had found Kate. He then made a quick call to Nick to call off the

149

search. Sam had been watching the tree, hoping Kate didn't try to run, then headed back to get her.

Kate wasn't sure what she would say to Sam as she watched him head her way. As he got closer, she could tell by the tone of his voice he definitely wasn't happy with her. "Why did you leave? Where did you think you were going?"

"Who was that? Who were you talking to?" Kate responded, hoping Ryan and Kevin were long gone.

"It was a deputy. The sheriff has put out a search for you. I told him he could call it off, since I had found you. I also called Nick to call off the ranch-hands' search. Now answer my question." He said angrily.

"Maybe I can hitch a ride with him." Kate said, still set on leaving, although she knew she needed to go back to the cabin and check the guitar case for the money.

"What do you mean? You're not going anywhere." Sam stated, irritated that she had tried to leave. If she left, she had nowhere to go and no one to help her. He didn't understand what she was thinking.

"Yes, I am! I refuse to put your life or anyone else's in danger."

"Just your own life, right?" Sam replied curtly.

"It's my life. I'm the one Ryan's after, not you or your family or friends. I can't put you all in danger. I already caused my brother to be shot by being there. I can't do that again."

Sam's voice softened and his anger lessened as he pulled her into his arms. "It wasn't your fault your brother was shot Kate, and I don't want anything to happen to you, I care too much; you're like family to me now."

"But I'm not family and I don't want you to care. I don't want to hurt you and I don't want you to get hurt." Kate replied.

"I'm afraid you're too late, I already care. I know I'm not good enough for you and someday you'll leave, but I want to enjoy the time we can have together." Sam said sadly.

"What do you mean 'not good enough for me'? Are you crazy? I just don't want to hurt you. I just graduated. I have no idea when or where I will find a job. I have no idea where my future is or even if I have one with a crazy agent after me for an insane drug-lord. I care about you, but I don't want you to get hurt." Kate responded.

"If you care about me and don't want me to get hurt, then stay and we'll see where it leads. You have a job here if you want it. Doc Porter, as well as Jake and Nick, were really impressed with you. Give us a chance Kate."

"I can't Sam, not until this nightmare is behind me and there is a chance I might live to see tomorrow." Kate replied.

"Okay, I understand and I'll try not to push you into a relationship you don't want, but I hope you'll reconsider once this is all behind us. I truly believe God brought you into my life for a reason and you know you're a lot safer here with all my family and friends to protect you; and me. You have to realize that." Sam stated worriedly.

"But what if someone gets hurt?" Kate asked.

"Then we'd get hurt protecting someone we care about. You have to trust us. Where were you going anyway?" Sam responded.

"I don't know; I just wanted to keep you and anyone else from getting hurt. I'm sure your dad would never forgive me if something happened to you."

"Did my dad say something to you?" Sam asked.

Kate didn't want to tell him what his dad had said, so instead, she told him she knew his dad was worried about him and she couldn't blame him. If the tables were turned, she would feel the same way his dad did.

Sam knew his dad had been angry about him wanting to stay with Kate and protect her, but now he wondered what he had said to her and if that was the reason she had decided to leave. He was going to have a talk with his dad tomorrow, but right now he had to try to calm Kate and get her back to the cabin.

Sam's voice was teasing as he responded. "Does that mean you care about me?"

"Of course, it does; I care about you, but you shouldn't have feelings for me, not now; not when my life is such a mess." Kate responded.

"But I do and I have a feeling, I always will; and I'll always be here to protect you, as long as you let me. Don't shut me out Kate. Come on, let's go back to the cabin and get some sleep. Things will look better tomorrow. Trust me Kate and trust that God has put you here for us to protect you."

Kate knew things wouldn't look better tomorrow. She couldn't explain to Sam that she knew it was only going to get worse. She should tell him about her encounter with Ryan and Kevin, but she was afraid because she believed Ryan when he said he would kill anyone she told. She knew Sam was right; she did need to put her faith in God. It was just hard with everything going on.

"All right, I'll go back to the cabin and I'll try to believe what you say and try harder to rely on my faith, but I can't handle a relationship right now. We both need to focus on the danger I'm putting you all in by staying here." Kate said.

"If that's what you want Kate, I'll try. It won't change the way I feel about you, but you're right, we need to focus on the danger for now. Let's go." Sam replied.

Kate reluctantly mounted behind Sam on his horse and they headed back to the cabin. She was glad Sam didn't try to pull her into a conversation, as she wasn't sure what she could say since she couldn't tell him anything that had happened.

Once they reached the cabin, Kate went in and Sam left to return his horse to the barn. She placed her bag on the bed, then walked back into the living room and sat down, knowing Sam would have more questions; she couldn't answer. She wasn't surprised to see Nick with Sam when he returned and Nick wasn't happy with her either.

She could understand, since Nick had been woken up in the middle of the night and had woken up most of the ranch-hands to help find her. She couldn't tell them anything though. She couldn't take the chance of causing the ranch to become a battle ground and people getting hurt.

"Why did you leave Kate? What were you thinking?" Nick asked, almost shouting.

"Ryan is after me, not you or anyone else at the ranch. I can't turn the ranch into a battleground and have anyone hurt. I need to get away from here." Kate responded.

Nick's voice softened. "The ranch isn't going to become a battleground and we're all being very careful, so no one gets hurt, but we want that to include you. We want to protect you, Kate. Didn't you think we'd try to find you?"

"I thought Sam was asleep when I left. I didn't expect him to call out a search party." Kate replied.

Sam finally spoke up. "I heard the door shut and saw you head up the path when I looked out the window. It just took me a few minutes to put on my pants and boots, but I thought for sure I'd catch up with you. I couldn't believe I didn't catch you before you got to the road. When I didn't find you, I really got worried. I backtracked calling out your name, but when you didn't answer, I wasn't sure what to do, so I called Nick."

"Kate, I understand your concerns for us, but you need to trust us. We really do want to protect you. I doubt Ryan would show up at the ranch, because there's so many people here, but if it looks possible that he might show up, Sam can take you to a safe place. You aren't alone and you won't be as long as you stay here with us." Nick said, although he understood Kate's concern.

Sam then pulled Kate close. "Promise you won't leave again without me. I want you to be safe too."

"You know how I feel about staying here, but if you promise to take me to a safe place away from everyone else

153

so no one else will get hurt, I promise I won't leave on my own again."

"You have my promise. I think we should try to get some sleep. It's going to be a very busy day tomorrow. I'll see you in the morning. Good night." Sam responded, then watched as Kate walked to the bedroom and shut the door.

Sam talked with Nick for a few minutes, before Nick left. He knew Nick wasn't happy with Kate trying to leave, but at least he felt Nick understood better, why she had left. Even with her promise, he knew he wouldn't get anymore sleep tonight. He wanted her safe in his arms, but she wasn't ready for a relationship with him. He prayed that someday soon she would be ready, although he knew it was an unrealistic dream.

If they did have a relationship, it could never last. She was way out of his league and she would eventually figure it out and leave. He was hoping they would at least have more time together, even if it was only for a few more weeks, he wanted as much time with her as possible.

Kate didn't want to take a chance on checking the guitar case while Sam and Nick were so close and might hear her, so she crawled into bed, her thoughts a jumbled mess. She couldn't believe Sam cared for her that much, how could he?

She was a mess, her whole life was a mess, but she had fallen for him too. She just wouldn't let down her guard and let him know. Not now; not until all of this was behind her, if it ever was and she lived to have a future, which at the present time, she didn't expect to happen.

What if she did find the money, then what? How would she get it to them and would they kill her then? She was so afraid of what tomorrow would bring and if Sam would really take her away from the ranch so hopefully no one else would get hurt. What about him, she didn't know what she would do if anything happened to Sam.

Kate couldn't sleep with everything racing through her mind. She had to do something, but what? She thought about what Ryan and Kevin had said and wondered where they were hiding out. If she didn't find the money in the guitar case; then what; would they just kill her and leave?

Were they serious about their boss maybe coming and turning the ranch into a battleground? She also wondered about what Ryan had said about trusting him. Was he just playing her for a fool; or was he serious? She didn't know what to believe.

Kate finally tried to clear her mind and prayed thanking God for all He had done to help her so far, but found it hard concentrating on her prayer as she kept losing focus and kept asking for forgiveness. She hoped Sam would take her away from here, before anything happened and she prayed about that too. She tried to sleep, but found it impossible.

Chapter 8

Kate was startled as she heard a tap on her door. "Hey sleepy-head, it's time to rise and shine. We've got a big day around here today."

She hadn't slept much as she was still worried from her late-night adventure with Ryan and Kevin, and she had a terrible headache, but she needed to get up. She didn't know what Sam had in mind for the busy day he was talking about, but she hoped it was to take her away from the ranch. "Just a minute. I'll be out shortly."

It didn't take long for her to dress and be ready for breakfast. Something she was really looking forward to, especially a good cup of coffee, which she hoped would help with her headache.

Kate was surprised Jake and Nick weren't at the table, but she was glad no one else was there either. She wasn't sure she could face them after they had been awakened in the middle of the night to search for her. Actually, there weren't very many people in the hall so she was curious and asked Sam where everyone was.

Sam laughed. "Well, for one thing we are a little later than usual since I let you sleep in, but most folks have already eaten and today is a very busy day around here, so they've already gone to work.

"What do you mean?" Kate asked.

"Well, you were saying you appreciated getting experience before opening your practice, so we thought you might like a bit more." Sam replied.

"You mean there are more colts or calves you need help with?" Kate didn't quite understand what he could be thinking about.

"You might say that; but if you're interested, you can get a lot of experience in worming and inoculating foals and calves today. It will be busy as we're inoculating and branding the ones that have been brought in already. Doc Porter will also be gelding the colts, that are of age, before we let them loose again and he may let you help. I hope you're up to the challenge."

156

Kate was hoping Sam had planned to take her away from here today, but smiled as she responded. She was sure there would be a lot of people around, so she wouldn't have to worry about Ryan. "Most definitely. I could really use the experience."

Kate wasn't surprised to see Doc Porter was there helping when they arrived at the corral, so she quickly went over to greet him and offered to help. Doc didn't hesitate in showing her what to do, so it didn't take long for her to start checking, worming, and inoculating the foals while Doc continued with the calves. There had been several foals and calves brought in since the weather had broken, over the last few weeks and Kate was looking forward to the challenge and experience.

Doc Porter also had her help geld the colts that were of age. Jake had always made it a practice to geld his colts before releasing them again. Only a few colts were ever kept as stallions to avoid battles and keep stronger bloodlines.

Kate was surprised when Sam said this wasn't anything compared to the work after the major herd would be brought in during the roundup. He then left her and went to help the guys who were busy branding. She hoped she would be able to help them with the major herd, but at the present time, she had little hope while having to deal with Ryan and now Kevin.

They were busy the rest of the day, only breaking long enough for lunch and then continuing. Kate was relieved when Nick said they were done for the day. There were still a few calves to check the next day, but for now they were all ready for dinner and relaxing.

It was hard work and Kate was exhausted. She and Sam headed back to the cabin to clean up and rest for a bit before dinner and she was definitely looking forward to dinner. The headache she had started the day with, from her lack of sleep, was worse, but she wasn't about to let Sam know how she felt. She didn't need him worrying about her any more than he already was.

She didn't envy the guys and the work they had ahead of them the next few weeks, although she was thankful for the experience she had gotten today. It was great practice for her future as a veterinarian working with large animals and there was no doubt, she needed the practice. She only hoped she still had a future.

The foals weren't bad, even though they were basically wild; but she had almost forgotten how ornery and stubborn calves could be. She had been reminded of this when she and Doc had traded places after lunch and she had given up the foals and started on the calves. It was definitely a change, she wished she hadn't made.

She was surprised when she realized she hadn't thought much about Ryan all day, although she again had felt as if someone was watching her. She wondered where he had been. She had been too busy and was thankful, but she knew it was too good to last.

As soon as they entered the cabin, she heard her phone beeping, letting her know she had a message. She was trying to decide whether to check the message but when she noticed the caller id was 'unknown', she finally listened to it.

"Getting a little slow there Kate. Having too much fun sticking those poor little colts and calves? Quaint little town, isn't it. You realize, there won't always be a large group of people around you, don't you; and the boss's patience is wearing thin, since it's taking me so long to get his money. I'm sure you'd rather not have to deal with him. He has a very nasty temper. We'll see you again soon; real soon and I hope you found the money."

The call only brought back her fear; she knew he was close and watching her. He had seen her yesterday at the rodeo as he had mentioned it last night when he had caught her leaving and taken her to the truck. There was no doubt he had also been watching her again today.

Why hadn't the sheriff been able to catch him? When was he planning to meet with her? Would she still be alive or be dead, since she didn't have the money? At least she didn't think she did, but she still needed to check out the guitar case.

Kate told Sam what Ryan had said. "He's close enough that he's been watching me, yesterday and today. I can feel it and he made it pretty clear. He knows exactly where I am. What should I do?"

"Let's get cleaned up for dinner so we can talk it over with Jake and Nick. Anyway, I'm so hungry, I think I could eat a whole cow." Sam replied trying to lighten her mood.

Kate jumped in the shower as Sam left to get ready, but he was back and ready to go shortly after she was dressed. They left for the gathering hall and after filling their plates, they sat down at the table with Jake, Nick, Joey and Sam's dad, John. Although Joey greeted them and spoke with them, their dad didn't say a word, and his eyes were sending daggers her way.

The conversation turned somber as Sam continued with what Ryan had said and told them they needed to come up with a plan to get Kate away from the ranch. He also thought it best to let everyone at the ranch know and to have them be on the lookout, since Ryan had somehow been getting close enough to be watching her.

Sam escorted Kate to the cabin and said goodnight before returning to the gathering hall to talk with Jake and Nick and try to come up with a plan. Kate was surprised when shortly after Sam left, her phone rang. Not thinking quickly enough she answered it.

"Kate, don't hang up. This is Ryan, I need to talk with you. I only have a few minutes as Dylan sent Kevin with me and he's watching every move I make. I don't want to hurt you, if I did, I could have just as easily killed you, as that mountain lion.

I'm just glad I was there as I'd hate to see anything happen to you. I just need you to get the money to me so Dylan won't come after you or your family.

He's really getting upset and talking about coming out here himself. He's afraid to fly, so even if he decides to come, it will take him a couple of days to get here. I don't want him having a chance to get to you, especially at the ranch where too many people could get hurt.

I'm not a rogue agent like you think, I'm undercover. Kevin is with me to keep an eye on me for Dylan. I don't think Dylan trusts me anymore. That's why I have had to leave messages, letting you know where we were and not talking to you. I couldn't say much last night either. Kevin is like a hawk and as you probably could tell, he's not a nice guy.

Kevin went into town, so I only have a few minutes. He took my phone, but doesn't know about this burner phone I picked up yesterday. You have to believe me, Kate. Dylan is definitely someone you don't want to mess with."

It took only a minute for Kate to regain her composure and shout. "Believe you? You shot my brother and then came after me!"

"I had to shoot him to save his life. We were being watched at the apartment by Dylan's men in a room across the alley and they had a bug in his apartment to hear what was going on. I didn't want to shoot your brother. I was trying to save his life.

They were planning to kill him and I had to make it look like I did it for them. I found out later they knew you were there and saw you take him out of the apartment. I put out a warrant for your arrest, hoping the police could find you before Dylan's men did. They knew you were going to the airport, so Dylan sent several men to look for you. He was really mad when they didn't find you.

I'm trying to save your life. You have to get the money to me before Dylan comes after you and goes to the ranch. They think Mike is dead. I put his ID on a John Doe corpse. That's why they are after you since they didn't find the money in the apartment."

"I don't know anything about the money or where it is." Kate responded. She still didn't believe him.

"Have you looked in his guitar case again?" Ryan asked.

"No, I haven't had a chance. Sam has been with me, up until a few minutes ago."

"Can you look. Maybe in the lining or in the guitar?"

As Kate responded she remembered Mike had insisted she take the guitar. "Give me a minute. Why should I believe you? How do I know you aren't working for Dylan and just feeding me a line about being undercover?"

"I don't know where your brother is now, but if you can reach him, ask him about me. He trusted me and you can too. Ask him where the money is. Please Kate, believe me. Do you remember the kitchen window shattering when you and Mike left the apartment?"

"Yes." Kate said as she remembered it and had wondered why.

"That was Dylan's men. They realized Mike was still alive and were trying to finish the job. Kate, you have to believe me." Ryan said emphatically.

"A DEA agent arrived yesterday and is with the sheriff, should I give him the money if I find it?" Kate asked.

"No, please no. I'm not sure who I can trust and it will blow my cover if I don't take the money to Dylan. Not everyone in the agency knows I'm undercover, which includes Matt."

"You know the agent who is here with the sheriff?" Kate asked.

"Yes, Matt and I have worked together before." Ryan replied.

"Can you give me a few minutes and call me back?" Kate asked as she placed the guitar case on the bed.

Ryan said he would, but for her to hurry. She then opened the guitar case as she hung up. She had to hurry because Sam could be back at any moment.

There was nothing inside the case except the guitar, so she pulled it out. The guitar felt extra heavy, so she looked inside the hole of the guitar. She was shocked when she saw a plastic bag taped to the bottom. She loosened the strings and reached in and pulled the plastic bag out. Inside was a stack of hundred-dollar bills. No wonder the case had felt so heavy. She thought.

She needed time to think about what Ryan had said and whether she could trust him, which would be difficult. She was still unsure of whether to tell Ryan she had found the money.

Should she believe him? She knew Mike must have trusted him before he had been shot, but should she? Should she tell Sam or the sheriff or Agent Matt? Ryan had killed the mountain lion instead of her, so could he possibly be telling the truth?

She pulled out her burner phone and called her mother. She really needed to talk to Mike. Fortunately, her mother answered and Kate quickly asked how they were and then asked for Mike, trying not to let on what was going on and worry her. Her mom seemed hesitant at first, saying he was still pretty weak, but then put him on the phone. He sounded tired, but appeared to be happy to hear her voice.

She told him about Ryan following her and that she had found the money, but hadn't told anyone yet. Ryan was wanting her to meet with him and give it to him so he could get it to Dylan before Dylan came after her and possibly their whole family. "He said I should believe him and trust him."

"He shot me and he's wanting you to believe and trust him. Is he crazy?" Mike quietly shouted back.

"Ryan said it was to save your life. That Dylan's men were across the alley with rifles aimed at us and they had your apartment bugged."

"What do you mean, us?" Mike asked.

"They knew I was there, but Ryan said he didn't know about me until your neighbor told him we had left the apartment. He had put out the warrant on me in hopes of finding me and getting me somewhere safe. He also put your name on an unidentified body at the morgue, so Dylan wouldn't go after you.

He said the kitchen window shattering as we left the apartment, was Dylan's men trying to finish the job of killing you. They were probably the men we saw running toward us, in the alley beside your apartment building when we left.

Mike, I'm not sure what I should do. He said I should call you, that you had trusted him. There's another DEA agent here with the sheriff, but Ryan said I shouldn't let him know since not all of the agent's know he is undercover. He said I should give the money to him to give to Dylan to keep his cover."

Mike hesitated for a few minutes, but it seemed like hours to Kate with the silence on the phone. "Please Mike, help me figure out what to do."

Mike finally said slowly. "I had trusted him and he was completely out of character when he got there that day, but if he was trying to save my life, he sure had a strange way of showing it. Kate, I just don't know. I don't want to put you in danger, but it looks like either way, that's what I've done. I wish I could be there."

"But you aren't and you aren't in any condition to be. Should I give the money to Ryan?" Kate said worriedly.

"If it came to trusting Ryan or Dylan, then I would definitely suggest Ryan. I don't know why I was so stupid. I figured Dylan had made enough money off me when I was an addict so I thought I deserved to get some of it back and get out of town. I wasn't expecting it to backfire on me, and especially not you. I'm really sorry Kate.

Now that it's too late, I understand it was a mistake trying to embezzle money from a drug-lord. I hope Ryan is trying to put Dylan behind bars but I'm still not totally convinced he hasn't gone rogue."

"I forgive you Mike. Please keep me in your prayers. I have to go, but I'll let you know how it turns out. Hope you are better soon. Love you!"

Kate had just hung up from talking with Mike when her phone rang and she wasn't surprised it was Ryan. She was afraid to tell him she had spoken with Mike, since she was still unsure of his connection with Dylan, so she simply responded with the facts. "I found the money, but I'm not

163

sure how to get it to you. I still don't trust you and besides Sam is always with me. We need to come up with a plan."

"Can you get in touch with Agent Matt?" Ryan asked.

"I can contact the sheriff and ask him to have Agent Matt call me." Kate replied.

"I need you to tell Matt to get in touch with Barry, he'll know who you mean. He's the special agent in charge of my assignment. Tell him you don't want him screwing up and shooting me again. He'll understand who it is coming from, if you say it just like that.

Barry can update Matt. Matt probably won't believe you but tell him everything, but don't tell anyone else." Ryan said.

As soon as Kate disconnected the call with Ryan, she called Dave and left a message for Agent Matt to call her. She still didn't like Agent Matt even though he had apologized, and she didn't really want to talk with him, but from what Ryan had said she thought she should. She was surprised when Matt called back almost immediately.

"Matt, I need to talk with you when you are alone." Kate said as she tried to remember exactly how Ryan had worded the message.

Matt said he was walking outside so he could talk without anyone over-hearing him. As soon as he got outside, he asked. "What's going on?"

"I have a message for you from Ryan." Kate responded.

"What? You've talked to him? Where is he?" Matt asked with concern.

"I don't know where he is, except he has been watching me the last couple of days at the rodeo and working at the ranch today. He was also close enough a few days ago to kill a mountain lion that was getting ready to pounce on me."

Kate then started telling Matt about last night when Ryan had picked her up and about Kevin threatening to kill her. She explained that Ryan somehow had convinced Kevin to let her go so she could get the money.

164

Ryan had said not to tell anyone, so I haven't. He said this is the first time he has been able to talk straight with me because Kevin is one of Dylan's men and has always been with him. He asked me to tell you to contact Barry and he said for me to tell you he doesn't want you screwing up and shooting him again. He also said for me not to tell anyone else."

"What do you mean?" Matt asked.

"I don't know, just that he wants you to contact someone named Barry and you'd know who he meant." Kate replied.

Agent Matt hesitated for a moment before he responded then told her he would contact Barry and call her back. Kate still didn't like his attitude, but if he could confirm what Ryan had told her, at least she would feel a little better about believing him. It wasn't long before Agent Matt called back and said he had gotten in touch with Barry.

"And what did he tell you?" Kate asked, wanting to confirm he had actually been updated.

"I can't tell you that, just that I spoke with him." He stated, as if irritated with her.

"Well, if you can't confirm what Ryan told me, I guess I'll just have to figure out what to do on my own." Kate stated sharply.

"Wait, he told you his situation and why he wanted me to call Barry?" Matt asked as if shocked.

"Yes, I know what Ryan told me is possible, but I need you to confirm it." Kate replied.

Matt hesitated for a moment and finally stated. "He's working undercover."

"Yes, that's what Ryan said. Do you believe it?" She said slowly, still unsure.

"Barry said he was, and Ryan and I have worked together before. Actually, that's when I accidentally shot him." He said with an embarrassed laugh. "He's always been a good agent, so I was having a hard time understanding why he would have changed. That's why I took this assignment. I need to know if he's gone rogue. Do you have a way to get in contact with him?"

165

"No, he's supposed to call later when he is free to talk again. Do you have a message for him?" Kate asked.

"Just give him this number and have him call me. Thanks for letting me know and I am sorry about the other day. I'm just worried about Ryan, but I shouldn't have taken it out on you." Ryan responded.

Kate told him she accepted his apology and then hung up. She hadn't told him about finding the money since she wasn't sure what Ryan's plans were and figured the fewer people who knew about that much money, the better. She taped it back in the guitar, tightened the strings, then placed it back in the case and slid it under the bed.

She had just sat down on the bed when she heard Sam enter the cabin.

"Did you come up with a plan?" Kate asked, trying to muss up the bed a little from her supposed rest, before he got to her room.

"Yes; I think so. Did you get some rest?" Sam asked.

She hadn't gotten any rest, but she didn't want to lie to him or tell him about the money or the phone call from Ryan, since Ryan had told her not to let anyone know. She answered vaguely. "I'm feeling much better now."

It wasn't a lie. She was feeling better after talking with her brother and knowing he was getting better and the drug-lord thought he was dead, and wasn't looking for him.

Finding the money was helpful and she really wanted to trust Ryan. She still wasn't quite sure about him, but at least Agent Matt and Mike seemed to feel she could trust him and that was a start.

"Do you feel up to checking on the foals and a couple of small calves that were just brought in with their mothers?" Sam asked.

"Sounds good, just give me a minute to freshen up." Kate replied.

They walked in silence to the barn. Kate had a lot on her mind and was still trying to figure out how she was going to meet up with Ryan. She did decide to tell Sam she had spoken with her mom and brother, and her parents were doing okay and Mike was feeling better.

She also told him Mike had been especially happy after finding out Ryan had said the drug-lord thought he was dead and was no longer looking for him. He said Ryan had identified one of the unidentified bodies at the morgue, as him.

Sam hesitated for a moment then asked, "So that's why he is after you instead of your brother? But why did he do that? Why would he have made it seem as if Mike was dead and come after you?"

Kate had to think fast. "Because the drug-lord had found out I was at Mike's apartment, as he had it bugged and was having it watched by some of his men. He thought Mike had given me the money, since they hadn't found it in his apartment. Mike said Ryan had been working undercover, so maybe he was trying to save his life."

"By shooting him and coming after you?" Sam was astonished as he asked.

"I don't know, but if he is undercover, maybe he is here to help me, instead of hurt me." Kate responded.

"It sure hasn't sounded that way in his messages." Sam replied.

They had arrived at one of the barns and Kate quickly changed the subject. She had definitely made a mistake telling Sam anything and should have just kept her mouth shut and hoped what she had said, Sam would think came from Mike. "Where are the new calves I need to check out?"

Kate could tell Sam didn't like changing the subject and still had lots of questions she couldn't answer, at least right now. He finally stopped with the questions, at least temporarily, and took her to the area where the new calves were being held.

A couple of the calves did seem a little small, but they all seemed heathy and the cows did too. She then checked on Lucky, the calf she hadn't expected to live and was happy to see her mother was now in the stall with her.

They then went to the barn with the foals and checked them out, then checked on her other patients. Little Katie was running around in the stall, and Snowball was nursing, which was a good sign. Kate was happy to see they were all doing well, so she told Sam she was ready to go back to the cabin to rest. She could tell he was reluctant as he responded, "Okay, but this conversation is not over."

On the way back, Sam told her the plans he, Jake and Nick had come up with, to take her to a safer place. He thought they would be gone for a few days which hopefully would give Dave and Agent Matt a chance to catch Ryan.

She knew that probably wouldn't happen now with Agent Matt knowing about Ryan's situation, but she figured they could work it out. She wondered if she should take the money with her.

Sam then turned to her and stated, "We'll leave tomorrow morning for the hunting cabin. You'll be safe there, while the sheriff hunts down Ryan. I'll give him a call now to let him know about the call with your brother and where we are going. I need to get some things ready for tomorrow, so I'll meet you back at the cabin in a little while."

Kate wasn't surprised Sam was giving her a little time before continuing with their conversation, but she still wouldn't be able to tell him everything. Her thoughts were all over the place as she packed her backpack to go.

She knew she wouldn't be able to use her computer at the cabin since Sam had said there was no electricity, which made more room in her backpack for the additional clothes she had bought at the store. She then laid down in the bed to rest until Sam arrived.

...

Sam was upset as he walked away from the cabin. Something wasn't right. There was something Kate wasn't telling him and he needed to know what it was. He was sure of it and he couldn't understand why she still didn't trust him. When he returned to the cabin later, he saw the light on in her room. He walked over and opened her door, but she was asleep.

He wanted answers, but he didn't want to wake her. He waited a few moments, watching her sleep, but when she didn't rouse, he quietly turned out the light and closed her door, then went to his room to pack.

He had everything ready to go at the barn so they would be ready to take off right after breakfast. The only thing he had left to do, was pray for God to watch over them and to thank Him for bringing Kate into his life, and how he wished she would trust him.

Chapter 9

After breakfast Sam and Kate saddled and loaded up the horses for their ride to a hunting cabin in the hills, where Sam thought Kate would be safe. They were just riding out when her phone rang and it was Ryan. "Get out of there. Dylan and his men are coming to town. I'm not sure how soon they will get here, but I don't want him to find you there."

Kate didn't waste any time before relaying the message to Sam and then tightening her legs to send Choco into a run, with Sam right beside her. When they got to the tree line, they finally slowed and stopped.

As Sam got down, he turned to Kate and stated frankly. "Okay, now what's going on? Why would Ryan call you like that? Come on Kate, I need you to tell me the truth and trust me."

"First, you call Dave and tell him Ryan said the drug-lord, whose name is Dylan, is leaving Las Vegas today and is headed for the ranch. Ryan doesn't know exactly when Dylan will get here, but he will be driving because he doesn't trust flying. I will call Agent Matt and let him know what is going on."

Sam understood and quickly called Dave, but he didn't understand how Kate was able to or why she would want to call Agent Matt, since she didn't like him. What else had she not told him. As soon as he hung up his phone, he looked over at Kate. "Okay, what's going on?"

Kate knew Sam needed to know everything, so she told him what had been said when Ryan had called the day before and that Ryan had told her not to tell anyone. She also told him about where she had disappeared to, the night she ran away, when Ryan and Kevin had found her. Lastly, she told him about finding the money; lots of money.

"I was going to bring the money with us to try to get it to Ryan, but when I took the money out of the guitar, I also found another package. When I pulled it out, it wasn't money; I think it might be drugs in small packages, but I'm not sure what it is, so I left it all there."

Sam was in shock and now understood why Kate hadn't known what to do or how much to tell him, but he was glad she had confided in him. Like her, he didn't know what they should do either.

He needed to contact Jake to let him know that the druglord, Dylan, was coming to town and he would probably be coming to the ranch once he got there. Sam told Jake they didn't expect Dylan for at least a couple of days because they knew he was driving.

Dylan had been the one to give Ryan Kate's location, which he got from a contact. Ryan didn't know who his contact was, but he planned to find out once this was over. Dave had been notified, so they could be prepared and come up with a plan.

Sam went on to tell Jake, apparently, Dylan didn't think Ryan was handling Kate to his satisfaction and wasn't getting his money quick enough. Sam then made it clear to Jake not to let on that he knew who Dylan was and to contact Dave as soon as possible, if he did show up at the ranch. They were all hoping Dylan wouldn't come to the ranch, but it was better to be safe than sorry.

Kate and Sam thought Ryan might possibly buy them some time to get a plan together by telling Dylan that Kate had left the ranch. Maybe Ryan could say he and Kevin would be able to grab her now without a ranch full of people around. Hopefully, this ploy would keep Dylan from going to the ranch. Everything was going to be crazy and, unfortunately, dangerous, but at least Jake could have the men armed and ready in case anything did come up.

Once all the calls were made, Kate and Sam remounted their horses and headed toward the hunting cabin. The ride was wonderful with all the changes in the landscape as they headed up into the hills. Kate found it wasn't unusual to see deer and elk now and then and of course lots of rabbits and squirrels.

She loved it here and prayed she would have a chance to see more of it in the future; if she had a future. They crossed several small streams, but when they arrived at a large stream, they stopped to water the horses. The sound of the water flowing over the rocks was calming and Kate was mesmerized watching the water bubbling and swirling around the rocks.

Sam interrupted her peaceful thoughts. "Beautiful, isn't it? Great fishing too."

Kate thought for just a moment as she looked upstream. "Yes, it is really beautiful. I think I could stay here forever. It's so calming."

Sam laughed. "I agree, but we're close to the cabin so we should keep going. We'll have plenty of time to check all this out later and maybe get some fishing in. Fresh fish over an open fire always tastes great."

Kate hesitated for a few moments, then nudged Choco to cross the stream. He was such a great horse. She was glad she had chosen him rather than a green-broke horse. It had made the rides more enjoyable, except for the few times he had been frightened.

She couldn't really blame him for being spooked since she had been frightened too. For the most part, Choco had been great and she hoped she would have a chance to enjoy many more rides on him, however, she worried that might never happen.

Kate could see the cabin now and it wouldn't be long before they could dismount and unpack. She was also looking forward to stretching her legs. She loved riding, but it had been a long ride. She was surprised when Sam stopped, motioned for her to be quiet and then told her to wait there. He dismounted and handed her the reins of his horse.

Now she was worried. She couldn't imagine what was happening. The cabin was supposed to be a safe place for her to hide out. Kate dismounted and held the horses as Sam pulled his gun and moved quietly toward the cabin while staying close to the tree cover.

She didn't see any other horses or movement, but something must have triggered Sam's alertness, she just didn't know what. She held her breath as Sam walked quietly across the porch, looked in the window and then opened the door.

She became even more worried when Sam disappeared into the cabin and she didn't know what to do. He had told her to wait, but how long? The minutes seemed like hours as she watched for Sam to come out of the cabin.

***

Sam could tell someone had been at the cabin because there were chairs on the front porch that had been moved from inside and there was trash and lots of beer cans in front of the cabin. No one from the ranch would ever leave the cabin in that condition. It didn't look like anyone was there now, but he wasn't sure. He didn't want to scare Kate, but he wanted her safe.

He tried to be quiet as he moved across the porch and looked through the window, but he didn't see anyone. He then went to the door and noticed the padlock was gone. There was evidence a gunshot had been used to break the lock. He slowly turned the doorknob, opened the door, and quickly entered the cabin. He didn't see anything at first, but as his eyes adjusted to the dim light in the cabin, he noticed a large object in the back corner.

He quickly aimed his gun in that direction and then stopped, as he realized there was someone lying on the floor and they were tied up. He quickly looked around the room, but didn't see anyone else. He walked over to the person, but couldn't tell who it was at first. He then realized it was the guy from the photo, the DEA Agent Ryan.

Ryan was lying awfully still and Sam hoped he was still alive. He wasn't sure if he could trust Ryan, but Kate had told him about Ryan being undercover and trying to help them, on the ride to the cabin and he hoped she was right.

Not sure if he should untie him or not, Sam holstered his gun, then using his knife, cut the ropes and shook him, but Ryan didn't move at first. "Ryan, can you hear me?" Ryan finally moved slightly, but only seemed semi-conscious, but at least alive.

173

Since Ryan had been tied up for some reason, Sam was thinking Kate was right and maybe Ryan hadn't gone rogue after all. Sam thought he had done the right thing by cutting him loose, although, Ryan didn't appear to be in any condition to hurt anyone at the moment anyway. Sam shook him again trying to bring him back to consciousness.

"Ryan, can you hear me?"

Ryan didn't open his eyes, but finally tried to speak. "Where am I? Who are you?" Ryan responded, his words slurred, broken, and barely auditable.

"I'm Sam, from the ranch. Are you okay? Can you move at all?"

"Where's Kevin?" Becoming more conscious, "You've got to get out of here." Ryan said, although still barely audible.

"There's no one else here right now. Can you get up?" Sam asked.

"Need a minute. Kevin drugged me. Don't know when he left. May be back soon. Get out of here." Ryan said as he struggled to get up, with Sam's help.

Sam was able to help him to a chair, but Ryan was very weak. Sam got him some water, praying he wouldn't fall out of the chair. "What happened?"

After a few sips of water, Ryan tried to talk. His words were still broken and slurred and hard to hear. "Kevin heard me call Kate. Knocked me out, tied me up. Where's Kate? She, okay?"

Sam was still leery about trusting Ryan, so he simply said. "She's safe for now."

"Get her out of here!" Ryan said emphatically as he tried to stand. "Kevin's dangerous."

Sam helped Ryan to a chair on the porch, so he could get some fresh air, hoping that would help, then motioned for Kate to bring the horses up. He had little doubt Ryan was right, they needed to get out of there before Kevin returned. Hopefully they could come back later and somehow get rid of Kevin, but Ryan was in no condition to do anything now and he had to get Kate to safety.

174

Kate had noticed Sam helping a person out of the cabin and was worried, but as soon as he motioned for her to come, she quickly mounted Choco and led Sam's horse toward the cabin. As soon as she stopped, she recognized Ryan, although his hair was shorter and his beard and mustache had been trimmed. She then turned to Sam. "What happened? Is he okay?"

"One of Dylan's men was with him and heard him warn you this morning about his boss coming. He knocked Ryan out, tied him up and then must have drugged him, before he left to go into town."

"That would be Kevin. I met him the other night. He didn't seem like a very nice person, so we should try to get Ryan out of here." Kate responded.

"We don't know how long he's been gone, so he could be back any minute. We have to hurry. Take the saddle bags off my saddle and put them over your saddle horn, then grab three sleeping bags out of the cabin."

Kate quickly did what Sam told her to do, then grabbed the sleeping bags and threw them across the front of the saddle. Sam was trying to get Ryan up so she ran over and helped him. They got him close to Sam's horse, then Sam lifted Ryan's foot into the stirrup and they both worked to push Ryan up into the saddle. Ryan was some help, but not much. They were happy he wasn't a big man.

Sam hoped Ryan wouldn't fall off before he could get behind him to hold him on. As Ryan fell forward, Sam removed Ryan's foot from the stirrup, then mounted. It didn't take long for Kate to saddle up, then moved the sleeping bags to lay across her lap. Sam looked around quickly, then said. "Let's go."

Kate followed as Sam led the way. She didn't know where they were going, but she had little doubt, Sam knew where to go. She was worried about Ryan. He was still slumped forward and she could tell Sam was working hard to keep him from falling off.

She hoped they weren't going very far and prayed she would be able to help Ryan once they stopped. Not knowing what kind of drug, he had been given was going to make it difficult to know what would help, but if nothing else, she hoped Sam had packed some coffee.

Fortunately, they didn't go far before Sam stopped and dismounted, still holding on to Ryan so he wouldn't fall off. Kate dismounted too. She didn't know where they were or why they had stopped, but she didn't hesitate to follow him when he started leading his horse up a narrow path.

As they rounded a curve, she understood what Sam had in mind. They were at the mouth of a large cave, that was well hidden.

Sam turned and smiled at her and then walked his horse into the cave. "We'll be safe here."

Kate followed and was surprised to see a hitching post just inside the cave. She tied Choco and Sam's horse to the hitching post then helped Sam get Ryan down. She then quickly grabbed a sleeping bag and laid it out against the wall and helped Sam get Ryan to it and sit him down.

Ryan still seemed dazed, but appeared to be coming out of his drugged state a little. He looked up at Kate as he tried to get up, and then asked with slurred, broken words. "Are you alright? We need to get you out of here before Kevin returns." Then he looked around. "Where are we?"

Kate felt sorry for him. He looked awful and confused and his slurred, broken words reminded her of someone who was drunk. She placed her hand on his shoulder to keep him from trying to get up.

"Stay still. I'm alright. We are in a cave not far from the cabin. Sam said we should be safe here. He's starting a small fire a little further back in the cave so he can make some coffee. Hopefully it will help you."

Ryan finally sat back against the wall, then fell over and passed out. Kate didn't know much about people strung out on drugs. It wasn't something that was taught in veterinary school.

She remembered her brother passing out the first time she had gone to see him in Las Vegas, when he was high

176

on drugs. She thought Ryan could sleep it off and be better when he woke up, but wasn't sure. She hoped so and prayed for his recovery. Kate finally walked over to Sam who had managed to get a small fire started. "He's passed out. What do we do now?"

Sam could tell Kate was worried. He was too, but they had to make the best of it. He reached over and pulled Kate into his arms. Just holding her close helped him think. "We just need to make the best of it and hope and pray Ryan recovers quickly.

It may take a while though, depending on what he was drugged with and how much. We just have to be patient. Why don't you help me unpack and unsaddle the horses, then we can fix up something to eat and make some coffee to hopefully help Ryan when he awakens again."

"Okay. Are you sure we'll be safe here?" Kate asked.

"Yes. I've been coming here for years. Nick and I found this cave when we were kids and used to stay here when we needed to get some time away from the ranch and all the visitors. We thought it was a lot cooler than staying in the cabin and it's well hidden, so very few people even know about it."

Kate only hesitated for a few moments, not really wanting to move out of Sam's arms as she felt safe there, but knew she had to. They then walked over to the horses, removed the saddle bags and sleeping bags, then unsaddled the horses. Once that was done, they removed the bridles and exchanged them for halters with lead ropes.

Sam told Kate about a small field nearby where they could take the horses to graze later. It was near a stream like the one where they had stopped to let the horses drink earlier. It seemed like Sam had thought of everything.

Kate walked over and checked on Ryan, but he was still out, so she unzipped and placed a sleeping bag over him, then went to help Sam. She was surprised to see all the things Sam had managed to pack in the large saddle bags. At least they wouldn't starve.

Sam placed a metal rack across the fire then filled a coffee pot with water from one of the canteens and placed it on the rack. Kate looked at Sam curiously. "Where did you get that rack?"

Sam laughed. "Leftovers from days gone by. I wasn't really planning on us roughing it quite this much, but under the circumstances, I think it will do for now. Hopefully Ryan will be better by tomorrow and we can contact the sheriff to take care of getting Kevin. We should be comfortable here for the night at least."

As Sam made a call to Dave to let him know about finding Ryan and about needing him to come get Kevin in the morning. He told him he would call him later with an update on Ryan's condition.

Kate couldn't see much further back in the cave because it was so dark, but she was really hoping nothing was back there. "Are you sure there are no bears or anything in here?" She asked Sam.

Sam laughed. "To make you feel better, I'll check it out further. There are bears in the area, but we've never found any in here before, so I doubt it. Might find a mouse or two though."

Kate didn't really find it funny, but was glad to hear bears hadn't been found in the cave before. Although, since Sam had said he hadn't been there in a while, that could have changed. Bears or anything else, like bats or wolves, could have found the cave and now be residing there.

"I can deal with mice, but I would really appreciate it if you would check it out." Kate stated flatly.

Sam stood and pulled Kate into his arms. "Don't worry Kate. We'll be alright. Just trust me." Then kissed her and was happy to feel her respond to the kiss. He didn't want it to end, but knew he didn't have a choice, so he finally pulled back and released her.

Sam found a lantern in the cave, that had been left in the stash he and Nick had left there long ago, and fortunately, it still had some fuel and he was able to light it. Kate was amazed at how large an area the lantern lit up and was glad

178

they had it. They took a short walk back into the cave to check it out, but didn't go far as it narrowed pretty quickly. Kate was really glad they didn't find any bears or anything else.

"Alright, what do you want me to do?" Kate asked as they returned to the area by the fire. She hadn't expected the kiss, before they had walked back into the cave. It had caught her off guard, but she didn't regret kissing Sam. It was wonderful, but they didn't have time for that now. She felt there was too much going on right now for... well for them to be getting so close.

"Why don't you pull some food out of those large saddle bags that came off of my horse?" Sam asked.

Kate was surprised when she opened the first side of the saddlebag; she found bread, apples, potatoes, onions, carrots, a salad mix and a plastic bag full of small packets of mayonnaise, mustard, and ketchup along with salad dressing, salt, pepper, and some other seasoning packets.

The other side had what looked to be meat wrapped in plastic bags that appeared to still be partially frozen, and some sliced ham and sliced roast beef in plastic bags. All the meat was sitting on a bag with a block of ice. There were also a few bottles of water.

When she opened the first side of saddle bags that had been on Choco, she found a loaf of bread, more bottles of water, tea bags, and she had watched Sam earlier remove a bag of coffee and a coffee pot. In the other side was paper plates, napkins, plastic utensils, a skillet, a pot, a pitcher and even a bag of chocolate chip cookies stuffed down in the pitcher, which she knew was Sam's favorite, but also hers. She couldn't believe Sam had thought of everything.

"I don't believe this." Kate finally said as she looked over at Sam.

"We aim to please at this dude ranch, so we always come prepared." Sam said with a smile. "How about fixing us up some sandwiches for now and we'll fix the steaks up later for dinner."

"Roast beef or ham?" Kate asked.

179

"Roast beef with mustard, please." Sam replied.

Kate quickly got to work preparing their lunch. She was also starting to get hungry. As she was packing the bags back up, she noticed some small bags of chips, so she pulled them out along with the cookies, carrots, and two cold bottles of water.

The cold water tasted great, but Kate wasn't sure if the other bottles of water would be cooled any time soon, so she placed three on the ice, just in case. It was hard telling how long the ice would last, especially since it couldn't be put in the ice box, Sam had told her about, at the cabin. The saddlebags however appeared to be make-shift coolers, so she hoped the ice would last until tomorrow and keep the meat, eggs, and water cold.

It didn't take long to eat and it had tasted great. Kate wasn't sure if it was the good food or if it was because she had been so hungry, but it didn't really matter; she was full. As they were cleaning up, they noticed Ryan trying to sit up and went over to help him and move him closer to the fire.

"What happened? Where are we?" Ryan asked.

"We're in a cave not far from the hunting cabin where we found you tied up. You said someone named Kevin had drugged you then left to go into town. We thought it best to get you away from there." Sam replied. He was glad Ryan seemed a little better. His words were not as broken and slurred, but were still not normal.

Ryan shook and rubbed his head. "Yes. Dylan, the boss, had Kevin come with me to get the money from Kate. I don't think he totally trusts me, even though Mike had introduced us and told him I was helping with selling the drugs.

When Dylan first started noticing some money missing, he thought it was me but then realized it was Mike. He bugged Mike's apartment and put men across the alley to watch him, hoping he would show them where he was keeping the money he was skimming.

They didn't find the money and not wanting to take a chance on losing any of his men, Dylan sent me to get the money and to kill Mike, with his men as backup in case I failed."

Ryan then looked over at Kate. "I didn't want to shoot your brother, but I couldn't think of any other way to save his life. I knew I could miss a vital organ, but doubted the sharp-shooters across the street, would.

I was planning to take him straight to the hospital afterwards, but Barry called. That's why I went out to my car, so I wouldn't be overheard.

I didn't know you were there Kate, but I'm glad you were or Mike probably wouldn't have made it. I've just been leaving you threatening messages so Kevin didn't catch on.

I was trying to let you know someone was with me and where we were, and we were definitely coming. I stalled as long as I could, before heading this way, but had to leave after Dylan found out where you were after you used your charge card."

"I know that was a big mistake, but I didn't even think about it until afterwards." Kate responded.

"Well, if there wasn't a leak in one of the agencies or police force, it wouldn't have been a problem. I'm definitely going to check into it when this is over and Barry, my boss, is already working on it.

Kevin was in touch with Dylan every day, so I couldn't take a chance on getting him out of the way. I'm sorry Kate. I'm sorry for everything I've put you through."

Kate thought for just a moment, hoping she could trust him and what he had said. "I understand, and thank you for trying to save Mike's life and mine."

Sam had given Ryan a cup of coffee and Kate asked. "Do you think you could eat something? It might help."

"I can try." Ryan replied.

"I can fix you a sandwich. We have ham or roast beef and mayonnaise, mustard, or ketchup."

"Ham, please; with mustard." Ryan responded.

181

Kate went over to the saddle bags to fix the sandwich, leaving Sam to talk with Ryan. She didn't like the way Ryan looked. His color wasn't good, especially with only the light from the fire and lantern.

He still appeared to be disoriented and dazed, but she wasn't sure what to do for him since they didn't know what kind of drugs he had been given. Hopefully he would be better after eating, if he could get the sandwich down. She knew fluids should help too, but didn't know what else she could do for him.

Sam wasn't sure what to do either, but he hoped with Ryan's help, they could work out a plan to get rid of Kevin and take back the cabin. Ryan didn't quite look up to anything just yet, but hopefully after he ate and rested a while.

Sam thought it best to let him know they would be gone for a while, so he wouldn't worry if he slept and then woke up again before they returned. Ryan definitely needed more sleep. "I know you're not up to it yet, but we need a plan to get Kevin out of the cabin. Hopefully tomorrow morning when you're maybe feeling better. We're safe here for now, but I'm sure we'd be more comfortable in the cabin.

Kate and I are going to take the horses to graze, but we shouldn't be gone long and we'll fix dinner when we get back. Why don't you rest but please don't leave the cave as it could put us all in danger."

"Don't worry, I don't think I'd be able to walk or go anywhere, even if I wanted to. Just be careful." Ryan replied.

Kate laid the plate in Ryan's lap and was glad to see him pick up the sandwich and take a bite. She hoped he would be able to eat it all, but she was sure, at least something on his stomach would help. She then refilled the cup of coffee Sam had given him and placed a bottle of water beside it. "When you finish, you really need to rest."

"Thanks Kate. I'm sorry I had to put you through all of this. I hope someday you can forgive me." Ryan responded.

Kate looked at him for a few moments before saying. "Your forgiven; and thank you for being there for Mike and me. I know it's been hard on all of us, but God will see us through. By the way, Mike is better, I spoke with him yesterday."

"Thanks for letting me know, you don't know how much that means to me." Ryan said.

"You're welcome." Kate smiled, then stood and walked over to Sam by the horses and untied Choco. Sam then led them to a small field not far from the cave, but in the opposite direction of the cabin, where the horses could graze.

"That was very nice of you, back there. I'm not sure I would have forgiven him so easily after all he has put you through." Sam said.

"Thank you. I have little doubt he's been going through a lot too, and he did save my life from the mountain lion or I wouldn't be standing her now." Kate replied.

"That's true, and I'm definitely going to thank him for that. I don't know what I would have done if I had lost you." Sam said as he thought about what he would do when she was gone; something he didn't want to think about.

Sam handed Kate his horse's rope. "Hold on to him for a minute. Nick and I made a makeshift fence around this area for the horses to stay in while we were at the cave. It's been a while since we've been up here so I want to check and see if I need to fix any of it.

We'll come back later and take them back to the cave before nightfall since there are so many wild animals around here." He gave Kate a quick kiss then started walking around the field.

Kate hadn't really thought about the wild animals up here, but she had no doubt there were some. She looked around for any movement, while hoping not to see any, especially a bear or a wolf or anything else that might prowl around up here. Not seeing anything, other than a few rabbits and squirrels, she finally relaxed some.

183

She was used to camping, but in campgrounds where there usually weren't any wild carnivorous animals. They had seldom seen any wild life at the farm, other than a few foxes, raccoons, and deer; oh yes, a few possums, snakes, mostly non-poisonous, and groundhogs too.

It wasn't long before Sam returned. "It's good. You can turn the horses loose. How about we check out the stream. If it looks like there's any fish in it, we can maybe come back tomorrow with the fishing poles, if not, I'm sure there are plenty in the larger stream we crossed earlier today."

"Sounds good, although I'm not much for fishing. I find it kind of boring, but I do like the taste of fresh fish." Kate replied.

Sam laughed. "Then you've never tried fly-fishing, have you?"

"No. Can't say that I have, but if it's more exciting than sitting on a dock or on the bank of a river or lake holding a pole, then I'm game to try, if we get the chance." Kate responded.

Sam took Kate's hand and they started walking. The mountain stream was nice and clear and definitely had some fish in it. They walked further up on top of a ridge, where the view was beautiful with the snow-covered mountains in the distance.

They sat on the ridge for a while and talked while watching an eagle flying around floating on the wind currents. It was spectacular. Suddenly, as they got up, a rattling sound behind them caught Kate's attention and she told Sam not to move.

He had heard it too and told her not to move, as he quickly turned, while pulling his gun and fired. The rattlesnake went flying, but Sam quickly grabbed Kate's hand and pulled her away from the area. He knew where one snake was, there were usually more and he didn't want to take a chance on Kate, or him, being bitten.

They decided it was time to head back to the cave to check on Ryan, hoping he would be feeling better after eating and getting more rest. They were really hoping

Kevin hadn't given him anything that would require a lot of time to recover from, but it was a guessing game at this point.

When they entered the cave, they didn't see Ryan at first, but then noticed him curled up near the fire, asleep. They were sure it was probably best for him, so they tried not to disturb him. Sam said he needed to go to the barn at the cabin for a couple of buckets for water for the horses later and he also wanted to see if there was any feed there.

Kate was really worried. The barn was awfully close to the cabin, so she suggested she go with him and watch the cabin, so he wouldn't be surprised by Kevin. She knew Sam wasn't happy about the idea, but finally agreed. She guessed he probably figured she would follow him anyway; and he was right.

Kate followed as Sam made his way down a narrow path, that was partially over grown with brush, toward the barn. They noticed a pickup was now parked near the cabin, but didn't see any sign of Kevin. Sam told Kate to stay where she was and keep an eye out for Kevin as he proceeded to the barn. Kate was worried as she watched Sam slowly open the side door and disappear into the barn.

Sam was glad the door hadn't made too much noise when he opened it and quickly went in. There wasn't much light, but he knew approximately where to find everything he needed. He hoped there was at least a little feed left from earlier in the year in the metal containers they stored feed in.

He tried to move quickly as he worried about Kate being so close to the cabin. He was armed and could take care of himself, but she was alone and vulnerable, although he had given her his rifle, he doubted she could or would use it.

Kate was thankful there was still no sign of Kevin, but she prayed Sam would make it back safely. It wasn't long before she noticed Sam peaking his head out the door and she motioned for him to come out. Sam quickly exited with two buckets and quietly made his way back to Kate, they then headed back to the cave. Sam told Kate that both buckets had feed and feeder masks in them.

Kate picked up a few pieces of wood on the way back to the cave, then they sat for a while watching the flames dance in the fire and talking quietly. Sam stood up and retrieved the feeding masks and dumped some feed into them before telling Kate they could get water from the stream when they went to get the horses.

The sun was starting to set, so they decided to walk back to the field to get the horses. They were happy to see the horses were content and still grazing as they walked over and fastened the ropes to their halters, and led them to the stream for a drink and to fill the buckets before heading back to the cave.

After they walked into the main area and tied the horses to the hitching post, Sam started placing the feed bags on the horses. Sam asked Kate to slice some potatoes along with some carrots and onions to prepare dinner, while he finished; then asked if she had ever had hobo potatoes.

"Isn't that when you take potatoes, carrots and onions and cook them in aluminum foil on the coals of the fire?" She asked.

He told her yes that was exactly what they were. She told him she had made them while at camp when she was younger. He then said she should be able to find aluminum foil and a knife in the saddle bag with the plates and things, which she did and began cutting the vegetables into chunks.

It didn't take long for her to get them ready and wrapped in the aluminum foil, then handed them to Sam to put on the coals in the firepit. Close to when the potatoes were ready, Sam started cooking the steaks and Kate prepared salads. They were not surprised when Ryan stirred and Kate had no doubt the wonderful smell of the steaks had helped to wake him. She was glad to see he looked better.

Ryan first looked around and then said. "Something sure smells good."

186

Kate smiled. "Think you could eat some steak, hobo potatoes and salad?"

"Not sure, but I'd like to try." Ryan replied.

"How do you like your steak?" Sam asked.

Ryan hesitated for a minute, then said. "Medium, I think. My mind's still a little foggy."

At least he looked and sounded a lot better and it put Kate's mind more at ease. She prayed he wouldn't have a relapse and would continue to improve, but at least she now had hope. She had been praying a lot lately and truly felt God had been listening, as they were all safe, at least for now.

Kate was glad to see Ryan was able to eat most of his meal, with the exception of half of his steak. He also appeared to be more alert, so after dinner they decided to work out a plan for how to capture Kevin. Sam contacted Dave and filled him in on their plan so he would be ready to pick Kevin up in the morning.

Kate hadn't realized how tired she was until she looked over at Ryan, who had crawled into his sleeping bag, and fallen back asleep. Sam had placed their sleeping bags on the other side of the fire across from Ryan, so she stood and turned toward Sam. "I think I'm ready to turn in too. It's been a great, but tiring day."

Sam stood and pulled Kate into his arms and gave her a kiss. "I think I'm ready to turn in too."

He watched as she crawled into her sleeping bag and then he put out the lantern, and used the light from the fire to make his way to his sleeping bag next to Kate's. He was glad she felt safe with him and it was wonderful lying next to her. He only wished it was a relationship that could last.

Chapter 10

It was still early the next morning when Sam called Dave to let him know they were heading to the cabin; and he said they were on their way. They waited for a few minutes before heading to the cabin, to be sure Dave was in position.

Sam moved to the side of the porch with his rifle ready, while Ryan went to the front of the cabin with Sam's revolver stuffed down the back of his pants. Ryan wasn't in perfect shape, but was definitely better than when they had found him the day before.

Ryan was posed with his arms wrapped around him as if he was hurting and yelled out. "Hey man, you up? I need some more of whatever you gave me. That was some good stuff. Kevin, hey man, can you hear me? I need some more stuff."

Kevin finally opened the door and looked out. He looked as if he was still half asleep, but had a gun in his hand. "What are you doing? How'd you get loose and where have you been?"

Ryan pretended to chuckle. "I found a knife under the bed and it took me a while, but I managed to get loose. I found a nice tree to curl up under. It smelled so good. But man, I need some more of that stuff you gave me. That was really some good stuff and I've got a terrible headache now."

"What about the sleeping bags; why did you take so many?" Kevin asked.

Ryan had to think quick, then responded. "I wasn't exactly thinking clearly and wanted a soft bed. That floor wasn't soft at all."

Kevin finally looked around and then walked out onto the porch. "Get in here man. I just shot you up with some pain killers. It should have done more than just knock you out; you shouldn't even be awake yet. Dylan told me to keep my eye on you and not leave you alone. He wants you alive until he can get to you himself tomorrow when we meet him at the ranch. I guess I'm glad you came back.

Dylan and his men won't hit town until later tonight and Dylan wants to check out the town and the sheriff's department to see what we will be dealing with before making a move. He didn't understand why you would warn that girl though."

"I was just trying to get her away from all those people so we could get to her easier; that's all. It worked, didn't it? Didn't you see how fast she rode out of there?" Ryan said.

"But where did she go? Do you know that?" Kevin asked.

"Yes, I do. She came here." Ryan replied.

Kevin had lowered his gun so Ryan stepped onto the porch as he pulled the gun from behind his back and pointing it at Kevin. "And now it's your turn to be tied up, so drop the gun." Fortunately, Kevin didn't hesitate for long before he dropped his gun as he had noticed Sam appear beside the porch with a rifle pointed at him.

Sam could see the pickup still parked near the cabin, but the camper had been removed and was sitting behind the cabin, which he hadn't noticed before. He now understood why Dave and his deputies hadn't been able to find a pickup with a camper and out of state plates, since there was also a Colorado plate on the truck.

Sam guessed they must have stolen the plate off another truck and put it on theirs. He now understood how they had been able to go into town without anyone suspecting them, as he guessed they also had western hats. Ryan also didn't fit the clean-cut photo or the description Kate had given, as his hair was shorter and his mustache was trimmed neatly; and the beard was now almost non-existent.

Sam moved up onto the porch to help Ryan tie up Kevin as Kate watched from a distance. She couldn't hear what was being said from where she was, but she was happy to see no one had been shot and Kevin was now tied up. She headed back to the cave to pack things up. At least this part of the plan had worked, she thought.

Soon after Kate had arrived at the cave, Sam appeared to help pack up. He had called Dave who was already at the turn-off to the cabin, with Agent Matt, waiting for Sam's call. He wanted to be sure to catch Kevin if he tried to escape, and it wouldn't take long for him to be at the cabin. Ryan had stayed at the cabin with Kevin and to meet up with Dave and Matt. It didn't take long for Sam and Kate to get everything together and head back to the cabin. Dave and Matt were there talking with Ryan when they arrived and Kevin was in the backseat of Dave's car.

They took the horses to the small barn, then quickly removed the saddlebags and saddles. They took the saddlebags to the cabin to be unloaded, and Ryan, Dave, and Matt followed them into the cabin so they could talk while unloading and putting the food away.

Ryan had told Dave to be sure and keep Kevin out of sight if possible so Dylan or any of his men wouldn't spot him. He knew Kevin had a big mouth and the plan they had come up with would require Dylan to be in the dark about Kevin being arrested. Fortunately, there was a cell in the basement of the jailhouse that Dave felt would work out nicely.

They sat down at the table and went over the plan, Kate had suggested, to keep Dylan away from the ranch. It all sounded like it would work, but they would have to wait and see. Everyone stood around and listened as Ryan made the call to Dylan using the phone he had taken from Kevin.

Dylan was skeptical at first and asked to speak with Kevin. Ryan told Dylan that Kevin was in the bathroom and that something he had eaten was really having a bad effect on him, and it sounded like he was throwing up his guts.

Ryan told Dylan he would have Kevin call him later, if he was able to stay out of the bathroom long enough. Ryan had then told Dylan he had called Kate to get her away from all the people at the ranch and it had worked.

They had been able to find her this morning and she was with them now and her boyfriend had gone to get the money where she had hidden it, and would be back later that night. He had told him they would kill her if he told anyone or brought anyone with him.

Ryan then told Dylan, Kevin almost screwed everything up by knocking him out, tying him up and drugging him and he wasn't very happy about it. They had worked it out this morning though, at least somewhat, so they were square for now.

Kate then screamed. "Let me go. You can have the dirty money. I don't want it. Just let me go." And then laughed silently with the rest of them.

Ryan said Kevin had told him this morning that the plan was to meet him at the ranch tomorrow, but since they now had Kate, they thought there would be a lot fewer people around if they met at the cabin they had found. It was where he and Kevin had been staying and it was very secluded and no one else would be around to hear that big-mouthed girl.

Ryan then went on to tell Dylan there were a whole lot of people at that ranch and they all carried guns, which was why they hadn't been able to get to Kate sooner. He also told Dylan they wouldn't have to worry about the people at the ranch, if they met at the cabin, unless Dylan wanted them to bring the money to him at the hotel in town, after he got there.

Dylan finally agreed to meet at the cabin and they set a time for 10 a.m. the next day. Ryan told him how to get to the cabin and said he or Kevin would meet them at the entrance to the drive leading up to the cabin because it was really well hidden.

The next step was to get the sheriff and his men there before Dylan, and not have cars that could be seen. They decided the sheriff and his deputies would come to the cabin before 8 a.m. and one of the deputies would drop them off. The deputy would then hide the car down the road a bit, and would block the drive once Dylan and his men had arrived. Another deputy would stay in town and follow

191

them at a safe distance in his own private vehicle, so they would know when Dylan would be arriving.

Once it was all set the sheriff and his deputies left. Agent Matt and Ryan stayed at the cabin with Sam and Kate. Sam called Nick and updated him on what the plan was. He then asked Nick to get Kate's guitar along with a laundry bag and bring it to them. He also asked him to bring a few more steaks, some hamburgers, and a new block of ice, since there were a couple more mouths to feed now.

Nick said he should be able to get there in about an hour, so Kate and Sam went inside to start cleaning up the mess Kevin had made in the cabin. Ryan and Matt also pitched in cleaning up the yard and straightening up the outside, as beer cans had been tossed everywhere. By the time Nick arrived, the cabin would be in pretty good shape both inside and out and they were ready for some food.

They hadn't had breakfast and were all hungry, so while Sam went to feed the horses, Kate started breakfast. Ryan and Matt sat on the porch talking and trying to tweak the plan for the next day, while they were waiting.

Sam was surprised when he came back from the barn, to find a large omelet on his plate, and even toast Kate had grilled on the wood burning stove since there wasn't an oven or toaster. "This looks good enough to eat."

Ryan then said. "Believe me, it is. Kate's a great cook."

Matt agreed. "Home cooked meals really beat eating out all the time."

"Thank you." Kate responded, her face beaming.

"Where did you learn to fix toast that way? I know we do it around here a lot when we're camping, but I didn't expect you to know how." Sam said.

"Well, I've been camping a lot over the years too. Jess and I used to camp out with the horses almost every weekend until I left for college. We still did a lot of camping on the weekends and during the summers when I was home from school. I've always loved to camp."

"Then you should fit in very well around here. We usually have a campout at least once a week with the guests and since you and Jess plan to be here for the roundup, that's a week of camping out." Sam stated.

"Wow, that sounds like fun. Can I join you too? I've never been on a roundup before." Ryan said eagerly.

"You're welcome to join us anytime Ryan. I'm sure you would find it interesting. Do you know how to ride a horse?" Sam asked.

"I can't say I'm great at riding and handling a horse, but I did ride a lot when I was younger. I think I could pick it up again pretty quickly, especially if you loan me a well broke horse." Ryan said smiling.

"I think we could find one of those around here, ask Kate." Sam responded.

"Yes, definitely. I've been riding Choco since I arrived and he's wonderful. If you think you'd like to try, you're welcome to try him out." Kate responded.

"I might take you up on that later, but I think for now I'm still feeling the effects of the pain killers Kevin gave me and I need some rest." Ryan replied.

"I'm looking forward to the roundup and the rodeo." Kate said.

Stopping, Ryan asked. "You have a rodeo here too?"

"Sure do. Biggest and best one in the county. You'll have to join us for that sometime too. It's always the Sunday before the roundup and everyone is welcome to participate, if you feel you're good enough on a horse. Kate's planning to ride Choco in the pole and barrel races, so if you're around in a couple of weeks, you're welcome to join us."

Sam turned to Matt. "And you are welcome to join us anytime too."

"I've never been on a horse, but I think I'd like to watch the rodeo." Matt replied.

"Never been on a horse?" Sam responded. "Well, we can take care of that too."

"What's on our schedule for today, Sam?" Kate asked.

"Now that the hard part of catching Kevin is over, I thought we'd do some target practice and then maybe catch some fish for lunch. What do you think?" Sam replied.

Kate remembered crossing the beautiful sparkling stream, where they had stopped to let the horses drink, just before reaching the cabin and Sam had mentioned how great the fishing was there.

"Do you think it's safe for me to be out of the cabin?" Kate asked.

"The only road up this way is to the cabin and the entrance is really difficult to find unless you know where it is. I honestly don't think we'll have a problem."

"You mean the road to this cabin that Ryan and Kevin found?" Kate teased.

Ryan laughed. "Yes, but it was only by accident. A deer ran in front of us the night we arrived. When I swerved to miss it, I ended up on the road leading up here. We decided to check it out and were surprised to find the cabin.

It sure came in handy since we were able to take the camper off the truck and then swipe some Colorado plates off a parked truck, that didn't appear to have been moved recently. With western hats on, no one even questioned us, so we moved around freely.

Fortunately, we found the road leading to the fire tower, not far from here, but I sure wasn't expecting you to show up. When Kevin took a shot at you and missed, it gave me a chance to take the rifle and supposedly try at scaring you so we could still get the money. When I looked through the scope and saw you and noticed the mountain lion ready to pounce. I prayed I wouldn't miss and thankfully, I didn't."

"I want to thank you for shooting that lion. It saved Kate's life and I'm eternally grateful." Sam said.

"I'm thankful too. I've never been so frightened in my life, as I was when that mountain lion leaped into the air toward me." Kate responded.

"It looked like your horse had a scare too. I'm glad you were able to hang on and I'm happy I was at the right place and at the right time." Ryan replied. "I figured you would call the sheriff, so we got out of there quick to go back to the cabin. We did pass them on the road before turning in the drive up here and was glad they didn't turn around and follow us."

"That's why Dave and the deputies couldn't find you. They were looking for a pickup with a camper and out of state plates, since that was the description, we had given them when we almost hit you in the road, and you disappeared." Sam said.

"Sam, I'm sorry. I didn't mean for you or Kate to get hurt, but I wanted to let you know we were there and Kevin thought it was a funny idea." Ryan responded. "He's got a pretty sick mind and unfortunately he was driving, so I couldn't do anything."

"I think we got the hint." Kate told Ryan, before turning to Sam. "Okay I'm ready, but I don't have any interest in shooting a gun, even if it is just at targets."

"Kate, up here guns are carried for safety. There are a lot of wild animals, most of which won't bother you, but occasionally, one gets aggressive, like the mountain lion that almost got you, the wolves, and the rattlesnake yesterday. It's like putting down a rabid animal, which I'm sure you've done, although maybe not with a bullet."

Matt then commented. "It really isn't a bad idea to at least know how to use a gun. I'm sure in areas like this, where safety could be an issue, it would come in handy to at least know how to use one."

"Alright, I'll do some target practice since I haven't shot a gun in quite a while and only a rifle. And just so you know, I have had to shoot at varmints attacking our cattle before, so I do understand, but I don't believe in shooting animals for sport."

Sam was surprised and was glad to know she had handled a rifle before. "I don't believe in shooting animals for sport either, but we do occasionally hunt for food in the winter, and it also helps to keep the deer population down. Venison is great to eat and so are rabbits."

195

As Kate cleaned up the kitchen, Sam sat up chunks of wood across a log while Ryan and Matt found seats on the porch to watch. Sam first handed Kate the rifle and watched as she loaded it, sited, and then pulled the trigger. He could tell she had used a rifle before, but was shocked when the first piece of wood shattered as it flew off the log.

As soon as Kate shot the rifle, her shoulder felt as if someone had slammed their fist into it. "Ouch, that hurt." But she was also ecstatic and screamed excitedly. "I did it! I did it! Did you see that? I haven't lost my touch."

"Nice job." Ryan yelled out.

"Sorry, some rifles do have a little kick, but you did great. Try again." Sam said.

Kate was reluctant, but took another shot. She then tried a few more times, realizing how difficult it was to hold the rifle steady, since it was larger than any she had used before, but she managed to clear the log. Her shoulder was killing her, so she finally asked. "Okay, so can we stop now and go fishing?"

"You did great Kate, but I want you to try with the pistol too. It doesn't have as much kick and you hold it in front of you with both hands, aim and just gently pull the trigger as you try to hold it steady. The first thing you have to do is take the safety off." Sam said as he handed Kate his pistol.

Kate was shocked when she actually hit a target on the first try, since she had never shot a hand gun before, but after that it was all downhill. No matter how hard she tried to aim and hold it steady, the bullets just didn't seem to go where she was pointing. After she shot all the bullets, Sam showed her how to reload and she tried again, but the best she got was to barely graze one of the targets. "I think I've had enough. Let's go fishing."

Sam laughed. "You did good. Remember, when you're shooting at wild animals, most of the time, the noise alone will scare them off. At least now you have the gist of how to handle the hand gun too and that's the most important thing, so you don't go shooting yourself or someone close by, by mistake.

"In other words, you've been standing behind me so I didn't accidentally shoot you."

"Pretty good guess Kate, I wasn't taking any chances." Sam laughed.

Kate could hear Ryan and Matt laughing on the porch as she looked at Sam. "Thanks a lot." She responded with a pout.

Sam laughed then handed her more bullets. "Now just be sure to reload and put the safety back on when you are finished so the gun doesn't go off unexpectedly." He watched as she reloaded the gun and then flipped the small bar to put the safety on. He was proud of her.

Sam smiled as Kate handed him the gun and he holstered it and picked up the rifle. "That wasn't so bad, was it?"

"Other than probably not being able to use my shoulder or arm for a few days, it wasn't bad, but I still hope I never have to use a gun. I prefer trusting in God to take care of me." Kate said.

"So do I, but I feel that sometimes He gives us the ability and the necessary tools to accomplish tasks." Sam responded.

"I never thought of it that way, but I still feel I'd have a really hard time shooting a living thing, especially a human and hope I never have to." Kate responded; she hoped she never would have to shoot anything or anyone.

She preferred helping animals and people and was hoping she would have a chance to do just that, but she still had doubts about her future, even though she now knew Ryan was on her side and there to protect her. Hopefully tomorrow it would all be over, but they had to get through tomorrow first.

"When it means saving your life or someone you care about, you may find it can make a difference. Hopefully, you'll never be faced with that dilemma. How about we get the fishing poles? I'm ready to go fishing so we can eat lunch." Sam replied, trying to make light of the situation.

As they neared the porch, they were surprised to see Nick had joined Matt and Ryan. Nick said he had already put all the food in the icebox and cupboards and had put the guitar case behind the couch. He then turned to Sam and told him there was a bag of grain and a bale of hay in the truck, if Sam would like to help him get it. Sam didn't hesitate and walked with Nick to the truck and then to the barn.

Once they returned to the cabin, Sam asked Nick if he would like to join them for their fishing excursion. Nick said it sounded like fun, but he had to get back to the ranch.

Sam then turned to Ryan and Matt and asked them. Ryan responded that they needed to work on the plan for tomorrow, and then he needed to rest. They both then said they would definitely like to join them for lunch, if they caught anything.

It appeared everyone loved fresh fish and were looking forward to eating some, but it looked like it was going to be just Sam and Kate actually fishing. Sam was glad they had turned him down. he was looking forward to spending time alone with Kate again, which he had hoped for when they had left the ranch.

As Nick drove off, Sam and Kate walked around the side of the cabin and Kate was surprised to find a storage shed attached to the back of the cabin. She was amazed at all the items inside for hunting, trapping, and fishing, and guessed they were probably used a lot around there.

Sam pulled out some really long fishing poles like nothing Kate had ever seen before. "What are those?"

"Fly fishing poles." Sam replied.

"Well, they're nothing like I've ever seen before, they look more like whips."

Sam laughed. "So, I take it you've never been fly-fishing."

"No; I've heard of it, but never tried it." Kate responded.

"You'll like it. It just takes a little bit of getting used to, but it's perfect for the mountain streams we have in this area. Here, can you handle the poles while I get the tackle box and cooler?" Sam asked.

"Sure; are we going to walk back to the stream we crossed yesterday?"

"We can walk or ride; what's your preference?" Sam asked.

"I think I'd like to walk. It's not that far and I've been sitting way too much since I've been here so I'm ready to stretch my legs." Kate replied.

"Fine with me, but first, let's put some liniment on your shoulder so it won't get too stiff and sore." Sam said as he helped Kate with the fishing gear.

They placed the fishing gear on the porch and went inside. Kate sat down on the couch as Sam got the liniment, then joined Kate on the couch and told her to turn around. She told Sam she could apply it herself, but he didn't offer to hand the liniment to her.

She was glad her sweatshirt had a V neck as it allowed more room for Sam to reach in and apply the liniment to her shoulder, but her body was responding to his touch making it hard for her to concentrate on anything else.

At first it was warm and felt really good, but the more Sam rubbed, the warmer it got. "Wow, that's hot. I thought you said it would just be a little warm."

Sam laughed as he stopped rubbing it in. He was enjoying the smooth feeling of her skin, but he knew how hot it got the longer it was rubbed in. "It'll only be hot for a few minutes then it will feel very cold."

He wasn't kidding, and it was only a few minutes after he stopped rubbing it in when Kate's shoulder felt as if it was packed in ice causing her to feel chilled all over. Kate was glad when Sam wrapped a sleeping bag around her shoulders then pulled her into his arms.

It didn't take long for the shivering to stop, but Sam still held her close. Kate knew she had to do something to get

199

away from the way he was making her feel. "Hey, I'm ready to go fishing; how about you?"

"Sounds great. Let's go." Sam replied as he slowly got up and headed to the sink to wash his hands before heading to the door. Once outside he picked up the fishing poles and handed them to Kate along with the empty cooler, he then picked up the tackle box and rifle and they headed toward the stream.

Ryan wished them good luck and told them to be sure to bring back lots of fish, as he was really looking forward to lunch.

***

The walk to the stream was downhill and easy. Kate felt wonderful stretching her legs and her thoughts wandered back to when she was younger. She decided to share how much she had always liked hiking as well as riding, and about how she and Jess had hiked a lot, when they needed a break from riding, while on camping trips. She told him about the beautiful trails they had taken that were so different from the hills and mountains here in Colorado.

Sam laughed when Kate told him that one time, since she wasn't able to make it home for a few weeks, she had rented a horse at a park not far from the campus. It was definitely not the same as riding her own horses, and very much unlike her own horses, as the rented horse was very docile and preferred slow walking to anything else.

It was difficult to even get it into a trot, much less a canter, until they were headed back to the barn, then it decided to speed up a little. She had found; however, she was glad it was such a short ride since the horse's gaits, especially at a trot, were horrible.

Sam said he understood how some horses had smoother gaits than others, but found it hard to believe there were horses that preferred slow walking to running. He had never found one like that even after they were old and well trained. He thought the horse must have been very old.

He did, however, totally understand and found it hilarious when she told him how all it wanted to do was head back to the barn and eat. It was a well-known trait of horses everywhere and it wasn't just to a barn, but wherever they had last eaten.

Kate laughed and agreed. When camping, the horses always knew how to find their way back to the campground no matter how far they had ridden, and they always got back to the campground much quicker than the ride away from it.

She also told Sam she wasn't sure what kind of horses they had at the riding stable, but they were not as nice to ride as her quarter horse or her Morgan, or even Choco. She wanted him to know Choco was truly a wonderful horse to ride. His gaits were smooth and his response to commands was great. She was really looking forward to riding him more. If she got the chance, she thought.

Sam asked Kate about her horses and she was happy to tell him all about them. Most of the horses throughout her life she had acquired as two or three-year olds and had trained them herself. She had gotten them after she had outgrown her pony and passed it down to her brother.

She had truly enjoyed training them, although her parents had been worried at first, they had finally given up and let her work with them. She was surprised when Sam told her she could get plenty of practice training horses at the ranch if she ever wanted to.

Kate thought about the black horse they had brought in earlier from one of their rides. She had thought the gelding would be perfect for Jess to ride, as Jess had always dreamed of having a black horse. Jess now had a beautiful black Tennessee Walker that she loved to ride, but he wouldn't be here for their vacation.

It would be great to try to work with the black gelding. It might take a while before she could risk getting on his back, but she would like to try. She wondered, if maybe the horse just didn't like the spurs, which was something she had never used when training her horses.

The gelding had been so calm when no one was on his back. He was even calm each time a rider got on his back, until they tried to get him to walk by touching him with their spurs, then he would go crazy. She doubted Sam would let her work with him, but maybe after Jess arrived, they would have a chance.

Kate told Sam about the Tennessee Walking horses Jess had picked up a couple of years ago and how different their gaits were from her own horses. She had ridden them a few times and had found it hard to believe how smooth they were, especially at a fast walk.

They never broke into a trot, but would go into a canter. One of Jess's horses had even been clocked at eight miles an hour at a walk, but she was sure there were others that were much faster and the side-to-side motion was different; almost like being in a rocking chair.

Sam said he had heard about walking horses, but had never ridden one. He was sure he would prefer his own horse, but wouldn't mind trying one someday.

The day had been wonderful so far, at least after Kevin had been captured and taken to jail. Kate was enjoying the time with Sam and was glad he was trying to keep her busy to keep her mind off Dylan and the plans to capture him tomorrow.

She was still worried about what was going to happen next. She really wanted to enjoy the day with Sam since she wasn't sure there would ever be another like it for them. She was trying hard not to think about tomorrow, but it kept entering her thoughts, so she prayed.

Kate was glad when the stream came into view. It hadn't taken as long to reach it as she thought it would and she was still amazed at how beautiful and calming it was. She enjoyed watching Sam prepare the poles, but she was anxious to try the fly-fishing he said was never boring. She just hoped it would be more fun and interesting than the type of dock and bank fishing she had done before with her dad.

Sam handed her one of the poles and showed her how to cast the line by wrapping her in his arms to help her try a few casts. Kate's whole body seemed to respond to his touch, but she tried hard not to let him know. "Okay, I think I have the idea, let me try on my own now."

Sam reluctantly stepped back. She had felt so right in his arms, but he didn't want to push her. It would work out in time if it was meant to be. He couldn't let his impatience cause him to lose her. He knew she cared; he could feel it each time her body responded to his kiss. He just had to be patient.

Boy was it hard though, Kate was the kind of women he had always dreamed of, but never expected to find. Now that he had found her, would he be satisfied with just a few weeks of fun with her?

He had told her he loved her, and when she was in his arms, he was sure he actually did, but was that enough for a real relationship? Would she ever love him enough to be happy with him and living at the ranch? He doubted it.

Sam watched as Kate cast her line out and was amazed at how quickly she had picked it up. "Great job, Kate. Are you sure you haven't done this before?"

"I'm sure, but this is fun. Although I think it would have been a lot easier and less painful if we had done this before the target practice." Kate replied.

"I'm sorry; I didn't mean for you to be hurt from shooting. I'll rub more horse liniment on it when we get back to the cabin."

"Are you calling me a horse now?" Kate asked.

Sam laughed. "Not at all, but it did help a little didn't it? Although it's a bit warm, it works."

"A bit warm!" Kate remarked. "I think that's an understatement, but you're right, it did help. I'm not sure I would have been able to cast this line if you hadn't rubbed my shoulder with the liniment."

Kate felt a tug on her line and then let out a scream of excitement. "I got one! I got one! Look at it? It's a good size trout we can have for our lunch."

"It sure is, now we need to get one for me and Ryan and Matt to eat." Sam replied as he brought out the net so he could take the fish off the line and throw it in the cooler. He then joined her in the stream and threw out a line so they could both work on getting their lunch. They caught several more fish before heading back to the cabin.

Matt was on the porch and said Ryan had gone in to lie down and rest while they were gone. He then asked if they had caught anything.

Sam and Kate didn't hesitate in replying they had caught more than enough for lunch and hoped he and Ryan were hungry.

"Yes, I'm hungry, and Ryan said to be sure and wake him when you got back. He didn't want to miss out on fresh fish." Matt replied.

Sam started a fire in the firepit, then gutted and filleted the fish before placing them on the rack to grill. While he was preparing the fish, Kate fixed a salad and some iced tea. Matt woke Ryan while everything was being prepared and then helped to set everything out on the picnic table near the fire.

The meal was terrific. Kate couldn't remember ever having fish that tasted so good and everyone else seemed to enjoy it too. She also enjoyed Sam telling them about hunting and fishing trips he had been on, which had often included funny experiences.

They especially enjoyed his story about the time he and Nick had just finished catching enough fish for dinner and had turned to pick up the cooler when they heard splashing in the creek. When they turned around, they saw a large bear headed straight for them.

They left everything and took off running and when they looked back, they saw the bear sitting at the edge of the water eating their fish. They waited until the bear wandered away and went back for the cooler and poles. They ended up eating peanut butter and jelly sandwiches for dinner.

Kate had found fly fishing to be a lot more fun than sitting on a dock or river bank holding a pole and was happy a bear hadn't shown up while they were fishing. She was glad Sam had waited to tell her the story about the bear until after they had gone fishing, rather than before. She was sure her concentration would have been broken. Actually, she had found the whole morning to be exciting and fun, except for capturing Kevin. Thank God it had been quick and no one had gotten hurt.

Kate decided to share some of her fishing stories about when she had gone fishing with her dad as a child. Although they were not as funny as Sam's stories. Everyone liked the story about her sitting on a dock fishing and getting bored after about five minutes and reeling in the line.

Her father had screamed at her to not pull the line out of the water, just as she did, and they watched a huge catfish continue under the dock and out the other side. Her father had never let her live down, the one that got away. She was surprised but delighted when Ryan and Matt shared a few fishing stories too. Lunch had been a great time.

Kate wondered what Sam had planned for the rest of the day, since things had possibly changed with Ryan and Matt being there. It didn't take long for her to get her answer. Sam mentioned to Ryan and Matt that he had planned to take Kate for a ride that afternoon and was wondering if they would like to join them on the ride.

Kate wasn't surprised when Ryan said he thought he needed more sleep and Matt offered to clean up while they were gone. He felt it was the least he could do since they had furnished and prepared the fish for lunch. They also told Sam and Kate about a plan they had worked out for the next day to arrest Dylan and had already called Dave to fill him in.

As they were getting ready to go to the barn, Sam was surprised when his phone began to ring. He noticed the caller ID was Dave. He let everyone know who it was, and quickly answered as he put it on speaker. They listened then Sam thanked Dave for calling before turning to Kate and the guys. He could tell they were glad to get the information.

Dave had called to let them know some strangers had arrived in town in a large SUV and he was pretty sure it was Dylan and four of his men. He and one of his deputies were keeping an eye on them.

"I won't rest easy until Dylan and his men are all behind bars." Kate responded.

"I don't think any of us will." Sam replied. "We just have to pray Ryan and Matt's plan works."

Sam put his arm around Kate. "Don't worry Kitten; there are a lot of good guys out there to help us. It won't be long now, since we know Dylan and his men are in town and Dave will keep us updated."

"I'm trying not to worry, but I know how dangerous Dylan and his men are, according to Ryan, and I'm praying no one gets hurt." Kate said, while trying to hide her fear.

"At least you're safe and away from the ranch for now and Dylan has agreed to meet here instead of at the ranch, which should keep anyone there from getting hurt. I'm really glad you thought of meeting here." Sam responded and Ryan and Matt agreed.

Kate really hoped it was true that no one would get hurt, but she still had doubts. When bad men were around, anything could happen and usually did. She knew she should be praying instead of worrying and trusting in God to take care of them, but it was hard to let go of the fear.

Sam told Kate he should apply a little more liniment on her shoulder before they took their ride. The ride sounded great to Kate, but not the horse liniment. Although she knew it would help, she wasn't looking forward to the burning. She finally headed for the couch to sit down so Sam could apply the liniment.

Kate thought about telling Sam she could apply it herself, but remembered how he had said his hands felt like they were on fire after applying it earlier, and changed her mind. His touch was gentle and felt wonderful as he rubbed her shoulder, but she was thankful he didn't rub it as long

206

as before. It was still hot, but didn't feel like it was on fire this time.

As Sam put the liniment away, Kate got up and headed for the door. "Hey, I'm ready for that ride; how about you?"

Sam hesitated for only a moment. "Yep, I'm ready. Let's ride."

Before heading to the barn, Sam told Ryan and Matt they wouldn't be gone long. It didn't take long to saddle up and afterwards Kate suggested they let Matt try to ride. "I think once he tries it, he'll be hooked. You could just take him down the trail a little way and give the horses a drink where we went fishing today. What do you think?" Kate asked.

Sam laughed. "I think it's a great idea."

They led the horses back to the cabin where Ryan commented that he thought that was an awfully short ride. As they laughed, they asked Matt to come down and check out the horses. He seemed skeptical, but then joined them. After petting Choco for a few minutes, Kate handed Matt the reins and told him to mount up.

Matt hesitated as Sam demonstrated how to mount the horse. Kate could tell Matt wasn't very excited about getting on a horse; however, he did seem happy once he was finally in the saddle. Sam told Matt to loosen the reins and to follow him. As Sam and Matt started down the trail to the creek, Kate joined Ryan on the porch.

Sam could tell Matt was apprehensive, but he was doing a fine job. They stopped for a couple of minutes to let the horses drink from the stream. Since the trail ahead was flat, Sam suggested they go a little further down it. They started slow then Sam coaxed his horse into a trot, which Choco matched.

The gait change, surprised Matt, but he stayed in the saddle. Once they slowed and turned back toward the cabin, Sam took his horse into a slow canter, which he knew Choco would once again join in. He wasn't surprised when Matt shouted. "Wow, this is great."

Sam could tell Matt really enjoyed the ride and was reluctant to give Choco back to Kate, but he finally dismounted and handed Kate the reins. Matt told Sam he was looking forward to someday soon, having a chance to ride again. Sam let him know he was welcome any time to come to the ranch and ride.

Matt was all smiles as he gratefully accepted, then walked up on the porch to join Ryan. Kate quickly mounted Choco and they rode out. Sam told Kate about Matt's ride and Kate was happy they had given him a chance for a new experience. Everything was so beautiful up here and she was really looking forward to their ride. Eventually, her thoughts turned troubled as she wondered what tomorrow would bring and if she would ever have a chance to ride with Sam again.

Kate had been surprised at how dense the area was at this altitude, but the path was wide and clear. They rode along quietly for a while, but Kate decided it was time to break the silence. "I'm amazed at how many trees there are up here. I didn't expect it, up this high." Kate said as she finally looked over a Sam.

Sam had waited patiently and was glad Kate was ready to carry on a conversation again. The silence had tormented him but he had been trying to keep her busy and not think about tomorrow. "The dense tree population is why this area is often referred to as the black hills. They are mostly conifers and aspens since we're at a pretty high elevation. As we climb higher, they will become sparser. There's a really pretty area up here, I think you'll like. It's only about an hour's ride."

"Sounds great; I know I'll love it. It's all so beautiful." As they rode, the trees did thin out and the majestic mountains in the distance, now visible, were breath-taking. "Oh wow! This is phenomenal!" Kate exclaimed.

Suddenly, Kate was caught off guard as Choco stopped and started snorting and shaking his head. Sam had also stopped and was pulling his rifle out of the sleeve while telling her not to move. She immediately froze as she looked ahead at a huge bear standing in the middle of the path. The horses must have seen or smelled it as they were both snorting and starting to dance around.

"You aren't going to shoot it, are you?" Kate asked quietly.

"Not if I can avoid it. Turn Choco around and start slowly back toward the cabin until you are out of sight of the bear, then run. I'm going to fire a shot to hopefully scare it away, but I want you out of range just in case it doesn't work." Sam said quietly.

"But what about you?" Kate asked frantically.

"I'll be okay. I'll shoot it if I have to. Now go! I'll meet you back at the cabin." Sam responded while trying to keep his eyes on the bear, that was now standing on its hind legs, which made it appear much larger.

While trying to calm Choco, as well as herself, Kate slowly backed Choco up and turned him around. When she felt they were finally out of sight of the bear, she punched Choco with her heels. They had just broken into a run when she heard the first shot. She then heard another shot; and then nothing. She was worried about Sam.

Kate slowed Choco to a walk hoping Sam would catch up. It had taken a few minutes to slow Choco, but she finally succeeded. She noticed a small stream ahead and stopped so Choco could get a drink. She looked around first to make sure there were no bears, then loosened the reins and sat back.

She waited impatiently, hoping Sam would appear. She thanked God when she saw him coming over the hill, she had come across a short while before. As he rode up, she jumped off Choco and into Sam's arms, barely giving him time to dismount. She had never been so happy to see anyone in all her life.

After a few moments, Kate finally asked. "What happened to the bear?"

"It's hard telling where it's at now. By the time I fired the second shot it was high-tailing it out of there."

"I'm glad you didn't have to shoot it, but I'm especially thankful that it didn't come after you. I sure hope we don't run into any more of them."

"There are a lot of bears up here, but we seldom have a problem with them. I think they prefer being left alone as much as we do. They're just coming out of hibernation, so they are probably hungry." Sam replied. "How about we mount up and head back to the cabin, enjoy some steaks and then a peaceful, restful evening?"

"Sounds wonderful." Kate responded as she backed out of his arms and mounted Choco.

They rode quietly back to the cabin and Kate was glad it was uneventful. She sure didn't want to run into another hungry bear.

Ryan and Matt were sitting on the porch when they returned and said they were surprised to see them back so soon. Kate quickly told them about the bear and how big it was, especially when it had stood up on its hind legs.

Sam laughed as he told them how quickly it had run off after he had shot his rifle a couple of times. Matt said he was glad he hadn't been with them and they all laughed.

After taking the horses to the barn, Kate and Sam joined Ryan and Matt on the porch. Ryan told them more about the plans for the next day and where they would all be positioned.

Sam called Nick to see if he would like to join them for a steak dinner, since he had been the one to bring up the steaks earlier. Nick had quickly agreed and said steak over an open fire was the best. He then said he would be there in about an hour. Sam started a fire in the firepit, then went inside to wash up, while the flames burned down and the coals got hot.

When Sam came out of the cabin, Kate went inside to freshen up and then started preparing the potatoes, carrots, and onions. She was looking forward to the steaks and hobo potatoes like they had prepared last night. Food sure tasted better cooked over an open fire. Nick had also brought hamburgers this morning, but they thought they could save them for lunch tomorrow, if everything went as planned.

Shortly after the hobo potatoes were put on the coals, Nick showed up with an apple cobbler for dessert that looked delicious. Sam came out with the steaks to put on the fire, along with a couple of pieces of fish they hadn't been able to eat at lunch. He told Nick, they had saved them for him, and he looked very happy. As Sam prepared the steaks and fish, Ryan, Matt, and Nick pitched in to get the picnic table prepared and set up, while Kate prepared salad to complete the meal.

After eating and cleaning up, they enjoyed a few card games, they had found in one of the cabinets. Nick said goodnight and left and it wasn't long after that Ryan and Matt said goodnight and crawled into a couple of bunk beds in the back corner.

Sam had started a fire in the fireplace and it was burning bright and warming the cabin. Kate was entranced by the flames dancing in the fire as she and Sam sat on the couch. She had enjoyed their wonderful day together and wished there could be a lot more. If it was meant to be, it would happen, she thought.

Sam finally said they should head to bed too since tomorrow was going to be an early and busy day. He got up, pulled her up into his arms and gave her a kiss, before saying. "I could get used to this. I love you, Kate."

Kate smiled, she loved him too and knew she could get used to being in his arms and him kissing her too, but now wasn't the time to let down her guard any more than she had already. She felt the loss of his arms around her as he released her and slowly walked away and found a bunk in the corner with the other guys.

Kate stood still for a moment then finally walked over and curled up in the bunk near the fireplace. Sleep didn't come quickly, and she prayed while watching the flames.

She feared what tomorrow would bring. Her thoughts were imagining all kinds of outcomes. She didn't want anyone to get hurt, but knew it was probably inevitable that someone would be hurt with the violent nature of Dylan and his men.

She wasn't sure what she would do if anyone was hurt or killed. It was her fault that Dylan and his men were there. She wished she had taken the initiative and looked for the money sooner and given it to Ryan even though he had told her earlier that this was a great way to finally put Dylan out of business.

Dylan was a criminal and was involved in a lot of bad businesses, not only drugs. Catching him with not only drug money but also drugs was a perfect way to put him away for a long time.

Kate had agreed, and she knew meeting Dylan at the cabin instead of the ranch was a safer option, but she was still afraid. She finally prayed, turning her worries over to God and fell into a restless sleep.

Chapter 11

The morning had gone as planned. Kate and Sam had prepared breakfast and the money had been transferred from the guitar to the laundry bag, along with the packets of drugs Kate had found with the money. The sheriff and a couple of deputies had been dropped off earlier and were enjoying coffee and donuts they had brought along.

The plan was for Matt and Dave to hide in the bathroom and occasionally flush the toilet so they could pretend it was Kevin still dealing with the stomach flu or something. Kate would supposedly be tied up in the shed since she had been too combative and making too much noise screaming at them all the time. Sam would be with her and have his gun ready if it was needed.

The deputies were to hide in the barn with the horses, where they wouldn't be seen and Agent Ryan would greet and talk with Dylan, and then give him the money along with the drugs. Everything seemed to be in place and they were all praying no one would get hurt.

Dave's phone rang, which was a surprise since it was only 8:30 a.m. and his deputy wasn't expected to call until Dylan had left town. Dave quickly answered and when he hung up, he told them all that Dylan and his men had just left town and should be there in about forty-five minutes, depending on how fast they drove. It didn't give them much time, but at least they were all prepared and knew their positions.

They had been waiting for about thirty minutes before Ryan's phone rang. It was Dylan telling him he should be at the turn soon so he or Kevin should get down to the road, as they didn't want to miss the turn.

Dylan asked about Kevin and Ryan told him he was still running into the bathroom a lot and he was worried Kevin might have caught a stomach flu or something. Ryan said he wasn't sure Dylan would want Kevin to come out of the bathroom while he was there, in case he was contagious.

Dylan only hesitated for a moment before replying he would rather not catch anything so he wanted Kevin to stay in the bathroom and asked Ryan if he thought he himself might also be coming down with whatever Kevin had.

Ryan told him 'No,' and laughed after he hung up the phone. He knew Dylan was really paranoid about being around anyone who was sick. Everyone then dispersed to their positions as Ryan went to the truck.

Ryan didn't have to wait long since whoever was driving, was driving fast. The driver almost wasn't able to stop in time to turn in and Ryan was sure Dylan wasn't too pleased with him slamming on the brakes.

Ryan hadn't seen the deputy but had little doubt he was somewhere nearby and would be blocking the drive once they were at the cabin. The squealing tires of the large SUV as it stopped, probably was a great heads-up for him.

Ryan led them up the drive to the cabin. When he reached the cabin, he parked then jumped out of the truck and walked onto the porch. He then turned and invited them in. There were no other vehicles in sight, so Dylan's men finally got out of the SUV, looked around, then entered the cabin.

They first appeared skeptical, then heard the toilet flush as they looked around the large one-room cabin. It didn't take long before they motioned an all clear to Dylan and his driver, letting them know they could get out of the car as the cabin appeared safe.

One of the men then walked over and tapped on the bathroom door and told Kevin not to come out. They heard a retching noise, then the toilet flush and the man quickly walked away from the bathroom door.

"I've made some coffee, if you'd like to have some." Ryan said, while trying to keep from laughing, as Dylan walked onto the porch.

Kate and Sam were listening to the conversation from the shed, attached to the back of the cabin. They could hear most of what was said and prayed everything would go smoothly from here on out.

"Where's the money and where's the girl?" Dylan finally said.

214

"The money is inside, in a bag behind the couch and the girl is locked in a shed behind the cabin. She wouldn't stop screaming and we couldn't find any tape, so we put her out in the shed. I didn't think you would want her seeing you anyway. It's bad enough she can identify me and Kevin, but I'll take care of her before I leave."

"Then it wouldn't matter if she saw me anyway, would it?" Dylan said.

"I guess not, but I didn't think you would want to take any chances. I can get her if you want, but I'll warn you in advance, she never shuts up." Ryan replied.

Dylan hesitated for a few moments. "Just leave her where she is for now. We aren't going to run into Kevin, are we?"

"No, I told him not to come out of the bathroom while you are here." Ryan replied.

Dylan finally agreed to a cup of coffee and said he liked his coffee black, as he walked into the cabin. Ryan poured Dylan a cup, along with one for himself, then told the other guys they could get their own. Ryan heard retching sounds and then the toilet flush again. He tried to hide his smile when Dylan looked toward the bathroom.

Once Dylan sat down in the chair next to the fireplace, Ryan pulled the bag out from behind the couch and handed it to him. "I didn't count it, but hopefully it's all there. He had stashed it in his guitar and then given it to Kate to take home with her.

Unfortunately, she found out the cops in Las Vegas had put out a warrant for her arrest for killing him, so she ended up hiding out here with friends. I guess she didn't even know she had the money at first."

"Guess it's a good thing she didn't know. She might have spent it all by now. You know how women can be." Dylan said laughing as he opened the bag and looked in. "I want to thank you for getting my money back, but I don't think I will be needing your services any longer, or the services of that idiot I sent with you." Dylan said as he closed the bag and pulled out a gun.

"Hey man, I got your money, what's wrong?" Ryan asked as he heard the toilet flush again. He knew everything was being recorded, with both video and sound, so if anything did go wrong, they would still have evidence of what had happened to help convict Dylan in court.

"But you didn't get it quick enough and I had to come all this way just to clean up your mess." Dylan glanced over at the bathroom and then back at Ryan, before turning to the two men who were inside the cabin. "Joe, go out and take care of the girl and Tom, take care of the idiot in the bathroom."

"But boss, Ryan said he was sick. I don't want to catch anything." Tom replied anxiously.

"You idiot! You can't catch anything just by shooting him." Dylan responded. "I want to take care of this idiot myself." He said as he looked back at Ryan.

The conversation between Dylan and his men, had given Ryan long enough to pull the gun from beside the couch cushion. He heard the door to the bathroom slam open and heard a couple of shots and prayed Matt and Dave hadn't been shot.

Ryan then told Dylan, "Drop your gun. You're under arrest."

"I knew there was something wrong about you. You're a cop." Dylan said angrily. "You don't have anything on me. You can't prove this is drug money."

"No; I'm not a cop, I'm DEA, but you forgot to look under the money. I guess Mike hadn't sold all the drugs yet, so there's a nice stash in with the money." Ryan responded.

Matt had told Ryan about a raid that was going to happen on Dylan's house that morning, and was hoping Dylan would give up when given the information. "And while we are here talking, your accounts have been frozen and your property in Las Vegas has been confiscated and a team is going through your house and businesses as we speak.

Believe it or not, they even found a large stash of drugs at your house, along with evidence of money laundering, prostitution, and human trafficking. I'm surprised you were stupid enough to hold some of the women at your house."

"You're lying. You have no right and there's no evidence of any of it. You're just guessing and trying to intimidate me." Dylan said as he took aim and shot at Ryan.

Ryan was expecting it and hadn't been surprised by the shot. He dove to the floor as he returned fire hitting Dylan in the chest. Ryan watched as Dylan fell to the floor; his large body shaking the floor as he hit. It took a minute, for the pain to kick in, but Ryan finally realized he had been hit.

His shoulder was on fire and blood was quickly staining his shirt, but he managed to sit up against the couch. Matt quickly ran over with a towel and applied pressure to Ryan's shoulder.

Tom had been shot, when he had opened the bathroom door and fired. He had dropped his weapon, and fell to the floor. Dave and Matt hadn't been shot, but Tom had come really close with his shot, since the bathroom wasn't very large. They had stayed out of sight and had been listening to Ryan and Dylan, but as soon as the confrontation was over, Dave bent down to apply pressure to Tom's shoulder wound.

Ryan was really worried about Kate and wondered if she was okay, since Joe had been sent out to take care of her. He hadn't heard any shots from outside and knew Sam was with Kate, but that didn't mean they had been able to stop Joe in time. Matt called out to Kate that it was safe for her to come in out of the shed and that Ryan had been shot.

***

Kate and Sam had been listening to all that was going on. They were expecting Joe, so they had hidden and managed to take him down when he opened the door. They heard a couple of gunshots and heard Dave telling someone to get on the floor.

217

They also heard Ryan and Dylan talking and were surprised at what Ryan had said regarding Dylan's business dealings. It was only a few minutes later they heard two shots and someone cry out. They didn't know who or if anyone had actually been shot.

Kate was worried. She didn't know who, if anyone was shot and if it was over or if they were still going to face Dylan and his men. It had been bad enough when Joe had entered and pointed the gun at her, before Sam had knocked the gun out of his hand, slugged him, then tied his hands behind his back and gagged him.

After a few minutes of silence Kate heard Matt call for her. "Kate, it's safe for you to come in and come quick. Ryan's been shot."

Kate didn't hesitate; however, Sam stepped in front of her, grabbed Joe and looked around before they exited the shed. "We need to make sure it's clear, just let me take him and go first." Sam told Kate.

Kate guessed Dylan's other two men had heard the first shots and had run to the porch, since the deputies had rifles pointed at them and their guns were lying on the porch. As soon as Dylan's men were handcuffed and taken to the deputies' cars, Kate and Sam ran to the door of the cabin.

Ryan was worried about Kate. He knew Sam was with her, but he still hadn't seen Kate or Sam, so he was happy when he saw them enter the cabin.

Kate and Sam noticed Dylan first, lying in a pool of blood, Kate didn't feel there was anything she could do for him or if he was even still alive. She then saw Ryan, who was slumped down on the floor by the couch and Matt was applying pressure to his shoulder.

Kate ran over to him as she told Sam to get the first aid kit. She also noticed Dave applying pressure on another man's shoulder, who she guessed also had a gunshot wound. She was thankful Dave and Matt were okay.

She asked Dave to call for the ambulance, that had already been on standby on a nearby road. He told her the ambulance was on the way up to the cabin, and they had sent for two more.

Kate was glad to see Ryan had only been shot in the shoulder and not somewhere that could have been fatal. She could tell the bullet was still lodged in his shoulder and hadn't passed through. It also felt like his shoulder bones were possibly shattered. She knew he was going to require surgery, so she didn't attempt to get the bullet out.

The ambulances were on the way and would take him to the hospital. She applied pressure, then packed and wrapped his shoulder. Her biggest concern was to stop or at least slow down the bleeding and try to make his arm stationary so he couldn't move it and cause more damage.

By the time the paramedics arrived, Ryan was ready to be transported. Dylan hadn't moved and Kate wasn't sure if he could be saved. He had been shot in the chest and had already lost a lot of blood. She decided to let the paramedics take care of him; and was happy Ryan wasn't as bad and should live.

The paramedics immediately ran to Dylan. They had noticed Kate bandaging Ryan and the sheriff was with another gunshot patient. They were trying to get Dylan stable enough to move, but could barely get a pulse or blood pressure, and his breathing was shallow. They had put an oxygen mask on him and were trying to stop the bleeding, but it didn't look promising that he would make it.

Kate didn't think the bullet had hit Dylan's heart, since he was still alive, but wondered if it had hit a lung. The paramedics were in constant contact with someone at the hospital and finally rolled him onto a stretcher.

They waited for another ambulance to arrive so they would have help carrying him to the ambulance. They planned to take him straight to the Colorado Springs hospital where more specialists and security were.

They heard the ambulance drive off shortly after with one of the sheriff's deputies following close behind. The pool of blood was large where Dylan had been lying, and

Kate was surprised he was still alive. She didn't expect him to make it to the hospital. She left Matt with Ryan and went over to the man Dave was with. Dave had been applying pressure to the wound, but moved back as Kate joined him. The man's wound was similar to Ryan's. She tried to stop the bleeding with the gauze pads she had left, and then wrapped his shoulder so he couldn't move it.

She was hopeful he would survive and he was now ready for transport too. The other two ambulances arrived and the paramedics placed the man Dave was with on a stretcher. Dave followed them out as he told Ryan and Matt, he would see them at the hospital.

Ryan was put on a stretcher and as the paramedics started carrying him out, he asked them to stop. He took Kate's hand. "Thank you. Thank you for everything. I'm sorry I put you through all this, but we couldn't have arrested Dylan without your help. I hope I'll see you again someday and tell Mike I'm sorry."

"I will and I'm glad I was able to help. Take care and get in touch when you're better. Mike and I both forgive you." Kate replied. She knew Ryan was in a lot of pain and his recovery probably wouldn't be quick, but hopefully he would feel better soon. She asked Matt to keep in touch and to let her know how Ryan was; and he said he would.

After all Ryan had put her through, Kate still felt sorry for him and was happy he had survived. He had actually saved her life twice that she knew of, and the nightmare she had been living in was finally over, because of him. Kate thanked God for being with them today and prayed he would watch over Ryan.

Kate was glad it was over and no one else had been hurt. She was happy when Sam put his arm around her as they watched all the emergency vehicles pull away. They knew it would still be a while before the forensic team left, but they were in no hurry now, except to sit back and relax on the porch.

Kate was surprised when Sam asked her. "Do you think we could possibly clean up this mess after everyone leaves and stay the night here, just you and me as we had initially planned?"

It only took Kate a few moments to answer. "I think I'd like that. Just you and me, sounds wonderful."

They walked out onto the porch to relax while the forensic team entered to start taking pictures, remove the surveillance equipment, and whatever else they needed to do.

Sam made a call to Nick to let him know it was over and all that had happened. He then let Nick know, he and Kate would be staying another night to clean the place up and would see them sometime tomorrow.

Kate could hear Nick laughing as he told Sam he didn't have to hurry. Sam also asked Nick to be sure and let his dad and brother know he was fine and wouldn't be back until the next day. Nick said he would and he was really happy everything had gone so well and no one else had been hurt.

It was early afternoon before the forensic team finished and left. Kate and Sam were finally alone and Kate realized she was starving. They decided to cook up some hamburgers to hold them over until later, and before tackling the mess in the cabin. It only took a few minutes to prepare over the fire in the firepit, along with some beans and chips. They sat on the front porch to eat so they wouldn't have to look at the mess inside.

They were surprised when they had finished their late lunch to hear a vehicle coming toward the cabin. They were even more surprised when they saw who was in the truck. Jake, Nick, Joey, John, and a few of the ranch-hands piled out of the truck cab and bed with buckets, sponges, and mops along with some bags and a cooler.

As they walked toward the cabin, Jake said. "We thought you two had been through enough already today and we don't let guests work around here, or at least much, so we're the cleaning crew which I have little doubt is needed."

Sam and Kate smiled as Jake came up and gave them each a hug and then Nick, Joey, and John, followed suit. Kate was surprised when John gave her a hug and told her he was sorry for the way he had treated her and hoped she would forgive him.

"Nothing to be sorry for. I don't blame you in the least for not liking me putting your son in danger. I hated the idea too. He just wouldn't listen to reason." Kate responded.

"That definitely sounds like my son. I hope we will become friends now, even though it's later than it should have been." John said.

"I'd like that." Kate replied.

John then gave Kate another hug and went inside to join the others. Jake then followed everyone inside and looked around before stating. "At least it's not as bad as I thought it might be. Only three puddles of blood. Not bad for the mess you were in Kate. And thank you for suggesting they meet up here instead of at the ranch. It might have been a lot worse and a lot more people may have been hurt."

"I'm just glad it turned out as well as it did. I've really been worried about people getting hurt. I want to thank you all for being willing to help protect me." Kate replied.

"God put you in our care Kate. We only did what we knew He expected us to do." Jake said. "And we're hoping once your vacation starts on Sunday, you'll have time to relax and enjoy it."

"Me too. I'm not sure how relaxing it will be with all the activities you say you have planned. I do still plan to help with the horses and cattle, if you need me too. The experience I've gained here, especially working with the foals and calves, has been priceless. I do plan to enjoy every minute of my vacation though and I'm sure my friend, Jessica, will too."

"We're looking forward to meeting Jessica on Sunday, so don't forget to introduce us." Jake said.

"I plan to and I think you'll really like her. She's like a sister to me and I know she's anxious to get here and meet all of you too." Kate responded.

Jake walked out to sit on the porch with Sam and Kate and they talked a little longer, while the cleanup was being completed. Kate was surprised when someone came out and restarted a fire in the firepit and then Nick walked out with a platter of steaks they had brought with them.

Kate was amazed as she watched the parade of guys come out of the cabin and place a table cloth on the picnic table, bring out all kinds of side dishes to go with the steaks and a chocolate cake, that looked scrumptious.

She had wondered what was in all the bags and coolers they had carried in when they arrived, and now she knew. Jake said it was his thank you gift to Kate and Sam. Kate gave him a hug, while trying to hold back tears. She definitely hadn't expected anything like this.

They all ate, laughed, and had a great time, but as dusk was settling in, Jake and the crew all climbed back into the truck and left. Sam and Kate were finally alone and were looking forward to a nice quiet evening together.

After feeding the horses, they decided to walk them down to the stream where they had fished and let them drink their fill and get some exercise. It brought back great memories of the time they had spent together fishing and gave Sam and Kate a chance to walk off some of the great food they had just enjoyed, especially the chocolate cake. It also gave them a chance to finally talk about all that had happened.

Kate had considered flying home for a couple of days, but it hardly seemed worth it and she didn't want to cancel or spoil the vacation she and Jess had planned almost a year ago. She decided instead to give her parents a call. While the horses were drinking, Kate borrowed Sam's phone and made a quick call to her parents to let them know it was finally over.

She was happy when Mike got on the phone and she could tell him about Ryan and what he had said about being sorry and having identified a person in the morgue as him, so Dylan would think he was dead and not look for him.

Ryan had thought they would find the money in the apartment and hadn't even considered the idea that Dylan would be sending him after her. Ryan wanted her to let him know how really sorry he was for everything.

She also told Mike about Ryan being shot and needing surgery and about Dylan being in critical condition. She could tell Mike was relieved and was looking forward to seeing Ryan again when they both were better.

Afterwards she gave a quick call to Jessica to let her know the nightmare was finally over and how she was really looking forward to seeing her on Sunday. She also reminded Jess not to forget to bring her some clothes because she was getting tired of doing laundry every other day. She knew Jess would be laughing before hanging up, since Jess knew how much she hated doing laundry.

After walking the horses to the barn, they went back to the cabin, took down a few games they had found in the cabinet and spent the evening playing games, laughing, and talking. They had decided not to rush their relationship and felt keeping busy would help.

Sam told Kate about the activities that were planned over the next two weeks, while she would actually be on vacation. It included a rodeo and a roundup, both of which she was really looking forward to, as well as, an overnight campout in the mountains and a ghost town.

After a few games, they sat down in front of the fireplace. They talked about where their relationship was now and both hoped their feelings would grow stronger over the next couple of weeks, when they planned to spend a lot of time together.

As Kate sat watching the flames in the fire, wrapped in Sam's arms, she felt wonderful. She was glad the nightmare was finally behind her and she could now look forward to a future that looked promising that she prayed, included Sam.

Mostly she was looking forward to spending more time with Sam and seeing where a relationship with him might go. She was also planning to let her guard down to see if a real relationship was possible with him. She knew she could trust him, which was in his favor and she was pretty sure she had fallen in love with him. He had even said he loved her and she prayed he always would.

Kate had seen too many of her friends go through failed relationships, including Jess, from an unfaithful partner. She hoped she never had to go through something like that and felt with Sam, she never would. He was the cowboy of her dreams and this ranch was the most beautiful place she had ever been.

She was also excited about the idea of possibly moving to Colorado and working at the ranch and with Doc Porter. It would be a dream come true, as she truly loved it here, along with the people she had met and come to know. A lot of possibilities were now in her future and she was happy to know she now had a future to look forward to.

Her faith had grown a lot over the past few days as she knew God had taken care of them all. She was thankful her future was in God's hands now and hoped to keep it that way.

Chapter 12

Kate was surprised she had slept in and the sun was starting to rise as she looked out the window. She looked around for Sam, but he was nowhere in sight; and guessed he was outside feeding the horses. She quickly got up, threw some wood on the fire to break the chill, freshened up and started breakfast.

Sam seemed surprised as he came in. "Quite the sleepyhead this morning, but something sure smells good."

"Sorry about that. I guess all that happened yesterday, wore me out. I did have a wonderful time yesterday after the events with Dylan were over. I especially loved being wrapped in your arms. It helped me to fall asleep knowing you were nearby."

Sam smiled as he pulled Kate into his arms and gave her a kiss. "Hopefully there will be a lot more nights with you in my arms in the future."

"I hope so." Kate replied.

As she turned to finish breakfast, Kate commented. "I'm just glad we were in the shed and not in the cabin. It was hard enough hearing the gun shots and all that happened, without actually watching it."

"Well at least, it's all behind us now and hopefully we'll have an even better day today, now that Ryan and Kevin are no longer hunting you down." Sam said as he sat down to eat.

They kept the conversation light as they finished breakfast and Sam asked if she would like to take the long way back to the ranch and check for any strays. At least today, they would no longer have to worry about Ryan or anyone else shooting at them.

Kate quickly agreed and was looking forward to it, but hoped they wouldn't run into any bears or wolves; or horse thieves either. As soon as they finished breakfast, they cleaned up the cabin, packed everything up to take back to the ranch, locked the door with the new lock Nick had brought, then saddled up. The sun was shining bright and Kate was looking forward to a beautiful day.

There was still some food in the saddlebags, so she was sure they would stop somewhere to eat along the way, and she was looking forward to it. She loved picnicking with Sam. The terrain was beautiful up in the hills where they were, but she had some bad memories of the area too. The nightmare was now over, but she had doubts that the memories would ever go away.

They headed in the direction of the beautiful area at the top of a ravine, overlooking the small lake, but Kate was worried as it was also the path they had taken when they had run across the bear. She finally asked Sam. "Do you think the bear will be gone by now?"

Sam laughed. "It was high-tailing it out of there when I last saw it, so I doubt it came back. Don't worry, if we run across another one today, I'll protect you."

Kate wanted to believe him, but that bear had been quite large and, if they were going to that beautiful lake again, it was also where the mountain lion had almost gotten her. This time, Ryan wouldn't be there to save her, so she would have to keep her eyes open and hoped Sam did too.

It was also where they had found and caught the horse thieves. Although the area was beautiful, it also had some bad memories. She prayed, this time, it would be uneventful.

They rode along in silence for a while and Kate was glad the only bear they saw was off in the distance and heading away from them; and she hoped it just kept going. Kate wasn't surprised Sam stopped when they reached the ridge overlooking the small lake.

"Would you like to have lunch here again?" Sam asked.

The view was phenomenal there, with the mountains reflecting in the lake, so Kate didn't hesitate to respond. "Sounds wonderful. It's so amazing here."

"We still have plenty to eat, as long as you don't mind sandwiches again and we'll have a real meal tonight at the gathering hall." Sam said as they rode over to the clearing where they had eaten before and dismounted.

Sam retrieved the tablecloth from his saddle bag and then handed Kate some food and water, before he spread out the tablecloth and they sat down. They had just finished when Kate noticed some movement by the lake. She watched for just a few moments, before mentioning it to Sam.

Sam was surprised to see a small herd of cattle, although only a few, he couldn't remember seeing any cattle the other day when they had rounded up the horses, but it was possible the horse thieves had run them off while getting the horses.

He thought they could round them up and take them to the ranch with them. It would be a few more they wouldn't have to get during the roundup.

Sam turned to Kate and asked. "So, are you ready to continue our ride back to the ranch?"

Kate laughed. "I'm ready for a nice quiet ride to the ranch."

Sam then handed Kate a pair of binoculars. "Did you notice the moose, deer and pronghorns at the end on the valley?"

"The what? I've never heard of a pronghorn before." Kate responded.

"Look near the other end of the lake. It looks similar to a deer, but its horns are shorter and pointed."

"Oh, I see them. They do look a little different from the deer; and there's a big moose there too." Kate replied excitedly. "It's hard to believe all the wildlife around here."

They mounted up and headed down into the valley to get the small herd of cattle. They were almost in position when they heard a low growl and turned to see a huge bear, standing where they had eaten lunch. It dropped to all fours and started running toward them.

Sam pulled out his gun and shot toward it, but it only slowed for a moment. The cattle had also heard the gunshot or smelled the bear and they had started running. The gunshot no doubt, would keep them running. Luckily, they were running toward the pass that led to the ranch.

After another gunshot, that didn't seem to slow the bear, Sam reached into his saddlebag and threw the leftover food behind him, as he and Kate rode fast behind the cattle. He hoped the food would slow or stop the bear so they could get out of range; and thankfully, it worked. As soon as the bear smelled the food it stopped and started eating and forgot all about them.

Kate had been frightened by the bear and was thankful when it finally stopped, but now she was worried because they had started through the pass where the mountain lion had been. She diligently watched the rocks as they rode through.

The cattle had slowed and they now had to coax them through the pass. She would much rather they could run, but she hadn't seen anything moving, except a few birds that had possibly been startled by them. She was truly thankful when they emerged from the pass with no incidents.

Sam turned to Kate and remarked. "You're not supposed to feed the bears, but I felt, under the circumstances, it was better the food, than us, and I really didn't want to shoot it."

Kate laughed. "I totally agree. I just hope that's the last one we see today or anytime while I'm here."

As they rode on, they ran across a few more cattle and quickly rounded them up and headed them toward the ranch. Kate thought the mountain lake was beautiful, but she didn't think she would be in any hurry to return to that area anytime soon. Too much had happened there, between being shot at, a mountain lion, horse rustlers, and now a bear.

Kate loved wildlife and all animals, but not when they were after her. She also knew the rangers needed to have access to the area for the fire tower, but she didn't want anyone using the tower for target practice, especially using her as the target again. Sam had possibly saved their lives today by thinking of the food, that fortunately, had stopped the bear and she was grateful.

Kate was happy when the ranch came into view and nothing else had happened along the way. She was looking forward to having dinner tonight at the gathering hall and for the companionship.

She knew the food was great there but nothing could compare to the wonderful steaks and fish, cooked over an open fire, they had eaten at the cave and cabin. She wondered why Sam had been so quiet on their ride back to the ranch and thought maybe he had just been thinking about all that had happened, as she had.

**

Sam had been thinking about all that had happened. He had really been frightened when the bear hadn't stopped when he shot towards it and was thankful it had stopped to eat the food he had thrown out. He hadn't been worried about his own safety, but about Kate's.

He was already so crazy about her and knew he loved her, but was that enough. They had talked last night about spending more time together and possibly having a future together, but for how long? He knew she cared, but doubted she loved him enough to stay for long in a small cabin at the ranch. It was only a dream that would probably never happen.

He needed to get away from her for at least a little while, so he could get his feelings for her under control. Instead of spending more time with her, he felt it would probably be better to try to avoid her instead. Now was as good a time as any and besides he was going to be very busy getting the horses and men ready for the visitors arriving on Sunday.

Kate would have her friend Jess to keep her company after she arrives on Sunday, anyway, so she probably wouldn't make time for him. It was going to be hard, but he knew he had to do it if he was going to survive once she left.

Sam had called ahead for the gate to an empty corral to be opened and when they got there Kate was happy to see some ranch-hands come out to help them get the cattle into the corral. They had been more difficult to deal with than the horses they had brought in, and they moved a lot slower.

Once they got to the barn, they dismounted and Kate walked Choco to his stall, unsaddled him, put some feed in his trough and started brushing him while he ate. Sam had told her, he wanted to check out the calves they had brought in, so she took care of Choco as she waited for him to return.

She was hopeful all the cattle had survived the run from the bear, and since they hadn't found any left behind as they followed them through the pass, she felt they had all made it. She thought it strange Sam hadn't ask her to go with him, but didn't ask.

Sam hadn't returned by the time Kate was finished grooming Choco so she walked toward another horse barn. She noticed a corral with horses she hadn't seen before and a beautiful, light-colored palomino colt. She wished she could take it back to Indiana, but knew that would be impossible. Maybe Jake would sell him to her, if she stayed in Colorado.

Unlike most of the other foals, the palomino colt had remained calm as she walked over to it, which was unusual for one that had been raised in the wild and never handled before. She wished Sam would let her name him, because she had already thought of a good name for him.

She felt that Dax, which meant strong and courageous, was the perfect name since the colt had been courageous enough to let a human touch it without the slightest battle even though he was slightly larger and possibly a little older than the other foals.

Sam finally met up with her and as they walked to the cabin, Kate mentioned the palomino colt to Sam and asked if she could name him. He only hesitated for a moment before responding, he was sure Jake wouldn't mind, which made her happy and she told him she had chosen the name, Dax, and why.

Sam thought it sounded very fitting for the little colt. He had been watching while Kate checked out the foals and had noticed how calm the palomino colt had been, but how it had held its head high. He told her she could tell Nick and Jake tonight at dinner and he was sure it wouldn't be a problem. Coming up with so many names around there for the horses had always been a challenge and he was sure Jake would like help naming the foals.

Kate was surprised when Sam, grabbed the things out of his room, then left her at the door of the cabin and didn't kiss her. He just left and said he would try to meet her at dinner tonight, but not to wait on him. Kate was surprised because dinner was still several hours away.

It was so unlike him, and he had been quiet most of the way back to the ranch and on their walk to the cabin. He had even taken his things from the room he had been staying in. She didn't understand and hoped later they would have a chance to talk.

Kate freshened up, then sat in the chair near the fireplace and called Jess. She knew Jess would probably be home since it was Saturday, unless she was still riding. She really needed someone to talk to who might understand her situation with Sam, so she was relieved when Jess answered.

"Hey Jess, have a minute to talk?" Kate asked.

"Sure, I need a break anyway. What's up? Are you okay?" Jessica asked.

"Actually, I'm feeling much better and even slept in today. Things here are a lot calmer, except for the bear we ran into on the way back to the ranch."

"Another bear?" Jess shouted.

"Yes. After lunch we went down into a valley with a beautiful lake and saw a moose, some deer, and pronghorns."

"What is a pronghorn?" Jess asked.

"That's the same question I asked Sam. They look similar to deer but with short pointed horns. Hopefully you'll get a chance to see one while you're here.

232

Anyway, when we went down into the valley to round up a small herd of cattle, we heard a low growl and looked back to see a huge bear where we had just been. It headed toward us and the cattle stampeded when Sam took a shot toward it.

It didn't stop, so Sam took another shot at it, but it didn't seem to faze it, and it kept coming. The funny part was when Sam threw out the food that was left over from the cabin, it just stopped and sat down to eat. I was relieved and it definitely made for an interesting ride back to the ranch." Kate replied.

Jess laughed. "I'm sure it was frightening, but something cool to see." She then became serious. "But something is bothering you, I can hear it in your voice."

"It's Sam." Kate answered hesitantly.

"Is he alright?" Jess asked.

"Yes, it's just, well, he's just acting different. He was so quiet on the way back and he seems to not care anymore; I mean not like he did, not like when he told me he loved me."

"He told you he loved you?" Jess screamed excitedly.

"Yes, when we were at the cabin. He kissed me and told me he loved me. But, at the time, everything was happening and I wasn't sure about what was going to happen to me, so I didn't tell him how much I love him."

"He's been through a lot since you arrived, Kate. You both have. If he told you he loved you, while he was under so much stress, he probably meant it.

I doubt his love has or will change, but now that things have calmed down, he may be analyzing his feelings since they happened so quickly. He may also be trying to figure out if you feel the same about him too, since you haven't told him."

"So, you think I should tell him how I feel?" Kate asked.

"Definitely; if you're sure you really love him, he needs to know it so he has all the facts while he's trying to understand how he really feels about you. Before you tell him though, be sure you understand your feelings. It all happened very quickly." Jess responded.

"I don't have any doubts about how I feel about him." Kate said. "I think I've loved him since the first time I laid eyes on him. It's like he's the cowboy I've dreamed of all my life and a man I know for sure I will always be able to trust."

"Kate, I've got to go, but I think you should tell him how you feel and I can hardly wait to meet him." Jessica replied.

"Thanks Jess. I can't wait for you to meet him too. I know you'll understand why I fell in love with him. You're going to love it here and I have someone special I want you to meet." Kate said.

"Oh, no you don't. I'm not ready for another heart-breaking relationship. Men you can trust are too hard to find and two weeks is definitely not enough time to build a lasting relationship. I'm glad you found a man to love and you can trust, though. I wish you the best. See you Sunday."

As she hung up the phone, Kate knew Jess was right. She needed to let Sam know how she felt, if she wanted a real relationship and future with him, which she did. Hopefully they would have a chance to talk tonight and over the next two weeks their relationship would grow, like they had talked about at the cabin. She was still going to try to fix Jess up with Nick because she knew they would be perfect together.

Jess had been hurt by an unfaithful partner and had basically stopped dating. The fact Nick was Sam's best friend and Jess was hers, would make it even better if they got together. She knew Jess needed to get out in the dating field too and hoped her dream cowboy would be Nick.

After Kate finished her call with Jess, she pulled out her computer. She had received messages from several friends and family members over the last week who had heard about her brother, Mike, but she hadn't responded to any of them. She decided it was time to finally update them and let them know she and Mike were safe, so she sat down to send a group email message, which would be quicker and easier.

It was difficult trying to find the words and even more difficult holding back the tears as she relived her ordeal and typed it as briefly as possible. The wonderful weekend in Las Vegas visiting with her brother, watching him be shot, being on the run, meeting the wonderful people at the ranch, and finally, a little bit about what had happened at the cabin to end her terrible nightmare.

She left out the messages and gory details. She didn't want to face reliving them or putting it into words. It had been hard enough writing what little she had written. She had left out meeting Sam and falling in love. She wanted to tell him first and see if he still wanted a relationship with her. She didn't know what had happened, but hoped they could work it out.

By the time Kate had finished her email, she was ready to get up and out of the cabin for a while, so she headed to the barn. She couldn't find Sam anywhere, so she walked out to one of the corrals. She noticed the black horse, she had thought Jess would like, standing near the fence around one of the corrals, so she walked over to him. She was surprised as she petted him, as he seemed so calm. He was definitely an outstanding horse.

Kate was surprised as someone walked up behind her and turned to see Sam's dad. "Mr. Nelson, it's so nice to see you."

"That's John. Mr. Nelson makes me sound old."

"But you're not old. Just in your prime." Kate said.

"Thank you. Flattery will get you everywhere." John said with a smile. "That's a beautiful horse there, isn't it?"

"Yes. It's just too bad no one has been able to ride him." Kate replied.

"Someone will someday, and he'll make a wonderful horse for them." John said.

"I think you're right. You haven't seen Sam around anywhere, have you?" Kate asked.

"I saw him ride out earlier, but I haven't seen him come back yet." John said. "If you're wanting to go for a ride, I'd be glad to join you. I get pretty tired of sitting around here sometimes."

"I'd love to join you for a ride." Kate said. "Just give me a minute to saddle Choco."

"We've got guys around here who can saddle him for you." John responded.

"Not necessary. I've been riding and saddling my own horses since I was a youngster. I grew up on a farm where my parents raise Black Angus cattle. All of us kids had our own horse." Kate said.

"How many is all?" John asked.

"I have three younger brothers and a sister. My older half-brother was the one who was shot. My friend Jess, also moved in with us when her parents were killed in a car wreck when she was sixteen."

"Wow, your parents must be something else. I thought I had it bad raising just two boys."

"But you've done a great job with both of them." Kate said.

"Thank you. I'm proud of them both. Let's get saddled up and take that ride." John responded.

They rode along for a while talking about family and the ranch. Then John asked if she would like to get down for a bit and stretch their legs and Kate didn't refuse.

It took a moment, before John finally said. "Has Sam ever told you much about his mother?"

"No, just that she wasn't around." Kate replied.

John hesitated for a few moments before he responded. "I think there's something you need to know, because if I'm not mistaken, you two have become very close. Actually, I think Sam is in love with you, and I can't say as I blame him."

"Thank you, John. I love him and I think he loves me too, but for some reason he suddenly seems to be backing away. I don't know what I've done and it worries me. I know our feelings for each other have happened really fast, but I thought he was hoping in the next two weeks to see where our relationship would go. It now makes me wonder if it will go anywhere." Kate responded.

"Sam and Joey's mother left when Joey was two and Sam was nine. Sam took it very hard, but his mother didn't like ranch life and made it pretty clear she wasn't happy. She up and left leaving me with the boys and she's never seen them since."

"John, I'm so sorry." Kate said.

"Water under the bridge. My sister moved in with us until Joey was five, then she married one of the ranch-hands. She's stayed around and would babysit off and on for a while, but when she moved out, Sam was hurt again, although he tried not to let it show.

Around here, you see a lot of marriages on the rocks, including Nick's. He and Cory grew up together and ended up getting married right out of high school. She was never happy living on the ranch either, so she ran around on Nick, trying to find someone to take her away from here.

She finally succeeded, but the day she left, she was in a car accident and didn't survive. Nick took it really hard and then got into a mess with his last girlfriend. She was a real work of art.

Anyway, what I'm trying to say is, I think Sam really loves you, but he is truly afraid of commitment. He's afraid if he was to marry you, he'd only be hurt when you left, like his mother, his aunt, Nick's wife, and a few others around here. Ranch life is definitely not for everyone.

If you really love him and are sure you would be happy living on a ranch, then I will wish you both the best, but if this type of life is not for you, then it's best to let him go now." John said.

Kate thought for a few moments and then responded. "I truly love Sam and I grew up on a farm with cattle and horses and that's the life I love. This is the most beautiful place I have ever been to. It's like a dream come true for me.

I became a large animal vet, because this is the lifestyle I love. I take marriage very seriously. It's a commitment I believe in and I don't believe in divorce, although I know there are times that warrant it. The only reason I'm single now is because I lost my husband when he was overseas in the military."

"Kate, I'm sorry." John said.

"Thanks John. It's been four years and I've accepted it. I believe God brings people into our lives for a reason, even if only for a season and he takes them home or away when they have met his purpose. I truly believe God brought Sam into my life for a reason, and I'm hoping it was for more than just protecting me, unless he's meant to protect me forever."

"That's a nice way to look at things, Kate. I think you two just need to slow down a little and see where your relationship goes. I truly believe you would be perfect for him and hopefully we can both work on him and make him see not all marriages fail. Some are good, like Jake and Sarah had.

I think I'd like having you as a daughter-in-law and I look forward to meeting your parents someday, but I think we'd better head back to the ranch now, before we miss dinner."

"Thanks, John. I think I have a better understanding now and I do hope the love between Sam and I grows, but I think I now know what I need to do to make it happen." Kate said as she gave John a hug and then said. "Let's go. I definitely don't want to miss dinner."

As they headed back, Kate told John about fishing near the cabin and how good the fresh fish had tasted, cooked over the open fire. She then told him about the huge bear they had encountered this morning and how Sam had stopped it by throwing out the rest of the food. "The sound of a bullet didn't stop it, but the food sure did." John seemed to get a real kick out of that story.

She told him how she and Sam had really had a lot of fun and excitement since she'd been there and she was

238

looking forward to more fun over the next two weeks, although she could do with a little less excitement. She wasn't surprised when John laughed.

Once they were back at the barn, they agreed to meet at the gathering hall after stopping by their cabins. Kate was hoping to find Sam at the cabin, since he wasn't at the barn, but he wasn't there. She quickly freshened up but wasn't surprised when the dinner bell rang, and Sam had still not shown up.

She waited a little longer, but finally decided to go to the gathering hall by herself. She filled her plate and joined Nick and Jake at the table and was surprised when they said they hadn't seen Sam either. John arrived shortly afterward and joined them.

Nick said he had run into Sam earlier and Sam had mentioned that Kate had a name she thought would be great for the new palomino colt. He asked her what the name was and Kate didn't hesitate to tell him she wanted to name the colt Dax and what the name stood for and why she felt it fit the colt so well.

Jake said he thought it was a great name and very fitting from what Sam had said about the colt. He then told her to feel free to name all the foals she wanted, as coming up with names was one of the hardest things to do with there being so many young colts and fillies each year at the ranch.

Kate laughed. "I'll keep that in mind. I understand it would be hard thinking up new names when there are so many. I don't envy you that job, but I think Joey could be a great help in that area too. He has already named one colt and one calf that I know of."

Jake laughed. "I heard that too. Snowball and Lucky, wasn't it?"

Kate laughed too. "And they were very fitting names. Snowball is all white and Lucky wasn't expected to live."

Kate hadn't been at the table long, when she saw Joey come in and was glad when he joined them. She asked Joey, "Is Sam with you?"

"No, he said to tell you he wouldn't be here tonight for dinner. He grabbed a sandwich earlier so he could check on the horses that came in today and said he would see you in the morning for breakfast." Joey replied.

"Thanks Joey. I'm sure I can talk with him tomorrow." Kate was hurt and wondered what had changed to cause Sam to no longer want to be with her. Talking with John had helped and she understood more now of why he might be trying to back off, but it didn't make it any easier.

Hopefully she could get him to open up tomorrow and she could tell him how she felt about him. She was worried though that it might not work out the way she wanted it too.

Kate tried to carry on a conversation with everyone at the table and not let her disappointment show, but it was hard. Trying to keep the conversation light, Kate looked at Nick "I'm looking forward to my friend, Jess arriving here on Sunday. I think you'll like her."

Nick laughed. "I'm sure I will if she's anything like you."

Kate noticed Nick seemed to be troubled. "Nick, is everything alright? I haven't caused anything else bad to happen, have I?"

"No Kate, It's not you. I just received a cable from someone I hoped was out of my life for good, and she's arriving tomorrow."

Kate remembered what Joey and Sam had said about Nick's last girlfriend and if that was who he received the cable from, she could see why he was upset. "Can't you just call her and tell her not to come?"

"That would make it a lot easier, but I already tried and her number's been changed. I don't know why she is coming back. I told Jackie last fall she wasn't welcome here anymore."

"Perhaps you could meet her at the airport and tell her to get back on the plane." Kate suggested.

"That sounds like a great idea, but I know she'll be flying in on a private plane and I don't know what time it will be arriving, so unless I spend the day at the airport, I'd probably miss her. She didn't say what time she would be here." Nick said with an emphasis on the 'private plane'.

"I'm sorry Nick, if there's anything I can do to help, let me know."

"Just pray. Maybe God can change her mind." Nick asked.

"I'll do that." Kate responded.

Nick then excused himself to go to the barn. Kate knew he had a lot on his mind with getting ready for all the guests arriving on Sunday, and now Jackie unexpectantly arriving. It was no wonder he was worried.

Kate listened to the other conversations for a little while then excused herself and walked around for a short time praying about Nick's problem and trying to think of a way to help. She ended up at the creek that ran beside the cabin, which she found comforting. She hadn't paid much attention to it before, but now, without the stress of someone possibly watching her, she could actually listen to the water as it raced across the rocks. She just wished Sam was here with her.

She had followed the path up to the road, the night she had tried to leave, but she hadn't noticed the path going the other direction led to a beautiful lake in the valley. Knowing how much Jess loved morning runs, she was sure it would be a perfect place for her to run.

Kate finally walked into the cabin. She looked in the room where Sam had been staying and noticed the bed was made and Sam's things were gone. She wondered why he had moved out so suddenly.

Was it because she no longer needed his protection or he knew Jess would be coming on Sunday to share the cabin with her. She stared at the bed for a few minutes, wishing he was there and then turned, locked the door to the cabin, then went to her room, and crawled in bed.

It was lonely without Sam nearby and she wondered if her life would always be without him or if he could find it in his heart to still love her after all that had happened. She wished he was there so they could talk, but she would have to wait until tomorrow. Maybe she could get him to go for a ride so they could be alone. She decided she would work on it in the morning.

All kinds of scenarios raced through her mind and she didn't understand what had happened for him to back off so suddenly, instead of talking with her. She finally turned out the light, pulled up the covers, and cried herself to sleep.

Chapter 13

The sun was just coming up when Kate woke up and she was surprised Sam was nowhere in the cabin. She then remembered he had moved his things out and that Joey had told her Sam would meet her at breakfast in the morning. She prayed Sam would be there and willing to talk with her. She hadn't expected to miss him so much.

She felt much better than she had for a while and thanked God for relieving the stress she had been under over the last week and for being with them, especially when Dylan and his men had shown up. It was hard to believe it was finally over, but she would never forget the fear she had experienced. She prayed she would never have to go through something like that again.

As she laid out her clothes, she began to wonder about the money that had caused all the problems. It was hard to believe her brother had gone from one bad situation of using drugs to dealing and hurting others. The scripture in the Bible that states *'money is the root of all evil'* really held meaning to her now.

It had almost cost her brother his life, her life and Ryan's life. With it being drug money, its hard telling how many other lives the drugs had ruined or taken. It made her sad to think how greed and the love of money could harm so many people.

Kate looked at her watch and was surprised when she realized it was already seven o'clock. She quickly showered and dressed then went to the gathering hall to see if Sam was there. She opened the door and looked around at the table where Jake, Nick, and John sat, but she didn't see Sam, so she turned and headed back to the cabin.

Sam was walking toward the gathering hall when he noticed Kate walk to the gathering hall, stand in the doorway for just a minute, and then turn and walk back toward her cabin. He wasn't sure why, but he had a feeling she had been looking for him.

He had been trying to avoid her, hoping it would make it easier if they didn't spend so much time together. He loved her, but there was no way he would ever be good enough for her. He could never make her happy, especially at the ranch.

Ranch life was his whole life and he couldn't see himself giving it up for anyone. He had seen the hurt it caused his dad and Nick and wasn't going to let that happen to him. He watched as Kate entered her cabin, and knew he had to check on her.

When Kate reached the cabin, she considered taking a walk, but decided to wait at the cabin since she wasn't sure when or if Sam would show up. The book she had brought with her to read on the plane, was still sitting on the stand beside her bed, so she picked it up and curled up in the comfortable chair in front of the fireplace. She hoped it would get her mind off everything that had been happening in her life recently and of course off Sam.

Unfortunately, it was a murder mystery and immediately brought back the memories of seeing her brother shot. She laid the book aside but she couldn't stop the tears that rolled down her face. She didn't know how long she sat there crying uncontrollably, but it had been long enough to give her the hiccups. She was startled and embarrassed when Sam walked in the door and caught her crying like a baby.

Sam was worried when he found Kate crying as he walked into the cabin. He knew he shouldn't have left her alone so long, but he had needed time to think. Seeing her like this tore at his heart and he quickly ran over to her. "What's wrong Kate? What happened?"

Kate struggled to talk through the hiccups, but it was difficult, so she just pointed to the book, lying on the arm of the chair.

Sam quickly picked it up and glanced at the title on the cover before he looked back at her. "You were reading a murder mystery, after what you've just been though. What were you thinking?"

"It was the only book I had with me." Kate managed to stammer. "And I needed a distraction."

"But a murder mystery, that was crazy don't you think?" He said softly.

"I know." Kate replied. "As soon as I read the first page, it brought back all the memories of watching Mike get shot and I couldn't hold back my tears."

Sam pulled her up and into his arms, struggling to find the right words, but he wasn't sure what they were. He was crazy about her; he knew he loved her, but she was way out of his league and she would never be happy here. He felt he didn't have a chance with her in a lasting relationship and should just give up now, rather than making it worse by spending more time with her, but right now, she needed him.

Kate might care about him, at least for a while, but a backwoods cowboy could never really make her happy any more than Nick had been able to make his wife happy, when she wanted to live in the city. He couldn't even offer Kate a decent home, just maybe a small cabin, and she deserved so much more. "We're all safe now. I know it's been hard on you, but you have to let it go and move on with your life.

Your friend, Jess, will be here tomorrow and you have a wonderful new career to look forward to. Life moves on Kate. Not always the way we want it to, but God has a path for all of us. We must look to the future, not dwell on the past."

Kate wondered why he had omitted mentioning himself in her future, as he had so many times in the past. He had told her he loved her, so what had changed? "I know you're right and I'm really trying to erase the memories and move on, but I also realize they won't disappear overnight. There will always be triggers that cause them to resurface.

I am looking forward to Jess arriving as she loves to stay active so I'm sure we will be too busy for me to dwell much on the past. I am looking forward to my future... and praying you will be a part of it." There, she had said she wanted him in her life, but would it make a difference.

Sam wanted her in his future too, but knew it wouldn't last, very few marriages he knew of ever had. Spending more time with her now would make it harder when she walked away, but was he willing to give up what time they could spend together now? "No one knows the future except God. We just need to bide our time and see where He leads us."

"And pray that the decisions we make are His and not ours." Kate replied, realizing his unexpected hesitancy.

"I agree, so are you ready for breakfast? I left Joey at the hall and told him we'd join him shortly and serving time will be over soon."

"Yes, just give me a minute to throw some water on my face and freshen up. I know I look a mess." Kate replied.

"I'm surprised you're not starving; and you'll always be beautiful to me." Sam said before finding her lips for a quick kiss. He wanted to fight his feelings for her, but it was difficult. God had brought her into his life, maybe just for a short-time, but he wanted to believe they were meant to be together, at least for now.

"Get a move on, I'm starving." He said kiddingly as he released her and gently shoved her toward the bathroom.

Kate quickly got ready, but was worried. She couldn't imagine what had happened to change the way Sam felt about her. He had kissed her, but it wasn't the same, something was missing. She wished she knew how to get his love back and what she had done to make him stop loving her. She thought her prayers of meeting a wonderful, loving cowboy she could trust, had been answered in Sam, but could she have been wrong?

Kate took one look at Sam standing near the window looking out, and decided that now wasn't the time to bring up her concerns, so she ran across the room and out the door as she said to Sam. "Beat you to the gathering hall."

Sam was surprised but immediately followed Kate out the door, racing to catch up with her. She was like a chameleon, going from one mood to another, always trying to hide her feelings rather than being open with him. He didn't feel it would be a good thing for a relationship, but he had decided not to have a relationship with her anyway, hadn't he?

As soon as they filled their plates, they joined Jake, Nick, John, and Joey at the table. Kate was surprised when Sam hardly acknowledged her or talked to her, and it hurt, but she tried not to let it show.

"I was wondering if maybe we could go for a ride this morning." Kate finally asked him.

"Sorry Kate. We're going to be really busy today getting ready for the guests tomorrow." Sam replied.

Kate knew he was still trying to avoid her and wondered why. Had his dad been right or wrong when he had said Sam loved her, but was afraid of commitment? She had to know so she finally asked him. "I need to talk to you about something important, so I was hoping maybe you could get away for a half an hour or so for a short ride."

Sam didn't want to be alone with Kate, not right now when he was making a little headway at trying to let go of his feelings for her. He wondered what she needed to talk with him about. At least he couldn't pull her into his arms while they were on horseback, well, not as easily.

"I can probably manage that." He finally said. "How about I meet you at the barn when you finish eating?"

Kate took one last sip of her coffee. She hadn't felt much like eating anyway, so she replied. "I'm ready now. I don't want to hold you up."

"You haven't finished eating." Sam said.

"That's okay. I wasn't very hungry anyway." Kate responded as she got up.

That worried Sam. Why wasn't she hungry? She was always starving. What had happened? It made him even more curious as to what she needed to talk to him about. "Alright, let's go."

They rode along quietly for the first few minutes, but Sam couldn't hold in his concerns any longer. "What's happened Kate? What's wrong?"

"Do you mind if we get off the horses for a minute? There's a nice spot over there."

"Okay." Sam replied.

Kate had been trying to gather her thoughts, to think of the right words, but nothing materialized. As she got off Choco and walked around to Sam and looked into his eyes, her frustration finally let loose. "I love you Sam and I don't understand why you said you loved me and now suddenly you don't even want to be near me." She tried not to cry, but the tears began to flow down her cheeks.

Sam quickly pulled her into his arms. "I'm sorry Kate. I didn't stop loving you or stop wanting to be with you, but I'm not right for you. You'd never be happy with a dumb cowboy like me. As soon as your life slowed down and you realized what ranch life was really like, you'd leave."

"Sam, I love you and you are not and never will be a dumb cowboy to me. My education didn't make me smarter than you. It just gave me training in different areas. You've had the advantage of hands-on training to prepare you for the job you have and you're great at it or you wouldn't be the foreman."

"Kate, I could never give you all you deserve. I don't own any land and can't give you a nice house for us to raise a family in." Sam responded seriously.

"I don't deserve or want anything more than your love. I don't care about a nice house, as long as I have you to raise a family with. We could live in a tent for all I care. Sam, I love you; that's all that matters to me."

"Kate, I can't offer you anything. I'm a poor cowboy."

"I'm not interested in material things. I only want you to love me, but I guess that's too much to ask." Kate said sadly as she pushed Sam away and walked around to mount Choco.

248

"Kate, wait." Sam quickly responded as he reached for her arm and turned her toward him. His thoughts were a jumbled mess, but he couldn't let her go, not if she truly loved him.

"I've believed all along God brought you into my life for a reason and I prayed he meant you to be with me, but I've had doubts because I didn't feel I was good enough for you. I've wanted to be with you since I saw your photo at the café and fell in love with you the first time, I held you in my arms.

I love you, Kate. I think I'll always love you. I'm sorry I let my doubts lead me away from what I believed to be God's path for us. I should have talked with you first. I truly believe we are meant to be together, but ranch life isn't enough for a lot of people."

Kate now understood, John had been right. Sam's fear of commitment was true, but she needed to let him know, his fears were not justified with her. "Ranch life is all I've ever dreamed of.

I was raised on a farm and loved it, along with all the animals. I wouldn't have gone to school to become a large animal vet, if living on a farm or ranch, wasn't part of my dream life.

I believe we're meant to be together too." Kate responded as she threw her arms around his neck and kissed him. This time his response was what she wanted and was wonderful.

When he finally loosened his hold on her, she asked. "By the way, how big is this family you're talking about?"

"As big as you want Kitten." Sam replied.

"We may need two tents." Kate responded.

Sam laughed as he pulled her back into his arms for a kiss, he hoped they would never forget. "I love you. We have a couple more weeks together, without the stress of the nightmare you've been under. Why don't we see where it leads?"

Kate happily responded, "I think that's a great idea. I love you too and I think it will put us back on God's path for us."

The ride back seemed much too short, but at least it had been worth it as far as Kate was concerned. She couldn't believe Sam thought she was too good for him. He was everything she had ever dreamed of and more. He was someone she felt she could always count on and trust and prayed their love would only grow over the next couple of weeks.

Sam joined Kate to check the horses, foals, and the calf they hadn't expected to live. He was surprised when Kate asked. "Have you talked with Nick and heard that someone named Jackie, that he thought was out of his life for good, is arriving today in a private plane?"

"He mentioned it this morning. It's the mistake of a girlfriend he met after his wife died. Believe me; no one at the ranch is happy about Jackie's return."

"Is she that bad?" Kate asked.

"Bad is definitely an understatement. A redheaded witch is more like it. I've never seen anyone with a temper like hers. If you're smart, you'll avoid her as much as possible." Sam stated.

"From what I've heard I'm sure that's good advice." Kate replied.

They were riding into the ranch when Kate noticed a large limo pulling to a stop and looked over at Sam. "I take it that's the unwelcome guest."

"Good guess. She flaunts her money every way she can." Sam responded.

Kate watched as a beautiful redhead stepped out of the limo. She was dressed in an amazing western outfit that showed off all her curves what little that was covered by it. It must have cost a fortune. "Wow, I can at least see what initially drew Nick's attention. She's beautiful."

"Unfortunately, it's only skin deep. Just beware Kate." Sam replied.

"I'll do my best."

After they unsaddled the horses, they headed to the cabin trying to avoid Jackie, but unfortunately, they weren't quick enough as they heard Nick call out. "Hey Sam, Kate, come here a minute. Someone would like to say 'hi'."

Sam looked at Kate curiously. "Believe me; she does not want to say 'hi' to me. She can't stand me and knows I feel the same about her. I don't know what she's up to, but be cautious."

As they walked up to Nick and Jackie, Kate was very surprised after all she had heard, that Jackie politely said 'hi' to Sam and then extended her hand to her. "Hi, I'm Jackie. I don't think we've met."

Kate was a little leery, but extended her hand. "I'm Kate; it's nice to meet you."

"Well, Kate, I hope we'll get a chance to get acquainted. I just love it here at the ranch with all that goes on. Have you had lunch yet? Nick said they had a lot to do to get ready for tomorrow, so maybe we can hang out for a while and get to know each other."

Kate looked at Sam and then Nick and they both gave her questioning looks as if they didn't understand, so she looked back at Jackie. "That would be fine. I just need to freshen up from my ride. How about I meet you in an hour at the gathering hall?"

"That would be perfect. It will give me a chance to get settled in to my cabin too." Jackie replied.

"Then I'll see you in an hour." Kate responded as she turned to walk to the cabin.

Sam joined her and when they arrived back at the cabin, Kate finally turned to Sam. "I was expecting something completely different. She actually appeared to be very nice."

"She's very good at putting on a good front and I'm sure it helps that you are with me and not Nick, but I'd be careful not to get on her bad side. She's definitely not the kind of person you can trust and I wouldn't put anything past her." Saam responded.

"I try never to get on anyone's bad side, so I should be fine." Kate responded as she put her arms around Sam's neck. "Don't you think?"

"I know you're definitely on my good side and I love it." Sam said as he pulled her close and kissed her. Happy he now knew where he stood with her, at least for now. There was a good chance of their relationship growing and possibly lasting, if she really wanted to live on a ranch or farm, that was in her favor, but he still had doubts.

"I love it too. Will you be joining Jackie and me for lunch?" Kate asked.

"No way, I'm going to grab a bite as soon as the food line opens, so I'm nowhere in sight when she arrives at the hall. Don't be surprised though if she shows up late. She's very well known for her late 'dazzling' entrances.

Kate had to laugh. "I'll keep that in mind. Will I see you later?"

"I'll pick you up around six for dinner. Enjoy your afternoon." He replied as he pulled her into his arms for a kiss before heading toward the door.

"You too. See you around six." Kate replied.

Kate was happy she had gotten Sam to talk with her and hoped she had convinced him of how she felt. She now had hope, they would be spending a lot more time together and stood a chance of building a lasting relationship. His kiss had been a lot better than the quick kiss with no feelings, he had given her earlier and it made her worries disappear, or at least mostly.

Kate hurriedly showered and changed, as she felt a little grubby after checking on the foals and calf, when they had returned from their ride. She made a call to Jess, to let her know, she had a talk with Sam that morning and everything was better between them now. She thanked her for her suggestion to tell Sam how she felt about him since it had seemed to work.

Kate told Jess she was anxious to show her the ranch and introduce her to all the wonderful people. She also told her about Sam's dad, John, and how they were now friends.

She could tell Jess was anxious to get there and was looking forward to meeting everyone. They talked a little longer, and finally Jess said that Emma, Kate's sister, was waiting for her to start exercising the rest of the horses.

Jess said they had just finished exercising her horses and were getting all the horses ready for Emma to take over exercising them tomorrow, and until she and Kate got back from the dude ranch.

Kate was glad her sister was following in her footsteps with her love of horses and she was planning to start college in the fall to become a veterinarian like her. She was proud of Emma for working so hard to reach her dreams.

After hanging up, Kate headed to the gathering hall. She didn't see Jackie anywhere, so she grabbed a cup of coffee and a few pretzels to hold her over while she waited. The little she had for breakfast had worn off and she was getting hungry.

Jake, Nick, John, and Joey joined her at the table and she enjoyed talking with them and learning more about the ranch. She could tell none of them were happy about Jackie being there and they hoped she would leave soon. It appeared Jackie had left a bad impression on everyone at the ranch.

It had been almost an hour and the pretzels were no longer working to keep her hunger at bay. The guys had already eaten and left, so Kate was getting ready to get up and fill a plate, when she noticed Jackie entering the hall.

Jackie was dressed in a different, but also outstanding outfit that put Kate's jeans and sweatshirt to shame. Jackie's smile appeared genuine as she approached, which was unexpected, after all Kate had heard about her.

"I'm so sorry. I just lost track of time after I unpacked and then realized I still needed to freshen up. Are you ready to grab a bite to eat?" Jackie asked.

Kate held back from telling her how hungry she was from waiting so long and that the serving line would be closing shortly. Instead, she politely said. "Yes, that sounds great."

When they returned to the table, Jackie began telling Kate about herself. She said she had come to check on a relative who was near here, so she decided to stop and visit Nick.

Jackie then told her how she and Nick had met in Las Vegas. She said they had a wonderful time at the ranch last year, and she was looking forward to spending more time there to see if she could put their relationship back on track after their little 'tiff.'

Kate had a hard time holding her comments as she listened, knowing full well about Jackie and Nick's escapades the previous year. Nick had finally escorted Jackie off the property and to her plane, once he had sobered up and realized what she was really like.

Nick had taken his wife's death hard, even though she had been leaving him when the accident had happened. His wife, Cory, had hated living on the ranch, even though she had been raised on one. Kate knew, Cory leaving the ranch was one of the reasons Sam was afraid of commitment, and after talking with John, she knew Sam's mother had left the ranch too.

Nick had met Jackie in Las Vegas shortly after his wife died. They had partied heavily and had started a relationship; however, Nick had sobered up not long after they came to the ranch and he realized the mistake he had made in meeting her. Sam had already told Kate all about it when they were at the hunting cabin, but she wasn't about to let on that she knew.

"I hope you two can work out your 'tiff' and you enjoy your time here. Are you planning to stay long?" Kate asked, when she was able to get a word in.

"No, unfortunately I'm only here for a few days; my daddy's getting married again and I have to get back to help with the arrangements. He just wanted me to check on his half-brother first, since he didn't have time to fly out here.

254

"I hope your uncle is alright and you have a chance to visit with him." Kate replied, but was surprised at the strange look Jackie gave her, before she smiled.

"I stopped by and saw him on my way here, but hopefully he will be better soon." Jackie responded. "I'm hoping Nick will attend the wedding with me."

Nick's going to be pretty busy starting tomorrow from what I've heard, but I'm sure he'll try to make it to the wedding, if he can get away." Kate replied.

"I hope so. I never realized how much I missed him until I saw him today. Are you and Sam a thing?"

"We've become good friends since we met and I'm hoping we can build a real relationship, but we'll just have to wait and see." Kate replied.

"I hope it works out for you two. You know, you look kind of familiar. You haven't been in Vegas recently and on the news, have you?" Jackie asked.

"I was in Vegas a couple of weeks ago with my friend Jessica, but only for a few days. I don't know anything about being on the news there." Kate could tell Jackie knew something, but she wasn't about to explain everything that had happened in Las Vegas, especially to a person like Jackie.

"You look exactly like the woman whose picture was in the paper and on the news. She was wanted for killing her brother, but then was stalked by the man who actually committed the murder.

The news said the stalker was finally shot in a battle with a drug-lord here in Colorado. How bizarre is that? It wasn't you he was after, was it?" Jackie said letting Kate know she was sure she was right.

Kate hesitated for a few moments. She wasn't sure she wanted to admit to it, but it was over now. She no longer had anything to worry about, so she finally confessed. "Yes, the guy shot my brother and I witnessed it, so he came after me. Sam and Nick hid me here, but he finally found me. The drug-lord and his men also came looking

255

for me and he shot the guy, but also got shot. At least, only one other person was shot."

"Wow that must have been scary knowing someone was after you. Do you know why he shot your brother or why the drug-lord was here?"

"No, not really. I'm just glad it's all behind me now. It's been like living in a nightmare. I'd rather not talk about."

"I understand. I'm sorry for your loss." Jackie responded.

"I guess we'll never know, with my brother gone; and the two guys who were after me too." Kate stated. She wasn't about to take a chance on letting anyone know her brother and Ryan were still alive, especially someone from Las Vegas.

"Hey, would you like to go for a horseback ride since the guys are busy? Or do you ride?" Kate asked as she was tired of sitting with Jackie and doing nothing.

"Sure, I ride; my daddy has a ranch too, although he spends most of his time at the casino he owns. Sounds like fun. Let's go." Jackie replied.

As they walked to the barn Kate told her about her best friend, Jessica arriving tomorrow, and she was sure everyone was going to like her, as she also loved to ride. Kate was surprised when Jackie gave her another strange look, but wasn't surprised when Jackie walked over to where a beautiful palomino was stalled.

Jackie then called over one of the ranch hands, even though pretty much all of them had scattered when she and Kate had walked into the barn. Jackie pointed to the palomino and said bluntly, "Saddle him for me." while looking irritated at having to call for someone and wait.

Kate was surprised when she looked over and noticed one of the guys was saddling Choco for her. She smiled as she approached him and spoke. "Thank you."

"Anytime Kate, it's always a pleasure helping you."

"I'm glad you feel that way. We're just going to take a short ride. We should be back in an hour or so."

"I'll let Sam know." Then he lowered his voice. "Be careful not to wander too far, especially with her."

"Thanks for the warning. I'll keep it in mind. We'll probably just take a short ride to where Sam and I went earlier. It's really nice there." Kate responded with a serious tone, but she was smiling, as the ranch-hand nodded his understanding.

Kate mounted Choco and Jackie mounted the palomino and they rode out. She figured it best to take the trail she and Sam had taken earlier since she knew the way herself. If anything happened, and Sam tried to look for her, he would know where she had gone.

Kate couldn't believe Jackie was riding in the expensive outfit she had on. It didn't seem practical, but it didn't seem to bother Jackie. At least she was wearing boots, although they were white and looked extremely expensive. She doubted if they were half as comfortable as the ones she had on, which she was glad she had bought at the little general store here on the ranch.

When Jackie finally stopped talking non-stop, Kate started telling her a little bit about her life on the farm in Indiana and going to college. She also told her about her friend, Jess and that she would be joining her at the ranch tomorrow.

"Does Jess live on the farm with you and your family?" Jackie asked.

"She did after her parents were killed in an accident, but she has an apartment now near where she works in Lafayette. It's still near the farm, so she's been taking care of my horses while I've been in college and while I've been here." Kate replied.

"So, she doesn't have any family?" Jackie asked.

"Yes, she has a brother, me, and my family. She's like a sister to me." Kate was surprised at the questions Jackie was asking, but guessed she was trying to make small talk.

After a few more questions, Jackie did most of the talking telling her stories of her family. She told Kate about her real mother, who had finally contacted her a couple

257

years ago, when she was away from home on vacation and her dad wasn't around. Her mother had asked her not to let her dad know she had talked with her because she had promised not to contact Jackie when she had left her dad.

Jackie had thought her mother was dead, so it had been a surprise when she showed up, but her mother had finally convinced her that she was who she said she was. Her mother had told Jackie she was sorry she hadn't been there for her while she was growing up, but she loved her very much.

She had confided that when she left Jackie's father, she hadn't had enough money to fight him for custody, so she had given up. Her mother had regretted her decision and had missed her, but knew she wouldn't have been able to give her all her father had; and she said she had been afraid of him.

Jackie had agreed not to tell her father, since she believed her mother after hearing the rest of her mother's story. She knew her dad and had no doubt of what he was capable of, even though he treated Jackie well.

Jackie was happy her mother had contacted her and they occasionally had a chance to talk now and then. Kate was glad to hear Jackie had a relationship with her mother even if it was brief. She understood Jackie better now and had no doubt why she might need a friend.

Jackie also told her what it was like for her living in Las Vegas and all there was to do there. She even invited Kate to visit some time so she could show her around, but Kate doubted she would ever take her up on the offer. Kate had no desire to ever return to Las Vegas for any reason.

Kate was surprised she had enjoyed the ride and talking with Jackie, although Jackie had done most of the talking. She hadn't expected to like Jackie let alone become friends with her. For some strange reason they had hit it off and seemed to enjoy many of the same things, such as riding and dancing, which they were looking forward to that evening.

258

They were laughing as they rode back into the barn and Kate could tell the guys were surprised. They rushed over to take the horses, not wanting to face the wrath of Jackie. Kate excused herself when she saw Sam near the back of the barn and Jackie left to freshen up for dinner.

Once Jackie was gone, Sam walked up to Kate. "It looks like you enjoyed your ride."

"Actually, I did; a lot more than I expected." Kate replied.

"That's surprising. I never considered Jackie to have enough of a personality to get along with anyone." Sam responded.

"She's had a lot of interesting things happen to her while growing up between the ranch and the casino, where she works for her father. Her stories were actually interesting."

"I don't doubt that. I hope she's not joining us for dinner tonight." Sam said.

Kate smiled as she replied. "I think you are out of luck, if you're planning to eat with Nick. She said she would be at dinner with him, so I figured we'd be with them. I hope you don't mind."

"I do, but I always eat with Jake and Nick, so I guess I don't have much choice. Maybe she'll be late enough we won't have to spend too much time with her and I don't doubt Jake will try to get away before she shows up, too.

He doesn't like her at all and is very irritated that she is here. He knows Nick didn't invite her and he doesn't want her here either, so it will be interesting to see just how long she stays." Sam stated seriously.

"Jackie said today, she would only be here a few days. She had come to see a relative near here and thought it would be a good time to see Nick and try to patch up things from what she called their little 'tiff.' Kate said.

"Little 'tiff'? That's definitely understating it. There's no way Nick would ever consider patching up their 'tiff.' It's too bad she doesn't seem to get the hint and leave now." Sam replied, then asked. "Did you have to wait long for her for lunch?"

Kate smiled. "Yes, I was starving by the time she got there. They were getting ready to close the line for serving and I was getting up to fill a plate when she finally showed up.

I'm glad you told me about her always being late or I would have thought she stood me up and wouldn't have waited. Although I did have great company until shortly before she arrived. They didn't waste any time eating and getting out of there though."

Sam laughed. "It would have served her right for you not to wait. I sure wouldn't have. Are you going to check on the foals?"

"Yes. How are they doing? Is little Snowball still nursing?" Kate asked.

"Yep, he's doing just fine and the others are doing fine too." Sam replied.

"That's good to know. I checked on most of them earlier after our ride, and was glad to see Snowball running around in the stall. I would like to check on Katie and Dax though."

Sam knew who she was talking about and was glad Jake had approved the name she had chosen for the palomino colt. "I take it Jake liked the name you chose?"

"Yes, and he said I could name all the foals I wanted." Kate replied.

Sam laughed. "I don't doubt that. Jake said it was getting harder and harder to think up names for all the horses and was beginning to wonder if numbers might work better."

Kate couldn't image Jake would ever consider numbering his horses, it would be so weird. She thought at least he would know how many horses there were, but at the same time, she was sure there was a turn-around with selling some each year.

"I think using a different letter in the alphabet each year might work better. That way he'd have to only start over every 27 years." Kate said as she laughed then headed toward the stall where Katie and her mother had been and was surprised it was empty. "What happened to Katie and her mom?"

Sam laughed. "They were turned out in the small corral for exercise today since they are doing much better. They're fine though. I like your idea, but how many names can you come up with that start with a Q or X?"

"Well, maybe he could skip those, but we could always suggest it to Jake." Kate wanted to finish checking on the foals and mares that had been in her care before they had left for the hunting cabin, and afterwards she headed for the corral to check on Dax.

It was great being here and getting a chance to see so many horses and all the activity going on around them. Several ranch-hands were riding horses trying to get them ready for the guests who would be arriving tomorrow, so there was a lot of activity in and around the barn.

Sam followed her to the corral, where they checked on Dax and she admired how much stronger he appeared. Katie and her mom were also there, and she was glad to see Katie running around.

They had just left the corral where Dax was, when Sam pulled her into his arms and fell back with her into a stack of hay and kissed her. She could have stayed there forever, but with other ranch hands around, she was embarrassed. She grabbed a handful of hay and stuffed it down his shirt and everyone started laughing.

After Sam practically buried her in the hay, she finally managed to jump up and started brushing herself off. Sam quickly joined her and then started pulling hay from her hair as they laughed. She did the same for him for a few minutes but there was so much hay she finally gave up. "I think I need to take a shower again and see if I can get the rest of the hay out of my hair."

Kate laughed as she looked at Sam. "I think you need to do the same. You kind of remind me of a scarecrow."

"That bad, huh?" Sam questioned.

"That bad." Kate responded.

"Okay, I'll see you at the gathering hall around six." He gave her a quick kiss and walked over to talk with some of the ranch-hands.

Kate walked out to the corral to check on the black gelding, she had thought would be perfect for Jess and she wished he wasn't so wild. She was surprised when he raised his head and then headed toward her. She was even more surprised when he hung his head over the fence and she was able to pet him. It was hard to believe it was the same horse, that had thrown several of the men who had tried to ride him.

Maybe someday, after Jess arrives, they would have a chance to work with the gelding. He was such a beautiful horse. He was all black, except for a small, almost perfect white star on his forehead. Kate wasn't sure if he had been named or if any other horse had the name 'Star' but she felt it would be a perfect name for him.

She left the black horse and headed to the cabin. She could still feel the hay in her hair, although Star had helped her get rid of some of it, and was sure it would probably take a while to get the rest out.

Kate was surprised when Sam joined her as she was walking toward the cabin. She wondered if the pool was open since the guests would be arriving tomorrow. "Sam, is the pool at the lodge open yet and is it heated?" As she thought about the new bathing suit, she had purchased her first day at the small ranch store.

"I'm sure the inside pool is open and heated. Would you like to go for a swim? There won't be life guards yet, but I could be your life guard."

"I'll always love having you as my life guard. I need to get this hay out of my hair first, but I'd love to go for a swim after that, if you can spare a little time." Kate responded.

"Sounds great. I need to get the hay out of my hair too. How about I stop by the cabin when I'm done and we can walk over together?"

"I'll be ready and looking forward to it." Kate replied.

Sam left Kate to get ready and told her he would see her in half an hour, which should give them an hour or so to swim before dinner. He hadn't been swimming in quite a while and was really looking forward to it; and he was especially looking forward to seeing Kate in a bathing suit. He was surprised she had a bathing suit, but remembered she had told him she had picked one up when she had purchased some other clothes, when she had first arrived.

***

It had been hard getting all the hay out of her hair, but Kate was finally ready to head to the lodge and take a swim. Sam was right on time and Kate couldn't wait for them to get to the pool. She loved swimming, almost as much as she loved horseback riding and hiking. It wasn't quite warm enough outside to go swimming, but with an indoor, heated pool, she felt it would be wonderful.

Once they got to the pool, Kate removed her jacket and sandals and walked to the edge of the pool. She was surprised as she then heard a wolf-whistle and turned around to face Sam.

"Wow!" Sam said. "You look amazing. I think we should come swimming more often. I also love the horses on your suit. It's really you."

"Thank you. I couldn't believe I found such a perfect suit when Joey and I went to the ranch store. I'm glad you like it." Kate replied.

"And I like you in it." Sam replied as he pulled her into his arms and gave her a kiss.

Kate didn't want the kiss, or being in Sam's arms, to end, but as soon as he released her, she dove into the pool. It was wonderful, but wasn't as warm as she expected. When Sam asked how the water was, she couldn't help but respond. "It's wonderful, come on in and join me."

Sam quickly dove in and when he surfaced, he immediately said. "I thought you said the water was wonderful; it's freezing."

Kate laughed. "It is wonderful though. I think it just needs a little more time to warm up. How about we swim a few laps and see if that helps warm us up?"

"Sounds good to me, but if that doesn't work, I'm sure I could help warm you up." Sam replied, as he pulled her into his arms for a kiss.

"I like that idea too, but let's get in a few laps first, since we're already here and see if it helps."

Kate then started swimming toward the opposite end of the pool and Sam joined her. She was surprised when she came up after a few laps, to see Nick standing at the edge of the pool. She had finally warmed up and was enjoying the swim and was sure Nick would too.

"Hey Nick, come in and join us. The water is wonderful." Kate said as she looked over at Sam and smiled.

"I didn't want to impose, but when Sam mentioned it, I thought it might be a good place to hide out for a while. I can only tolerate Jackie for so long before I have to get away. You don't mind, do you?" Nick asked.

"Not at all." they both answered looking at each other playfully.

They watched as Nick dove into the pool and both laughed when he quickly came up out of the water and stood up.

"I thought you said it was wonderful! It's cold!" Nick said, surprised, noticing that Kate and Sam were both laughing.

"It's not so bad after swimming a few laps, but I think the temperature needs to be turned up a little more before the guests arrive tomorrow." Sam responded.

"Believe me, I'm going to let the staff know. How about a race to the end of the pool and back?" Nick asked.

"I'm game!" Kate and Sam both said simultaneously.

Kate quickly said "1, 2, 3, go." And they all took off.

Nick finished first and Sam next with Kate close behind. They were all laughing, when they heard the door to the pool area open and Kate noticed Nick's smile completely disappear. Kate turned to see who had entered, pretty much knowing who it would be from the look on Nick's face.

Jackie had found them and was wearing a very skimpy bikini. "I saw you heading this way Nick, darling, so I thought I'd join you. It looks like you're having so much fun."

We had been, Kate thought, then Nick looked over at Kate and Sam and smiled. "Yes, the water is wonderful; and it would be nice to have a fourth for volleyball."

Nick noticed Jackie starting to put her foot in, to walk down the steps. He thought quickly, and stopped her saying. "Just dive in so you can show off."

Jackie smiled and walked over to the spring board. "You're right, I do prefer diving in."

Kate was amazed as Jackie's form was perfect as she did a jack-knife into the pool. Kate couldn't help laughing as Jackie came up looking almost blue, kind of like she, Sam and Nick had all felt when they each dove in.

Jackie's eyes were throwing daggers at all of them. "I thought you said the water was wonderful. It's freezing. I'm leaving and I don't appreciate being laughed at." She said huffily, as she headed for the steps to get out of the pool.

They could all tell Jackie was angry, and not doing a good job of trying to control her anger.

"It's just fun Jackie." Nick said. "We all had the same experience. It is good once you swim a few laps and warm up."

"Well, I'm not interested in trying to warm up or be a fourth for volleyball." Jackie said as she stepped out of the pool, grabbed a towel and her coverup, before stomping toward the door.

Nick had his smile back as he turned to them. "Thanks, Sam, Kate, I think this was a wonderful idea. How about that volleyball game. Me against the two of you. I think that should even up the game."

"You're on." Sam said

Sam went to get a volleyball net and a ball from the storage room, and it didn't take long for them to put the net up and start playing. Nick and Sam didn't know Kate had played volleyball in high school, especially since she hadn't done very well when they had played the other day.

They were amazed at how well she played. Kate knew the warm up practice at the volleyball game the day of the practice rodeo had definitely helped.

Nick finally gave up after being skunked twice. "OK, I think I learned my lesson. Never underestimate your opponents, especially when they have a wringer." Nick said.

"I haven't played since high school, other than last Sunday and I'm definitely not a wringer, but I always enjoy a good game of volleyball. Maybe we can try again after Jess arrives and you won't be outnumbered." Kate replied. "She was really good at volleyball too, when we were in high school.

"I'll look forward to it; and if she's anything like you I'm sure I will enjoy meeting her." Nick responded before he grabbed a towel, dried off a little, put on his jacket and boots, and then headed for the pool door. Before he left, he let them know he was stopping by the front desk on the way out to have someone take care of turning up the thermostat on the pool.

Kate and Sam both laughed, then decided to stay a little longer swimming and playing around. They finally decided to get out of the pool and get ready for dinner; hopefully they would be finished eating by the time Jackie showed up, if she did show up.

They hadn't meant to make Jackie angry, but had just been teasing her in fun. They had all accepted the teasing when they had first gotten in the pool, but Jackie hadn't considered it fun. It appeared her sense of humor was lacking when it came to joking around, but at least Nick had really been happy to see her leave and they had a great time playing volleyball.

Sam walked Kate to her cabin, gave her a kiss, then told her he would be back to get her for dinner in about half an hour. He hoped it would be long enough for her to get ready, as he really wished they didn't have to tolerate Jackie at dinner. He kind of hoped Jackie wouldn't show up at all and would just pack her bags and leave, but he doubted they would get that lucky.

He was glad he had taken the ride with Kate this morning and now knew where he stood with her. He still wasn't sure their relationship would last, but they could at least have some great times together, like today at the pool. Kate was so much fun, especially now that her traumatic experience was over.

Sam wondered if their relationship would grow over the next two weeks and if so, whether he would be able to take a chance on asking her to marry him. He wanted her in his life, but how long would it last? Was he willing to take the chance? Even if it turned out to be only two weeks, he was going to enjoy every minute he could with her. His idea of avoiding her had only made him miserable. He had missed holding her in his arms and kissing her. He wanted her in his life for as long as possible.

Chapter 14

It was almost six and Sam would be arriving soon, so Kate took one last look in the mirror and thought it was too bad she only had jeans and a sweatshirt to wear. She knew Jackie would be dressed to the hilt.

At least she would have a little more variety once Jess arrived tomorrow with her clothes. She had never thought much about her wardrobe before and jeans and a t-shirt or sweatshirt had always been comfortable and fine as far as she was concerned, but was it good enough for Sam, she wondered.

She didn't have to wait long for the answer; when Sam walked into the cabin, he noticed Kate looking in the mirror and commented. "No worries, Kate, you're as beautiful as ever, and perfect for me." He then walked over and took her in his arms and kissed her.

Kate was happy Sam thought she was beautiful and hoped he always would. She could have stayed wrapped in his arms forever, but she knew he wanted to get to the gathering hall and hopefully finish eating before Jackie arrived.

She had been fortunate Jackie hadn't shown Kate her bad side, other than at the pool. At lunch and on their ride, Jackie had been nice and interesting to talk with or at least listen too, but her stories had been interesting. She just hoped Jackie had calmed down and wouldn't create any problems at dinner.

Sam and Kate talked for a few minutes, then headed for the gathering hall. They were both hungry from a busy day and swimming, so it didn't take long to fill their plates and head to the table. Jake, Nick, John, and Joey were already there, but so far there was no sign of Jackie.

Kate was happy to see a smile on John's face as she and Sam sat down together and were smiling and laughing. She could tell he seemed happy to see them together.

"Chow down." Jake said, as if very annoyed. "No since in waiting on our other 'unwanted' guest to arrive. I don't think she has ever been on time to anything before and she'll probably even be late to her own funeral."

Kate was surprised as she had never seen or heard Jake this upset before. She understood why after hearing all the stories from Jackie's last visit, including how badly she had left the cabin she had stayed in.

Kate felt sorry for Jake and especially Nick, as she knew the predicament, they were in. She hoped, under the circumstances, Jackie would be late, really late, in joining them. She had little doubt Jake would disappear once Jackie did arrive. She was surprised she hadn't seen Lorrie this weekend and wondered if that was part of the reason Jake was upset too.

Kate felt maybe changing the subject would help, so she asked him about Lorrie. He said she had taken a vacation to go visit her daughter in Florida, before the weather got to warm there.

Kate then told him she thought Lorrie was a wonderful lady and she was looking forward to seeing her again. She wasn't surprised when Jake smiled and said he thought so too and he was looking forward to her return next weekend.

Kate felt Lorrie was really good for Jake and hoped they might have a future together. She then told Jake about checking on the foals and calf and how they were doing much better.

She also told him about the black gelding, that had thrown the guys the day of the rodeo, and how he had come to her today and seemed so gentle. "It's hard to believe it's the same horse. I noticed he has a white mark on his forehead that is almost a perfect star, so I was thinking his name should be Star, if he hasn't already been named."

The conversation had seemed to work, at least a little as Jake replied. "I'm sorry Kate. I didn't mean to take my frustration out on you. It's just I was hoping we'd never see Jackie again. She is definitely not the nicest person to have around.

And about that gelding, he's pretty ornery and you should probably stay away from him; but with that said, if you think he should be named Star, then that's what his name is. Don't forget what I told you earlier, you're welcome to name as many nameless horses, on this ranch, that you want."

Sam then spoke up. "Kate had a great idea for you naming the horses today. She thought you should use the alphabet, with a different letter of the alphabet each year. That way you would only have to start the alphabet over every 27 years."

Jake laughed. "Not a bad idea, but there are some letters I would definitely need some help with; like Q and X."

Kate smiled as she replied. "That's what Sam said, but I told him you could always skip a letter if you had to."

"Sounds good to me, but I think we'd better consider starting next year as the names you and Joey have come up with, don't start with an 'A' Jake responded.

They all laughed, then Kate responded. "Sound good to me and I will try my hardest to stay away from Star but he seems gentle when no one is trying to ride him.

I understand about Jackie putting you in a bad mood though. I've heard several stories and I know Jackie must have been quite a problem the last time she was here. I hope she doesn't do anything like that again, but she said she was only planning to be here a few days, so hopefully she won't be here too long." Kate replied.

"The fewer hours she's here the better." Jake stated angrily. Calming down he added with a smile, "I want to thank you for checking on the foals and calves, and for all your help around here. You've become a wonderful guest and I'm glad you'll be around for a couple more weeks, at least."

"Well, there's no doubt I've made it interesting since I arrived, but hopefully all the bad experiences are behind us now. Thank you for all you've done to help me through the mess I was in. I've truly enjoyed working with the horses and it's been a great experience, which I'm sure will come in handy when I open my own practice.

I think Star is a great name for the black gelding so I'm glad you like it and if I think of any names for any new horses, I'll let you know. I think Joey would be great at naming the foals too and he is really looking forward to working with Doc Porter in the future."

Joey then spoke up. "That sounds great. I can think of a lot of perfect names. Just let me know when to start."

Jake laughed. "You can start right away; just make me a list. I'm looking forward to you working with Doc Porter too, Joey, but that's a few years down the road." He then turned to Kate. "You know, Kate, you've always got a job here at the ranch if you'd like to start your practice here. I know Doc Porter would really appreciate your help, even if you just worked at this ranch." Jake stated.

"Thank you, Jake. I'll keep it in mind. I love your ranch. It's so beautiful here and the ranch layout is perfect." Kate replied.

"Well, you'd have to thank my wife for that. This was all her idea and she designed the layout with all the cabins for guests and employees, and then later we added the lodge. She loved it here and although she is no longer with us, we've tried to keep her memory alive."

Kate had heard about Jake's wife, who had battled cancer and lost, and about his strong faith that had given him strength and gotten him through the ordeal. "I'm sorry for your loss, but I think you've done a wonderful job of keeping her memory alive. By the way, did Nick tell you about our swim today?"

Jake laughed. "Nick said it was a bit cool and that Jackie hadn't thought it funny, when you all coaxed her to dive in. I wish I had been there to watch. Too bad she didn't just, pack up and leave then, that would have made the day great for all of us."

Suddenly, Jake, along with most of the others at the table, stood up. "Thank you, Kate, for the pleasant company, but I think it's time for me to depart. Our late 'dazzling' guest has decided to bless us with her presence and I'd prefer not having to deal with her. I'll see you in the morning. Take care and try not to get snake-bit."

Kate turned around and noticed Jackie had just entered the gathering hall dressed in another fantastic outfit. She wasn't surprised to see Jake walk right past Jackie, not saying a word, or even acknowledging her existence.

Jackie had arrived just in time to get something to eat. Kate was glad the servers had stopped clearing up when they saw Jackie arrive, because she was sure there would have been a commotion if Jackie hadn't been able to get something.

It wasn't unexpected when Jackie got to the table and sat down next to Nick and told them how dried up and terrible the food looked. Kate was surprised when Nick told Jackie, "If you had arrived before they were closing down, your selection would have been fresher and better." Which didn't seem to faze Jackie in the least.

Kate was amazed at how quickly Jackie's features could turn from irritation to a smile, and her tone turn to sickeningly sweet. "Oh, Nick darling, you know I'm just kidding. The food here is always... interesting, and I'm really looking forward to the band playing tonight so we can dance."

It seemed Jackie had forgotten about the earlier incident at the pool. She had been so angry that Kate had expected her to still be angry or gone. Kate guessed it would have been too easy and made too many people happy if that had happened.

Kate wanted to apologize so she said. "I'm sorry about earlier at the pool Jackie; we were just having fun and we had all experienced the cold water when we dove in. We weren't laughing at you, just hoping you would laugh with us."

Jackie looked at Kate with a smile, but daggers were coming from her eyes, as she spoke. "I understand and I'm sorry I didn't stay around for the volleyball game, if you actually did play volleyball."

Kate responded, trying to keep the conversation light. "Yes; we did play a few games and it was lots of fun. Sam and I took on Nick by himself and skunked him, but I think he still enjoyed it."

"Perhaps I should have stayed, but I was freezing. I don't know how you all stood that cold water." Jackie said.

Sam finally spoke up. "When you live where it's cold, you often end up in cold, wet conditions and swimming in cold water is not unusual."

"I'm not sure I would ever get used to cold water. In Vegas, with a heated pool, you can swim comfortably all year round or jump in the jacuzzi, which is wonderful when the weather is cooler." Jackie responded.

"That sounds wonderful. I guess there's good and bad situations everywhere." Kate said.

Nick then questioned Jackie. "Kate mentioned you had come to visit a relative. I didn't know you had any relatives around here. You never mentioned it when you were here before."

Jackie hesitated for a few moments before she finally answered him. "My dad's half-brother was in Colorado on vacation and had an accident, so my dad asked if I would check on him.

I don't know him very well, but since it wasn't too far from Las Vegas, I told daddy I could check on him. Then I thought since it was so close to your ranch I would stop by and visit you and hopefully straighten everything out between us."

Nick looked at Jackie, and Kate could tell he wasn't happy. "There's nothing to work out between us. It's over. I told you that when you left last fall, so I don't know why you came back."

"But Nick, darling, I've been thinking about you and I don't want it to be over. I think we should give us another chance." Jackie responded with a pout on her face, which Kate felt was pathetic.

Kate thought it was crazy when, not waiting for Nick to respond, Jackie turned to her and sweetly said, "Kate, I so

273

enjoyed our ride today. I am really looking forward to meeting your friend Jess. Do you have a picture of her so I will recognize her when she arrives?"

Kate wondered what Jackie's game was, but she pulled up a photo of Jess on her phone and showed Jackie. Kate was surprised when Jackie showed the picture to Nick and Sam. She then pulled out her phone and took a picture of the photo, which surprised Kate. Jackie then said it would help her recognize her.

Kate could tell by the look on Nick's face, he was impressed and Sam even said "Wow!"

Kate could tell Jackie wasn't pleased, as she commented. "Jess is pretty. I guess I'm going to have to put blinders on Nick when she gets here."

Jackie laughed, but everyone could tell it was fake. she then changed the subject as she handed Kate her phone back. "Didn't you say you were in Vegas when your brother was killed? And that the guy who had really shot him had stalked and kidnapped you?

It was all over the news in Vegas and your photo was on the news for a while. I guess they thought you had killed your brother but then found out it wasn't you but your kidnapper. I'm so sorry to hear it was you they were reporting about."

Kate was surprised Jackie had brought up the shooting again. She could tell by Nick's and Sam's expressions; they were surprised too. Kate tried to play along without giving Jackie any complete answers. "Yes."

"You were actually stalked and then kidnapped?" Jackie asked. "That must have been horrible."

Kate didn't like having to remember her ordeal. It had been terrifying, but replied, hoping it would satisfy Jackie and she would change the subject. "Yes, it was horrible, but I'm okay now."

"But what happened to the man who was stalking you?" Jackie asked.

Kate thought for a moment trying to think how best to answer Jackie without telling her anything she probably didn't already know. "There were two men stalking me. They finally found me, while I was riding and kidnapped me. They took me to a cabin where they had been staying and locked me in a shed that was attached to the house, so I could still hear them talking and arguing.

From what was being said I figured out their boss had shown up and was upset because the men hadn't gotten whatever they were supposed to be getting before getting rid of me. I heard them arguing, so I stayed quiet. The boss told someone to shoot one of them and he'd take care of the other, then I heard four or five shots.

I guess the sheriff had followed them since they were strangers in town, because he showed up and they arrested some of the men. I was let out of the shed and I watched as three men were brought out on stretchers and the other men were handcuffed and put in the sheriff's cars.

I'm not sure what happened, but there were three large pools of blood on the floor. I don't know if any of them were killed, but they all lost a lot of blood, so it's possible. It was really terrible."

"It happened here, at the ranch?"

"It happened at a cabin near here where I had been staying since Sam and Nick had offered to hide me so the men who were after me wouldn't find me."

"I'm glad Nick and Sam were willing to help you. I'm sure it helped." Jackie said and then asked. "You didn't know any of the men or what they were after?" Jackie then asked as if horrified.

Kate tried to be evasive and not give away any knowledge of the money. "No. I recognized two of the men brought out on stretchers. One was the man who shot my brother and the other, was the man who helped him kidnap me while I was out for a ride, but I'm not sure who the third man was.

I thought they were after me since I saw the one who shot my brother, but I don't know why their boss showed up and the shooting began. They were all his men from what it sounded like."

275

Kate could tell Sam and Nick were surprised at her story by their raised eyebrows, so in hopes of ending the questioning she hadn't really expected, Kate finally said. "That's all I know, and I prefer not to have to relive it again. I want to put it all behind me and pray nothing like that ever happens again."

"I'm sorry your brother was killed, Kate. It sounded like such a horrible thing to happen when it was on the news; I was just curious after finding out it was you. I can't believe it all really happened; and here. I'm glad you're alright now and no one else was hurt."

"Thank you, so am I." Kate replied, then was relieved when Jackie changed the subject.

Kate could tell Sam and Nick were also relieved as Nick gave a nod and a smile, while trying to conceal it from Jackie. Kate had no doubt Sam felt the same way as he gave her hand a slight squeeze under the table.

Jackie then went on and on about her father and his upcoming wedding to a woman she knew was only after his money like her father's other wives, except maybe her mother. She was sure she had her pegged right, she was young and pretty, just like the others.

Jackie had tried to talk her dad out of marrying the woman, but he wouldn't listen and had forbid her from saying anything to his future bride or he would cut off her allowance. He had bought her a beautiful condo though and let her move out. She knew it was his way of getting her out of the way, but she said she loved being on her own.

Fortunately, the music started and Sam quickly stood and asked Kate to dance. She knew he had been irritated since Jackie had arrived, so she didn't waste any time before jumping up and joining him. She loved being in his arms and was really looking forward to dancing with him. She wished it could last all night.

It wasn't long before Nick and Jackie joined them on the dance floor. Kate could tell Nick had very little interest in being there, but was tolerating the situation. Jackie however seemed to be relishing the idea of being back with Nick and dancing.

Kate felt sorry for Nick, but couldn't think of any way to help him. She just hoped Jackie would soon be on her way back to Las Vegas because she really wanted to introduce Nick to Jess. She had little doubt they would hit it off, if they had the chance, and she didn't want Jackie around to mess things up.

Sam and Kate danced the rest of the evening, although Kate thought for sure it was because Sam had no intention of going back to the table and listening to Jackie's never-ending stories. She didn't really blame him; Jackie was starting to get on her nerves a little bit too.

Once the music stopped, they returned to the table for just a moment to say goodnight and then left for the cabin. Kate had never danced so much, without a break, but she had loved being in Sam's arms and he was a great dancer.

"I think you wore me out Kate." Sam said as they walked into the cabin.

"Excuse me. I think it was you who didn't want to take a break and go back to the table." Kate replied.

"Well, maybe it's because I love having you wrapped in my arms." Sam said as he pulled her into his arms.

Kate laughed as she responded. "Or maybe it's because you didn't want to listen to Jackie's stories anymore."

"You might have something there, but I do love having you in my arms."

"And I love being here." Kate replied before Sam pulled her close and gave her a kiss.

"I'm sorry Kate, but I really need to go. Tomorrow is going to be a very busy day and I still have a lot to finish up before the guests arrive."

"I understand, but please be careful and get some sleep." Kate responded.

"You too." Sam replied before giving Kate another kiss and then heading for the door.

Kate was really excited about tomorrow and seeing Jess again and having someone to talk with about Sam. She loved talking with Sam, but it wasn't the same as girl-talk.

Kate was surprised when her phone rang. She noticed that the caller ID was Agent Matt, so she quickly answered. He asked how she was then said he had called to tell her Ryan's shoulder replacement surgery had gone well and he was expected to make a full recovery.

She was so relieved to hear Ryan was going to be fine, even though he had put her through a lot of bad times, he had turned out to be a great guy after all. She was thankful he had saved her life and had really hated he had been shot.

She asked Matt about Dylan and he said his room was being well guarded, although he wasn't in any condition to go anywhere and was still in critical condition. The doctors didn't have much hope for him and were surprised he had held on this long. Matt said he would let her know if anything changed, then ended the call.

Kate had inadvertently found out from Ryan, the day of the confrontation, that Dylan not only dealt in drugs, but also money laundering, prostitution, and human trafficking, which were all horrible. She hoped, if he didn't survive, no one else would take over his awful, sick life and dealings. She was sure if someone didn't take over his businesses, someone else would probably start their own horrible businesses in his territory, which made her sad.

If Dylan did survive, hopefully he would be locked up for the rest of his life. All his accounts had been frozen and his assets had been confiscated, including his home, so at least for now, no one else could use it to carry on his business dealings. It was too bad there are horrible, evil people like him, existing in this world today, she thought.

It had been a busy day and Kate was tired, so it didn't take long for her to lock the door, crawl into bed, and pray, thanking God for His wonderful love and hope for a better world. She was happy Sam was now part of her life and willing to work on their relationship to see if it would grow over the next two weeks.

She was going to do everything she could to hopefully convince him she loved him and loved this ranch. She so much wanted everything to work out between them. She hoped for wonderful dreams of Sam tonight and it didn't take long for her to drift into sleep.

Chapter 15

Kate had enjoyed dancing last night with Sam. It had been great and her dreams had been wonderful dreaming about him and what their future might be. It was a nice change from the nightmares she had been having, and prayed they were over now.

Although Agent Ryan had been responsible for most of them, if not all, she had been happy to hear his surgery had gone well and he was expected to make a full recovery. She couldn't wait to tell Sam and the others and was sure they would be happy to know too.

It was finally Sunday and Kate was really looking forward to Jess arriving later today, so there was no way she was going to waste any more time lying in bed. She quickly jumped up and dressed for the day, of course that meant blue jeans and a sweatshirt, but it was at least one of the new ones Jess had never seen. She thought it was really beautiful, with horses running all the way around from the front to the back.

Kate was surprised when her phone rang; and then happy as Sam asked her to meet him for breakfast in fifteen minutes. She was ready so she knew she wouldn't be late and she was starving.

Sam was waiting for her at the door and gave her a quick kiss before they headed to the buffet. Everything smelled so good, as usual, and Kate couldn't wait to sit down and enjoy it.

She did however, wonder how long it would take her to lose the unwanted pounds she was sure she would have by the time she left, although hopefully only for a short time. She had already decided though, she was going to enjoy it while she had the chance.

They joined Jake, Nick, John, and Joey at the table and Kate was glad Jackie wasn't there yet, since she knew it would put a damper on their breakfast. She didn't hesitate in sharing the great news from Agent Matt about Ryan and they were all happy to hear about it. Sam then asked about the drug-lord and she filled them in on what Matt had told her about him.

They weren't surprised he wasn't expected to live, and although he was a horrible person, from what Ryan had inadvertently told them, they would pray for him. Kate wasn't surprised, as she had prayed for him too. She knew it was crazy in a way, but bad people were the ones that really needed God's help to change them.

They had a great breakfast and weren't disappointed Jackie hadn't shown up at all. They were getting ready to head to the chapel when Kate's phone rang. Kate was surprised when she noticed it was her mother's number, which was totally unexpected. She quickly answered it, and was shocked at the news.

She hung up and turned to the others at the table. "Jess was in an accident this morning on her way to the airport. It seems, someone ran her off the road and didn't stop. Her truck was totaled, but mom said Jess called and told her she was alright and one of the police officers drove her to the airport. Hopefully, that means she is still coming. I guess we all need to keep her in our prayers too."

"There's no doubt we will keep her in our prayers. I'll let the pastor know too so everyone here will also be praying for her. Don't worry Kate." Jake responded.

Kate looked around for Jackie as they headed to the chapel on the hill for the church service, but she hadn't shown up by the time the service started. Kate wondered if Jackie hadn't shown up, because she wasn't a Christian and wondered if she had ever been introduced to the scriptures and knowledge of Christ. If not, she really felt sorry for her.

Kate was hoping Tucker Thomas would be preaching again today, and wasn't disappointed. His sermon was great and once again, he seemed to be speaking directly to her. It was about love and how there are always ups and downs in all relationships, but if you have faith in God, all things can be worked out.

Once the service was over while she was getting a cup of coffee and a donut, Sam gave her a quick kiss and said they had a lot to do today and he would see her later for an early lunch before the bus arrived. It didn't surprise her in the least that Sam would be busy, since she had noticed ranch-hands already working in the cabins getting them ready and others were working in the barns.

She was sure people were working in the lodge too. Getting everything ready at such a large ranch would take a lot of preparation and work. She hoped the people in the lodge were going to take care of the temperature in the pool, so it wouldn't be so cold the next time she went for a swim, which she hoped would be soon.

Kate finished her coffee and then headed to the barn to check on the foals she had helped deliver, as well as the calf she and Sam had saved. She also now had several others she was checking on. She loved it and was happy to see how well they were all doing and how much stronger they appeared, including the small white colt, Snowball, and the calf Joey had named Lucky.

Joey and his friends had done a great job at bottle feeding Snowball and he was now running around in the stall. The mare was doing amazingly well too, which was a wonder after thrashing around on the ground when they had found her.

Kate had found several bite marks on her back and legs from the wolves trying to take her down, but fortunately they hadn't made it to her neck, and there were no major injuries. She had been lucky they had spotted her in time. God had truly been watching over her.

Kate was surprised to see a cow in with Lucky, the calf they had saved, and the calf was now nursing. He looked so much better than when she and Sam had left for the cabin.

As she was walking out of the last stall, she noticed Nick and Jackie walking toward her and Nick didn't look happy. She understood how upset he was about Jackie being around, but she didn't know what she could do to help.

"It's nice to see you again, Kate." Jackie said. "I was wanting to go for a ride, but Nick said he's too busy. Would you like to join me?"

Kate first glanced at Nick who was standing behind Jackie and appeared to be pleading 'Please' with his hands folded as if in prayer, so she accepted the offer to join her for a ride. Kate loved to ride and it would help pass the time and hopefully get her mind off Jess's accident for at least a little while. She was still very worried about Jess, and since Sam was going to be busy too, she was hoping a ride would help.

It didn't take long for the ranch-hands to get their horses saddled and ready and Kate was happy to once again be on Choco. He was such a great horse and she really enjoyed riding him.

As they were riding out, Kate told Jackie they should not be gone too long since Sam had told her, lunch today would be served early, so everything could be made ready for the guests to arrive around two. Kate was happy that Jackie had agreed, and was surprised when Jackie took off at a run.

Kate went along with it and joined her, but was glad when they finally slowed. Jackie's sudden stop had surprised her and she was happy Choco was able to maneuver around her horse, instead of plowing into them.

Jackie seemed caught off guard, when Kate pulled up beside her. Jackie said she loved to run and feel the wind in her hair and Kate understood. She had always thought a canter was great, rather than a run, but she felt everyone had their own idea of fun. As they finally pulled the horses to a walk, Jackie seemed surprised that Kate had kept up with her and said she didn't realize Kate could ride so well.

Kate told her she had grown up on a farm and had ridden most of her life. Jackie was quiet for a few minutes, and then started asking questions. Kate was surprised at the change since yesterday when she had talked non-stop about herself and her excursions and Kate had barely gotten a word in, but today was just the opposite.

Kate still didn't let down her guard and let Jackie know, Mike had survived. Ryan had made sure everyone thought Mike was dead and she thought it best to keep it that way. She also thought it wise not to let anyone know Ryan was a DEA agent working undercover and that he had also survived being shot.

Mike had sort of changed his name, since Michael was his middle name anyway. He was now going by Scott, which was his first name and he had changed his last name to Davis, like the rest of the family. Kate had been happy to hear that 'Scott' had been making a lot of headway in his recovery and was planning to find an AA type drug group in Indiana to help him stay clean, which was the best news of all.

He was also planning to stay at the farm and work with her dad. She knew that would be a blessing since the help was needed, especially now, since she and Jess would no longer be living there to help, and neither would her sister Emma, once she started Purdue University in the fall.

Kate and Jess would both be working full-time once their vacation was over. Kate was now hoping to move to Colorado and help Doc Porter until she could set up her practice here, but only time would tell. Her thoughts were all things she couldn't let down her guard and tell Jackie or anyone else who lived in Las Vegas.

Kate thought Jackie was trying to get to know her better, so she didn't hesitate to tell her about her family in Indiana and more about Jess, who for some reason, Jackie was anxious to meet. Jackie said she thought they would all get along great and could have a lot of fun together.

Kate was a little surprised, but since she had met Jackie, she wondered if she had any friends and if she really wanted to change that. It was hard to tell, but in some ways, she actually felt sorry for her.

Jackie's father didn't appear to have time for her, her mother had been out of the picture until recently, she didn't have any siblings, but had gone through several step-mothers, and it also appeared she didn't have any friends.

The best thing Kate could think of, was to pray for her and offer Jackie her friendship while she was at the ranch.

Kate was surprised when Jackie asked if she had heard from Jess today. She hesitated for a moment, then told Jackie about the accident Jess had been in this morning, but that Jess was at the airport and still planning to come to the ranch.

Jackie was quiet as they headed back toward the ranch and Kate wondered why. It had been an interesting ride, but the riding was what Kate loved best, so she had enjoyed the distraction since it made the time fly by.

As they arrived at the barn and dismounted, Kate told Jackie she had enjoyed their ride and would see her later; as she was planning to meet Sam for lunch. Jackie said she was planning to meet Nick for lunch too, so they might run into them at the gathering hall.

Kate knew Sam wouldn't be happy if Jackie showed up to spoil their lunch, so she hoped Jackie would be her normal self and be extremely late. Not that it would bother her, she had gotten used to Jackie, but she was sure Sam and Nick would appreciate a quiet lunch.

Kate decided to freshen up at the cabin before going to lunch and was surprised when she walked in. The cabin had been cleaned and there were flowers in the vases in each room, the bedspreads had even been changed to beautiful flowered ones and her clothes had been stacked neatly at the foot of her bed.

She was amazed and knew Jess was going to love it here. She moved her clothes to the dresser drawers and placed her backpack, in the closet. She hadn't thought of it before, but she had pretty much been living out of her backpack since she arrived.

She knew she would probably be using it when they went on campouts and definitely when they were on the roundup, but she decided to make herself at home since she now knew she would be at the ranch for at least another two weeks. Up until now, she had doubts, not knowing if Ryan would find her and end her future or even her life.

Thank God he had turned out to be there to protect her instead.

If everything worked out with Sam, then she would hopefully be accepting Doc Porter's offer to work with him here in Colorado. It was wonderful to have hope again of a happy future, but a lot could happen over the next couple of weeks.

Kate quickly freshened up and then headed to the gathering hall for lunch with Sam. She didn't see him when she first arrived, but it wasn't long before he walked in. They went through the line for food and then joined Jake, Nick, John, and Joey at the table. It didn't take long before Nick thanked her for taking Jackie off his hands this morning and then asked how her ride had been.

She told him the ride had been fine and Jackie had been fun to talk with, and she had actually been able to talk with her and share things about her life. She could tell Nick was surprised, but then he thanked her again.

Jake then spoke up. "And speaking of thanking you Kate, I want to especially thank you for all you have done around here. I'm so glad you are going to be here for a couple more weeks and we can't wait to meet your friend, Jessica. Don't forget, you've got a job here anytime you want one, so I hope you give it a lot of thought."

Kate was happy everything had turned out so well and Jake was offering her a job. "I should be thanking you. You all stood behind me and helped me through the horrible mess I was in and I'm truly grateful. I've enjoyed working with the foals and calves and truly appreciate getting so much experience, as it will definitely help when I go into practice.

And Jake, thank you for the job offer. I will be sure to keep it in mind. I love it here and I'm truly contemplating moving here in the future, now that I have a future. You've all been so wonderful. I'll be here for another couple of weeks and hopefully I'll know by then where I will settle down."

Sam then stood and pulled Kate up from her chair and put his arm around her. "I hope our love grows over the next couple of weeks and I'll be a part of that future you're planning. Shall I walk you to your cabin?"

Kate didn't hesitate to accept his offer. She was hoping he would be a part of her future and that the time they would have together over the next two weeks, would bring them closer together and their love would grow, but only time would tell.

Once they got to the cabin, Sam pulled Kate into his arms and gave her a kiss. He said he would meet her later when the bus arrived and he was looking forward to meeting her friend. He was hoping Jess would be alright and would be able to enjoy her vacation.

Sam was happy Kate had come into his life. He had never expected to meet someone like her, and although he still had doubts, he hoped they would have a future together.

Kate was worried about Jess and even though the nightmare was over, she couldn't help wondering if someone had run Jess off the road this morning on purpose. Everyone liked Jess, so it was truly a mystery, but hopefully everything would be fine once she arrived. Surely if it had been on purpose the person wouldn't follow Jess here.

Kate felt her dream since childhood, had come true, and God had brought her to this beautiful place and to Sam. She felt Sam met all the qualities she had hoped for in a husband. He was a loving cowboy, who she felt she could always trust. She had found the love of her life and was looking forward to a wonderful future with Sam in the beautiful mountains of Colorado.

Watch for 'Dude Ranch Dreams,' Jessica's Suspenseful Adventure at the ranch, coming soon in the Colorado Dude Ranch Series.

By: Barbara Clay

Chapter 1

Jess was excited about leaving on her dream vacation. She and her friend, Kate, who also shared her dream of going to a dude ranch, had planned their vacation almost a year ago. They had reservations at Jake's Dude Ranch, a working dude ranch in Colorado for the next two weeks.

Their dream also included riding beautiful horses, and riding to their hearts content. They had also talked about possibly meeting and falling in love with a cowboy, but neither expected that to really happen, although it appeared, it may have for Kate.

As part of the package, there were plans for a rodeo and a roundup while they were there. They could even participate, if the owner felt they were experienced enough at handling the horses.

Due to unforeseen circumstances her friend, Kate, had inadvertently arrived at the ranch almost two weeks early. Jess was sure by now the dude ranch owner knew Kate was an experienced rider. Jess would still have to prove how well she could handle horses, although she didn't expect it to be a problem.

She was so excited to get the vacation started that she couldn't sleep. The apartment was clean, and she had been packed for hours, so she decided to leave early and miss the rush hour traffic.

It was an hour and a half drive from Lafayette where her apartment was located to the airport in Indianapolis. She had five hours before her flight left, which should give her plenty of time to get there, check in, and have time to stretch her legs before boarding the plane.

As Jess loaded her suitcase into the back seat of her pickup, as well as a suitcase for Kate with the clothes she had requested Jess bring, she noticed a big black SUV in the parking lot of the apartment complex. She was sure she had never seen it there before.

The SUV had dark tinted windows, so she couldn't tell for sure if anyone was even in it. Without another thought of the SUV, Jess got into her pickup, quickly locked the doors, started the engine, and headed out.

As Jess pulled out of the parking lot, she was surprised to see the lights of the SUV turn on and the SUV start moving. She watched in her rearview mirror and noticed that the SUV had turned in the same direction she was going. It seemed to be following every turn she made as she navigated the back road shortcuts to get on Interstate 65 South to get to the Indianapolis airport.

When she glanced in her rearview mirror, she noted the SUV was picking up speed, and closing the gap between them. It was right behind her; almost on her bumper. This is insane. She thought and was really getting scared, especially since she knew there was a curve in the road up ahead.

She was just going into the curve when suddenly the SUV pulled beside her, then flew around her and cut in close, clipping the front side of her pickup, causing her to lose control. Her truck flipped over several times before finally coming to rest on the driver's side, blocking the door.

The side and steering-wheel airbags had both inflated which took her breath away. It took a few minutes for her to understand what had just happened. She was scared, and worried that the SUV was still nearby, but she knew she had to get out of the truck in case the gas tank caught fire.

Jess didn't smell any smoke yet, but that didn't mean it wasn't going to happen, since she had a full tank of gas. She dug at the airbags, pushing them to her side and tried to free herself from the seatbelt so she could try to escape from the wreckage.

It was really a struggle, but she finally managed to get free. The windshield had shattered and there was an opening where the glass had been, so she felt the quickest way out would be to crawl through that opening, although there was still some glass remaining of the windshield.

As she started struggling to get out of the seat, she saw a person look in through the windshield opening, which practically scared her to death. Jess was afraid it might be the driver of the SUV, but she hoped they were long gone by now.

"Hey lady, are you alright? I called 911, so the police should be here soon with an ambulance."

Jess caught her breath and responded. "I think I'm okay. Just trying to get out of my seat so I can get out of the truck through the windshield."

Jess then wormed her way out of the seat, around the steering wheel, and started climbing out. Fortunately, her rescuer had a coat that he laid across the remaining broken glass and then reached over and helped her out.

Her legs were weak and she could hardly walk, but the teenage boy who had helped her get out, helped her over to a tree and sat her down. Jess didn't hesitate to thank him for his help.

Soon after she escaped from her pickup, the police arrived and quickly came over and asked what had happened. She told them about the SUV that had followed her from her apartment complex and that it had hit her pickup, causing her to lose control and the pickup to roll.

Unfortunately, she hadn't gotten the license plate number because they had stayed behind her until they went to pass and swerved in to her, causing her accident. She said she was sure they were probably long gone, at least she hoped so.

One of the officers asked if she knew who was in the SUV or if anybody might want to hurt her, but she told them she had no idea who was driving. As far as she knew, she didn't have any enemies, and hadn't seen the SUV before. The officers asked her a few more questions, before one officer headed over to check out her pickup truck.

Jess had no doubt it was totaled, as it really was a twisted mess of metal. The first officer stayed with her and told her the paramedics would be there shortly to check her out and take her to the hospital.

Jess thought about what he had said for only a moment, before she responded. "No! I can't go to the hospital. I don't have time. I was on my way to the airport for a vacation to a dude ranch in Colorado. My best friend and I planned it last year. I had decided to leave early to be sure I didn't have any trouble catching the plane so I can meet my friend. I'm fine. I just need to find a ride to the airport."

"Miss, you don't seem to understand, you've been in a really bad accident. You need to be checked out." The officer stated worriedly.

"I'm ok. I feel fine, just maybe bruised a little, but I had my seatbelt on and the airbags deployed, so no broken bones. The only thing that hit my head was the airbag, which I must admit, was bad enough, but probably saved my life." Jess responded frantically. She didn't want to go to the hospital and miss her flight.

The officer, showing concern, looked at her questioningly, before he responded. "Well, if the paramedics check you out and say you are alright to travel. I'm about to get off work and I'll take you to the Indianapolis airport if you want."

He then told the other officer. "Can you get this crazy lady's luggage out of her truck? She says she was on her way to the airport to catch a flight to Colorado and no matter what, she is still going."

Kate laughed, then said to the officer, "Thank you. I really appreciate it and I'd be glad to pay you."

"That won't be necessary. I'm glad to help and I figure it might be safer for you, in case we run across that SUV. If they were waiting for you at your apartment, they might also know where you were headed and could be waiting somewhere else for you along the way." The officer responded.

"I didn't think about that. I would probably feel safer riding with you. I really do appreciate your help." Jess replied. "Would it also be possible to arrange for my truck to be taken to Ed's Repair Shop in Lafayette, so my friends can clean my things out of it? I know he has a junk yard too, so it would probably be best to have it towed to his place."

The officer said he would make that call. It wasn't long after he made the call to Ed's, who said they were on their way, that the paramedics arrived and checked Jess out. They thought she should go to the hospital, but gave in and told the officer she was clear to leave, with instructions for her to check with a doctor when she reached her destination, just in case.

Jess was thankful they were willing to compromise and release her, so she could still go on her vacation. The officer who had been checking out her pickup, soon returned with her luggage, so she could now be on her way to the airport.

Thank God she had started early and she hadn't been badly injured. Her friend, Kate was never going to believe this, especially after all Kate herself had gone through recently.

The officer dropped her off at the airport departures without further incidents and helped her with her luggage. As she turned to thank him, she noticed he was looking around and wondered if he was checking the area for a black SUV that could be the one that followed her and hit her truck. She couldn't imagine why they would be at the airport, but it made her wonder how they would know she was there? She then thanked the officer and went inside to check-in.

The airport was busy, but Jess didn't have any problems checking in her bags. She would have had only one suitcase but she also had Kate's suitcase, since Kate had been limited on clothes at Jake's Dude Ranch, and she was sure Kate needed them. Jess knew there were laundry facilities in the cabin, and she could probably shop nearby to pick up a few things, so she hadn't packed much.

Jess got through security pretty quickly and still had a little time before her flight boarded, so she went to the restroom to check her appearance. She wasn't surprised to see her long blonde hair was a mess, so she pulled it back into a ponytail. As she looked in the mirror, she noticed bruises starting to form on her arms, from when the airbags had deployed, and on her neck from the seatbelt.

She was also starting to feel sore, pretty much all over, but thankfully she didn't seem to have any serious injuries. She stopped at a vendor station for water and a breakfast sandwich, to hold her over until her plane landed in Colorado, and found a seat in the boarding area to wait for her flight to be called.

It was eerie, but she kept feeling as if someone was watching her. She didn't see anyone suspicious in the area and she didn't see anyone actually watching her, but she was nervous and alert. She hoped nothing else happened before she got to the ranch. She didn't need a nightmare like Kate had just gone through. Thankfully, Kate was now at the ranch and was okay and it sounded like she had made some great friends.

Jess's thoughts then wandered back to the SUV wondering who might have been driving it and why it seemed they had targeted her. She couldn't think of anyone she had upset enough to harm her. Her mind was still a little foggy and it suddenly dawned on her she needed to make some phone calls before she got on the plane.

She first called her insurance agent to update him on her accident, and then called Kate's parents to let them know she had been in an accident but was okay. She explained to them what had happened but said very little about it being an SUV that seemed to target her.

She didn't want them to worry; they were the closest thing to parents she had, after losing her parents in an accident. She then told them where her truck was being taken, and asked if they would get her things out of it.

As soon as she finished her calls, her flight number was called and she quickly got in line to board. She still had an eerie feeling that someone was watching her, but it was probably just her imagination. She needed to let it go and focus on her dream vacation and the fun she and Kate were going to have horseback riding at the dude ranch.

About the Author:

Barbara Clay always loved to read and write when she was younger. She especially loved books about horses and always dreamed of someday owning a horse of her own. She grew up in Indianapolis, Indiana and attended the University of Indianapolis where she achieved a Bachelor Degree in Chemistry. She worked for a large pharmaceutical company in Indianapolis until she retired.

She married and had one son and eventually they bought a farm where she could have horses. Her first horse was a Morgan, then a mostly black Appaloosa, before ending up with Tennessee Walkers. She loved to ride with her son and rode as much as possible. Another one of her dreams was of going to a dude ranch. Although she never made it to a dude ranch, she always imagined what it would be like.

She especially enjoyed reading Romance Suspense books. One day she decided instead of reading, she would try writing. She loved writing but never considered publishing her stories until her son convinced her she should try.

Dude Ranch Protectors is the first in her first series.

Dude Ranch Dreams is second in the series.

Dude Ranch Roundup is the third book

Dude Ranch Christmas is the fourth

Barbara Clay doesn't have a website set up yet, but she can be contacted at blclay2748@gmail.com. She would love to know what you think of her first series of books.

Made in the USA
Monee, IL
10 August 2024

63050695R00164